The Portal

Donna Eimer Villani

Strategic Book Publishing and Rights Co.

Strategic Book Publishing & Rights Co., LLC
USA
www.sbpra.com

ISBN: 978-1-68235-703-3

Dedication

As always, I am beholding to the intercession of Our Blessed Mother for the blessings from the source of her Son that make my writing possible. A very special thanks to a woman who does not know the meaning of the word no, Carol O'Brien (nee Villani), my "sister"-in-law, who has given more than she knows. Thanks to my brother-in-law, the late Denny O'Brien, for his valuable input, and my brother, Jim Eimer. My dear friend and confidant, Alvera Sonsoucie, who with her smile, knows the crazy me. The list is endless with family and friends, especially Smart, where life's future journeys instill patience and endurance. But will always end with the love of my late husband, Ronald Frank Villani, who listened with his own kind of down to earth understanding, and now still, with his spirit, keeps my feet on the ground.

Acknowledgement

If it were not for the love of these four individuals, I would be nothing at all: My parents, August John Eimer Junior and Rosemary (Cookie) Eimer (nee Schuler), and my husband Ron's parents, Frank and Juanita Villani (nee Powell).

Tribute

Abigail Peregoy on her unique rendition book trailer for "The Portal" on my Facebook page.

The Moving Words LLC for the creation of donnavillani.com Website.

TW my 5th brother.

Introduction

The Portal depicts fictional phenomena events in the unusual life of Colleen Armstrong as a futuristic pioneer. A new age begins for her and her family when Earth becomes their frontier. Present techniques along with historical methods from the old West are used when a wagon train is formed and they travel through the wilderness in search of their dream to find a peaceful place to call home. Even with the threat of death all around them; these seekers find the strength to face the challenges of torrential storms, bandits, abnormal cats and natural disasters, yet keep up their courage to move towards their dream.

Colleen's mother, Beatrice, bestows to her daughter for safekeeping, a chest that was given to her as a child. Beatrice advises her daughter that the chest cannot be opened until the secret knowledge of what she calls "the compost" is understood.

But, there is another mysterious phenomenon that Colleen has lived with all of her life that she finds hard to explain, not only to herself, but also to those who love her. That is until she meets the Indian, Kuruk, who immediately recognizes her as The Portal.

As Colleen travels in the wilds, daily life brings new adventures as she searches for a love to fill her heart; the secrets of the chest; and the mysterious meaning of her role as The Portal.

Note: Just as many elevators omit the thirteenth floor, I have skipped numbering a chapter as Thirteen. It's okay; nothing's missing.

Part 1

❁

Chapter One

Birth of Ricky/Geoff Leaves

She sat quietly, by herself, at the dining table. The northern lake's frigid March winds howled and shook the tiny door and wooden shutters that covered the windows of the cabin. The burning logs crackling in the stone fireplace barely warmed the rooms, so she kept the wood fire in the cast iron stove lit.

"I know it's needed and I know it's important to keep it coming, but I wish I could do more to help than tend a pot of fresh water," Impatiently, she went to the stove, and covered a large vat of boiling water. She carefully, moved it to the slower burning side of the fire.

"In all my dreams I never thought water would be the thing she'd need the most from me. I feel so helpless," She felt completely frustrated and alone as she looked around the tiny room.

She hugged herself. "It's so cold," She tucked her mohair sweater into her denim trousers, and went to the hook by the door and grabbed a thicker woolen sweater. "I'm already weighed down with all these layers, but this feels a little better," She took another log from the wood box, and placed it in the stove.

She could smell the strong coffee as it started to perk. "Good, about ready," She knew no one would hear her as she spoke to herself. "Or maybe something stronger," She remembered the whiskey on the shelf in the cupboard for anyone who wanted it. 'Maybe later…' she thought about the whiskey.

"These are done," She knew they would be in the cabin for some time, so she decided to make a batch of buttermilk biscuits. She placed them in the warmer of the wood stove.

"God this is taking forever," She continued to busy herself. "Please give her the strength," She knew it would be difficult, but realized all she could do was pray and wait.

Colleen Belle Armstrong had turned sixteen only one month prior to this time, but she felt like fifty. Her older sister Jeanette had married against her parents' wishes, and now in this tiny cabin's bedroom was about to give birth to a baby.

Colleen tried to forget her present surroundings, and focus on a more pleasant time with her sister. Jeanette was five years older than Colleen, and they always shared a special sister's friendship.

She could envision herself and Jeanette as youngsters running in the meadow on Driftwood, their parent's ranch. In her mind she could again picture the clear blue sky, and remember how the hot sun prompted them to take off their shoes and let the grass tickle their toes.

She could see her sister in her long, gingham dress running ahead of her. "You can't catch me," She remembered Jeanette yelling to her. Jeanette was turning her head to look at her. She had a big grin on her face. How happy she looked with the long, dark tresses of her hair gently slapping her in the face.

"Oh yes I can," She remembered yelling back to her. She noticed Jeanette's deep hazel eyes sparkled with joy as she looked at her. Colleen thought she looked so much like her sister that she could have been looking in a mirror, and watching herself run far ahead.

'We had a good life back then. We worked hard, but we were happy,' Colleen thought. She then remembered some of the tales her mother, Beatrice had told her about their life.

Homesteading was tough for everyone, and Hiram Armstrong along with his wife Beatrice had worked hard to build their legacy they called Driftwood. Driftwood started out just as its name explains with piles and piles of assorted, uprooted trees that had ended up on the land. This sought after lumber was milled on the ranch.

But Driftwood was also their home, and a profitable horse and cattle ranching business for their family of six. Their two oldest sons Brice and Harry were content to remain on the land, and continue to work the ranch with their parents. And when they both married, their parents relinquished a portion of Driftwood to them to live on.

It was different for their oldest daughter, Jeanette; she fell in love with Geoffrey Banks, a quiet, homeless man they hired to help on the ranch.

To Jeanette, Geoffrey Banks was the man for her. He was good looking with his jet black hair, soft dark brown eyes, and tall stature. But he appeared to lack the upbringing that Hiram and Beatrice dreamed of for their daughter.

Geoffrey would never speak of his life before coming to work at Driftwood. And besides their not liking his slight British accent, which he sorely tried to hide; Hiram and Beatrice believed his poor attire screamed that he came from poor stock.

'I always knew Geoff was the one for you,' Colleen thought to herself. She knew nothing could ever change how she felt about her sister.

And when Jeanette married Geoffrey Banks, Colleen also went against her parent's wishes, and remained forever loving and giving to her sister. Their sisterhood meant more than the legacy they would inherit from their parents. "Even if you both hadn't invited me to go with you, I think I would've followed you," she said.

"Thank God Mama loved us enough not to hold it against us when we left home," She knew she and Jeanette were very thankful that their mother did not demonstrate the same bitterness as their father. But instead, Beatrice showed both of her daughters her endless love and kindness, and especially her expertise as a midwife by taking the journey, with their hired man Benjamin Dollar, BD, for short, to be with Jeanette at this time of her baby's delivery.

"Oh God, I know she's having a hard time of it in there," She was thankful for the loud shrill whistles of the wind that blocked the torturous screams from her sister. Waiting was not one of Colleen's virtues, and knowing Jeanette would be in pain for some time did not help matters.

She opened the cupboard next to the stove. She glanced at the bottle of whiskey on the shelf, and thought of the many times her mother had made her a hot toddy to calm her aches from a winter illness.

She reached for the bottle and a tin cup. Uncorked, the whiskey flared her nostrils with its potent stench. "Yuck," she said, with a shudder. "The feel sure outweighs the taste," She downed her first swallow, when the door from the bedroom opened, and Geoffrey came into the room.

"That's pretty potent stuff for such a young stomach," He saw his sister-in-law with the bottle and cup in her hand.

"This waiting's killing me. I think I'm old enough to learn how to birth a baby. We can't depend on Mama all the time," She started to put another slug in her cup.

"That's true. Maybe for the second baby! Right now it might be harder on your sister to have you in there than out here. Can you understand?" He walked next to her, and put the cork back in the bottle, and placed it back on the shelf. "Besides, Jeanette might need a bit of this in a little while, so let's save it, okay?" He gently put his arm around her.

"Okay. It tastes awful anyway," She shrugged her shoulders. "I just wanted to calm myself down, and this stuff helps me sleep. Not like that's going to happen with my sister in there in so much pain," She had a slight slur in her voice. "I must've drunk more than I thought, I have to sit down." She reached for one of the chairs by the table, and walked next to it and sat down.

"Don't worry, Jeanette's doing fine," He checked the warmer of the stove and saw the biscuits. "I'll wait until Jeanette can have one," He did not even feel hungry. He closed the oven warmer.

"Your mother said everything's going as it should. And she's young and strong," He sat down on one of the hard chairs.

"I know, like Mama always says 'Comes from good stock!'" She looked at him with tears in her eyes, but a slight smile on her lips. "You come from good stock too, Geoffrey, I can tell. Papa always said he had his doubts about you, but I can tell you hide your education," she said.

He sat back in his chair, and seemed to drift away in his own private thoughts. "You've always been the one who seems to possess that third eye, so to say. You're a good judge of character. I don't think I've ever thanked you for believing in me. That has always meant a lot to me and your sister," He reached across the table, and patted her hand.

"I guess when you're ready you'll tell me about yourself. I can wait. I'm not going anywhere,"The whiskey was making her speak a bit more openly than she normally would have.

"Some things are better left in the past. But I can tell you my father was not unlike your own. He worked very hard to maintain the ways of our ancestors. The stories passed on from generation to generation always made my father want only the best for his family," He noticed she fully understood where he was coming from.

"I know what you mean. But sometimes it's hard to think that times back then could've been so glorious, and then so disastrous so fast. Mama says she remembers everyone talking about how it was gone in a snap of the finger," She was trying to snap her fingers, but could not, as she was still feeling the effects from the whiskey.

"I've heard a lot of different stories, and everybody has their own past they have to deal with. That's what makes life so interesting, and gives us a goal to achieve a better future for our children," he said. He got up from his chair.

"I'm going to take in some fresh water. Can you fix a biscuit for your mother, I'll send her out. She needs a break and this is going to take a while," He went to the vat on the stove and dipped some hot water into a pan.

"Thanks for loving my sister Geoffrey, it means the world to me," She went to him, and hugged him.

"She's everything to me, and I'll never forget all she's going through to have our baby. She's resting right now, but I know the labor will start again. I better get this in there, and send your mom out before it starts again," He felt he was getting his second wind, as he rushed into the bedroom.

"Thank God for coffee and powdered milk!" Beatrice shouted after she closed the door to the bedroom. She then went to the stove, and poured herself a cup of coffee.

"You always say that Mama. I'm so happy you're here," Colleen hugged her mother from behind. "Here, you sit down and I'll fix that for you. You must be beat," She took the cup from her mother, and caringly put a teaspoon of the powdered milk into the cup of coffee, and placed it on the table for her mother.

"Here's a hot biscuit. We don't have butter, but here's some honey. We have lots of honey," She did not want her mother to be concerned for them.

Beatrice went to one of the tiny windows, pulled back the drape with her hand and looked out into the night. "Honey's fine Honey, or should I say Sweetie...No I like honey's fine Honey. See I'm making a joke. You look and act just like your father, always doting after me," Beatrice said. As she continued to look out the window she placed her hand on her forehead, and then ruffled her shoulder length, black with many strands of silver hair, as if she didn't have a care in the world. Her light brown eyes had lost their sparkling lightheartedness during this trying time.

Beatrice Armstrong was a petite, trim woman, who never really cared about her appearance, and believed age was just a number. "Has BD been in? You know him, feels more at home with the animals in the barn than with people. I can see the light's still on out there. I'm sure he's keeping warm out there with the wood stove..." she said, in her always caring way.

"He's quite the card isn't he...You want it he's got it. Did I ever tell you our family knew him before your father came into my life...Benjamin was always so kind to the family..." Beatrice preferred calling BD by his given name. She came away from the window, and sat down at the table in front of the biscuit and coffee her daughter prepared for her.

"Mama, are you okay? Is it Jeanette? Is something wrong with the baby?" Colleen noticed a grave, concerned look come over her mother's face.

"I've never seen anything like this. Her labor's so hard but she's not opening up. It's been over five hours now, and something should be happening, but it's not. I wish I had more education. I'm a mid-wife not a doctor," She started to wring her hands. Quickly, she acted like she was warming them. She then picked up the biscuit and rose from her seat.

"But she's going to be all right isn't she Mama, she's going to be all right?" Colleen kept asking.

Her mother continued to walk around the room. "I don't know daughter. At this point I just don't know. If something doesn't happen soon this could go bad," Her uncertain eyes looked straight in her daughter's distressed eyes. "She keeps going to sleep or passing out I don't know which, but it sure would help if she was awake to help," Beatrice continued her pacing.

"Geoffrey didn't seem too concerned," Colleen said. She knew her brother-in-law just seemed to think the process was going on as it should.

"I haven't told him. The boy's never seen the birth of a baby, he doesn't have a clue what's going on," Beatrice also did not want to tell her young daughter this distressing prognosis, but believed they had better be prepared for the worst.

"Can I help Mama? Don't you think I'm old enough to do something? Geoffrey seems to think if I'm in there it might be harder on Jeanette, but I think it'd help. What do you think?" She watched her mother, seemingly in deep thought, as she nibbled on the biscuit.

"I think maybe you're right, you might be able to keep her spirits up, and get her going enough to get that baby out," She chewed the last piece of the biscuit and swallowed her remaining coffee. "Besides, I was close to your age when I had Brice," She looked at Colleen. "Grab me a couple more of those soft towels, and come with me," she said. Colleen went for the towels, and followed her into the dim lit, tiny bedroom.

Besides the double bed, there was a tall, thin chest of drawers and a long dresser, with a potbellied stove positioned in a corner near the door. They had two small kitchen chairs in the room for anyone to sit on during the delivery.

At that moment, Jeanette just seemed peacefully asleep. "God, she looks so pale," Colleen said. Geoffrey looked at her with worry in his eyes. "I'm sorry. I'll keep it to myself," she whispered. Geoffrey's wrinkled forehead seemed to relax.

"Is that my Collie?" Jeanette whispered Colleen's pet name. She opened her eyes and tried to scoot herself up to a seated position in the bed.

"Yes it's me Sissy," Colleen said. She used her nickname for her sister. She came next to the head of the bed and knelt next to her sister. "It's getting close, are you ready to help get this little one born into this crazy world?" she softly asked her sister.

Jeanette reached for her hand. "I'm trying Collie, I really am," Jeanette replied. Just then a stabbing pain wrenched Jeanette's lower back. "Oh God, the pain," she screamed. "I can't bear the pain," She squeezed Colleen's hand so hard Colleen screamed too.

"Scream, Sissy scream, just let it all out," Colleen watched Jeanette arch her back with her knees bent.

"Don't push just yet Jeanette…" Beatrice cried out. She came to the other side of the bed and got right in front of her daughter's face. "You can't push yet, it's not time. Can you hear me daughter?" Her Mother had the authoritative tone Jeanette remembered in her voice.

"Yes I hear you, but I sure want to push Mama," Jeanette replied. Her perspiration drenched her flannel nightgown.

"Geoff, Honey I'm so cold," she whimpered. Her tears fell down her cheeks. "I'm trying not to push Honey," she sobbed.

Geoffrey slightly bumped Colleen with his hip, so she would move, and he came next to his wife. "Sweetheart, I'm going to cut your gown off so I can warm you with these towels. Just keep the sleeves on they'll help warm you," He looked at Colleen and she reached for the scissors and gave them to him.

He easily removed the material away from her swollen body. "Here you go…this should warm you up," he said. He gently laid the warm cloth over her stomach, and with slow strokes wiped her, as her body started to shake.

"This is not right. Her body's not reacting the way it should," Beatrice said.

Geoffrey stopped and looked at his mother-in-law. "What should I do?" Geoff yelled. "Colleen…here…take this and get some blankets," He pulled the cooled, wet towel from his wife and threw it at his sister-in-law.

He tried to cuddle his wife to warm her until Colleen brought him the blankets. "I can feel her heart. It's racing out of her chest," Geoffrey said. Beatrice went to check to see if she had dilated, but she had not.

"Here Geoffrey," Colleen said. She handed him the blankets he asked for, and she helped him unfold them and cover her sister.

"She's passed out again, Beatrice. Even I know this isn't right. What in God's name can we do for her?" Geoffrey asked. He held his wife's hand to his chest, and looked at his mother-in-law.

"I've never performed a Caesarean, but I think that's what she needs. Geoff, you stay with her. Colleen you come with me…" Beatrice ordered. She hurried out of the bedroom with Colleen right on her heels.

"Colleen, I don't know if I can save her…" Beatrice said, with a slight hesitation in her voice. "But with God's help, we might be able to save the baby," she added. Her eyes seemed to glass over.

"Honey, I've read journals on this procedure, but I've never performed one," She searched her daughter's eyes for any doubts. "It's not pretty. I'll have to cut into her stomach, and then into the uterus to get the baby out…" She noticed Colleen's eyes widen.

"We'll need to boil these instruments," She placed her utensils in the already boiling water.

"Colleen, it's very important that you keep this fire going and the water boiling. We're going to need plenty of both," She stirred her unusual soup.

"Oh Mama, we can't lose her..." Colleen was saying. She watched her mother take a small clean towel, and systematically place the sterile utensils on it. Beatrice counted and overviewed them, while making a mental picture of them, and then she folded the towel and rolled the utensils together. "Mama, I'm scared. What if she..." Colleen was saying.

Her mother came next to her, and put her arm around her. "Now listen daughter, we can only do our best. I learned a long time ago from my great-grandmother that life's journeys don't always turn out the way you might think they should. The world changes on a dime, and we have to be thankful for the time we've been given to live," she said. She softly put her hand under Colleen's chin, and tilted her eyes to hers. "Remember we can only do our best, the rest is up to Him," she said, as she pointed to the Heavens. "The water's fine right now. You come with me," Beatrice then said. They both went back to the small room.

In the bedroom Geoffrey was holding his wife in his arms. "She's passed out again. Her heart's still racing. I'm scared. I don't mind telling you both I'm scared to death for her," He noticed his mother-in-law place all of her instruments on the tiny dresser. "What are you going to do?" he asked. He held Jeanette closer to him as if he were protecting her.

"Son, we have to get that baby out, and we have to do it now," Beatrice said, not approaching her son-in-law. "Geoff she's my first daughter, you know I love her. I wish I could trade places with her, but I can't. She has to bear this on her own, and with the help from God this baby will be born," She slowly came next to him.

"What can I do?" he asked. He relinquished his defending hold on his wife. "I'll do whatever you say," he said.

Beatrice checked Jeanette's pulse and pupils. "She's unconscious! I'm going to do this as fast as I can. In short Geoff, I'm going to have to cut the baby out," She saw fear in his eyes. "I have to tell you I've never done this before, but I know it works. You're going to have to trust me son," She was trying to send a sense of calming to him.

"I've read about the Caesarean section, and I know she's at risk. All I can say is I trust you. Just tell me what you want me to do," He wanted to hurry, and get it over with.

"Well, first, we have to make sure she stays unconscious. I have these knock out drops. If she starts to wake up you just put a few drops on this cloth, and keep it by her nose until she passes out again. I can't have her thrashing about..." she was saying. "Do you understand?" She looked him in the eye for any signs of hesitation or misunderstanding.

"I can do that," He took the cloth and drops from her. "She's so cold," he said, as he felt her face. "But she's not shivering. Don't you find that odd?" He looked at his mother-in-law with questioning eyes.

"I think it's because she's passed out. But let's just focus on this right now, and worry about other things later," She turned and looked at Colleen.

"Now daughter, you're going to have to be my third hand. You've helped me with the animal's giving birth, and you know the instruments, so just listen, and I think we can do this," Colleen nodded to her.

"Let's begin," Beatrice calmly said.

The wind howled outside, and the cold night slowly turned into dawn. Later that morning Beatrice was tenderly rocking her new baby grandson, Erick Jonathan, in a chair placed by the hearth of the fire place. "He looks a lot like your brother, Brice when he was first born; so we know he has a lot of Armstrong in him," Beatrice said to Colleen.

Colleen slowly raised her head to acknowledge her mother from where she sat at the table. "Mama, I'm really worried about Jeanette. She was so out of it that Geoff never even had to give her any of the knock out drops," she said. "He's been in there a long time. Should I go check on them?" She looked at her mother with the baby in her arms. She thought she looked so peaceful, and the baby only softly whimpered every once in a while.

"Daughter, why don't you go to your bed behind the partition, and get a little sleep. You need it," she was saying, as Geoff came out from the bedroom.

"How's she doing?" Colleen asked. She became more alert when Geoffrey walked into the room.

"She's very groggy, but wants to see you Colleen. Can you try to get her to eat some of the broth?" he asked. "She won't for me," He felt totally worn to a frazzle. "How's the boy...I'll take him in when Colleen comes out. But she wants to see Colleen first," He went next to Beatrice, and looked down at his son in her arms, while Colleen went into thc bcdroom.

The room was lit from the opened doors of the pot belly stove in the corner. They could never keep enough wood in it to make the room toasty warm so Jeanette was mounded with plenty of downy quilts.

At first Colleen thought her sister was asleep so she thought maybe she had better leave her to rest. "Is that you Collie?" Jeanette softly asked. "Don't laugh, but even under the blankets I think I can smell you," She slowly lifted the covers from her head.

"I don't stink. I washed this morning," Colleen said. She knew her sister was playing with her, like she had so many times before.

"I know you don't stink, Honey, can you sit by me for a while?" Jeanette patted the bed up close to her.

"How're you feeling?" Colleen asked. "That was some kind of an operation. Mama was fantastic, she really knows her stuff," She hoped to make her sister understand that she was well taken care of.

"Collie, I'm sure Mama did her best, but something just doesn't feel right. I don't know how to explain it. I'm not myself," She did not want to scare her sister, but maybe prepare her.

"It might take a while for everything to go back into place. I'm sure you'll be just fine." She held Jeanette's hand. "I want to see those pretty eyes," She gently pushed back a tiny curl next to Jeanette's eye.

"Collie, just promise me you'll look after Geoff, and take care of my little Ricky. We named him after Geoff's great-grandfather. A proud name, Erick! And Jonathan after Mama's grandfather," She looked deep in her sister's eyes. "Promise me Collie." She squeezed Colleen's hand.

"Please don't talk like that, Sissy, you'll be fine. I just know it," She tried to hug her sister.

"It makes me feel better knowing you're here for them," Jeanette winced from a pain in her abdomen.

"I'll always be here for all of you. So don't worry, okay?" Colleen was trying to make light of the situation.

"I love you Collie. You're my best friend. I don't know how I ever would've survived without you. You're my happiness. You can never know how much you mean to me," She was trying to find a more comfortable position. "Whenever Daddy was on my case I always had you by my side. You stood up for me so many times. I especially remember when we were very young, and I forgot my baby doll. Remember that time we were going over to Grandma Armstrong's for the week-end…" Jeanette seemed to get a faraway look in her eyes.

"Yes I remember," Colleen said. She again swiped a curl away from her sister's face.

"I was afraid to ask if I could go back in the house to get my favorite baby doll, but you asked, and Mama went, and got her for me. That touched me so much, more than you'll ever know," she said, as a single tear dropped from her eye.

"Boy you're really out of it. That was a million years ago. Come on Sissy you have to fight. You have spirit, and a beautiful baby boy who'll need his mother," Colleen was saying. Her sister seemed to go to sleep. "Jeanette, don't you leave me," she cried out.

Jeanette opened her eyes. "Not just yet. I'm fighting Collie. I want to be with my family. Just know, I'm fighting the best I can," she softly whispered. "Geoff said he'd bring Ricky in. Can you see if he's ready?" she asked. She noticed Colleen looked at her with a sort of fear in her eyes. "I'll be fine Collie. We believe in a higher power Collie, so I know I'll be just fine," She mustered up a smile for her sister.

"I love you Sissy," Colleen bent and hugged her sister the best she could, with all the blankets and her in the bed. "Keep up your spirits, and I know you can beat this," Colleen felt like she was going to cry, but held back her tears to show her sister she was strong for her. "I'll go get your husband and your sweet baby. He's a whole lot better than your baby doll," Her voice quivered.

"I know he is. I'm fighting for him and for you Collie. I love you," Jeanette looked in her sister's eyes as Colleen wiped the tears from Jeanette's face. She then kissed Jeanette's cheek, and hurried from the bedside.

"Keep up those spirits sister," She slowly backed out of the doorway, while watching her sister's eyes, so full of love for her. Silently, Jeanette blew her a kiss with her hand and Colleen blew one back to her. Softly, she shut the door.

"She wants to see you and the baby Geoff," Colleen said. She went next to them as her mother was gently giving the tiny bundle to Geoff, and he went into the bedroom.

"She's fighting the best she can Mama, but she really doesn't think she's going to make it. It was so hard just walking out of the room and leaving her there. I wish I could just jump in her and keep her with me and help her get better," She went to sit on her small bed in the corner.

"Jeanette has always been the tender spirit Colleen. She doesn't have the fight that you have. Daddy always said you were a spit fire. Always ready for action. But that doesn't mean she doesn't have the grit to live. She's got that. It's just that the odds may not be in her favor," Beatrice sat next to her daughter on the small bed.

"Mama, I'm completely exhausted. Can you stay with me while I try to get some sleep?" Her mother got up and tucked her in with the blankets.

"That's my baby. You get some rest daughter," Beatrice said. "I'll keep watch and yes I'll wake you if anything happens," She perceived these same words in her daughter's eyes.

"Thanks Mama," was all she said. Beatrice gently massaged her back and stayed with her until she could hear her softly snoring in her sleep.

As she slept Colleen could see herself and Jeanette tunneling through a long dark portal which launched them into space. Happily, they were thrust past the stars. The feeling of freedom was all around them. The sweet scent of gardenias filled Colleen's lungs. It was Jeanette's favored scent of perfume.

They were one. They could see, feel and touch the same. It was awesome. They soared like eagles higher and higher until they were out of the universe as they knew it.

"We believe in a higher power Collie, so I know I'll be just fine," She could hear Jeanette saying. She then could hear Jeanette say over and over again "You are in my heart forever," They soared throughout the heavens until a gentle tug seemed to pull Colleen. She looked at Jeanette, who was floating away from her. She watched as the flapping lifeline that held them together wrapped around her and held her tight, while Jeanette freely, floated away from her. "God's lifeline, grab it Sissy..." She heard herself scream.

But she watched as Jeanette floated higher and higher away from her. She could not help but notice the peaceful look on her sister's face as she grew smaller and smaller and then was out of her view.

Suddenly, she could see herself falling down along the side of a huge, silk, gently waving, silver colored ribbon. She could feel a sort of magnetic flow hold her close to the ribbon. As she slid down next to the ribbon she could hear voices of those she loved and some that had spoken harshly and betrayed her during her life. She saw a vision of the little kitten that she loved, but had died. She tried to reach for it but it disappeared.

Finally, a high-pitched shriek startled her and she could feel herself fall on her bed. It felt as if the wind had been knocked out of her and she quickly opened her eyes.

The room was pitch-black, but she could see a large, cobalt blue ball darting around the room. She lay completely still wondering if she was dreaming or awake. But then she heard the familiar sound of the wind howling outside so she assumed she was awake.

The out of place ball seemed to slow and went up and towards her left. She felt compelled to watch this phenomenon with her eyes wide open. It then stopped, and a thin veil appeared as the ball disappeared. The shear veil was inlaid with what appeared to be sparkling glitter. The veil hid someone or something she could not make out.

She did not want to move a muscle but could feel the presence of a great love. She did not want to blink for fear that the presence would leave. But then the cobalt blue ball appeared again, and proceeded to dart about the room in front of her again. Then it came directly to her. It seemed to pass right through her and blast out the roof and up into the heavens she had just returned from.

This should have scared her, but she felt a great peace come over her as the ball disappeared.

But then a real nightmare came to life as Geoffrey started to scream and the baby started to cry. "Oh no, no don't leave me," Geoffrey was screaming over and over again with such a blood curdling shrill that Colleen jumped straight up and out of bed.

"Oh God, she's gone…" Beatrice was saying. She stood in the bedroom doorway, with the baby in her arms and saw Geoffrey holding her daughter's limp body. "Dear God be with us," Beatrice prayed. Prepared for this, she did not cry.

Colleen came next to her mother, and went into the bedroom. She went to Geoffrey and calmly put her hand on his trembling shoulder.

"Geoff, she's gone," She could only say to him. She also felt prepared for the worse, but still had a feeling of peace in her heart for her sister.

His tearful eyes reflected his broken heart. "My life's over. She was my everything Collie," He also used Jeanette's pet name for Colleen. "I was nothing before I met her, and now I'm nothing again," He buried his head in his wife's lifeless body.

"Geoff, Jeanette would hate to hear you talking like that. She's counting on you to take care of your baby. Ricky needs you Geoff," He lifted his head, and she could see hate in his eyes.

"She wanted a baby so bad. And I could never say no to her, you know that Collie. She had me wrapped around her little finger. But I should've told her we should wait, at least until we got to a larger settlement with a doctor. Not that your mom didn't do her best, but a doctor…" He was trying to make some kind of rational sense out of her death.

"Now Geoff, you know that wouldn't have made a difference. It's not your fault. It's no one's fault. Come on Geoff let's go in the other room with your baby. Come on now," Colleen was saying in a very adult way. Her mother continued to silently watch from the door-way.

"Just leave me alone with her. Please just give me some time alone," he shouted. He abruptly pushed Colleen away from them.

"Come on out Colleen. Like he said, let's give him a bit of time to be alone," Beatrice quietly said. Colleen came next to her. Beatrice put her arm around her daughter's shoulder and gently escorted her out of the bedroom.

"Mama, we can't afford for him to lose it. He's got a baby to take care of. I don't want my Sissy gone out of my life, but I do know what has to be done," Colleen knew she would terribly miss her sister. But, she also realized, through this tiny baby, a part of her sister would live on and have to be taken care of.

"You have grit baby girl. Just like your sister. I'm proud of both my girls," Beatrice stood rocking her grandson in her arms.

"We can't stay here now. We'll have to go back home. I can't live here alone with Geoff,"The finality of her lose hit Colleen in the pit of her stomach. "We had so many plans. We were going to go west and seek our fortunes…" she was saying.

Geoffrey came out of the bedroom and softly shut the door behind him. "Last night Jeanette spoke of the Valley of Pines at Driftwood. I didn't like her talking about it but I believe that's where she wanted to be buried. We'll have to pack and get started in the morning," He then turned, and went back into the room and again closed the door.

"We'll just take personal belongings, and all the food and water," Beatrice gently placed the baby on Colleen's bed and covered him. "We'll load the wagon at first light," she added.

She took a fluffy down filled comforter, and made a make shift bed on the floor next to Colleen's bed. "Colleen, Geoff's most likely going to stay in the bedroom all night. We're all exhausted. You get in bed with the baby, and I'll get some sleep right here," She lay down on the quilt.

The entire world as they knew it seemed to be eerily quiet. The wind had stopped its howling, and the deep silence put them to sleep.

***

It took them three weeks to return to Driftwood. The spring weather was in their favor for the entire trip. BD drove their Conestoga with Beatrice and the baby tucked snug inside the protection of this covered wagon. From the back of their wagon, Colleen constantly kept a vigil on Geoff, who traveled on horseback behind them.

It was hard for Colleen to see her sweet Sissy tightly wrapped in blankets and oil cloth, and gently placed and bound on the travois, BD had quickly made out of used wood and straps of leather. The travois was tied to a pack mule that Geoff towed behind his horse. Colleen's heart ached as she watched Geoff hang his head, unable to hide his total remorse. It made her cry and was a sight she knew she would never forget.

After Jeanette's burial at the Valley of Pines, Geoff pulled Colleen aside. "Colleen, I'm not returning with the family to Driftwood," He took her by surprise.

"Geoff, you have Ricky. He's your responsibility," She loved her nephew dearly, but he was not her child.

"I would not be a good father right now Collie," He bowed his head. "I have to go and find myself. I'm lost. I don't know how else to explain it to you," His tears started to flow down his cheeks, and he could feel his throat start to constrict.

"Where will you go? What will you do? What about Ricky, I'm not old enough to be his mother. I love him but..." she was saying when he cut her short.

"Collie, Ricky will be better off with you and your family. You're wiser than you know. I trust you with my son's life..." he was saying.

She outwardly showed him her anxiety when her face burned a bright red and her eyes squinted at him. "I know I'm throwing you a curve, but I just have to get a hold on my life. Please say you'll help me," In his heart he believed she was his only hope. He looked so alone standing there, his long arms hanging at his sides and his head drooped to his chest.

"I'll do my best," Was all she could say. She knew he was not capable, at this time, to accept his responsibilitics or change his mind. "But you must come back to your son. Geoff, you have to promise me you will come back," she said, with conviction in her words.

"I will Collie. Just as soon as I get my head on straight, I'll be back," He knew he was asking a lot of his sister-in-law.

"Where will you go?" She started to wonder about his family he never wanted to talk about.

"East," he said. I'll keep in touch and let you know when I get there. Right now I just have to get away from it all and live with nature," he lethargically said.

He led her to a large boulder at the edge of the pines where his horse and a packed mule awaited him. "Thank you Collie. You will never know how much this means to me..." he was saying, as he mounted his horse. He could not look at her.

"Take care Geoff..." Colleen called out to him. She watched him spur his horse to a gallop with the roped mule in tow. "You come back to us. Like you promised, come back to us," she yelled.

Colleen's heart felt frozen. She could feel her hot tears rolling down her cheeks as she watched him until she could see him no more. Finally, she sat down on the ground next to her sister's grave and just prayed that she would have the wisdom and the courage to be a mother to her little nephew. She knew in her heart that Geoff would one day return and she knew she would present to him the son that he and her sister would be proud of.

Chapter Two

Mitch Arrives With a Mission

Eight years passed and there was no sign of Geoff. He had written a few times but never left a forwarding address. He did not know that his son had grown into the image of his Jeanette. He would have fallen in love with his generous personality and funny sense of humor. But he made it clear that he didn't seem to want anything to do with them so Colleen always did her best to tell Ricky about his parents and how they sacrificed to bring him into the world.

It was a cool September evening. The sun was setting and Colleen could see the dark silhouettes of the trees against the bright orange sky. She expected Ricky to come riding in soon with her brother Brice and his son Keith. They were showing horses to prospective buyers.

It didn't surprise her to see a fourth rider coming in with them. "Mom looks like we only have one extra for supper," she yelled. She was standing on the porch at Driftwood. The front door was open but the screened door was closed to keep the insects from making the ranch house their home.

Beatrice was always ready for unexpected guests for supper. It had been a year since her husband, Hiram had tragically died during a round up and Beatrice continually wanted to keep herself busy with her family and the dealings of Driftwood. It helped keep her mind from her losses.

Since the individual family homes on Driftwood were at least five miles apart it was always understood that if a family member was overdue they would stay at the closest home for the night. Tonight it looked like Brice and Keith, and possibly this stranger would be staying with them; this was something else Beatrice enjoyed. 'The more the merrier.' She always said.

Ricky waved to Colleen, as they all rode into the barnyard. They then, unsaddled and led their horses to the open corral.

"Mama I'm going out to meet them, okay?" Colleen yelled again to her mother from the porch.

"Okay Sugar, but don't be long, tell them supper's about ready," She put a large batch of corn muffins in the oven.

Colleen was twenty four, and felt very happy and healthy. She missed her sister but loved to watch Ricky grow. He reminded her so much of Jeanette with his dark black hair and hazel eyes. His eyes expressed so much of his personality. He would always wink at her and tease her until she could not help but laugh. He was a very important part of her life.

"Hi Sweetness," Colleen said. Ricky ran up to her and hugged her as she neared the fence of the corral.

"Hi Collie, guess what? I made my first sale today. What'd ya think about that?" He looked up at her, his eyes beaming with joy over his accomplishment.

Colleen had always asked him to call her by the pet name her sister gave her. She told him his mother used that name and she was always happy to hear it. "Your first sale, why I think that's just fantastic, mules or horses?" She knew that was the agenda for the day.

"Well, actually driftwood." he said. She noticed a bit of reluctance in his eyes. "But it's a big sale Collie. Uncle Brice says it's the biggest wood sale he's ever seen," he said, with happiness in his words.

"Honey, be proud of a driftwood sale. That's why Grandma and Grandpa named our home Driftwood. We have the largest stock in the countryside." She did not want him to feel belittled by not making a sale on stock.

"I know Collie, but I would've liked to have made my first sale with horses," He was grinning up at her with his toothless smile after losing his two front teeth over a month earlier.

"Now you listen here buster you did a fine job, I'm really proud of you," Colleen said, as she ruffled his hair. "So introduce me to your first client." He started to run in front of her.

"And you'll never guess what, he has the same last name as me, Banks," he yelled. He ran to the corral where the men were wiping down their horses for the day.

"Hey guys!" She neared her brother as he continued his chore. "Ricky's sure excited about his first sale..." Just then the stranger, with the same last name as Ricky's, turned to face her.

"Well, howdy ma'am," He had a big smile on his lips that lit up his sparkling hazel eyes.

Colleen thought he looked like a true cowboy. A thick mustache topped his upper lip and he had at least a weeks' worth of whiskers on his face. His curly brown hair hung to his shoulders under his broad brimmed cowboy hat. He looked right at home and very comfortable in his red checkered flannel shirt with worn out blue jeans covered with leather chaps.

"Watch your step, I wouldn't want Ricky's first customer to mess up his boots," Colleen was saying. She noticed he was about to step in a fresh dung heap.

"Wouldn't be the first time!" he said. He started to wipe his hands on his pants to clean them up a bit. "You must be Colleen. I would know you anywhere," he said. He neared her with his hand outstretched to shake her hand.

"I'm afraid you have me at a disadvantage..." she was saying as Brice interjected.

"Colleen this is Geoff's brother, Mitchell Banks," Brice said, bringing a stunned look on Colleen's face.

"Please just call me Mitch," he said. They continued to shake hands. "Oh I can see I've taken you by surprise, and for that I'm sorry," he said, with genuine concern in his eyes.

"Where's Geoff, is he okay..." He gently dropped her hand. She looked him deep in the eyes for any trace of grief. Then she looked at her brother.

"Geoff's fine, Collie," Brice quickly said. This sent a surge of relief throughout her body. "Mitch has come here, as he's told me, on a mission," he added.

Ricky came up next to them. "Yeah, Collie, Mitch is going west that's why he needs the driftwood," Ricky said. She could tell he did not really comprehend that Mitchell Banks was his uncle, his own father's brother.

"Is that right?" Colleen was saying.

Beatrice rang the dinner bell. "We better get up there. Mama can become really testy if her hard day's work gets cold on the table," She noticed Mitchell go to the fence and throw his saddle over it.

"You're very welcome to join us Mitch. Maybe you can answer a lot of the questions we all have about Geoff," she said. They watched Ricky run ahead with Brice and his son, Keith.

"I'll do my best. He's kind of a recluse," he said.

He pulled his saddle bags down. "Do you think it'd be okay to freshen up some ma'am? I'm not really in the best of shape for feminine company," He motioned if it would be all right if he brought his bags to the house.

"Yes, you're welcome to our home. We welcome all, who come to Driftwood, to stay with us. We have a guest house, and it seems it's used just as much as the main house," she said.

They started to walk to the guest house. "How long has it been since you last saw Geoff? I'm sure you know Ricky's his son and your nephew?" she asked. She saw a flicker of remorse in his eyes.

"Yes, I know Ricky's Geoff's son and my nephew. Geoff's had a really hard time of it, as you already know…" Mitch was saying. "And he told me he entrusted Ricky to your care. I think because of you and your kindness he was able to continue his life, and build on the dreams he and your sister had," He had a genuinely, sincere tone in his voice.

They made their way to the guest house where he could dispose his bags and freshen up.

"So what exactly has he been up to? You know he hardly keeps in touch with me. Ricky doesn't know any other family than us, so he's not very concerned. But Geoff was my sister's husband, and my friend. It was really hard to lose my sister, and then Geoff," She felt her throat constrict. She turned her head from him to hide the tears in her eyes.

"Colleen, I have much to tell you. I know a lot of questions have to be answered and I'll do my best…" he was saying.

They reached the guest house. "Well here you go," She opened the door to the guest house.

They walked into the main living room of the house. It was comfortably fitted to house at least eight guests. It was equipped with a wash room and four separate bedrooms, each furnished with two single beds.

"Mother has always served all the meals at the main house. Here's the washroom and you can pick either of these two bedrooms. Brice and Keith always settle in the front rooms," She pointed out the rooms to him.

"And of course the outhouse, you can find down the path in the back," She pointed to the door at the back of the house.

"Thank you for your hospitality ma'am!" He tipped his hat to her just before he removed it from his head.

"Please call me Colleen," she looked at him.

"Yes ma'...okay Colleen...I'll be up shortly," He opened the door to the closest bedroom, and almost had to duck to enter the room. "This is just fine," He returned to the main living room.

"Well, I'll just leave you to a little privacy. You come on up for supper when you're ready," She started to leave.

"I hate to detain the family, please ask them to eat without me," He did not want to impose any more than he already had.

"Mother, would never hear of it. You take your time, we'll wait," She purposely hurried from the house so he could not protest.

***

After supper they all remained in the living room of the main house. Colleen was anxious to ask about Geoff. But she also could not help but notice how handsome a man his brother, Mitch was, especially after he cleaned up. He wore a light blue flannel shirt, which brought out the blue in his eyes, and washed out jeans that made him look comfortable in his own skin.

"That was a mighty fine meal Mrs. Armstrong. It's been a long time since I've sat down to such good home cooking," Mitch said. He waited for everyone to be seated before he took a chair.

"Why thank you Mitch, and please call me Beatrice," she said. They all got comfortable. "And what can you tell us of Geoff? He has been in our prayers all these years," Beatrice added. She ruffled Ricky's hair as he sat beside her.

"Grandma told me you're my dad's brother," Ricky said. He took a hold of Beatrice's arm, and shied away from Mitch.

"Yes, I am Ricky. And may I say you take a lot after your dad," Mitch said, perking Ricky up.

"Collie always said I look a lot like my mom," Ricky spoke in almost a defending sort of way.

"Honey, you favor your mom a lot, but you also have some traits of your dad and maybe that's what your Uncle Mitch sees," Colleen said. Ricky looked at her with many questions in his eyes.

"Your dad's a handsome man Ricky," Mitch said. Ricky lit up like a Christmas tree. He sat up next to his grandmother trying to look important.

"So I guess that means you're handsome too my little Ga Ga!" Beatrice said. She again ruffled her grandson's hair. "He couldn't say Grandma when he first spoke; just called me Ga Ga, so now he's my little Ga Ga," Beatrice commented. She smiled at Mitch. Ricky's face turned a bright red when she took him in her arms and gave him a big hug.

"Grandma," Ricky said, placing a hard emphasis on his wording. "Mitch is going to think I'm a baby," he added.

"I don't think so Ricky," Colleen interjected. "A baby can't make a driftwood sale. That takes a man. Wouldn't you say so Mitch?" Colleen asked. She looked at Mitch, and noticed he had been staring at her, which sent a flush of excitement throughout her body.

"That's my take. And I have to say Ricky sure knows his driftwood. I don't know the difference between Oak or Pine. And the Birch, Ricky told me about and showed me, is really going to come in handy for our mission," Mitch said. He noticed Ricky again proudly sit up straight in his seat.

"Does Geoff play a part in that mission you keep talking about?" Colleen asked. She perked up everyone's attention.

"Yes, as a matter-of- fact, he does. I am. How can I put this; I'm kind of here on Geoff's behalf. He would've come himself, but I'm guessing, even as I speak, he's getting together some very important supplies and most likely receiving his doctor's diploma," Mitch said. He took them all by surprise.

"Oh my word, how wonderful," Beatrice said. She clapped her hands together and reared back in her seat. "I always knew that boy had grit. Takes grit to hold fast to such an idea," she said, bringing smiles to them all.

"Geoff, a doctor, now I can understand," Colleen said. She remembered the guilt and loss he felt when he lost his wife. "We need good doctors, and Geoff will be the best," she added. They all nodded in agreement.

"Wow, my dad's a doctor. But Uncle Mitch you said my dad would've come here. Does that mean he still will?" Ricky asked, with hope in his words.

"Yes Ricky, your dad will be here as soon as he can. But for now I'm on the first part of our mission, and that is to put together a wagon train to head west. My brother and I want to invite anyone who's ready for that adventure and a new beginning to come along," Mitch said. They all looked back and forth at each other.

"Gosh, I'd sure like to go," Ricky said with enthusiasm in voice. He jumped up and looked his grandmother square in the eyes.

"Now Ricky that's something we'll have to talk about. A person doesn't just pick up and leave their home and head west," Beatrice said. Disappointed, Ricky sat back down on the sofa.

"Your grandmother's right Ricky. This is a new life change. And I can tell you all, Geoff and I have been planning this for some time. This is too important not to give a lot of thought," Mitch said. They all seemed to silently contemplate his words.

"I'm sure Geoff already told you that when my sister was alive that was also our plan. We were set to travel west…" Colleen said. She felt that old spirit of adventure rise again in her heart.

"We had the maps and our route planned, but fate intervened as we all know," She did not mean for her words to offend or hurt anyone's feelings.

"I think I'm that fate you're talking about Aunt Collie," Ricky said. They all knew he only called her Aunt when he was serious about something.

"Ricky, you let me tell you something. If you were fate, you were a true fate of good luck because you've given our whole family a joy that could never be surpassed. Do you understand me young man?" Colleen seriously asked. She knelt in front of him with her arms around his waist. "When your Mom and Dad first found out they were going to have a baby all they kept saying was how they were blessed," She ran her fingers through his soft hair. "We all will talk about this move west. It's not like it's not an option," She noticed her mother gave her a surprised look.

"I know I have my work cut out for me and I would appreciate any help I can get from any of you," Mitch said. He was glad that Colleen at least did not put a negative energy on his mission. He was also happy that they all seemed to want to welcome Geoff with open arms back into the family, and they did not show any animosity about him not keeping in touch with them all these years.

"Uncle Mitch, I'm ready to help all I can," Ricky said. He wiggled out of Colleen's cozy grip and stood on his feet in front of Mitch.

"Well, that's mighty nice of you partner. That is if it's okay with everyone else?" Mitch asked. Ricky looked back and forth from Beatrice and Colleen.

"It's fine with me. Keep this young man out of trouble," Beatrice said. She also rose from her seat and went to pour herself a fresh cup of coffee from the corner buffet. She didn't want them to see any regret in her eyes. All of a sudden she had the feeling she would be losing her family and that was something she was not prepared for now or maybe ever in her life.

"What about you Collie?" Ricky asked his aunt.

Colleen felt like she was on the spot for a quick answer. "Well, you know I have my own responsibilities, with the ranch and all, but I will help whenever I can," Colleen said. She knew she would actually want to be a part of this mission rather than just a helper.

"I've met with several new families to the area, who have asked about future wagon trains," Brice said. He remembered over the past years more than ten families had inquired at their church, but then had settled in town to wait for any talk of a wagon train west. "Most folks venture out on their own, but that has been ill advised by some who return and a lot of the old folks," he added.

Beatrice came back and again took her seat. "Now who are you calling old folks…" she said. They all laughed. "You know I wouldn't be so quick to think someone like me wouldn't be up for this mission of a wagon train or whatever you call it," she said. She took a sip of her coffee, knowing she had surprised them all with her statement.

"Mama, really..." Colleen blurted out. "I was thinking the same thing, but I didn't want to leave you here all alone," Colleen said. Her statement almost confirmed to Mitch that she would be leaving with him and Geoff.

"Age is just a number daughter. You know that old saying 'you're as young as you feel'," she said.

Shocked, Brice stared at his mother and sister, Colleen in disbelief.

The stars started to twinkle bright in the evening sky before any of them even spoke of retiring for the night. Many plans were made, and before the sun rose in the morning some of their lives were changed.

Chapter Three

Geoff Returns/New Plans Made

For the entire night the cool rain steadily battered the windows. Getting out of bed was not easy. Colleen struggled to separate herself from the warmth of her downy quilt. The clouds covered the sun making it seem earlier than it really was. Finally, she forced herself to get out of bed, and slip into her house shoes and cotton robe.

She hurried with her personal morning chamber needs, dressed, and then went straight to the kitchen. She stoked the fire in the stove and added another log. She went to the kitchen sink, and filled the porcelain caldron with water for any utility needs. Then she filled the coffee pot to the full line with water, and scooped the appropriate amount of ground coffee into the drip basket. She finally placed the pot next to the caldron on the wood stove, and made certain the fire was set.

For a moment she relaxed by the sink. Sleepily, she looked out the window above the sink, and noticed that after the night rain; a morning fog had settled in around them. Suddenly, through the milky mist, a figure, on horseback slowly entered the barnyard. Quickly, she rubbed her eyes to see if the figure was true or some kind of sleepy illusion.

The figure arrived at the rear hitching post, dismounted, and started to walk to the back door of the house.

She recognized his stride, but could not believe her eyes and immediately let out a soft shriek. Quickly, she ran and opened the back door. "Oh dear God, Geoff, it's you," she said. She stood frozen in the doorway, completely astonished to see him.

"Am I allowed to come in?" he asked. Embarrassment showed on his face and he bowed his head in front of her. He could not look her in the eyes.

"Yes, yes come in its cold out there," she said. He passed in front of her, and entered the kitchen; she could smell the scent of musky smoke on his clothes.

"Here let me take your coat. You go by the fire and get yourself warmed up," she was saying.

He slowly backed away from her. "Colleen you're as kind as you've always been, but I really can't stay," he said.

She felt an ice cold knife, colder than the morning air, hit her heart. "What do you mean you can't stay?" she almost yelled. "Mitch told us you were coming, and he told us about your mission. We have made plans Geoff, you can't just leave us again…" she was saying.

He interrupted her. "Let me explain," He took her up on the warmth of the stove as he removed his gloves, and opened his hands over the heat. "Colleen, I have to tell you how much I appreciate all you've sacrificed in my name. You've been a mother to my son, and you've given me more strength than you could ever know. It's really hard for me to stand here and face you…" he was saying. Tears filled his eyes and rolled down his cheeks.

"Geoff, please don't say anymore. What I've done was for love. Love for my sister and love for your son. Wait until you see him, Geoff, he's a ray of sunshine. He gives me so much joy," she said. She pointed for him to take a seat at the table.

He neared a chair and pulled it away from the table and slowly sat down. "You are making this too easy on me. I know I didn't keep in touch with you like I said I would. And I want you to know I had full intentions when I left to do just that. But I couldn't find the strength to do it," he said. He took off his wet, leather cowboy hat, and buried his head in his hands. He openly sobbed in front of her.

"Now you stop that, I'm fine. We all are fine. Here now, get up, and let me help you out of that soaked coat," She coaxed his weary body up from the chair.

"Collie you should be a married woman by now, with a family of your own. I took all that away from you..." he was saying.

She helped him out of his heavy tanned leather coat, and hung it on the rack near the back door. "Oh forget that, I haven't met the man who could match my wit much less put up with it..." She teased. She went for two mugs and filled them with the perked coffee. "We still have honey! That is if you still take it the same way..." she looked at him. She put some in hers, and then in his when he nodded a yes to her.

"You're too good to me. I don't deserve any of this," he said. He felt he was allowing her to mother him, but was enjoying her attention, as he accepted the mug of aromatic coffee.

"You've turned into a true cowboy from head to toe," she said, in a kidding way. "Leather hat, leather coat and chaps, and even your boots," She stood in front of him pointing out his apparel. "And not to be surprised a cotton plaid shirt just like your brother's. I guess you learned to dress like this from him?" she asked. She took a sip of her coffee, while she continued to stand in front of him.

"Mitch is another wonder. He found the way to help me through that desperate time in my life. Collie, I'm truly ashamed to tell you this, but Mitch stopped me from taking my life," he told her. He watched her for any signs of animosity towards him. "I was in a sorry shape, and my brother helped me see that my life was worth living, not only for myself, but for my son," He lowered his head.

She went for the coffee pot, and refilled their mugs. "Geoff that would've been a good time for you to be here with us, we all could've helped each other. But I understood why you had to get away back then, so please don't fret on it, it's over, and now it's time to move on. Right?" she caringly asked. She was trying to put him at ease after telling her such a tragic personal experience. "I'll tell you one thing that is very obvious about you, and that is that you don't try to hide your British accent like you used to do," She looked at him for an explanation.

"That's another tribute to my brother. We can't hide our heritage or take on the sins of our ancestors. I am who I am. Mitch made me see that what our fathers and grand-fathers did at a time in history when men struggled for independence, and just to stay alive, should stay where it is in the past. I am the man who I am, and I make my own future," He knew she could respect his comment after remembering stories from her own past.

"You're right there! The world changed. People and nature had to learn how to live together again," She had a look of acknowledgement on her face. "And that brings up another point your brother told us about how your life has changed..." she was saying. She noticed he sat up straight in his chair just like Ricky.

"Oh yeah, well knowing my brother that could be just about anything," He waited for her to reply.

"He told us you've studied and received a diploma as a doctor," she said. She pulled a chair in front of him, and took another sip of her coffee.

"Yes, it was a struggle Collie, but I had great motivation," he said. He knew she would understand that he meant after the death of his wife and her sister, Jeanette.

"I know you did, and the whole family is very proud of you," She rose from her chair and went to the stove. "You're staying for breakfast..." she said, in a stern voice. "I won't take no for an answer," She looked him straight in the eye.

"You really don't have to twist my arm Collie. I'm famished," he said. She came next to him, and was filling his mug again, when they heard a noise near the kitchen entrance way.

"Hi!" was all he said. He stood in his footed pajamas rubbing his sleepy eyes awake. "It's so dark outside. Is it morning already..." He sluggishly walked up to Colleen right past the man in the chair.

"Ricky, Honey this is your dad," Colleen said.

Ricky shyly turned to face the man in the chair. With questioning eyes as big as saucers he then looked up at Colleen to make certain he had clearly heard what she said. Seeing the confusion in his eyes she nodded a yes to him as tears welled in her eyes.

"Hi Ricky," was all Geoff could muster up right then. He sat eye level to his son.

"Hi," Ricky returned. He courteously extended his hand to his father, as he had, to many strangers in his lifetime.

"Well, this is a time for celebration. I think I'll go to the smoke house, and get one of those prime hams we've been saving," Colleen said. She watched Geoff take his son's tiny, tender hand into his large strong hand. With tears flowing down Geoff's cheeks he rose from his chair. He then picked his son up, and lovingly hugged him in his fatherly arms.

"Are you really my dad?" Ricky asked, with true admiration in his voice. "Wow you're a cowboy just like my uncle Mitch. That's neat," Excitement filled his body, as he hugged his father's neck.

"Yes, I'm really your dad, son," Geoff said. He held Ricky up in the air, and admired him as his son. "What a handsome young man you are," he added.

Saying that brought an uninhibited grin to Ricky's lips. For the first time in his life he felt a natural connection with someone other than the family he already knew, which gave him an instinctive awareness that this stranger truly was his dad.

"What's all the commotion?" A fully dressed for the day Beatrice was saying, as Colleen was going out the back door.

"Look who's here Mama. I'm going for a smoked ham. We're celebrating today," Colleen said. She hurried from the house to the smoke house.

"Oh my God, is that you Geoff?" she asked, with astonishment in her voice. "My prayers have been answered," She neared Geoff, and her grandson.

"My dad, Grandma," Ricky said. He had a proud look in his eyes.

"I see that Honey," She reached and tasseled Ricky's soft hair with her fingers. "So good to see you Geoff," She reached around both of them, and gave them a great bear hug. "You've been sorely missed my boy," Tears rimmed her eyes and spilled down her cheeks.

"Don't cry Grandma. This is a happy time..." Ricky was saying.

Colleen banged open the back door. "Look who I found in the barnyard," Colleen and Mitch entered the kitchen.

"Breakfast will be ready in a little bit." Colleen said. She grabbed the huge ham that Mitch had carried in for her. "Why don't you men go to the dining room," She noticed Ricky's face light up when she included him as a man. "Give us women some room to get a good breakfast cooked," She started to slice the ham.

"And Ricky you get yourself dressed it's kind of nippy today," Beatrice said. She started to flip the cut up ham in a large cast iron skillet on the stove.

"Collie, Grandma was crying when she saw my dad," Ricky was saying. Geoff and Mitch were greeting each other, as they were getting ready to leave the kitchen for the dining room.

"Those are happy tears, my boy, and you're most likely going to see some more before this day's over, so get used to it," Beatrice said. The men left the kitchen with Ricky still in his father's arms smiling from ear to ear.

"Collie I'm going for BD. He needs to be here for this," Beatrice said. Her daughter only nodded a positive reply.

BD had his own, one room cabin, not far from the main house next to the barn. He always said, 'the animals are the pulse of Driftwood,' and he always wanted to be close to them.

With her mother gone, all at once Colleen could feel the emptiness in the kitchen. Although the kitchen was large in size so were the men who had just left, and their absence in the room gave her a lonely feeling deep in the pit of her heart. At that second she decided she would cherish every moment in time with those she loved.

It was right at that time, when those she loved were on her mind that a great blue streak of light passed right in front of her. She watched it fly straight up through the ceiling and then return and shoot right into her. Instantly, she had an intense remembrance of her first recollection of BD. Of course he was much younger, but still portrayed his gruff, yet witty personality.

Just then her Mother rushed in the back door. "Collie, get Geoff, something's wrong with BD," was all she said. She turned and ran out the door.

Colleen removed all the cooking food from the stove, as the men hearing the commotion, hurried into the kitchen.

"What is it Collie?" Geoff asked.

Colleen ran up to him, and grabbed his hand and lead him out the back door with the rest following. "Mama said something's wrong with BD, she needs you as a doctor," she was saying.

"Mitch, get the black bag in my saddle bags," Geoff asked. He hurried out of the house with Colleen and Ricky right on his heels.

"Hey Ricky, come on over here and give me a hand will ya?" Mitch calmly asked.

Colleen turned towards Ricky. "Go on Ricky, help Mitch," She did not know what they might have to tend with in BD's cabin.

"Here you go partner. Hold on to that until I can find that bag your dad asked for," Mitch said. He feverishly rummaged through his brother's personal belongings.

"There it is Mitch," Ricky saw the black doctor's bag from his lower vantage, and pointed it out.

"Thanks partner. Can you put this stuff back in the saddle bags?" Mitch asked. "Don't want to just leave it on the ground," He winked at Ricky, feeling even at his young age; the boy was capable around horses, so he hurried to the cabin.

"Wow, that was a bad one," BD was saying when Mitch entered the small cabin. "Thanks Bea," he added. Beatrice handed him a cupful of water, as she studied his cool, steel gray eyes.

"So you've experienced this before?" Geoff asked. He looked at BD with concern written all over his face.

"Well, yeah, but not as bad as this one," BD replied. Perspiration was dripping from his soaked, graying brown hair, and off his face. "This one was a doozie," he added. He felt slightly light headed.

"Here's your bag," Mitch said. He handed his brother the black leather doctor's bag.

"Let's take a listen," Geoff said. He removed the stethoscope from his bag, put the earpieces in, and gently placed the chest-piece on BD's chest to listen to the activity of his heart.

"Sound like a pow-wow going on in there does it Doc?" BD jokingly asked.

Beatrice came next to him, and sat by his side. He was a big strong man, who now looked very out of place slumped over in his bed. Normally, he was the one always in control around the ranch, riding high on his horse. Beatrice could always pick him out from the others. His shape so broad with his cowboy hat always pointed tip down; she could even distinguish his silhouette in an evening sunset.

"You have something funny to say about everything, don't you Benjamin?" Beatrice asked, with concern in her voice. "This is serious," she added. She had a caring tone in her voice that Colleen had never heard her speak to him before.

"I know...I know, but a guy doesn't have to scare the wits out of everyone now does he? I'm sorry you had to see me like that Bea, but I'm fine now, right Doc?" He was eyeing Geoff.

Geoff sat back, and took the stethoscope from his ears. "It appears to me that you've suffered an acute angina pectoris or in other-words an insufficient supply of blood to your heart. I have some nitroglycerin that will help relax the blood vessels and increase the blood flow," He looked through his bag for the bottle. "I always keep this medicine close by for such emergencies," He took one of the pills out, and placed it in the palm of his hand.

"I don't think so Doc. Nobody's going to blow me up. You're an okay guy, but pardon me for..." BD was saying.

Beatrice interjected. "I'm sure Geoff would never give you something that's going to blow you up now would you son..." Beatrice said. She put her arm around BD's shoulders to comfort him.

"No BD, this is not dynamite, this is a medicine. Please trust me," Geoff said, with kindness in his words.

"Well if you're sure it's okay, I guess I can take it," BD said.

Ricky opened the door and peeked in. "Come on in," Colleen whispered. She motioned for him to enter the room. "Your dad's taking really good care of BD. He's feeling a lot better now," Ricky stood next to her and watched his father.

"Just place this under your tongue and try not to swallow for about a minute. This should help prevent another attack for now. But we're going to have to have a little talk about your life style," Geoff said.

Colleen noticed BD take a hold of her mother's hand and give it a tender squeeze. "You know it Doc. Why I'm feeling like my ole self already. Can't keep a good man down," He tried to get up, but fell back on his bed.

"Not just yet. I think you better rest for the day," Geoff said.

Beatrice rose from her seat and stared down at him in the bed. "You're not going anywhere. I'm going to take care of you. Are you listening to me mister?" she sternly asked. "I'm going to get you some good food. That'll fix you up," She was trying to hide her apparent emotions from coming to surface.

"Ricky you sit here next to BD, and make sure he doesn't try to get up. Come on Colleen let's get the breakfast finished and I'll relieve Ricky, and he can come up and eat with all of you," She was making fast plans, in front of them, to hide her deep concern.

"Mama, are you all right, you seem…" Colleen was saying. They were walking up towards the house.

"I'm fine daughter. It's just that I've known BD for so long, and to see him like that," She waved her hands about her head with tears starting to flow, when she remembered how frightened she felt when she found him on the floor of the cabin. "I care for him Collie I have known him for a long time…" she was saying.

"I know Mama I care for him too. You know, it was really weird, just before you came in the house to tell us about BD..." she was saying.

Her mother cut her short, just when she was about to tell her about the blue flash of light, and the thoughts she had about BD.

"Let's not dwell on it now daughter. Let's just get this food cooked, and our men fed," she said. She scurried ahead of Colleen leaving her with an unexpressed empty feeling.

***

Later that evening, after supper; they all sat in the living room making their future plans.

"I brought three families with me," Geoff said. Everyone in the room seemed relaxed and ready to listen.

Even BD was comfortable sitting in Hiram's lounge chair, where Beatrice insisted he sit. After one day he was his ole self, but Beatrice was persistent, that he take it easier a little longer, and Geoff agreed with her.

"The families I brought with me are camping near the north bluffs," Geoff explained. He could feel a tingle of excitement rush through his body knowing they were truly going to head west.

"That's a good spot. Lots of protection there," BD interjected. "Are they going to need more supplies for now?" he asked, in his always caring for others, voice.

"No they're set for now, BD. But I'm going to check on them in the morning, and let them know what's going on with the wagon train. Have any other families come forward?" Geoff asked. Ricky was sitting next to him. He looked up at his father, and Geoff put his arm around him, while his son snuggled in next to him.

"Brice said several families have been asking and waiting in town for the next forming wagon train," Beatrice said. "I've been talking with both Harry and Brice, and when we leave; they will be taking over Driftwood," This did not really surprise anyone.

"It is a big responsibility. And besides the hired hands on the ranch, and at the mill; they're planning to hire some more help. That will be good for the town too," Colleen said. She was always well informed on the business of Driftwood.

"Tomorrow we can look into the driftwood and lumber, and of course we're going to have to round up some horses, mules and cattle. This is going to take some time. We will need more wagons to carry our supplies. I have sent for medical supplies, and I will need one entire wagon for them. I want to make sure, we..." Geoff was saying.

Colleen interjected. "We know how you feel Geoff. Whatever you want you got it. I'm sure I speak for everyone..." she looked around. Everyone nodded in agreement.

"Firewood is one of the biggest problems," Geoff said.

BD joined in the conversation. "Well, I have been giving that a lot of thought, and I think I've come up with an idea that you all might agree on," BD said, perking their attention. "From what I've heard over the years, sage brush is plentiful in some areas, but scarce in others. So I thought pressed sawdust nuggets and dried maze might come in handy to keep the fires smoldering for cooking and heat," he said. "I have several airtight safes that I've used over the years that we can take with us. All we have to do is before the fires go out gather up the embers and keep them in the safe. They turn to charcoal and are easier to light," he said.

Looks, like light bulbs flashing, regarding BD's good idea, sparked grins on everyone, even Ricky. "That's a swell idea BD. I can help with the gathering of the embers. And the nuggets and dried corn are not as bulky as driftwood, and can store pretty easy," Ricky said. They all laughed at his remark.

"My son the business man," Geoff was saying.

Beatrice added. "Why of course…comes from…" she started to say. They all cheerfully chimed in. "Good stock," Beatrice's favorite saying. "Oh my, I guess I do say that a lot, don't I…" Beatrice said. She turned a bright red, as they all smiled and nodded in agreement. "Oh well, I'm proud to say I can't hide the truth," She got up from her seat. "Who's ready for cake? How about you Ricky, want to help Grandma with the dessert?" She asked. Her grandson left his father's side, and went to the kitchen with her.

"The sawdust nuggets and dried maze sound like a good idea BD. Besides our water, fire is a big concern. We can store them in a dump wagon and build false bottoms under each of the wagons for extra storage. Everyone will have their own supply to be used sparingly," Mitch was saying.

Colleen went for a journal, and started to write down all their plans. "First off for now I will write down how many in our family who are going," She neatly wrote each of their names.

"We can get the other families later, but Geoff if you could give me the names of the three families…" Colleen asked. Beatrice and Ricky came in with the refreshments.

"Well, we have the Bolovich family. Yerik, he is the father, with his five sons. He lost his wife after the birth of their last son, Bohdan," Geoff said. He tried not to make too much of the resemblance to his loss.

"Let's see then; the first born is Gavrie, and then we have Andrey, and there is little Pavel, and second to last Alek," He remembered the quiet loving family. "They are a fine addition to our train. Not to mention the boys are very strong," he was saying. Colleen asked him if he could spell all of their names for her.

"There are three in the O'Donnell family. We have Brady, and his wife Briana, and their five year old daughter Abaigeal," He then started remembering conversations with them wanting to start a new life with their daughter.

"Lastly we have the LaFarge family of four. A nice family but a bit spirited for me, but ready for the adventure. Let's see, we have Claude and his wife Camille, with their fraternal twins a daughter Antoinette and a son Olivier," he was saying. Ricky offered him a large piece of chocolate cake with a sweet butter frosting.

"Oh wow, I haven't had anything this good for a long, long time," Geoff was saying.

Mitch agreed with him. "I know what you mean brother. I think I've put on a couple pounds since I've been here," He openly showed he was thoroughly enjoying his piece of cake.

"Geoff, I would like to go to the campsite with you in the morning. I would like to meet everyone and welcome them to Driftwood," Colleen said.

Ricky eagerly added. "Me too, please Collie can I go too?" Ricky asked. He was so excited he could not keep his seat.

"I guess it would be okay. What do you think Geoff?" Colleen asked. She could not help but smile at the eagerness of her nephew.

"Sure. Besides I think one of the Bolovich boys is about your age. You two can get acquainted," Geoff said. He was finishing off the rest of his cake.

"I would like to go too," BD was saying.

Beatrice interjected. "Benjamin, I think you should give yourself another day of rest. We have a big trip to get ready for, and plenty of time to do it. Isn't that right Geoff?" She looked at her son-in-law. She came close to BD's chair, and sat on the arm of it.

"I think she might be right. One more day should do it. And I do want you to let me know right away if you have any out of the ordinary feelings, right?" Geoff asked the older man. He was looking at him with a deep concern on his face.

"You'll be the first to know," BD said. He felt strange to be put in the position of others caring mainly for him.

"And I'll tell you another thing mister; you might as well get used to me being around. Somebody has to take care of you; seems you don't take care of yourself," Beatrice said. She was speaking in a kidding way, but meant it from her heart.

"Holy cats Bea, I think I can..." he started to say. His face flushed a bright red, and she rose from the arm of the chair and looked him straight in the eyes.

"You better give it up BD, she gave you the look," Colleen said.

Ricky noticed it too. "Yeah BD, I'd back down if I were you," Ricky said. They all started to laugh.

BD fidgeted in the chair. "Fine, fine, but you know I'm a very private sort of guy," he said. He shyly looked up, with a slight smile on his lips.

"You'll be okay. I won't hurt you too much," Beatrice said. She again sat on the arm of his chair, and patted his hand.

"More like she'll smother you with kindness," Colleen said. She noticed her mother slightly blush.

"Enough of this, let's get on with our plans," Beatrice said. She slowly took her hand from BD's, and felt him relax.

"You know I'm not sure everyone is familiar with the flint rock fire starting. I know Ricky could use some tips," BD said as Ricky nodded positively. "Well, in a couple days, when Bea, uh I mean, when the doctor thinks it's okay I'll teach him some of my methods, and he can teach the families that need to learn," BD said. Beatrice playfully but gently smacked the back of his chair when he teased her.

"Wow that sounds like fun," an excited Ricky said. "I'm a fast learner BD. You won't have any troubles from me," he said. He was ready to start right on it.

"In a few days son, okay…" Geoff was saying. He felt so proud to talk to his son as a father. His heart leaped in his chest when he saw a flicker of his wife in his son, as Ricky turned and looked at him with a hint of disappointment in his eyes. "We want to make sure BD's ready," He could tell he had successfully curbed his son's anticipation, and realized Colleen and his mother-in-law had disciplined him well.

"Okay, Dad," Ricky begrudgingly said. "But can I still go to camp tomorrow?" he anxiously asked. He was looking forward to meeting everyone especially the younger children more his age.

"Yes that's still on, and we'll be starting pretty early in the morning so I think it's about time for you to hit the hay young man," his father said. He rose from his seat, and went next to his son. He held his arms out to his son and Ricky jumped into his father's loving arms. "Think I can bunk in your room tonight?" Geoff asked. He noticed Ricky's eyes lit up.

"Holy cow Dad," Ricky shouted. "Wouldn't that be great Grammy?" Ricky asked with pleading eyes. He wiggled with excitement in his new found father's arms.

"That's a great idea my little Ga Ga. Let's go get some fluffy quilts, and make up a mat for your Dad right on the floor next to you. Will that be okay Geoff?" Beatrice asked. She was happy that he would be with his son, but sorry he would have to sleep on the floor.

"Anyplace by my son's fine with me, we're going to be in harder places than a floor pretty soon right son…" He was playing with him. He snuggled into his son sending giggles of joy from Ricky.

"Yep, just like real cowboys," Ricky said. They followed Beatrice. "See you in the morning," he added. He waved to everyone in the room. Geoff did not turn around; he just raised his hand with his back to them. They could not see his happy tears flowing down his cheeks.

"Yeah see you both in the morning," Colleen said. She also could feel her throat constrict as she watched the two of them leave the room. Ricky waving and Geoff with one farewell arm in the air.

"Well I think I'm going to hit the hay too," BD said. He rose from his seat and started for the door.

"Breakfast at five too early BD?" Colleen asked.

BD turned from the doorway and faced them. "Sounds great Colleen, see you all then," he said. He started out the door as Beatrice was walking into the room.

"Hold on a second BD I have a few things I'd like to go over with you if you don't mind," Beatrice said. BD stopped in his tracks. "Here I'll walk with you to your cabin we can talk on the way," she said. She purposely put her arm in his, and they started for the door. "I'll be back in a little bit Collie, don't wait up," she said. She shut the front door of the house.

Colleen felt comfortable left alone in the room with Mitch. "You know I think something's going on between those two," she said to Mitch. She felt a little awkward saying it out loud though she had thought it for some time.

"They do seem to meld," Mitch said. He had seen their closeness from the first time he met them. Never knowing Colleen's father, he was able to see them as a couple, who deeply cared for each other, unlike those who knew them to be longtime friends. "I hope that doesn't offend you Colleen?" He noticed a shocked look on her face.

"Well, it does a little. I've known BD all my life. He's always been around as part of the family. My Dad trusted him completely, and it just feels odd that my Mom and him, well…" she was saying. She got up from her seat and started to pace the floor. "Well, you know like you said meld," She picked up her glass of water, and took a sip of it.

"I wouldn't make too much of it. Like you said he's been a part of your family all your life," He tried to set her mind at ease, but knew from the way they acted that her mother and BD meant more to each other.

"Yeah, and my Mom knew BD before she knew my Dad. He started out working for her parents. I never knew my grandparents. And not much has ever been said about them, but from what I gather when Mom's parents died a long time ago and my parents married, BD stayed on and worked for my Mom and Dad. He's been here ever since," She sat in the chair across from Mitch.

"You know, if you're not too tired, I sure would like another piece of that chocolate cake. I've never tasted anything as good as that," He was trying to lighten up the conversation.

"Sure," With her glass of water in hand; she picked up his plate and a few other items and started for the kitchen. "Hey, would you mind picking up some of those plates for me, and bring them in the kitchen?" He rose from his seat, and gathered some plates and glasses.

"You can just put them over here," She was filling a dishpan with some hot water from the kettle and added some soap. "I love the kitchen. It's my favorite room in the house. So warm and cozy," She whipped the suds with her hand.

"And smells so good," He placed the dishes on the counter where she asked him to.

"I'll go get the rest of them, while you fill the pan," He felt a surge of pure joy fill his body. Or never having experienced the feeling before, that was the feeling he thought it was, as he watched her methodically continue her chore. He could tell she was in her element.

He came back in the room. "I cut you a piece of cake over there on the table. Care for some more coffee?" She turned from the sink with the coffee pot in her hand.

He thought she looked like a beautiful angel standing there with the soft lantern light glowing around her like a halo. She was breathtaking yet so far out of his league.

Mitchell Banks was a lady's man. When he saw what he wanted he got it. He knew the ladies looked at him with a sort of adoration. He never asked for this, but just seemed to possess it with his good looks and self-confident demeanor.

But Colleen was different. He thought Colleen, in her soft denim overalls and white cotton blouse could give him more than any other high or low society woman ever tried to satisfy in him. She possessed a nonchalant personality, and never found it necessary to put on airs to attract him. She had a way of making everyone believe they were important to her. He could tell by her lighthearted actions that she was a take me or leave me kind of woman. And what interested him even more was that she did not seem to realize it.

"Thanks for the cake but I'm kind of full up on coffee," He patted his flat muscular stomach. "Oh and just to let you know I left some candles lit but blew out the lantern in the other room," he said.

"Thanks, one less chore," she said.

"You wash and I'll dry," He came next to her and picked up the dish towel.

"I don't know you look kind of out of place in the kitchen," She replaced the coffee pot on the stove. "You look more like a get waited on kind of guy," she teased. She found her Mother's apron, and tied it around his waist.

"Oh yeah," He raised his arms in submission, "Trying to tame the wild cowboy," He kidded her, and enjoyed the feel of her tying the apron.

"No, just don't want you to get those pretty jeans of yours all wet," She teased him as she started to wash the dishes.

"I was thinking about what you said about my Mom and BD. You know about them seeming to meld," She felt free to speak to him in confidence. "Between you and me, now that you've mentioned it I should've seen it all along," She looked at him with trust in her eyes.

"Colleen, unless you otherwise tell me, you can be at ease that anything you say to me stays with me, okay?" He confirmed a feeling she already had about him.

"I already kind of figured that out or at least I hoped you were like your brother on that count," She saw a flicker of hurt in his eyes. "I'm not saying I completely compare you with Geoff, but you are brothers, and there must be things about you two that are alike," She hoped she had not put a damper on the beginnings of the friendship she was establishing with him.

"We are brothers but we're farther apart than we seem. In our younger days there were reasons why we both took off to be on our own," She noticed a bit of hesitation in his voice.

"Well, I guess you could say I was more of the renegade and Geoff was the evangelist," He continued to dry and stack the dishes that she washed and rinsed.

"I hope you don't think I'm prying," She was glad he seemed at ease to still speak with her.

"Our Mother died when Geoff was born," He noticed a shocked look on her face. "I can see you didn't know that," he said.

They both stopped what they were doing and looked in each other's eyes. "No I didn't know that. Geoff has always been very, I don't know how else to say it but secretive about his life before he came to Driftwood. Whenever we would start to talk about his past he always got a depressed look on his face so we would drop it. I figured whenever he was ready he would let me know. I don't even know if my sister knew everything about him," She was happy to now understand some more about her brother-in-law.

"Colleen, when everything happened, our family was on the other side. And when our father decided to come East, Geoff and I were just wet nosed babes. Our journey here was treacherous. We saw our father do things I can never repeat. But he vowed to us that what he did he did for our survival. Men were fighting to be free, and the world, as we knew it, not only died, but our family did too. Our country was overwhelmed with patriotism and regular human beings just trying to survive. I'm sure you know where I'm coming from," He could tell by the look on her face she did. "As a free patriot, I know your family had to fight and work hard to make ends meet, and still have your life here on Driftwood," He started to wave his hand above his head. "Oh boy, now I almost feeling like my brother, the evangelist," he said.

They both slightly giggled. "Yes, life is really hard and we're always trying to keep things going around here," she said. "I still remember some of the stories my parents told us about survival and trying hard to keep our freedoms," she looked at him. "But it's all been worth it for us. We lost a lot but we keep on trying," she was saying as he interrupted her.

"Look, wow, I've spoke up now more than I ever should have. I guess it's just that you're so easy to talk with. I feel like I can be very honest with you Colleen. I hope I haven't offended you in any way..." He searched her eyes for any sign of animosity.

"No, but you might offend my Mom if you don't finish off that cake," She thought she would rather tease him and get away from the political subject.

"Heck no, I wouldn't want to offend her. I'm caught up with the dishes anyway," He put the dish towel down, and went to the table to finish his cake. "I really should just wrap this up and get out of your hair for the night," He looked around for something to wrap the cake in.

"No, you just sit down and enjoy," She came to the table and sat in the chair across from him, and motioned for him to sit. "I wanted to tell you a little bit more about when my Dad died," She situated herself in her chair. "My Mom was devastated. Her pain was overwhelming. She almost had to reinvent herself. BD was always there for her, but really no more than he was before. In a way maybe he has always been in love with her, but never would admit it to himself much less her," She got up from her chair.

"Now I'm saying more than I really want to hear, but I guess it's just something I have to face. So they say life goes on," She placed her hands on the back of her chair and looked at him. "I really want my mom to have some happiness in life. She's a strong woman, and has given so much to her family and the land that now I think it should be her turn," She put her elbows on the back of the chair and her hands innocently under her chin.

"You also deserve it to be your time too," He wondered how he got the nerve to say such a thing to her. "Oops, now I'm stepping out of line. I think it's about time I called it a night," He rose from his seat and she came next to him. She was so near to him that he could smell the naturally fresh scent of her hair.

"I'll walk with you to the door. I don't know what to do about leaving a candle lit for her. I guess with the globe it will be alright..." she was asking. They entered the living room.

"Maybe just leave the one closest to the door lit, so she can grab it when she comes in," he said. They both blew out the other candles.

"Thanks for sticking around, it was nice to have someone to talk with," she said. They stood awkwardly near the door. "And I don't think this is a part of your wardrobe," She went behind him, and untied the apron and then faced him with a sly look on her face holding the apron in front of him.

"No, I don't think that would look good with my chaps. And Colleen this evening was my pleasure. See you in the morning," He stepped back from her and opened the door, while taking his hat from the hook on the wall by the door and placing it on his head as he left.

"Yes, nice and early all bright eyed and bushy tailed," she teased. "Good night Mitch," She spoke in a softer voice as he turned and walked into the night.

"Nice, full moon tonight; can see a mile," He hoped she would understand he meant for her not to worry about her mother walking back to the house in the dark.

"Yes, I see," She stepped onto the edge of the porch and looked up. "Almost as bright as sunshine," she whispered. She continued to watch him walk towards the guest house. "Good night," Not wanting to disturb the quiet of the night she muffled her words.

"Good night," He raised his arm in the same fashion that his brother had earlier. But unlike his brother, who had tears in his eyes, Mitch was so full of joy he couldn't stop himself from grinning. It was at that very moment he knew this beautiful creature in the moonlight, who was whispering good night to him, would one day become his wife.

***

The soft dim fire light in the cabin created a romantic ambiance that stimulated the love they expressed.

"The lights in the kitchen, I should go help Collie with the clean-up," Beatrice said. She felt a bit remorseful leaving her daughter with all the mess.

"Just as I've seen it for so many years knowing it was you doing the clean-up," Benjamin said. He lovingly caressed her cheek and gently kissed her soft lips as she lay next to him.

"You can always take away the guilt. You know you are my peace don't you Benjamin…" She cuddled up next to him.

"Bea, you shouldn't have a guilty bone in your body. Why, you're the most giving person I've ever met, and you've taught your children well. I'm sure Collie doesn't feel like you should be tied to the kitchen. She can take care of things. That's how you raised her…," he was saying.

She started to pout. "Yes, I know, but…" She was about to say another guilt feeling, when he got up from beside her and straddled her naked body with his.

"Benjamin, you savage," she cooed to him. She had a shameless look in her eyes as she slowly ran her fingers through his hair. She watched as his eyes searched her eyes and then looked down the length of her body. "One might think you want something…" She placed the soft fronts of her worked calloused hands on his unshaven face. "You move me in a way I have never…" she was saying.

He lowered himself to her, and purposely kissed her tender lips to silence. Easily, they expressed their love.

***

The morning sun burned the early fog away and brightly rose in the eastern blue sky. It was a fresh new day, and spirits in the house were high.

Colleen was busy starting the morning coffee, and keeping an eye on the crackling bacon in the iron skillet.

"Ricky, you might want to start getting dressed as soon as you get out of bed. Footy Jammies aren't a cowboy's way to dress on a wagon train," She smiled at her young nephew as he slowly entered the room rubbing his sleepy eyes.

"I will Collie," He went next to her, and hugged her hip, as she filled a glass with milk for him.

"Here maybe this will help wake you up..." She handed Ricky the milk as Geoff entered the room. "Coffee should be done in a bit. How'd you guys sleep last night?" she asked.

Geoff sat at the table and Ricky came next to him. Geoff let him sit in between his legs facing the table. "Best night's sleep I've had since I can't remember," Geoff said. He ruffled his son's hair.

Ricky looked up at him with a milk mustache topping his smiling upper lip. "Me too Dad," Ricky said.

They could hear the front door open and close. "Morning everyone," Mitch said. He entered the kitchen with his hat in his hand.

"Mitch, you can hang your hat back there next to the back door," Colleen said. She motioned the rack to him. "Coffee's about ready. Hope everyone is hungry we're even having biscuits this morning," she said.

Ricky got up from his seat. "Oh boy, Collie's biscuits this is a celebration," Ricky said. He turned and faced his dad. "Wait until you taste Collie's biscuits. She puts honey in them. They're the best," he was saying when Geoff interjected.

"I know son, I've had them before," Geoff said. He smiled at his son's jubilation. "She's sure a good cook..." Geoff added. Colleen brought him a cup of steaming coffee.

Mitch came next to the stove and filled his own mug. Colleen came next to him and started to turn the bacon. "Just to let you know the candle by the door was still there and burned completely down," Mitch said. He knew she would understand the significance of what he said.

"Oh I see..." she was saying.

Just then her mother and BD entered the back door walking hand in hand. "Everyone, we have an announcement to make..." Beatrice said. She purposely held BD's hand up with hers. "This wonderful man has asked me to be his wife and I said yes," She put her hand on his shoulder and looked around the room. She then vigorously and openly hugged and kissed him in front of them all.

"Oh boy, does this mean I'm going to have another Grandpa?" Ricky shouted with glee. He started jumping up and down.

"It sure does," Beatrice said. She opened her arms to her grandson and he happily let her pick him up. "You're almost getting too big for this..." She patted his bottom as she held him in her arms. "But today I could do about anything. Grammy has some added strength today," She kissed Ricky's cheeks.

"This is just great," Ricky said. He hugged his grandmother.

BD shyly tried to edge his way towards his wife-to-be and her grandson. "I hope everyone is as happy as you are Ricky," BD said. He intentionally looked at Colleen.

"Who wouldn't be happy? I haven't seen Mama this happy in a long time..." Colleen said.

She went up next to the trio and hugged them all. "I'm happy for you both Mama," she said. Tears spilled from her eyes.

"Happy tears my daughter?" Beatrice softly asked. She placed her hand on her daughter's face and wiped away her tears.

"Yes Mama only happy tears," she said. She smiled at her, and then hugged her.

She then hugged BD. "I know you will take care of her," she said, with trust in her eyes.

"With my life Collie, with my life," He said, tears glistening in his eyes. "She means the world to me," he added, as Beatrice smiled up at him.

"Well let's get us some vittles I'm starving," Beatrice said. She relinquished her loving hold on Ricky to his father. She then went to the stove and took over the cooking. "We have a lot to do to get ready for our trip. And, oh, by the way Geoff, I think BD is up to just about anything today," She looked at her future husband and winked, which brought a red blush to BD and an outburst of laughter from Geoff.

"I think on this occasion I will let you make that call," Geoff said.

Colleen hurriedly went next to her mother deliberately not looking at her, but went about her business of getting the table set for their breakfast.

***

Beatrice and Benjamin married on the hillside overlooking Driftwood. Geoff besides receiving his doctorate had obtained a justice of the peace certificate, and officiated at the ceremony. Besides the family the entire wagon train and a few friends attended.

And by this time they had started to live at the campsite to accustom themselves to the rigors of outdoor living so later that evening they celebrated their nuptials with a reception at the campsite.

"This is the way we're going to live for some time to come daughter," Beatrice was saying to Colleen. They were sharing a private moment away from the celebration.

"I know Mama. I think we're ready for it, don't you?" Colleen asked. She had a bit of hesitation in her voice.

"I know I am. It's going to be a challenge, but what the heck! And Daughter, who would of thought at my age I would be a blushing bride," Beatrice said. She scooted next to her daughter where they sat on crates near Colleen's wagon. "I'm so happy I can't tell you how much," She put her arm around Colleen.

"Just knowing that makes me happy Mama. You truly deserve it," Colleen delighted at the love and happiness she saw in her mother's eyes.

"You know, I'm kind of sorry you have to have your own wagon, but I'm sure you understand," She was about to say something about becoming a newlywed, when Colleen interjected.

"Mama, you don't have to explain and I have plenty of help," She did not want her mother to feel any kind of embarrassment.

"Honey this might be a good time to tell you something about my past," Beatrice said, peaking Colleen's attention. "It's not that it's been a secret or anything but it's just that it's never really come up in conversation…" She saw a startled look on her daughter's face.

"I'm not adopted, or something, am I?" Colleen asked. She thought that to be the worst thing she might tell her.

"No you're not adopted but even if you were, why would you worry yourself about that?" she asked. She looked at her daughter with only love in her eyes. "I had you the normal way and I couldn't love you anymore if I picked you out myself. What I have to talk with you about is Driftwood and my parents," She saw a confused look in her daughter's eyes.

"What about them?" Colleen asked. She knew she had never met her grandparents.

"Well, I was young and don't remember all of it. But my parents never owned Driftwood," she looked at her daughter. "Driftwood actually belonged to my Aunt Frieda and Uncle Thomas Stilles, who never had any children. They willed

Driftwood to me after their passing," Beatrice was saying. "It's a long story Colleen, but my parents lived out west, and sent me here to visit with my Aunt and Uncle. Well then everything happened and I never saw my parents again," She knew she had Colleen's complete attention.

"Honey I really don't know if my parents are dead or alive. I know it has always been said that BD was asked to stay here when my parents left but I just never thought it was important to tell the real story. And land sakes I was so young back then I barely remember much. But Honey I do remember this…" She reached behind her and pulled out a tiny wooden chest.

"Wow, I've never seen that before," Colleen said. Her mother placed the chest in Colleen's hands.

"Now, this is yours Colleen," Beatrice said. Colleen began to open the box.

"That's one thing you can't do daughter," she said. She placed her hand on top of Colleen's hand to prevent her from opening the chest.

"Why, what's the purpose?" Colleen asked. She felt she was taking in more new information than she really wanted to. "This is all so confusing…" She put her hand to her head.

"I'll tell you why. My life was all turned upside down back then. What I thought was going to be a summer vacation staying with my aunt and uncle turned into a lifetime. And since I was so young when my parents sent me to Driftwood this was left with my aunt Frieda for me to have later in life," She patted the chest. "Since Aunt Frieda never had any children she said her sister, my mother loved her so much that she sent me to spend the summer with her. And it was supposed to only be for the summer…" Beatrice seemed to make it sound very important that she was not just dropped off. She was loved by her parents. "And daughter, that is why this has a special importance to me. It was from my parents," Beatrice had a look of trust in her eyes.

"When my aunt gave it to me she said, my mother wrote to her to give it to me, but my mother insisted that I could only open it when I got to the compost. Honey I can see you're as confused about this as I am. But I was so young when I was given this, and life was really confusing back then..." she was saying.

"The only reason I'm giving it to you now is because I'm getting older, and I'm hoping one day you'll figure out where or what the compost is and then and only then can you open the chest with this key," She handed her daughter a necklace with the key on it.

"But what if I never figure out where or what the compost is, then what do I do with it?" Colleen asked. She thought this to be a crazy situation. "Why don't we just open it up right now, together?" Colleen asked. She hoped to change her mother's mind.

"No, Honey, please understand I have to abide by my mother's wishes. Will you do this for me?" Beatrice asked with pleading eyes. "This is my legacy, and in time if you don't find the compost I want you to pass it on to your children or someone you trust. It is very important Honey, and my mom honored me when through my aunt she entrusted me with it," she said, curbing Colleen's anticipation.

"I will do my best Mama. If you've been carrying this thing around with you all of these years I guess I can too," Colleen said.

Her mother let out a yelp, and vigorously hugged her daughter. "You make me proud daughter. You make me proud..." she hugged her again.

BD walked up to them. "I've been looking for my bride. I think it's time we retired to our wagon," he said. He extended his hand to the woman he loved.

"My knight in shining armor," Beatrice said. She playfully bowed in front of him. "Your lady awaits," she said. She winked at her daughter, and they left Colleen sitting alone with the chest on her lap.

"Isn't this just something else, and what in the world is this compost?" she was asking herself. "It sounds like some kind of pile of garbage, but this box looks like it belongs to something very important not a pile of garbage," she was thinking.

"I wonder what else I don't know about my mother or my family! Oh well, we're going to have a lot of time in the future to talk about it anyway," she thought. Then she smiled, when she remembered her mother's sly little wink to her as she went off with the man she loved, Colleen's new step-father.

Life as they knew it was changing fast. The journey they were preparing to embark on would take them to places they had never before seen with people they were only starting to get to know. Sand would take the place of wood floors. As they traveled, their wagons would protect them from the light of the scorching sun. The cool evening's twinkling stars would be their night time ceiling. They all had one thing in common, they would trek their way to the place some called home. They would do this for themselves and for their ancestors, and in the end the unknown would finally be answered.

Chapter Four

Ricky Bonds with Pavel

The wagon train was coming along and their journey was only weeks away. Ricky had spent many days and nights with the Bolovich family. Although he was two years older than Ricky, little Pavel had become Ricky's best friend. But Ricky also liked spending time with his new friend's brothers, Alek and Bohdan.

"Grandpa, BD rigged this up for me," Ricky held up his fire making kit for his friends to see. "He said, he will fix up as many as he can before we head out," Ricky said. "Look at this Pavel, Grandpa BD put a wooden handle on this steel rasp to make it easier to hold, and he made this box for me to keep my stuff in. He showed me how to make this box and I was going to make some for all of us, would you guys want to help?" Ricky asked, perking their attention.

"Wow that would be great," Pavel said eager to learn and have something to do. "And maybe we can work some more on fire making too…" he was saying as their Father, Yerik called them to help with the animals. "I guess maybe later Ricky," Pavel said. He waved to Ricky as he ran with his brothers to help their Father.

Feeling a bit disheartened Ricky crammed his box in his saddle bag and started for their Conestoga wagon to start on his projects when Pavel came running after him. "Ricky, Ricky Papa said I should come help you he has plenty of help," A panting Pavel yelled reaching Ricky.

"All right..." Ricky shouted. "Come on, Grandpa has all the stuff ready to go," Ricky felt so happy as the pair walked with one arm draped across each other's shoulders, "And we'll work on fire starting too," Ricky was excited to be with his new friend. "See how this fits?" When they reached Ricky's campsite he placed some of his workmanship in Pavel's hands. "Grandpa BD showed me how to use the hand drill to make these holes and how to hammer the wooden doll pins in..." He pointed out the holes. "We'll make as many boxes as we can," he smiled at Pavel, and watched as Pavel shifted the box in his hands and looked it over. "Look at this stuff, Grandpa calls it char cloth," Ricky placed a piece of the tender charred cloth in Pavel's hand.

"Is that what starts the fire?" Pavel asked. He could tell he had to be careful not to play with the flimsy cloth. "It's sure light and fluffy," Pavel examined the cloth.

Ricky gently took it from Pavel's hand. "We don't have much of this but we'll put some in each box. It's mainly for emergencies when the hemp rope's not available," Ricky said, remembering the importance BD put on the char cloth. "Let me show you how my box is set up and we can go from there," Ricky pulled his box from his leather saddle bag. "Grandpa says the box should be kept in a place that follows you," He noticed a confused look on Pavel's face. "You know if you're going to be riding your horse you keep it with you in your saddle bags. And if you're riding in the wagon keep the saddle bags there. So I guess in other words where you go your saddle bags go, cause you don't want to be without fire, and you never know when an emergency might come about," Ricky explained. He had a feeling of being in charge and grown up.

"So then we should make the boxes just like this one?" Pavel continued to look over Ricky's box. "What's this?" He picked up a tiny magnifying glass.

"My Dad brought those. He said we can use them when the sun's out. But it's important to know both ways so you'll always have fire," He winked at Pavel. "Come here I'll show you how they work. You see it reflects the sun's light as it filters through the lens and makes the sunbeam hotter. Watch this." Ricky positioned the magnifying glass towards a tiny pile of tinder he had placed near the campfire. Within a few minutes the tiny twigs started to flame.

"Wow," Pavel shouted. "That's neat," He looked at Ricky.

"I know," Ricky said. He took a shovel and stirred the small fire into the bigger campfire.

"Ready to get started on these boxes…" Ricky was saying as Colleen rode into the campsite.

"Hi Collie," Ricky yelled, as Colleen trotted her horse next to the wagon and dismounted and tied him to the wagon wheel.

"You boys look hard at work. Are those the boxes BD showed you how to make?" she asked. She pulled up a wooden crate and sat next to the pair.

"Yeah, we just got started and we're going to try to make a hemp fire in a little bit," Ricky said. He saw a concerned look on her face. "It will be our supper fire. I know to only make a fire that we can use Collie," He knew the importance of conserving their supplies.

"I know you do Honey, just want to make sure cause you know we won't have anything but what we can carry out there, and whatever we can scrounge up in the wilderness," She was trying not to make a scary deal about it but just an important one as she ruffed his hair.

"Collie…" Ricky blushed when she showed him an endearment in front of Pavel as Pavel kind of shied away.

"Sorry, but you know I love you," She went to hug Ricky when Pavel started to cry. "Pavel you come here I have plenty of love for you too…" she was saying, as the boy missing the tenderness of his mother dashed into her open arms and bitterly sobbed.

"Gosh," Ricky said. He backed off and looked away giving his friend some privacy.

"I miss me Mom so much," Pavel said. He looked up at Collie with tears streaming down his cheeks.

"I know you do sweetheart and you just come to me anytime you want to talk and we'll talk about your Mom…" Colleen was saying. She noticed Ricky was crying too. "You come here too," She opened her arms to him and Ricky came to her. They all comforted each other. "Now you both got me going," Colleen had tears of empathy starting to flow as Mitch came up on the three of them.

"Everything okay here?" Mitch asked. They all looked up at him at the same time with wide eyed startled looks on their faces.

"Oh we're just fine. Just doing a little bonding, isn't that right guys?" Colleen said. They all jumped up and simultaneously started to brush off their clothes.

"Yeah, just bonding," Ricky said. They all nervously started to giggle while Ricky and Pavel started picking up the box making materials and they both headed for Pavel's wagon to continue the project. "Collie, we'll be back after while to make the supper fire," He waved goodbye to her. "Here you go Pavel," Ricky handed him his saddle bags. "See you later Collie," he said, as they ran out of sight between the wagons.

"Hey Ricky what's bonding anyhow?" Pavel asked. He noticed Ricky looked at him with a bit of laughter in his eyes.

"I'll tell you later, it's no big deal," he said, hoping Mitch didn't see his tears and think of him as a baby. "Let's just work on the boxes now," he said, as they reached Pavel's wagon.

"Pavel was missing his Mom," Colleen said to Mitch.

Mitch gave her an understanding look. "I can relate," Mitch took off his hat and automatically started to hit it on his leg to get the dust out when Colleen started to sneeze.

"Oh geeze, I'm going to have to get used to dust and cooking outdoors," she said. She took a handkerchief from her pocket. "I'm really going to miss the kitchen," She softly blew her nose into the handkerchief.

"I should've waited to clean my hat. You okay?" he asked. He thought life around a wagon train was going to be different than what he was used to with just the guys during a round up.

"Don't worry about it. Like I said I'm going to have to get used to it," she said. She went to the wagon to get a drink of water. "Mitch, do you think this is going to work? I mean the wagon train. Do you think we might be biting off more than we can chew?" Saying aloud what she had been thinking for some time. "I know, with your experience, you understand about the wilderness and everyone is sure antsy to get going, but can we ever really be completely ready?" She had a wondering look in her eyes.

"I don't think anyone can ever be completely ready for anything. We don't know what we're going to run into out there. But I believe we're as prepared as we can be, and I'm glad to see you continue to wear your side arm…" he was saying, as Antoinette LaFarge entered Colleen's encampment.

"Pardonnez-moi, Mademoiselle Colleen, Monsieur Mitchell, mon père. Pardon me I must speak in English. Mitch, my Father has requested that if you might have the time could you please stop by he has a matter with the storage of the…" She was trying to describe the pressed sawdust nuggets storage compartment. "You know this," She pointed to the one under Colleen's wagon.

"You mean the sawdust and maze?" Colleen tried to help the young woman with her speech.

"Oui, yes, the sawdust and...My Father has a, what you call, a leak," She appeared slightly embarrassed. "And has requested when your visit with Mademoiselle Colleen is completed could you come by our wagon?" She gave Colleen a curiously mischievous look.

"He can go right now," Colleen hurriedly said. She looked at Mitch with raised eyebrows her eyes wide as saucers.

"Why sure, I can take a look," Mitch said. He could not help but notice the look of embarrassment on Colleen's face after Antoinette's insinuating look of his assumed personal involvement with her.

"Perfect," Antoinette said. She went next to Mitch and slipped her arm in his and gently led him from Colleen. "Au revoir, Mademoiselle," She turned inwardly towards Mitch and gave Colleen a passionate look of possession.

"Excuse me," Mitch said, as her bold move made him think he had been jabbed with a hot poker and he openly dropped her arm.

"Oh no, pardonnez-moi," Antoinette awkwardly acted like she tripped and quickly grabbed his hand and purposely brushed his hand across the bodice of her dress. "I'm so clumsy. You must forgive me Monsieur," She pretended to straighten herself.

"Well, let's get on with it," Mitch said. He had an agitated tone in his voice as he hurried to the LaFarge campsite with Antoinette following him like an attentive puppy.

"So that's what a tramp acts like," Colleen thought to herself. "And what was that look all about, like I'm Mitch's kept woman but she wants him. The nerve of her," She thought when she started to think of how their relationship must look to others. "Oh my God I'll have to talk with Mama about this," she said, aloud as Ricky and Pavel came back to her campsite.

"Don't ask Grammy Collie, maybe I can help," Ricky said. He thought she might need some kind of physical work done in her campsite, when he overheard what she had said.

"Oh don't you worry yourself about it. I just have some woman stuff I want to talk over with Grandma. You boys back here to start the supper fire?" She noticed they were carrying some sawdust nuggets and firewood.

"Sure are," Ricky said as they both dropped the wood. "Here Pavel hold this for me while I get this ready," Ricky gave Pavel his rasp and a piece of flint stone.

"Do you think your Grandpa will have these handled rasps for all the boxes?" Pavel asked. He watched Ricky unravel and cut off a piece of the hemp rope and carefully pull it apart until he had a small fibrous ball in the palm of his hand.

"He said, he would, he's making them back at the ranch in the smithy," Ricky replied. He reached for the rasp and securely placed it in his hand with the wood handle between his fingers and then took the flint. "The idea is to create a spark from the rasp as you strike it with the rock," Ricky said as Pavel closely watched.

"I'll get the tinder set up with the sawdust nuggets," Pavel said as Ricky continued to strike the rasp as sparks sprayed down on his hemp bird's nest and started to smoke. "It's going to go Ricky…" Pavel was saying, as Ricky gently blew on it and got a single flame. To keep it going, he hurriedly placed more hemp on it.

"Here Ricky, set it under here," Pavel said. He lifted a small twig and cupped a hole in a mound of sawdust nuggets, while Ricky carefully placed the now burning hemp in the small hole and they placed more twigs on it and then the larger logs.

"Grandpa says start out making the fire real hot to get the dust going cause once it's lit it will smolder and make a nice cooking fire. But use the dust sparingly," Ricky said, as Pavel shook his head in a positive way.

"Doesn't that burn your hand?" Pavel asked, as he watched Ricky tend the fire.

"Not really. The flame goes up but you have to act fast. When Collie says this one's okay, if you want, we can go over and you can start the one at your campsite," Ricky said as Pavel's eyes lit up.

"That'd be really swell Ricky," Pavel said.

Colleen came next to them with her pot of stew meat ready to be cooked. "You guys did a good job. The fire is just right for my pot to fit on this angle iron swivel. See look at this," She placed the pot on the angle iron and swiveled it over the fire.

"Collie, if you're set we're going over to Pavel's and I'll help him with their supper fire…" Ricky was saying. Both boys looked excited at their progress.

"That's fine Ricky and if you see Grandma could you send her over here?" She watched as the pair picked up their saddle bags and fire making kits and eagerly ran from her encampment.

"Will do Collie, see you later," Ricky yelled.

Colleen smiled to herself and felt a sense of happiness for her nephew. He was adapting and enjoying his new special friend. She was about to put some pared carrots into her pot of stew when her Mother entered her camp.

"Smells yummy, what is it?" Beatrice said making her daughter chuckle.

"Mama I would think you would recognize your own stew recipe," Colleen said. She finished with the carrots and started to stir the concoction.

"Are we going to have corn muffins too? Have to have corn muffins with stew," her Mother said. She went to one of the crates and sat down.

"Yes we are if I don't burn them in the Dutch oven," Colleen said. She set the lid on the pot of stew. "Mama something happened that has me kind of confused," she said. She went up to her Mother and slightly whispered to her. "Could you come up here next to me while I get the muffins ready for the oven I don't want the fire to go out?" she asked.

Her Mother came next to her. "Daughter you're so secretive, what's up?" Beatrice had a concerned tone in her voice.

"Well, it might not be anything, but the young LaFarge girl came to my camp a little while ago and Mitch was here and she asked if when he was finished with me could he come and help her Father…" Colleen felt her body flush and she thought she must look as red as a beet. "Mama it was embarrassing and you should've seen the look she gave me, like I was his woman or something," She hastily mixed the cornmeal with some milk and eggs.

"Is that it, I thought somebody died or something," Beatrice said with a laugh. She noticed a shocked look on her daughter's face. "Now then, Honey don't get upset but you and Mitch do seem to have some kind of chemistry and you're around each other a lot…" she was saying.

Colleen interrupted her. "Mama, we have a lot to do to get ready for this trip and he helps everyone not just me," Colleen said. She continued to stir the batter longer and harder than she should.

"Slow down girl you're going to beat the life out of the flour. You did use the baking powder right?" Beatrice asked trying to make light of the conversation.

"Yes Mama I know how to make corn muffins," Colleen replied. She felt a bit flustered when she thought that her Mother was trying to connect her with Mitch.

"Calm down Colleen, don't get so upset. You know you could do worse," Her mother picked up a carrot peel and chewed on it.

"I've never even thought about him like that. We all have been so busy getting ready for the trip that something like that just never entered my mind," She spooned the batter into the muffin pan and put it in the Dutch oven and placed it on the fire.

"Well maybe you should step back a moment and take a look, cause from where I stand you two would make a perfect match," she said. She noticed her daughter pretended not to hear her as she lifted the lid from the pot and stirred the now boiling stew. "And he's sure not bad to look at either," Beatrice commented.

This sent a hot flash throughout Colleen's body. "Mother," Colleen almost shouted. She was trying to hold in her emotions. "I don't have time for any of that kind of stuff," She wished she could just leave the room like she used to be able to but this kitchen had no walls and the fire and food had to continuously be tended.

"Find the time Daughter. Love is worth the time and it sounds to me like if you don't find the time someone else might just step in and…" her mother was saying.

Colleen understanding her interrupted. "I get the picture Mama, but I don't even know if he's interested in me," she said, as Ricky and Pavel entered the camp site.

"Wow, you should see all the horses and cattle Dad and Grandpa rounded up. Dad said we might be ahead of schedule and starting out sooner than expected," Ricky said.

Colleen looked at her Mother with a nostalgic look in her eyes. "It will be fine Daughter. It will be fine…" Beatrice was saying. She knew Colleen, at that very moment, was having the same thoughts that she was; that their time at Driftwood would soon be coming to an end and a new way of life and home would start.

Chapter Five

Lake Polymer/Bees

By this time, after they had started their journey, the wagon train had seen many bright orange glows of the setting sun disappear in the western sky. This evening, as they settled in, the slow moving air filled with smoke and mingled with a variety of aromas from different supper fires. The camp was quiet and the gentle sounds of the evening were starting to filter in like soft music. The day had been long and all of the travelers would most likely have their meals and retire for the night.

That day they had just traveled from the settlement where Ricky was born. It was a painstaking journey and brought back many sad memories for Colleen and her family, but for them and the entire wagon train it was a path they had to take.

"Wow, I'm bushed," Ricky said. He plopped down on one of the crates near the fire. "And I think I could eat a horse," Colleen gave him a piece of hardtack with a biscuit. "Think I could have some honey with this? That really would hit the spot Collie," He had a coaxing look in his eyes.

"Sure. I know it won't mess up your supper," Colleen said. She gave him a little saucer with some honey in it for him to dip. "You did take care of your horse right?" She looked at him and watched him almost devour his biscuit and lick up the honey.

"Yes, Pavel and I both wiped down and tied our ponies together at the rope corral," He showed her his empty saucer. "More please," He had another one of those looks in his eyes she found hard to resist.

"Just a small one, you have to save your appetite for more nourishing food sweetheart," She wanted to dote and spoil him, but knew she had to teach him to conserve.

"Well, maybe just a bit more honey and I'll wait for supper…" He was saying as his father came into the encampment.

"Lots of memories huh Collie," Geoff approached his sister-in-law and whispered. He knew she also had to be reminiscing about the last time they were at the settlement where Ricky was born and they lost Jeanette.

"Yes, lots," She did not want to linger on it with Ricky present, and she knew that Geoff would understand where she was coming from.

"Take care of your horse son?" Geoff asked changing the subject. He sat next to Ricky on the crate.

"Yeah Dad, sure did," Ricky said. He was finishing the last of the honey he had drizzled onto his saucer. "You know it sure was neat that you and Grandpa picked horses with identical markings for me and Pavel," Ricky was commenting.

Colleen brought a grate to the fire and Geoff got up from his seat to help her place it over the fire. "The boys got enough birds for the whole train today. I'm going to fry ours with some potatoes on the side," She went to get her skillet. "Have you boys named your ponies yet?" Colleen asked when she returned with the skillet and placed it on the grate.

"Yeah and this is neat too. I named mine Pavel and he named his Ricky. That way when we're not together we can always feel like we're talking with each other," He looked proudly back and forth from Colleen to his father.

"Why, how unique," Colleen remarked. She looked at her nephew; in the firelight he seemed like a little imp when he licked the honey from his fingers.

"That is unique..." Geoff was saying as Beatrice and BD slowly walked into Colleen's encampment.

"Evening everyone," Beatrice said, as BD raised his hand in greeting to them all. "Long day hmmm?" she said. She was looking directly at Geoff knowing he would understand she meant leaving the settlement.

"Yes it was! One I will always remember," Geoff said. He ruffled his son's hair. He could see a reflection of Jeanette in his son's actions. For a second a flash of her last moments of life filled his mind, but then a peace settled in and he remembered the fun times they had together. He remembered what a loving woman she was and her great sense of humor. "Hey, you better go wash up, you look like an all-day lollipop," he said. Everyone laughed as Ricky begrudgingly got up and went to wash his sticky hands and face.

"Yeah, honey and dirt sure don't mix," Colleen added. She brought Ricky a soft towel to dry with. "Supper's about ready is Mitch on his way?" Colleen asked. She looked at Geoff, but noticed her mother glance her way.

"I drove the wagon today and he was coming from the corral when I started over here, so he should be here shortly," Geoff said. He watched as Colleen started to get their dishes ready for supper.

"How's the alternating working for you?" BD asked. He went up to the fire to check out how it was holding up for Colleen.

"It works pretty well. I'm sure it's the same for everyone. Walking and riding the horse or in the wagon are easier on the body when we rotate. How are the Bolovich boys working out for you and Colleen?" Geoff asked. He watched as Beatrice took a hot pad and checked the potatoes.

"It seems to be a good system don't you think Bea?" BD asked.

His wife came next to him and sat closely beside him on a crate. "Yes they're very accustomed with the horses and it helps not having to ride on the wagon all the time, as long as we have enough people to tend the cattle and horses…" Beatrice was saying. She could not help but notice that Colleen seemed to be getting a little agitated.

"Well, I'd say we have a good system in place…" BD was saying.

Beatrice went up next to her daughter while the men continued to talk amongst themselves. "Honey, what's up, you seem upset?" Beatrice caringly asked. She noticed Colleen shied away from her and continued to set up the buffet. "Was it the settlement?" Beatrice whispered. She knew it was a trying personal day for all of them remembering where and how Jeanette died.

"Yes Mama it's about my sister but it's also about Mitch," Colleen whispered. She had a perplexed look on her face. "I don't know if it's on purpose or what, but he seems to be avoiding me. Or at least that's the way it feels to me…" she was saying. She looked towards the fire at the men to see if they were paying any attention to her conversation with her mother.

"That's nonsense. We've all been busy," Beatrice said. She tried to comfort her daughter, but also knew Mitch had been spending a lot of time away from the family meals especially their evening gatherings.

"All the while we were at the settlement he was always off doing something and a lot of times Geoff just brought his food to him with some kind of an excuse why he wasn't joining us," She was starting to get more agitated, when she realized they would have to start supper soon and Mitch most likely was not going to join them again this evening.

"Could one of you boys check on the food? We're busy over here..." Beatrice asked.

BD jumped up first to help out. "Always ready to help out the woman-folk," he said. He winked at his wife and she puckered her lips sending him a pretend kiss.

"Honey I wouldn't make too much about it, I'm sure he's not seeing that LaFarge girl, she's not his type," Beatrice whispered.

Colleen's eyes widened. "I never even gave her a thought. You don't think they might be..." Colleen looked completely amazed.

Her mother interrupted her. "She's too young for him. She's so flippy..." Beatrice started to toss her arms about trying to imitate the girl.

"But I know she has a crush on him. She's always throwing herself at him. And those low cut blouses don't leave much to the imagination," Colleen had a hint of jealousy in her voice.

"Boobs don't make the woman," Beatrice commented. She never minced her words with her daughter.

"Mama you always come straight to the point," Colleen turned a bit red about the two of them gossiping.

"Yeah that's me straight to the point. Get it boobs, point," Beatrice put her arm around her daughter's waist and playfully tapped her with her hip as they both started laughing.

"Mama you are such a hoot; you can always make me laugh," Colleen said. She continued to laugh.

The guys started to chant. "Eat, eat, eat..." They continued until the girls motioned that they could come up and get their plates and fill them with the supper.

"Everything will work itself out Honey, it always does," Beatrice said to her daughter as everyone was sitting down to eat.

"Thanks Mama," Colleen said.

They all sat on crates and ate. But even with her loved ones around Colleen could not help but perceive the vacant seat and her empty heart.

***

"I've been waiting a long time for this," he passionately whispered. He approached her wanton body. "God you're beautiful," he lustfully panted. His passion was mounting as he fondled her breasts through the cotton material of her blouse. Quickly, he unbuttoned it; slipped it off her and threw it aside.

"It's about time I got your attention," she purred. She purposely rubbed her breasts against his bare chest. "I know you can satisfy me," she seductively whispered. She stroked the inside of his naked thigh. "Just thinking about you makes me hot," She quickly took off her pants.

"When I saw you riding in this evening I could almost taste you. Does that sound crazy?" He gave her an almost hungry look when she straddled his leg and urged him to pet and lift her stimulated breasts from her camisole.

"Crazy, that was me when I saw you. I could almost feel your hands all over me," she softly whispered to him. She started to giggle and press her body closer to his. "I guess we can't be heard?" Giggling again she thought at that moment she really did not care.

"I'm past worrying about who the hell's nosy enough to snoop around here. I've been waiting a long time for this and you smell like a woman ready for a real man," He nibbled the tender spot of her neck. Purposely, he slowly went to her lips; he licked and parted them with his tongue as they openly engaged in an intense, sexually stimulating kiss.

"Now..." she coarsely whispered. She wiggled and squirmed. "I'm going to lose my mind..." She suppressed a scream as he quickly rested her on the tiny bed and skillfully satisfied their mounting desires with overwhelming pleasure.

After their love making they lazily lay in each other's embrace. "You always know what I need," she whispered. She cuddled next to him in their wagon and he tenderly caressed her back.

"It's fun to make it seem like the first time," He gave her a playful pat on her naked bottom.

"I think so too, and it takes me away from all the problems," she said. She hoped she could now maybe peacefully fall asleep.

"What was all that about with Collie?" he caringly asked. "You two seemed in deep conversation," He knew anything that involved his wife also involved him.

"It's Mitch again. He hasn't been around much lately. I think she's fallen in love with him," She looked at her husband. "But, I think she believes she just cares for him, you know like family," She cuddled in next to him. "There's just so much going on..." she sighed. "And then there's the LaFarge girl always flitting around him," She was happy she had her husband to talk with. He always seemed to have a solution to any problem.

"Want me to poke around and see if I can find something out?" he asked. He noticed the outside camps were settling down and the sounds of the night were getting louder.

"I don't think so Honey. It will work itself out. Besides I think you've done enough poking around..." She quietly giggled. She relaxed when he started to massage her lower back. "Oh that feels so good," She sighed again as he snuggled closer to her.

"You know, who would've known that after all these years we would've wound up together. You're right, if it's to be they will find each other," He noticed she was completely relaxed. "Good night my love," He kissed her cheek and heard a gentle snore from her. Finally, he could feel himself drifting off to sleep.

***

The maps and journals they were using had been accurate. And according to the last landmark they came upon, they should be approaching a spring fed lake. After their day's hunt, Ricky and Pavel had just met up with each other. They had an abundance of prairie chickens and rabbits draped over their ponies.

"Have you noticed when we're closer to water we get more game?" Ricky was asking Pavel.

"Hell yeah, I got a shit full today and we're not too far ahead of the train. Got enough so we can head back?" Pavel asked his buddy and hunting companion.

"Hell yeah, take a look at this bunch..." Ricky held up some of his game. "Hey, want some of my jerky?" Ricky passed a piece to Pavel.

"Thanks," Pavel accepted the jerky. "Boy, we're sure in for a feast tonight," Pavel could feel his mouth watering. "But this'll help tide me over," He took a bite of the hard, cured meat and chewed it, while they rode side by side. "Later when we get by the lake we can set up some snares," He noticed Ricky just nodded in agreement.

They were great buddies and could almost read each other's mind. They loved the adventure and independence they were allowed with the hunt.

"Do you think we're something like scouts?" Pavel asked. He laughed when he saw Ricky with his mouth full of jerky again only nodded in agreement until he could maneuver his chew to speak.

"Hell yeah we are. We have a compass. We find the food and we let them know what's up. Yeah we're scouts all right even if Mitch or someone else is out there too, who cares we're scouts too," Ricky was enjoying his buddy's companionship and their freedom to speak their minds, even with colored language. They both enjoyed their unsupervised indulgence to say whatever they wanted especially the un-reprimanded thrown in use of profanity. As they took another chew of jerky, they smiled at each other. They thought of themselves as men as they spurred their horses back to the wagon train.

The wagon train was heading to what the maps referred to as Lake Polymer, one of the largest fresh water, spring fed lakes in what was called the Gyre District. It was their intent to replenish their water supply and allow themselves some much needed rest and relaxation.

"Thank God for Lake Polymer and the fresh water spring that feeds it," Beatrice said. She and Colleen were walking with their horses towards a secluded spot where they could bathe and wash their hair.

"It seems like forever that I sat in a bath. This is going to be pure luxury," Colleen said. She tightened her grip on the reins of her horse as she guided him behind her. They both had packed their personal toiletries and clean clothes in their saddle bags. "But not quite the same as a peaceful bubble bath while toting this around," She patted her side arm.

"But necessary Daughter," Beatrice said. She had a serious look on her face.

"I know Mama. I'm getting used to it, even if I haven't used it yet," She noticed they were nearing a clearing close to the water.

"Geoff said Ricky and Pavel are going to check out the honey bee Apiary a few miles from our campsite," Beatrice said. She had a slight look of concern in her eyes.

"I know Mama I worry about Ricky too. He's been taking on such big responsibilities. He acts like he's a man, but he's still a child," Colleen said as her Mother only nodded in agreement.

"Looks like someone beat us to this spot Daughter," Beatrice said. She stopped walking and turned to pat her horse's nose to stop him. "That looks like Geoff and Mitch's wagon," She squinted to make it out more clearly through the tall green bushes and dead brush.

"What's that hanging on the side of the wagon? It kind of looks like some kind of a canvas tent or something..." Colleen was saying. Then they noticed someone riding up on horseback. "Oh my God Mother it's the LaFarge girl. She's out here to meet Mitch. We have to get out of here," she hurriedly whispered.

They both tried to steady their horses as Antoinette dismounted her horse and tied it to a bush.

"What's she doing? I can hardly see from here," Beatrice said. She was trying to stand on her tip toes. She noticed a horrified look on her daughter's face. "What's she doing Daughter?" She forced her daughter to speak.

"God Mama she's taking her clothes off. Right out in the open she's completely naked and now she's taking some kind of silky scarf or something and wrapping it around her shoulders. I can't watch any more they're having some kind of rendezvous," Her tears started to flow from her eyes. Quickly, she untied her horse and pulled the reins turning him back towards the train. "Come on Mama," she whispered. She mounted her horse and quietly retreated.

"I'm coming Daughter," Beatrice said. She still tried to make out, through the thick foliage, exactly what was going on, but the figure had disappeared into the odd looking canvassed tent so she mounted her horse and followed her daughter.

When they reached the wagon train they both noticed a commotion. "What's going on?" Colleen asked BD when they reached Colleen's wagon. "Isn't that Ricky's horse?" She noticed everyone was hovered around the rider-less horse.

"We can't tell; his and Pavel's are exactly the same..." BD was saying.

Colleen dismounted her horse and ran next to the horse. "No saddle bags. He has them with him. Both of the boys always take their saddle bags," Colleen surmised.

Yerik came next to her. "She's right. My Pavel always has his bags with him. So I can't tell whose horse this is. But they went to the bee Apiary; so we do know where to find them," Yerik shouted. He was happy that they all shook their heads in agreement.

"BD, where's Geoff?" Colleen asked. She looked around for her brother-in-law. "We have to find Geoff and look for the boys," She wanted to act fast.

Beatrice stepped in. "Mitch is down by the lake, I'll get him. Colleen, you help BD saddle his horse. I'll be back as fast as I can," Beatrice said. She looked at her daughter with a glance of understanding and then authority in her eyes. "It's best if I go daughter," She held her daughter's shoulders and looked in her eyes. She knew she did not want her daughter to have to face Mitch and interrupt him with the LaFarge girl.

"I know Mama," Colleen said. She watched her mother mount her horse and gait out of the campsite. Just then, another one of those blue balls, that she was becoming accustomed to, flashed in front of her. It came near her and she almost fell backwards as it entered and flew out of her. Suddenly, she had the feeling of Pavel. She looked at BD. "BD, we can't wait for them. I say we go, and let them catch up," Colleen quickly said.

"You're right let's go," BD said. One of the Bolovich boys brought him his horse and when Yerik, Claude and Olivier LaFarge, and Brady O'Donnell joined them they rode off towards the Apiary.

At this same time, on her way back to the lake, Beatrice met up with Mitch; he was driving the wagon and Geoff was riding his horse alongside the wagon. She looked around, but did not see Antoinette. "One of the boy's horses returned to camp. We don't know if it's Ricky's or Pavel's; they both left camp," she shouted.

Mitch jumped from the wagon and went near Beatrice and her mount. "Drive the wagon; we'll ride ahead to the Apiary..." Mitch was saying. He reached for Beatrice, and helped her down from her horse and then mounted her horse. "Follow us," Mitch, looking at Beatrice shouted.

He and Geoff sped off and Beatrice climbed onto the driver's seat and slapped the reins. They would be far ahead of her, but she also realized they might need the wagon for emergency transport.

"Yes, they were here," the beekeeper said. "I told those young whippersnappers not to mess with the bees, but they said they knew what they were doing. And then I saw the horse running wild. I couldn't catch him and I didn't know where to go look for anyone," He explained to the group after they asked him the whereabouts of the boys.

Just then, Mitch rode up and listened to what the beekeeper was saying. He cut him short. "Which way..." Mitch shouted. Quickly, he darted off in the direction the beekeeper pointed with Geoff right behind him.

"You're better off to just let the two of them go," the beekeeper yelled. He stepped in front of the rest of the riders waving his arms above his head. "You don't want to stir up my bees," he told them.

They all stopped in their tracks. "My son," Yerik cried.

BD dismounted his horse and came next to him and motioned for him to dismount his horse. "They're fine men they will find the boys," BD tried to comfort Yerik.

Beatrice was driving the wagon into the yard. She noticed there were several small cottages, two large barns with what looked like miles and miles of bee hives behind and on either side of the buildings. "BD," Beatrice shouted. She jumped from her seat and ran to her husband. "Where's Colleen?" She looked around.

Colleen came to her from behind the group of men in the yard. "Mitch and Geoff went looking for the boys Mama. The keeper didn't think we all should go. We might stir up the bees," Colleen put her arm around her mother.

They looked at each other hardly able to fathom the enormity of the Apiary and the constant loud humming noise of the bees.

Time seemed to slow down, but nature continued as it always does. They watched the sun starting to set. They noticed that the hum of the bees sounded like it was dwindling as the beekeeper lit a large bonfire.

"Oh Lord please deliver my son," Yerik prayed. He knelt on the ground near the fire when they all noticed in the shadows the slow movement of horses. "Thank you Lord," Yerik said.

They all patiently waited for the riders to come to them. "Quickly, take Pavel," Mitch said. He was carrying the boy on his horse.

Yerik took his son from Mitch's arms and laid him on the ground near the fire while Beatrice brought some blankets from the wagon and placed one on Pavel.

Geoff had Ricky on his horse and BD was taking Ricky from Geoff's arms when Geoff started shouting orders. "Beatrice, my bag's under the wagon seat," Geoff shouted. He ran to Pavel and checked his vital signs, as she went for the bag.

"Oh my God he's so swollen…" Pavel's brother Alek was saying, as Beatrice came next to Geoff with his bag.

"Here, help me with this," Geoff said, to Beatrice. He took a bottle of Diphedryl from his bag and tried to administer a dose of the elixir to the boy.

"Is he going to be okay Dad," Ricky asked his father. He came next to them with Colleen holding him close to herself.

"I don't know son. At this point I just don't know. But if he can swallow this, it should bring down the swelling..." Geoff was saying.

Just then Claude and Olivier started to yell for some help with Mitch.

"Bring him over here," Geoff shouted.

The men carried Mitch's large heavy body and laid him next to Pavel, while Beatrice covered him with another blanket.

"He's swollen too," Yerik said. The flicker of the firelight made Mitch appear like a terrifying ogre.

"Dear God Geoff how did this happen?" Colleen asked. She knelt next to Mitch. "What can I do to help?" she asked, with anticipation in her eyes.

"Sit him up," Geoff said. Colleen straddled behind Mitch's head and BD helped him into her arms. "Open your mouth Mitch," Geoff said. His brother slowly opened his swollen eyelids with only a slit of his eyes showing. "Here take this and swallow it hard," he commanded. His brother opened his mouth and did what he was told. "Water," Geoff looked around and Beatrice brought him a cup of water.

"My son's convulsing," Yerik shouted.

Geoff gave the cup to Beatrice. "Only let him sip it, but make sure he drinks all of it..." Geoff patted her shoulders.

Quickly, he went beside Pavel to try to blow air through his mouth into the boy's lungs, while Brady and Claude tried to hold Pavel's violently jerking body down so Geoff could help him.

"Pavel..." Ricky cried. He showed deep remorse as he watched his father try to save his friend.

'God help me,' Geoff thought. He looked up from what he was doing and saw the fright in his son's eyes. Just then Pavel's body went suddenly still and collapsed to the ground.

"My son," Yerik wailed, from where he knelt near the head of his son. "My son is with his mother," he cried. He buried his head in his hands and sobbed for the loss of his child.

"Oh God Yerik, I tried he was just too far gone. He must've been stung hundreds of times," Geoff told him. He continued to sit next to Pavel's lifeless body.

Ricky came near his father and knelt next to his friend. "Pavel, talk to me Pavel," Ricky cried, with a whimper. "Talk to me buddy," He took his friend's small hand and placed it in his own, as they all cried for the loss of this gentle spirit.

All at once Mitch started to cough vehemently and Geoff turned his attention to him. "Spit out anything in your mouth," he commanded. Mitch compulsively regurgitated all over the blanket. "I was afraid of that, but that's a good sign," Geoff stood near Mitch.

Colleen noticed Mitch's blanket seemed to be moving. "God he threw up bees," Colleen could see many bees from her vantage point behind Mitch's head.

BD picked up the blanket and threw it in the fire while Beatrice replaced that blanket with a fresh one.

"Hopefully, any others will be digested," Geoff looked at his brother. "I'm going to give him another large dose of the Diphedryl and some mineral oil to coat his throat," Geoff administered the drug. "Here, rub some of this mineral oil on his body…" Geoff was saying. He handed the bottle of oil to BD as he stripped off his brother's clothes and boots.

Right away, BD with the help of Beatrice rubbed the oil over his entire bee stung body, while Colleen cooed and coddled his head as her tears flowed uncontrollably. "With any luck his large body will save him," Geoff had confidence in his voice. He replaced the blanket on his brother.

They huddled around Mitch as the night dew put a chill in the air, while the beekeeper and his family reverently assisted the

Bolovich family with Pavel's remains. Later, they sat on blankets and unconsciously sipped hot coffee that the beekeeper and his family also provided for them. "Do you have any idea what happened?" Beatrice asked Geoff.

"When we got there, Ricky was standing away from Pavel, and he told us Pavel's horse must've been stung and threw Pavel onto one of the hives. Pavel's horse ran off and he could only watch as the bees attacked Pavel. Ricky said he tried to help Pavel but he slipped down and there were so many bees on Pavel that he couldn't get near him," Geoff was explaining. "He said he wanted to help Pavel because he was screaming, but the bees were all over Pavel and then after a while the bees just swarmed around and never touched Pavel again and he was surprised that they never came near him." Geoff looked at his son who, completely exhausted, slept in his arms.

"My poor baby, he must've been terrified," Beatrice said. She brushed her grandson's hair away from his warm, red cheeks.

The beekeeper and his family kept the bonfire going throughout the night. They fed the group and brought plenty of fresh water. By morning Mitch's swelling had gone down immensely but he still was not out of the woods.

"May I speak with everyone?" The beekeeper, raising his arms, got their attention. His wife and family were passing around homemade buttermilk biscuits, served with honey and apple butter. "This has been a very sad time for all of us and my family and I extend our deepest, heartfelt sympathy to Yerik and his family…" he was saying.

Ricky clung to Colleen while Geoff carefully attended Mitch in his wagon.

"Thank you my friend you are very kind," Yerik replied. His son's hovered around him and embraced each other with Pavel's tiny, covered body, on a pallet in front of them.

"Yerik, we have a beautiful apple orchard that signifies to us the beauty of life after the bitterness of a hard winter. The pink blossoms shower us with a fragrance so invigorating that it renews our beliefs in a much higher source. Our orchard is full of life and peace and we would be honored to make it your son's final resting place," the beekeeper said.

Yerik sobbed openly and went to the man. "You honor me. Thank you so much," Yerik said. He shook the man's hand and then vigorously hugged him.

So they could attend the funeral service that afternoon the entire wagon train was invited by the beekeeper and his family to camp just far enough from the Apiary as not to disturb the bees. Yerik and his sons picked a beautiful spot in the middle of the orchard, depicting life all around little Pavel's gravesite.

"Much of my little Pavel's life will never be written in the book of life but, by God, the beauty of his big spirit will always be etched in our hearts..." Yerik was saying. His sons and those who cared surrounded him and bowed their heads. "I can feel the arms of my beloved Verna, his Mama embracing him," Yerik's burning tears streamed down his cheeks. "Let it not be with heavy hearts we leave this gentle spirited boy, but with hearts full of memories and love," He went to the deep grave and threw a handful of soil onto his son's blanketed body. "Remember man that thou art dust and to dust thou shall return," He stood still while his sons and then the others filed in line to pay their last respects to the little boy who loved life, who loved to learn and who would be sorely missed by them all especially his true, best friend.

"Good bye my friend, my buddy scout," Ricky said, with a constricted voice. He watched the soil fall in slow motion from his hand onto the blanket that covered his dearest friend. He felt he wanted to jump in next to him to be near Pavel, but slowly backed away. "I love you Pavel," Not wanting anyone to see the tears that burned his eyes, Ricky turned and ran from the congregation.

Colleen was right on his heels. "Ricky, please hold up," Colleen shouted, stopping him in his tracks. "I know this is hard Honey. It is for all of us, but I know Pavel was your best buddy," She turned him to face her. "Honey no one can ever take away the friendship you had with him. It will always be here in your heart," She patted his chest.

"But my heart hurts really bad Collie. He was like my shadow. We did all the scouting and hunting together. Now I'm just all alone..." he was saying. His head hung low, as the flowing tears dripped from his face to the ground.

"I'll scout with you and be your buddy," Five year old Abaigeal O'Donnell said, startling them.

"Abby, you're a girl, you can't be a scout," Ricky said, using the nick name everyone used for the young girl. He turned from them both and ran to his father and Mitch's wagon.

Giant tears formed in Abby's eyes, as she looked despairingly at Colleen. "Abby don't cry Honey. Ricky didn't really mean what he said. This is real hard on him. You know Pavel was his best friend," She knelt in front of Abby.

"I know Colleen, but he sounded like he hates me...I could be his friend too," Abby tried to rub the tears from her eyes. "I don't have a friend and now he doesn't and I would be a good friend," She spoke in an unusually adult manner.

"I don't know Honey, maybe in time, but right now I don't think it's a good time to press it," Colleen said. She hoped the child understood. "Let's go find your mom," Colleen held onto Abby's hand leading her back to the congregation.

"Come here son," Geoff said, to a sobbing Ricky after he had climbed in the wagon from the front. "I'm sorry I couldn't be there with you…" Geoff was saying with tears forming in his eyes.

Ricky let his father take him in his arms and they both cried for their loss. "I loved him Daddy. He was like my brother. We did everything…" Ricky was saying. He could not control his sobbing.

"I know son, you two were great friends and believe me I know what it means to love a brother," his father said, as they both looked at an unconscious Mitch.

"I tried to get him out, but the bees just kept coming at him," Quickly, Ricky rose from his father's embrace and started to pace around in the limited space of the wagon. "I should've done more to help him," Looking completely lost, he stood in front of his father, with his arms limp at his sides.

"Ricky it wasn't your fault. It could've happened to you just as easy as it happened to poor Pavel. You see son, when bees think the hive is being disturbed they put a scent on the one that is doing the disturbing and the bees instinctively follow that scent until they get rid of the intruder. Can you understand what I'm saying?" Geoff was trying to explain. He hoped to ease his son's feeling of the guilt for not being able to save his friend.

"So that's why they only went after him because his horse disturbed the bees? Then why did they go after Uncle Mitch and not me?" he asked. He tried to wipe his nose on his sleeve.

"I'm guessing they were calming down and then Mitch disturbed them again. Hard to say, but I'm glad you're okay son," Geoff said. He handed his son a handkerchief.

"Daddy, why does Uncle Mitch keep on sleeping?" Ricky asked. He again snuggled with his dad and for the moment turned his attention towards his uncle and away from his loss.

"It's his body's way of healing son," Geoff said, holding Ricky close to him.

"It was horrible Daddy, I missed Pavel so much I could've jumped in the hole with him," Ricky started to think of all that had happened, which again prompted him to uncontrollably sob.

"Come on son calm down," Geoff tried to ease his son's pain. He did not really know what to do to help his son bear his grief. "I know your pain Ricky, and son I can't say it will go away soon, but trust me Honey it will," He held his son's chin in his hand and made him look him in the eyes.

"Daddy we were together, we did it all. Nobody knows what we did. We believed we took care of everyone. Without us, you guys wouldn't have ate or known about shit," At that moment, he did not care about cussing in front of his dad. He was a man with Pavel and Pavel was a man with him. They truly believed they cared for everyone and took pride in their achievements, and now his comrade with whom he could do anything was gone. This was a loss he found unbearable, and believed no one would ever understand.

"Ricky, it was like that with me and your mom. Son, your mom and I were like; how can I say this so you'll understand... we were like an oak tree. We were together like a strong, straight tree, but we also branched off. Our love for each other made us strong, but as it turned out it was cut short," He noticed Ricky was paying close attention to him. "But son, that love we had for each other, lives on in you. Ricky you are one of our branches, but still part of the whole strong tree. Just like Pavel is a part of your branch. Love goes on son, and builds other branches. Can you understand some of this?" Geoff looked at his son. He thought he might be getting too deep for his young son.

"Well, if he doesn't get it I sure do," Mitch softly mumbled. He startled them both. "How long have I been out?" he asked. He started to scratch his head and rub his eyes.

"Longer than I care to say brother. Are you hungry?" Geoff asked. He went next to his brother. "Ricky light the lantern and bring it here son," Geoff asked his son.

Ricky brought the lantern closer to them. "Wow Uncle Mitch, sure glad to hear your voice again," Ricky said.

His uncle reached to him and ruffled his hair. "Yours too," Mitch said, feeling like he could eat a horse. "And to answer your question I'm famished but my throat sure hurts," he said. He massaged his neck.

"The bees stung you all over," Ricky was relating to his uncle, while his father checked his brother's vital signs.

"Bees?" Mitch asked. He did not seem to remember what had happened.

"Yeah bees, don't you remember me and Pavel…" Ricky was saying.

His father interrupted. "I think that's enough talk for right now. Here, you take this," Geoff said, handing Mitch a mild sedative and a cup of water. "Colleen has been keeping a fresh broth going for you. I'll go get some. Ricky you stay here but no more talking, just let your uncle rest okay?" Geoff gave his son a stern look.

"Okay Dad, I'll take care of Uncle Mitch. You can count on me," Ricky said. He wanted to care for his uncle as the man who had tried to save his best friend's life.

"I'll be right back," Geoff told them.

He left the pair and went to find Colleen at her campsite. "Oh good you're still up," Geoff found Colleen sitting next to the fire. "Mitch woke up Collie…" he was saying. He watched her jolt up from her seat. "And he's really hungry," he told her.

Colleen went for one of the jars of broth she had earlier canned for this purpose. "How is he, can he talk?" she asked. She was prying the hardened wax from inside the top of the jar and pouring the contents into a pan.

"Yes he can talk but his throat's sore, which is to be expected…" he was saying. He watched her place the pot on the grate over the fire. "Do you want to bring the broth to him yourself?" he asked her. He knew, even though she had never openly spoke of her feelings for his brother, he felt he could read her like a book, and she was head over heels in love with Mitch.

"Geoff I don't know if I can do that," she said, taking him aback. "Maybe he wants someone else to bring him the broth," she said. She continued to stir the warming liquid.

"I don't know who or what you're talking about. I thought you figured out by now that Mitch loves you," He calmly said. He then plopped his weary body onto one of the crates near the fire.

"Loves me, I don't think so. You don't know what I've seen…" she was saying. She went for a bowl and spoon.

"What are you talking about? What do you think you've seen?" he asked. He looked at her with great concern in his eyes.

"It was just before all this disastrous bee stuff and we lost our little Pavel…" she was saying. She noticed the broth started to simmer so she stirred it.

"Yeah, well what happened?" he asked. He was paying close attention to her every word.

"Well, Mom and I were on our way to the lake to bathe and we came across Mitch's wagon…" She placed a lid on the pot and put it to the side of the fire to let it slowly heat. "Well his wagon had this funny looking tent built out from the side of the wagon and then, while we were looking, the LaFarge girl rode up and, and…" she was saying.

Geoff broke into loud laughter. "Oh my God you saw that…" he was saying. He noticed tears welling up in Colleen's eyes and she turned her back to him. "Colleen you know that's my wagon too," he said. He went to her and put his arm around her.

"But you have to let me finish..." she was saying.

He turned her to face him. "Collie you don't have to finish, cause I know what happened. She walked into the funny tent, you're talking about, and she was stark naked..." He could not stop his laughter.

"It's not funny Geoff, right until that moment I thought I loved Mitch too...huh, what did you say...how could you know she was naked, there hasn't been enough time for you to have spoken with Mitch to know that..." She looked at him with bewilderment in her eyes.

"I know, because I was there...The girl walked in on both of us," He held his stomach. "And if you'd stuck around long enough you'd of seen her run out just as fast as she came in," He could not help but continue to laugh. "Collie, I'm sorry for laughing but it just struck me funny. I guess I've been needing a good laugh lately," He tried to compose himself. "Collie that funny tent is the reason Mitch hasn't been around for suppers lately. He's been making it for you ever since we left the settlement. I'll let him tell you about it, but it sure has nothing to do with the LaFarge girl," He thought she seemed to calm down.

"Oh my God Geoff, he's been making it for me..." She could hardly believe what he said. "I don't care how funny it looks, he made it for me," She held her hands to her heart. "I think this broth is ready, I'm going to take it to him," She poured it in a bowl and grabbed a towel and a spoon. "Can you help me out here a bit?" she asked.

He followed her to the wagon. "Hey son, come on out here with me for a while," Geoff said. He opened the back flap of the canvassed wagon and helped Colleen in as Ricky jumped to the ground next to his dad.

The lantern light dimly lit the inside, but Colleen could see Mitch partially sitting up in the make shift bed of the wagon. "Colleen, you're a sight for these ole sore eyes," he hoarsely said.

She placed the bowl of broth next to the bed. "So are you," She sat next to him. "And I'm happy to say your eyes are close to the way they're supposed to be. Your brother has taken really good care of you," After groping for and then finding the bowl of broth she handed it to him.

"And from what Ricky's said to me so have you. He said, you've all but moved in with me," he said. He noticed a flash of embarrassment on her face. "Even in this light I can see you turn red Collie," He started to cough and she quickly took the broth from him.

"Better let me have this before you spill it all over yourself," She took the bowl from him as his coughing stopped. "Feel okay now? You've been coughing a lot, but Geoff said the swelling has gone down in your throat..." She noticed he was staring at her. "Here take a sip of this," She spoon fed some of the broth to him.

"That's good. Seems like it's been a while since I've eaten, I really think I could handle a thick juicy steak though instead of this broth. Not to say that it's not good I'm just famished," he whispered. He looked at her with pleading eyes.

"Well that's for Geoff to say. You've been through a lot and the swelling isn't completely down; you may not be able to swallow that big juicy steak," she said. She prompted him to take another spoonful of the broth.

"Spunky aren't you?" he said.

She sincerely looked at him. "Mitch you could've died. And poor little Pavel..." Her tears welled in her eyes.

"Yeah Ricky told me. I wish I could've saved him..." He started to cough again.

"I think that's enough for now," she said. She placed the spoon and bowl down. "Maybe you should get some rest..." she was saying.

He reached for her and pulled her next to him in the small bed. "Maybe enough broth but not enough you," He looked her straight in the eyes. "Colleen Armstrong I believe I've been in love with you since the first day I laid eyes on you," he whispered.

She laid her head on his chest. "Oh Mitch I was so afraid I would lose you," She tried to suppress her tears. "I knew I had feelings for you but until this happened, I really never knew how deep they were," She felt compelled to confess her feelings to him after he had also shown her a part of his heart. "You know, I feel as if I've always known you, like you've always been a part of my heart. Does that make any sense?" She did not look at him. She could hear the thump of his beating heart. It filled her with joy.

"Colleen, I might not be a very good catch. I mean I've done some things in my life and there have been many…" He was about to surrender his past, passionate affairs.

"I don't want to hear it. That was then and this is now. We didn't know each other then…" She was saying when Ricky startled them.

"Aunt Collie hurry up, something's wrong with Grandma," Ricky was shouting from outside the wagon.

"Oh my God," Colleen said. She jumped up from Mitch's hold on her. "You stay put. I'll let you know what's going on…" she said, as Mitch tried to get up with her but fell back onto the bed. "I mean it Mitch stay put," She shuffled towards the back exit.

"I guess I really don't have any say so," he abruptly mumbled. Impatiently, unable to get up; he knew he could only think about what was going on with Beatrice, but helplessly do nothing about it.

"What's going on BD?" Colleen hurriedly asked BD when she reached his and her mother's campsite with Ricky right beside her.

"I haven't a clue. Geoff and Ricky were here telling us how Mitch woke up, and next thing we know Bea fainted. Luckily, she fell right into my arms. Geoff's checking her out; we took her into our wagon," he told them.

They went by the fire to sit and wait. "God I hate waiting. It seems I've been doing it all my life," Colleen said, as Ricky put his head on her arm. "It'll be all right. Your daddy will take real good care of Grandma," She hugged Ricky close to her.

"I know Collie," Ricky replied. He tried to truly believe it in his heart. He didn't think he could take another loss.

"BD, your wife wants to see you," Geoff said. He left the wagon and came to them by the fire.

"She all right?" Looking at Geoff, BD asked. He sprung from his seat and went next to Geoff.

"I'll let her tell you," he could only say, as BD rushed from them and went to his wife.

"What is it Geoff?" Colleen asked, with panic written all over her face. "Mama has never fainted that I can remember…" she was saying. Then she saw a look in his eyes like she had never seen before.

"Your mom's fine. She wants to talk with you both herself…" he was saying, as Colleen started for the wagon. "No just a minute Collie, she'll be right out," he said, stopping Colleen in her tracks, as BD and her mother were climbing out of the back exit of their wagon.

"Oh Mama are you okay?" Colleen was asking. She had a skeptical look in her eyes, as she and Ricky came close to her and BD. BD had a gentle arm around his wife's waist.

"I'm fine Collie. Just got something that around six months or so can cure," Beatrice calmly explained.

Colleen had a shocked look on her face. "Six months or so," Colleen shouted. Her eyes almost bugged out of their sockets.

"Wow Grammy, six months or so is a long time to be sick," Ricky said.

Beatrice and BD nervously laughed and went to sit by the fire. "Come here Honey," Beatrice said. She patted the spot in the middle of her and BD on the crate while Colleen, still in shock, sat across from them to listen with Geoff next to her. "Well, I'm just going to tell it like it is. You see in about six months or so you're going to have another aunt or uncle and your aunt Collie is going to have another brother or sister," she told them.

Ricky looked even more confused than before. "Huh, and that's why you're sick cause someone's coming all the way out here to visit," Ricky was asking. He had a look of innocence written all over his face.

"No Honey, not visit. You see Grammy's going to have a baby," Beatrice said. She looked at BD and patted his hand. She could tell he was still trying to grasp onto the reality of it all.

"A baby?" Ricky yelled. He looked over at his dad and Collie. "Did you hear that; Grammy's going to have a baby..." he said with a smile. He snuggled in the loving arms of both Beatrice and BD.

"Yes I heard," Colleen said. She put her hand under her chin and could only stare at all of them facing her, as they sat on the crate with the glow of the fire light all around them and the night air starting to chill her. "I'm sure with such a good doctor in the house, or should I say the open, everything will just be fine," she softly added. Unconsciously, she wiped away the tears that started to flow down her cheeks.

"Yes everything will be just fine daughter. Come here to Mama," Beatrice stood up and opened her arms and Colleen went to her and they hugged.

"Oh Mama," Colleen said. She had a bit of panic showing in her red tearful eyes.

"It's up to him Honey," Her mother pointed upward. "Come on now, no worries," She tried to calm her daughter.

"I'll never leave her side Collie," BD said. He had a deep look of love and admiration in his eyes.

He came next to his wife and Colleen. Ricky then jumped in the middle for a group hug; while Geoff watched and prayed that he could live up to the reputation Colleen had so faithfully spoken of him.

Chapter Six

Omar Arrives/Bandits

Time seemed to pass slower than the sand in a watched hour glass. The travelers, bored with their surroundings, yearned for the open road and the journey's end. They knew they could only go forward with the guidance of Mitchell Banks, and although he was near a complete recovery the wagon train waited throughout the winter at the bee apiary.

"Mama, your baby should be born any day now," Colleen said.

Her mother rubbed her protruding belly, as she sat on the rocking chair her husband made for her comfort in place of the hard crates. "Yes, daughter, and I'm surely ready," Beatrice said. She watched her daughter mix fried potatoes with sausage and eggs for their breakfast.

"The biscuits are ready. I'm going to put everything in the warmer," Colleen looked at her mother. "Unless you're ready for a bite now..." Colleen reached for her mitt and started her task.

"No, I'll wait," Beatrice replied. "How was Mitch this morning?" She did not wait for her daughter to answer her. "You know with springtime here I can almost feel the tension around here," She knew everyone in the wagon train was itching to be on their way. But for right now, in her condition, she was content to lazily ease back in the rocker and just stare out beyond the wagons to the open land, while her daughter continued her task.

"I know Mama; I can feel spring in the air too. And Mitch is getting stronger every day. He's really come a long way," She almost felt like she had to defend him. "He's a good, caring man Mama, and he wants to be at his very best before we head out again," She finished the breakfast meal and sat on a crate next to her mother. "So much has happened in these past months. Life is different yet still the same," She knew her mother was one person who could understand what she meant.

"I know daughter, life goes on and on and praise the Lord for that," Beatrice again rubbed her familiar bulge. "One day it will be your turn daughter," She looked at Colleen.

Colleen turned her head from her mother's stare. "Oh Mama, you're always right to the point. Oh no you don't, I'm not falling for that one again. You always try to get me to open up by changing the subject," Colleen said. They both started laughing. "Mama, Mitch is such a wonderful man and maybe one day..." She placed her hand on her mother's belly and gently massaged her as the baby kicked. "Maybe one day..." She started to remember the day Mitch proposed marriage to her.

She recalled it was the second month after his attack by the bees. He finally felt steady enough to do a few chores around the camp. Geoff had been on him to take it easy and he followed his brother's instructions to the tee, but on this particular afternoon he wanted to surprise the woman he loved with the gift he had been making for her since they left the settlement where Ricky was born.

Geoff drove their wagon to the spot by the lake where Colleen had first seen the funny tent that was attached to the wagon. Geoff helped Mitch set it up and returned to Colleen's campsite.

"Collie, Mitch is down by the lake and asked me to invite you there. He has something he wants to show you," Geoff said, with a bit of a smirk on his lips.

"What's this all about? You look like the cat who swallowed the canary," She was curious about her brother-in-law's actions.

"Oh...um...it's a surprise. Just go to the lake. You know the spot..." He had a sly look in his eyes. "You know where the LaFarge girl bared it all," he whispered. He started to laugh like he had the first time she told him what she had seen.

"So I'm finally going to get to know what that silly tent's all about," She did not want him to think he had the upper hand and embarrass her again about her misinterpretation of the LaFarge girl's presence back then at Mitch's wagon down by the lake.

"Well, I guess the only way to find out is for you to get on down there. But maybe if you wait until the sun goes down your face won't look as red as it does right now," He kidded her again and started laughing. He could not control himself.

"You need help..." She too started to laugh. She then continued to shake her head at him as she mounted her saddled horse and rode out of camp towards the lake.

Reaching the lake she dismounted her horse and led him behind her as she had done the day she was there with her mother. Reaching the campsite she tied her horse and came next to the tent to inspect it. Quietly, she walked around it scrutinizing how it was attached to the wagon.

Mitch came behind her and gave her a start. "Looking for something?" he whispered.

She turned, and almost hit her face in his chest. "What in the world is this all about?" she asked. She gestured her arm towards the tent.

"This is about you," he said, relishing in the moment. He had made this for her with love in his heart.

"About me, I don't get it..." She knew she was kidding him, since she already knew, from Geoff, that something about this bizarre looking display was about her.

"With your permission…" He lifted his arm with a scarf dangling from his hand.

"Now what are you up to?" She looked at him with hesitation in her eyes.

He gently shushed her and turned her around to blindfold her. "I won't hurt you…" He said. He placed the blindfold on her.

She could almost see his big smile. "Come on Mitch, is this necessary?" She started to giggle and get involved with his surprise.

"Too many questions…just trust me," He put his arm around her waist and guided her towards the tent. "Watch your step. Step up," he said.

She giggled again loving the feel of him so close to her. "What's this?" she asked. She stamped her foot on what she felt was a hard floor beneath her feet. "Sure doesn't feel like anything I've had my feet on in a long time," She reached to un-blindfold her eyes. "Oh Mitch, this is just beautiful," She could not believe her eyes. "It's my kitchen," She looked at him with tears glistening in her eyes. "You can't know how much this means to me. Just look at this intricate work," She could feel herself blush, like Geoff teased her she would do.

"Oh yes I can. Collie, you come alive in a kitchen. I remember the first time we were alone in the kitchen at Driftwood. You gave me a feeling of belonging. You were so at home, and that was something I had never felt before, a sense of home and a place to want to be…" he was saying. He watched her check out the portable cupboard he had made that pulled out from beneath the tailgate of the wagon.

"And you painted the walls?" she said. She touched what looked exactly like her kitchen window painted on the tent canvas. She could see the backyard of Driftwood in the background of the window; it looked exactly as she remembered it. "I have never seen anything so beautiful," she walked around the tiny room.

"I really didn't know I had it in me, but Geoff did. He reminded me how I loved to paint when we were kids and it just came back to me," he said, enjoying watching her admire his artistic workmanship.

"This is really unbelievable. You even have the cabinets painted here that look so real. Wouldn't it be nice to really have this much space for things? I feel like I'm home," She went next to him. "You're an incredible man, thank you so much. And this floor, how does it travel?" She tapped her foot and loved the secure feeling it gave her.

"I know it's not very big, just pallet size. And it fits right under the wagon floor. I made a little compartment so it can just slip in and out," He was delighted that she was so pleased with his work.

"And I'm sure this all will fit on my wagon?" she asked. She turned to admire the walls again.

"Collie, I made this kitchen for you. And I made it to fit only on this wagon," He went behind her and put his arms around her.

The feel of his embrace sent a thrill of excitement throughout her body. She had loved him for so long that his gentle hold on her felt very comfortable and very right. "Oh Mitch I love you," She turned to face him. "I feel at home in your arms and in this room," She felt her tears welling in her eyes and flowing down her cheeks.

"Happy tears?" he asked. He started to wipe her tears from her cheeks, but then he too had tears falling from his eyes.

"Yes happy tears," She looked in his eyes and could see her reflection in them. She could see her happy face and she could see his love looking back at her.

"Colleen, I'm not too good at this," he said. He looked like a shy school boy. "Well, it's just that I've never done this before," He stumbled on his awkward words.

She innocently looked at him. "Mitch, you can say anything to me. I love you…" she was saying. She took her small hand and softly caressed his cheek sending a spark down his spine.

"I hope I can always live up to that love, and as your husband I would always give you my love in return," He knelt down on one knee. "Colleen, Armstrong, will you marry me, will you become my wife?" he boldly asked, with hope in his eyes.

The morning sun warming the chilled air made her body twitch dispelling her day dream of that special day, when Mitch proposed to her, bringing her back to the present time. She knew her family would soon be coming in from their morning chores to have their breakfast.

"You looked far away daughter. Only good thoughts?" her mother asked.

Colleen got up from the crate and went to check on their breakfast. "Yes Mama only good thoughts. I was remembering when Mitch proposed to me," Colleen said. She left her mother's side.

"Wonderful time…just wonderful," Beatrice said in her always joyous voice. She looked at her daughter who still seemed to be daydreaming of that time in her life. 'I have a good daughter,' Beatrice thought to herself. She continued to look out at the distance. But then she noticed a figure that seemed to be approaching their campsite. "I hope Ricky didn't wander off that far. But knowing that boy…" she said aloud. But then she realized the figure was much larger than her grandson, and looked like he might possibly be injured.

"Collie, take a look over there. It looks like someone is coming in and he might be hurt," she said.

Colleen looked in the direction her mother was pointing. "I'll get one of the men to check it out," Colleen said. She left her mother to tend the breakfast.

"Mitch there's a traveler making his way in and it looks like he might be hurt," Colleen said. She met Mitch near the horse coral.

"I'll check it out. Geoff is on his way in, send him out when he gets here," he said. He carefully mounted his saddled horse. "Better let the others know," he said. He was thankful she always carried her side arm.

"I'll do it," she said. She knew the safety of the train was everyone's responsibility, as Mitch rode off towards the stranger.

Nearing the stranger he seemed to hail Mitch with his hand; but then he slowly went to his knees and fell to the ground. Mitch immediately noticed, like a chameleon he seemed to fit in the environment. Had he not seen where he fell; he could have been mistaken for a mound of earth.

Finally, reaching him Mitch saw the stranger was covered from head to foot. He thought he looked like he was his own pack mule. Then he heard a faint cry from beneath the stranger's coverings. Quickly, he dismounted his horse and went next to him. Gently he turned him on his side, and just as quickly the stranger was on his feet.

"Hold on, I only want to help…" Mitch was saying. But then, he quickly backed away from the man who aimed what appeared to be a handmade spear in Mitch's direction. "I can see you need help stranger," Mitch said in a caring way. But he did not attempt to near the man. Mitch kept his distance, but kept his wary eyes on the armed stranger, who continued to aggressively protect himself.

Just then Geoff rode up on the scene. "What's the trouble here?" Geoff shouted. Keeping up his guard, he purposely did not dismount his horse, as he evaluated the situation.

"No trouble, just yet…" Mitch was saying. He again heard the faint cries coming from the stranger. "Do you speak English?" Mitch asked. He watched as the man reached out to him. But then, the stranger again fell to his knees and then, face-first, down to the ground. "Geoff, I think he might need some of your doctoring," Mitch said, as Geoff dismounted his horse and neared the man. "Wait a sec, let's get this out of the way," Mitch said. He carefully removed the homemade weapon and tossed it some distance from them.

"You know, I think he's got a baby tucked in there somewhere," Geoff said. He could hear faint cries coming from the stranger. "Here help me get this canvas wrapping off of him," He was pleased that the passed out man never moved.

"Holy shit, you're right," Mitch said. He un-wrapped the swaddled infant that was tied to the man's back.

"I think I'll be fine here. Go on back and get some help and a wagon for transport," Geoff gave his brother a confident look, and watched Mitch quickly mount his horse and leave him with the stranger and the tiny bundle.

"Here you go, that's all right little one…" Geoff was saying. He noticed the stranger cautiously turned onto his side and glared at him. "You're fine. You're with friends," Geoff said, to the stranger. Then, he gently lifted the whimpering baby into his arms. He noticed the stranger seemed to get a look of relief in his eyes. "What happened, where are you from?" Geoff was asking.

The stranger looked at him with trust in his eyes. "Bandits…" he was saying. He reached towards the child as tears welled in his eyes. Suddenly, he could feel himself starting to profusely perspire, as his world went black and he lost consciousness.

***

Later that evening they all were meeting at what they called their community camp bonfire. At this time they were discussing the stranger's appearance with the child.

"We can't have a black man in this camp. And what about that baby, she's white, where did she come from…" Camille LaFarge was saying.

"Mrs. LaFarge, I think we should be more concerned about the bandits he spoke of than his color. Did he say any more about what happened, Geoff?" BD asked. He was very concerned about what the man had said. He was seated on a crate and had brought along the rocker he had made for his wife and she was next to him.

"No, he hasn't said a word. He's been unconscious ever since we brought him back here, but that might be a good thing. His body needs some rest. Who knows how long he's been alone out there or how far he's traveled," Geoff said. He took a sip of the coffee Colleen had given him.

"Mari, il est noir," Camille LaFarge again stated, in French, to her husband about the color of the stranger.

"My wife has discriminating feelings concerning the Negro race," Claude LaFarge said. "We know that ways have changed and that after it happened, for self-preservation, ethnic prejudices were almost nonexistent, but for her and almost her entire family such ideas die hard," Claude said.

"I just don't see why we have to let him join our train. He's so different. And I'm sure he's uncultured…" Camille crossed her arms in front of herself, and stiffly sat on a crate next to her husband.

"I don't know what you're talking about…we're all different… we all come from different backgrounds and ethnic groups," Beatrice said. She looked coldly at Camille. "Why, you speak a different language all the time; so that makes you different, but you don't see anyone asking you and your family to leave," She noticed Camille snubbed her nose at her.

"But we don't look different. He's so…so…well, he looks like a big oaf," She tried to hold her ground about the stranger's presence. "I simply do not like his race," she shouted.

"Well, if you ask me with all our world's been through we should be proud to get along with any upstanding person who's survived…" Beatrice was saying. "And Camille, why can't you just accept him as part of the human race…we all have to help each other," Beatrice noticed, even in the darkness and with the limited firelight that Camille turned red.

"I want the best for my children. Not this uneducated…oaf," She curtly said. "I know his type," Camille looked at her husband.

He did not want any part of her conversation. "Don't look at me…" Claude said. He got up and walked to stoke the bonfire.

"Well…" Camille put her hand to her eyes and tried to turn her head from them all.

"Well folks, I have to say, for now I think such ideas have to be put on the back burner. If what he says about bandits is true, we have bigger problems that may lie ahead," BD said. He was happy that most present shook their heads in agreement.

"Maybe our family is lucky that you all have been forced to stay here," The beekeeper added to their conversation.

They all agreed. "Better here than out in the open," someone said.

They all started to talk between each other.

"Dad, hurry he's waking up," Ricky yelled to his father.

"I might need some help…" Geoff was saying. He was happy that the men followed him with the women not far behind.

"Theresa, where's my baby?" The stranger was screaming. He tugged at the soft tethers that, for his own protection, bound him.

"Collie, bring the baby," Geoff shouted to his sister-in-law, after he entered the back door way of the wagon.

"My child, please bring me my baby,"The man cried out. His tears fell from his cheeks as he uncontrollably sobbed. "I beg of you," he pleaded. He placed his large, loosely bound, black, hands over his eyes to cover his humiliation of the situation.

"We have your child. She's safe. We've cared for her while you've been recovering," Geoff explained to the stranger. Cautiously, he approached the man. "It was only for your safety that we tied you down. You've been...how can I say it...out of your mind. We didn't know what else to do. Can you understand?" Geoff came and sat closer to him.

"Yes, I understand. But I heard the woman talk about my color. Sir, yes I'm black, can't hide that. But I'm an honorable man," he said, with pleading eyes. "The bandits tested me to the limits, and now from the bottom I must rise," His tears continued to fall, but he tried to compose himself. "The baby, she's the only thing left. She's my own flesh and blood," He looked at Geoff. "I must see my baby. She's all I have left. Please God, my child..." he humbly whispered. He bowed his head.

Colleen entered the wagon with the child still asleep in her arms. "She's fine," Colleen caringly said. She uncovered the face of the child, but to keep her warm quickly put the cover back over her.

The stranger could see that she was peacefully sleeping. "Oh, thank God," he prayed. His sobs continued. "Her mama, my wife, she was slaughtered. Dear God, right before my eyes they killed her," He seemed to be remembering that time. "They wanted me to lead them, but I escaped with my baby," With his hands still tied he reached towards Colleen for his baby.

Colleen looked at Geoff. "It's okay," Geoff said to Colleen. Geoff went next to the stranger and untied him.

Colleen knelt next to the stranger and gave him his child. "She's a good baby. She ate well..." She wanted him to know the condition of his daughter. She looked and saw that some of the men were peeking inside to see what was going on with the stranger.

"My Theresa, our baby," he softly said. He gently took her in his huge hands. He uncovered her face when he felt her slightly squirm in his loving hold on her. "How long have I been out?" he asked. Openly, he showed his adoring love for his child.

"We only found you this morning," Geoff said. He watched the man in awe. He had never seen a man, in public; show such complete love for a child. He could empathize with him, when he remembered the loss of his own wife, and how he had missed his son when he left Driftwood. But he knew the circumstances were not the same.

"They will come..."The stranger looked at Geoff. He seemed to be giving his child all of his love and strength.

"Can you tell me more about what happened to you?" Geoff asked. He believed the man could be more in control of his situation. "Can you start with your name?" He noticed the man seemed to relax a bit.

"I'm Omar Turnbow, the wagon master for Turnbow Trails. I've made this trip many times. But after the birth of Theresa, this was going to be my last trip West; and I was making it with my family," he explained to Geoff. He gently kissed his daughter's forehead and again started to sob, as he softly clutched her to his bosom.

"You know the land?" Geoff asked. He looked at Collie. "We might be on our way sooner than we expected," He smiled.

"Yes, I know the land. And those bandits wanted me to guide them. Even after they murdered everyone," He started to sweat. "First they murdered my sons," Omar could see in his mind the savages beating his boys. "And then…" He hesitated. "Right in front of me; they violated and murdered my wife," He wiped his brow. He caressed his child. "And they still expected me to lead them. They're ruthless," He looked at Geoff and Colleen. "And they're led by a woman meaner than I've ever seen," He was controlling his emotions.

Colleen felt a cold spike flow down her spine. "You are a brave man," She said. She had tears welling in her eyes.

"You have to get ready. I know they're following me," He had a look of fear in his eyes. "They will come like shadows in the night. You won't even know they're here," He was starting to fidget in the bed. "May I…" He wanted to sit on the side of the bed.

"Of course," Geoff said. He and Colleen gave him some space. "Please tell us more," Geoff asked.

"First they pilfer and then they kidnap. It was only when they took the first woman that we knew something was wrong, but by then it was too late," he related. He noticed the men at the rear opening started to chatter. "She's all I have left of my family," He let out such a loud, mournful, keening howl, that Geoff and Colleen and those near the wagon stepped back.

"Please, for your baby's sake, for little Theresa, try to calm down." Colleen, feeling safe enough to approach the man, put her hand on the infant. She noticed Omar calmed down, but still had great concern in his dark eyes.

"You must get ready, they're not far behind. I tried to cover my trail, but I know they'll find us. They're like animals; they smell you out," he said with pleading eyes.

Suddenly, they heard Ricky yelling from outside the wagon. "Collie, Dad, its Grandma, it's time," he shouted.

Geoff looked at Colleen. "Hand me my bag," he asked Colleen. She gave him the bag. He hurried from the wagon.

"The others heard what you said. We'll get ready…." Colleen put her hand on Omar's shoulder. "You're a good man. I'm so sorry for you loss," Her tears fell from her eyes. "Geoff went to help my mother. I have to go…" With trust in her eyes she looked him right in the eyes. "We will prepare," She left to find her mother.

For her safety and comfort during her labor and delivery, the beekeeper and his wife had graciously taken Beatrice to their family cottage. Inside, the living quarters were lit with several hanging oil lamp chandeliers. The kitchen was combined with their large living room and fires glowed in the spacious stone fire places built in the north and south walls.

"She's in our bedroom," the beekeepers wife said. She was showing Geoff the way, as Colleen entered the cottage and followed them to the room.

"Oh, boy its time…" Beatrice almost shouted. Her face was red and her hair was matted from perspiration. She was trying to control her words.

She gave her husband's hand a hard squeeze. "Give it to me Honey, I can take it," BD said. He winked at her.

She looked at him knowing he would give up his life for her. "Oh boy, here we go again…" she yelled.

Geoff came to her where she lay in the bed, and checked her progress. "Almost here Bea," Geoff told her. "One good push…" he was saying.

Colleen came to the other side of her mother and took her other hand. "Can I help?" Colleen asked.

Geoff started moving faster and the beekeepers wife assisted him. "Nothing to help with," Geoff said. He looked at Beatrice. He held up the baby in his hands. "You have a son Bea," The baby started to cry, when he tied and snipped the cord.

"Our son," Beatrice said. She looked at her husband, as she opened her arms and Geoff placed the naked boy in her arms and BD coddled them both. Immediately, the baby stopped his first cries.

"Oh Mama," Colleen said. Tears formed in her eyes when she saw the joy on her mother's face.

"Isn't he a sight for sore eyes? My easiest delivery ever..." Beatrice was saying. She looked at her daughter and then to her husband. "Your son, my husband," She handed him to BD.

"Oh Bea, I love you," BD said. He openly cried, happy tears, in front of all present. "Our joy, our Joseph," He accepted from her the love they shared in the form of this little child, their son.

"Can I bring Ricky in?" Geoff asked. Beatrice and BD shook their heads in agreement. Geoff went to get his son.

The beekeepers wife came next to BD with his baby's first wardrobe in her hands. "Here, I'll take care of him," Colleen said. She took the clothes from the beekeeper's wife and accepted her half-brother from her step-father. She cleaned and dressed him on the bed next to her mother when Geoff came in with Ricky.

"Lookie here Ga Ga, your uncle Joseph," Beatrice said. With pride in her eyes and a little chuckle in her words she looked at Ricky.

Colleen placed Joseph in his mother's arms, as Ricky came next to them by the bed. "Wow Grammy, I'm older than my uncle," Ricky happily said. He looked down at him and took a hold of his tiny finger. "Wow, what a grip. I'll teach him how to make fire and hunt and everything Grammy..." he was saying.

Suddenly, a burst of thunder broke their merriment and Mitch hurried into the room. "Geoff, can I see you," He was too much in a hurry to even greet anyone. With Geoff in the other room and the door shut behind him he whispered to Geoff. "The LaFarge girl is missing. We have searched the whole camp and can't find her. Her parents are beside themselves," Mitch related, as Geoff with Mitch right beside him, quickly left the cottage and headed outside to the wagon where Omar was recuperating.

The rain was steady and hard and belted the canvas of the wagon making it hard to hear. Omar lay with his baby in his arms and seemed fast asleep. "Omar," Geoff shouted, but the man did not budge. "Omar," Geoff again yelled. He shook the man.

Omar shot straight up, yet held his baby girl close to his bosom. "I slept, I should've stayed alert," Omar turned his body and sat on the side of the bed. Hurriedly, he woke his half asleep mind and listened to Geoff.

"Omar, a woman's gone. They have checked the whole camp and she's missing," Geoff said. He saw such a fright in the man that he wished he could have taken back his words.

"Oh my God, I led them to you. God forgive me..." Omar was saying. He had such a feeling of remorse and a sense of guilt that he tried to hide his face from Geoff and Mitch.

"It's not your fault. You had to find safety for yourself and your child. We have to join together and fight them," Geoff said.

Omar, with his hand near his eyes, trying to hide his grief shook his head in agreement. "I will give my life for my child and your people. We must hurry. They work fast. I can't tell you the horrors they will do," Purposely rising from his seat he bowed in the low ceiling and motioned for Geoff and Mitch to leave so he could follow.

Omar relinquished his daughter to Mitch; who took her to the beekeeper's cottage for Colleen to tend. He informed them of the missing LaFarge girl, and her most likely being kidnapped. BD went for guns and ammunition and would stay with the women and children inside the protection of the crowded cottage.

For their protection against the rain, the men gathered under a canvas canopy erected from ropes stretched from several wagons. "I know these savages. They will take their time and play with her and then..." Omar knew they would understand what he meant without saying it. "We do not have much time, they work fast..." Omar was saying.

All the men listened to his every word. Although his words were harsh; they believed he spoke as an educated man.

"Please, tell us everything. We have to be prepared," Mitch asked him.

"I'm only telling you what I know. They did it to my family, and my friends," Omar looked at the men in front of him. "Oh God, they will torture her. They will do it slowly, obeying the commands of a woman who seems to hate life itself. She gives her followers the spoils for their pleasure. And for their amusement..." He bowed his head, but shouted. "They will kill her..." Omar again shouted. "If we don't act fast...They will kill her," He turned from their gaze.

Claude LaFarge let out a cry. "Oh God, my daughter," he cried aloud.

Omar turned to face them. "I hate to say these things, but that's how it is. This woman who leads them seems to thirst for blood. There are about fifteen of them, but they fight like a hundred. They have no fear, so they fight and kill with no feelings for themselves or others. The only way we can get them is by surprise," he was informing them.

Mitch neared him. "Should we make a frontal attack on horseback, or sneak in and surprise them?" Mitch asked Omar.

Claude LaFarge abruptly interrupted him. "They'll kill her, the second they know we're there," Claude said. He looked at Omar for confirmation in what he said.

"Unfortunately, you're right," Omar replied. His words sent a dagger down Claude's spine. "I know their set up. I know how they work," He looked at the men. "When the bandits attacked my wagon train, they always retreated back to the East. So I say that's where we'll find them," He only paused for a second. "And with the help of only two others I believe we can get her out of their camp," Omar knew he had their complete attention. And he knew what he had to say next was going to be hard to say and hard to understand, but something they had to accomplish. "And then, we all must make a last, united attack," He wiped his brow. "To save her and all of us, and I truly mean all of us, we have to destroy all of them," He noticed they all looked around at each other. "Trust me, if we don't...they will rape your women and kill all of us," Omar was speaking with a strength that bonded them with a determination to fight for their lives.

"I have an idea that might work," the beekeeper stood up and said. "We have an armory of weapons. We have guns, rifles, knives and swords. But our best weapon is our bees. We have many protective suits and netting that we can wear. And if we all rub our bodies with mineral oil and tar the bees won't bother us as much..." he was saying. His words sparked hope in their hearts.

"Hurry, give me your plan," Omar took the beekeeper aside.

The beekeeper's son approached Mitch. "We always use these methods to keep the bees from stinging us," he said, to Mitch, as the rest of the men listened.

"Can you show us where to get these extra weapons and supplies?" Mitch asked.

"Sure. Follow me," the beekeeper's son said.

Mitch and the rest of the men left the protection of the make shift tent and followed him, while Omar and the beekeeper made their plans of attack.

***

The rain was non-stop into the night. But Omar assured them it was on their side. With Omar's guidance: he, Claude and the beekeeper crept and found their way to the bandits' campsite with the others waiting at a safe distance.

The storm did not discourage the evil ways of this band of derelicts. They showed no inhibitions. They kept their huge bonfires ablaze; which seemed to beg anyone to come and challenge them.

The queen of the bandits had her band completely under her control. She demanded that her drunken subordinates scurry around the muddy plain and bring her sagebrush for her fire. It did not matter that the brush was wet; they wanted to please her and continued to keep the gigantic bonfire, in their camp, ablaze. Their intoxicated merriment sounded more like a party than a killing spree.

From a short distance Omar, Claude and the beekeeper watched the bandits, while the rest of their company of men continued to wait a short distance from them with a live bomb.

"I asked you before and I have to be certain, can you kill?" Omar asked. He was looking directly at Claude, who was hunched next to him in the brush.

"Yes I can kill…my daughter's in there...I can kill," Claude replied.

Omar was not completely assured. He saw some hesitation in Claude's eyes. He then turned his head and also peered in the eyes of the beekeeper; instantly, he knew by his look he was ready. Again, he looked at Claude. "Damn it LaFarge you can't let your feelings get in the way," he peered intently at Claude. He wanted to see more from the man than revenge. He had to be capable to act on impulse and be ready to defend and kill. Many lives hung in the balance of their actions, so his reasoning depended on his instinct to again evaluate Claude. "They're playing with her now. Do you understand me man?" Omar spoke in a low whisper.

Claude looked him straight in the eye and sharply nodded an affirmative response. "Damn it man, what do you want me to say? I know, these bastards are raping my daughter, but I will keep my wits about me, for her sake," Claude hoarsely whispered. His tar black face looked at Omar with an understood purpose in his eyes.

"Just listen to me. The queen will give your daughter, as a gift, to one or two of her favorites. She will let them use her tent..." Omar was saying. As he spoke these words, he felt the palms of his hands sweat when a flash of his own experiences of her tent, entered his mind. "I've seen and heard it more times than I want to say," he said, as both men turned and bowed their heads. "That's when we make our move," he quietly said, as they listened to his every word. "We just watch and wait till we see which tent they go to. Then we'll crawl to it and cut our way in," Omar put his sharp knife in his mouth and clamped down hard on it. "Just follow me, we have to get closer; you'll know what to do," he softly mumbled, still holding the knife in his mouth.

Slithering, like snakes, they made their way along the muddy, rain soaked slush. From their vantage point they watched the naked savages dance around the gigantic bonfires.

Finally, they picked out the queen, as she purposely made her domineering presence known to her subjects. They saw Antoinette being held by two guards, as the queen danced around them. The queen did not display a modest bone in her body. In a quick thrust, she threw her long, black, rain drenched hair away from her exposing her completely nude body in front of Antoinette. Antoinette tried to turn her head but the cruel bitch smacked her face. "You look at me brat," She sinisterly spat in her face.

She took Antoinette by the chin and made her face her. "Come on..." she purred. "You're a pretty little thing. I know you've seen your share," The queen softly stroked Antoinette's face and forced her to look at her. "See what you get," She motioned to the naked men holding her. She started to pet them, but she did not take her eyes away from Antoinette. "Of course, they're not my best, but they'll do," She made Antoinette look at the naked men.

"I'm in a mood tonight. I want my best for me," she shouted. She left Antoinette for the moment, and started to playfully dance around. Openly, she fondled her horde, even the three women in her band. "I love you all. We will celebrate with wine," she yelled, sending a drunken cheer from them all, as she held up several stolen bottles from her booty.

Purposely, she went in front of Antoinette and poured a little wine in Antoinette's mouth, as she ripped off the front of her dress exposing Antoinette's bare breasts. Seeing this Claude almost lost it. He started to go towards his daughter but Omar hurriedly stopped and muffled him, as the queen continued her quest.

"Your bitch," The queen shouted to the men who held Antoinette. She neared her and squeezed Antoinette's cheeks. "You look at me bitch," she yelled at Antoinette; her hot breath reeked of wine. Then she wrapped her leg around Antoinette's leg and mockingly humped her. With evil, lustful eyes, she looked Antoinette straight in her eyes, and laughed when Antoinette shook her head and tried not to look at her. "She's a feisty bitch. Take her..." she finally yelled. She grabbed Antoinette's shoulders and shook her.

"No..." Antoinette fiercely screamed, sending stabbing pains through the hearts of her hidden saviors, who silently watched which tent her captors led her to.

The rest of the bandits started dancing and building the fire's glow. "Come, my puppies," Their queen squealed. They all came to her. They picked her up on their shoulders and then down to the muddy ground where their animal passions indulged in a drunken orgy.

Quickly, while the band was distracted, Omar and his close entourage crept to the tent where Antoinette was held.

Omar waited for a bolt of lightning and when the thunder started he hurriedly cut a slit in the tent. Entering the tent Antoinette let out a frightening scream.

"Good puppies...take her..." The queen yelled thinking the rapists were enjoying their treat, as she indulged in her own sexual debauchery.

Antoinette could not stop her death fearing screams. In the dark she could not see her father. With another flash of lightening she saw Omar raise his knife and slice into one of the rapist, while the beekeeper killed the other.

With another flash of lightening Antoinette saw her father and ran to him. She could see the fear in his eyes as he gently took her in his arms. He nodded to her and put his fingers to her lips to silence her. With warm tears flowing from her frightened, wide eyes, she quietly shook her head in agreement, as Omar led them from the tent.

Covertly, they ran hand in hand from the camp and met up with their comrades in arms. Geoff brought a blanket and a canvas for Antoinette to huddle under, as they all readied themselves for the attack.

Geoff gave each of them a triple dose of the elixir, Diphedryl to help prevent the swelling from any bee stings.

"You have to stay here," Claude said to his terrified daughter. "We have to take care of this. Can you understand me daughter?" He was afraid to leave her alone, but knew his help would be needed.

He calmed down when she positively shook her head. "Yes father, I understand," She had a faint smile on her lips. He patted her cheeks.

"Quickly," Omar, whispered and with a wave of his arm they were off.

The Bolovich boys galloped in for the first attack. Kegs of gun powder were thrown onto the blazing fires. The surprised bandits dispersed in fear, when they blew up.

And then, as fast as they left, the second attack came, but this time the attack was more deadly than the first. Mitch, Yerik, and the beekeeper's eldest son, dressed in the beekeeper's protective garb, quickly rode in and threw down wooden containers filled with angry bees. The drunken bandits scrambled and fumbled for their weapons.

With God's armor on their side, the rain stopped and when the containers of bees cracked open on contact, the bees instantly swarmed the naked bandits stinging them. The more the bandits carried on by jumping around and trying to get away, the more the bees swarmed and stung them distracting the bandits from the invading group.

Finally, with the last attack, the group entered the bandit's camp firing fatal gun shots and swinging the long, deadly swords that the beekeeper armed them with. Fortunately, the bees paid most of their attention to the naked bandits.

Then, with a flash of lightening Omar saw her. She ran a short distance from the group.

At the same time, Claude saw her too. "The queen," he whispered to himself. With a sharp sword above his head, Claude spurred his horse towards her. Nearing her he reigned in on his horse when the queen raised her hands and turned to face him. Abruptly, his horse reared up and Claude fell to the ground. His sword slipped from his hand and landed next to his side.

Viciously, the queen ran next to Claude and picked up his sword. She was about to ram him with it, when Omar's horse galloped next to her and knocked her several yards away, but not before the sword, missed its first target and cut into Claude's arm.

Omar turned his horse and went next to Claude. Quickly, Omar extended his arm to him, while Claude, jumped up and with his good arm grabbed a hold of Omar. He mounted the horse right behind the saddle.

Within a split second, Omar's horse neared the queen and reared up on top of her, knocking her down. As the horse reared up again, both he and Claude looked down at her. They could not keep from looking at the queen's cold, black fish eyes stare at them, as the hooves came down and crushed her skull. With this came the end of her rule, which rid the world of this heartless, scum of the earth.

***

While this was taking place, BD, along with the women, waited at the beekeeper's cottage. They were armed and ready for the bandits.

Beatrice felt helpless. She could only lay in bed with her newborn tucked in close on one side, and a knife and pistol on her other side.

BD, kept watch outside the front door; the beehives naturally protected their backs and sides.

Colleen kept her vigil by her mother's bedroom door, with Theresa sleeping peacefully in a cradle the beekeeper's wife brought to her.

Suddenly, Colleen saw the blue ball streak in front of her. It was the same phenomenon she experienced with her sister, BD and then Pavel. But this time when it came near her and passed through her and then back again, she had the thought of Antoinette.

Quickly, she turned and looked at her mother, to see if she had seen it. But by the look on her face she knew she did not, so she turned to continue her watch.

There was such a hush in the house that it almost gave her goose bumps. She couldn't help but look at Camille LaFarge, and feel her pain knowing the predicament her daughter faced.

But she wondered: "What could the blue light mean? Did Antoinette die? Was that what the blue light meant?" But then she remembered the light did not leave her. It stayed the same way it had, long ago with BD. And he is still alive. 'So maybe Antoinette's okay,' she thought. "And why didn't anyone else seem to see it?" She looked around. 'I know nobody else saw it,' she thought. At times she had tried to talk about the blue light with her mother. But it seemed every time she tried to bring it up, something else of importance took its place in the conversation. So she was never able to have a discussion about it. It was something she just lived with.

After some time, BD opened the front door of the cottage. "They're coming," he shouted. He put up his arms and everyone stood at attention and ready to fight the bandits. "It's our men," BD then shouted.

Happily, they all put down their arms. Colleen hurried to her mother's room and with Joseph in her mother's arms; Colleen helped her from the bed. "Thank God, Collie. Thank God," Beatrice said.

Colleen then picked Theresa up from the cradle and they all went outside to greet their warriors.

As they rode their horses closer to the cottage Camille LaFarge first caught sight of her husband. She noticed he was slightly slumped in his saddle. Running to him she noticed his bloody shirt and his arm in the first aid sling Geoff had put on him. But looking around she could not see her daughter. "Oh

God no, my baby, mon enfant," she screamed. She thought the worst had happened.

"She's coming wife," Claude LaFarge shouted to her. "Go to her," He knew she must see her child.

Just then Omar rode up and quickly dismounted his horse. He reached up for Antoinette to dismount the horse into his waiting arms. Gently, in a very protective way, he had tight hold on her. He held her like a baby.

Camille ran next to them. "Merci, merci," she said to him. She bowed her head, almost ashamed to look him in the eyes. "I have been a fool, vous êtes notre ami, you are our friend," She was sobbing. She noticed Antoinette hung on to him and had her head buried in his chest. She acted like she did not want him to let her go. Omar carried her into the cottage.

Omar looked like a tall tree standing in the middle of the room. Antoinette continued to keep her arms around his neck. She wore Omar's buckskin shirt over her torn dress.

Finally, Colleen came next to them with Theresa in her arms. "Antoinette, Omar must hold his daughter," Colleen calmly, whispered. She made Antoinette look at the baby. But Antoinette only held on closer to Omar.

"Dearest Lady of Guadalupe, mystical rose, virgin Mary and yet mother of our true God, obtain for us from thy most holy Son the grace to keep our faith, sweet hope in the midst of the bitterness of life, burning charity and the precious gift to hold fast to final perseverance. Amen," Omar prayed. He bowed his head.

"How is it you know that prayer?" Camille asked. She had a completely surprised tone in her voice.

"I'm a Christian, ma'am," Omar said. He felt Antoinette slightly move in his arms. She turned her head and glared at her mother to stay away. She would or could not turn loose of Omar.

"She's been through a horrible ordeal. I think she feels safe in my arms," Omar said. He knew the feelings of fear and safety, and he was glad he could give her the latter.

Claude entered the cottage. "My daughter," A huge smile lit up his face. He neared Omar. "Come to me child," Claude whispered. He lifted his one, good arm to his frightened daughter. "Come child," he again whispered. He motioned for Camille and Olivier, Antoinette's brother to come next to him. Finally, Antoinette relinquished her hold on Omar. With tears flowing from her red eyes she fell into her family's opened arms.

With her out of his arms Omar teetered and became faint. The beekeeper's wife, hurried to place a kitchen chair in front of him. "Thank you ma'am," Omar said. After he sat down he could feel the perspiration pour from his spent body.

"Omar, I owe you for my daughter's life and my life. Without you we all could've died," Claude put his hand on Omar's shoulder. He and his family openly cried and nodded in agreement to Omar.

"Merci, merci," Camille cried. "You are a great man," She neared Omar and hugged him. "From the bottom of my heart, I thank you," She gently stroked his cheek. "You're bleeding. I will tend you…" she was saying.

Geoff came into the cottage. "We were lucky. Not too many stings and just some cuts and bruises on the men…" Geoff was saying. He noticed Camille was cleansing Omar's head wound. "I have some ointment and bandages you can use on that. It doesn't look too deep," Geoff looked over Omar's laceration.

"Here Omar, I'm afraid no one wears your size, but this might help," the beekeeper's wife said. She gave him a large poncho.

"I will get my daughter some fresh clothes and clean up your buckskin shirt," Camille said. She looked Omar straight in his eyes. As he sat on the chair; she was at his height. "I cannot thank you enough…" She spoke with her French accent. Her tears again filled her eyes. "You and your baby will live with us. That is the least we can do. Am I right husband?" She turned to her husband. Finally, she looked at Omar; not seeing a black man, but a selfless, man.

"Absolutely," Claude replied. He again hugged his daughter.

"With your permission, I believe it would be a good idea if I examined Antoinette," Geoff said. He neared the LaFarge family. "Could I use the bedroom?" he asked the beekeeper's wife.

"Certainly, I will prepare it for you," she said, as she went to the room.

"Mrs. LaFarge, I think it would be best if you accompanied me," Geoff said. He watched her finish bandaging Omar's wound.

"Of course, just let me finish up here and get her some fresh clothes," Camille checked Omar's bandage. "There you go," She patted Omar's hand and then left the cottage.

"My Theresa," Omar said. He turned his kind eyes towards Colleen.

She was patiently holding the baby, waiting for the right moment to give her to Omar. "She's a good baby. No trouble at all," Colleen said. She gently released the infant into her father's loving arms.

"She has the spirit and look of her mother," Omar said. He accepted his only living child in his arms. "Her mother and I were blessed with four sons, God rest their souls. And Theresa, our only daughter," He caressed her tiny, pearl white face with his large, black hand.

"She's beautiful…" Colleen was saying. She stood next to Omar and his baby.

Camille returned with Antoinette's clothing. "Come with mother," Camille extended her hand to her daughter and they followed Geoff into the bedroom.

"Omar, you must be hungry enough to eat a bear..." Colleen was saying. She noticed Mitch come in the cottage.

"Haven't had much time to think about food ma'am. But now that you bring it up; I'm sure I could eat just about anything you could rustle up for me," Omar looked at Colleen. "And thanks again for taking care of my Theresa," he said.

Colleen smiled at him. "It was my pleasure. She's precious," she caressed the baby's cheek. "I'll be right back," She then patted Omar's shoulder.

She and Mitch left the cottage. "Oh my God Mitch, I was so scared. If I had lost you I don't know what I would've done," Colleen said. She had a look of fright in her eyes.

Mitch grabbed and hugged her. "It was horrible Collie. Those bandits lived like wild animals, only worse. They didn't act like normal human beings," He shook his head in despair. "It had to be done. They had to be killed," He bowed his head and looked at her. "Otherwise, I'm certain they would've killed us," He felt a sense of calm when he looked in her compassionate eyes.

"I know it had to be done," she whispered. She continued to hug him as close to her heart as she could. "But I can't understand what made them like that? We would've helped them and shared with them," She had a bewildered look in her eyes.

He gently caressed her cheek and slipped a lock of her hair behind her ear. "I saw people like that when we crossed the first time with my father. And I made the trip two times after that. But this was the first time I've ever seen a murderous woman have so much power over people..." he was saying.

She saw a faraway look in his eyes. "Honey, it's over now. Try not to think about it," she said. She held on to him as if she would never let him go. "Let's go rustle us up that food Omar was talking about," She put her arm around his waist. She looked up at him and giggled when he put his arm around her waist, and they went to prepare the food.

After the twilight seeped in around them, and the last bright orange rays of the sun disappeared in the West like they always had, every soul in the encampment quietly said a prayer of thanks to their God.

Chapter Seven

Falling Stars

The early morning sun reflected off the calm lake with an eye penetrating glare. She had a soft quilt not far from the edge of the water. She disrobed and placed her clothing neatly on the quilt, with a towel at the water's bank.

She enjoyed this little time of self-indulgence with an uninhibited feeling of freedom. Carelessly, she dipped the tip of her toe in the lake to check the warmth of the water. Satisfied, she slowly waded out to her favorite spot and dove into the clear, tepid liquid.

He watched her from the bushes. He saw her holstered pistol next to her clothes on the quilt.

She was breathtaking. "She looks like a little water nymph," He pondered to himself. He watched her swift movements make the calm water sparkle, with each stroke of her arms and flutter of her long, trim legs.

As she turned and played in the crystal clear water he could see her fully nude body, which sent a thrill throughout him. Her lack of concern and unpretentious frolic made him yearn for her.

Finally, she came out of the water and picked up a bar of soap and gently worked it between her hands. With her legs slightly parted she gently massaged the sudsy foam between her legs and then up to her breasts. This pleasurable sensation made her body ache for more, so once again she bent to the water and worked the soap into another slippery lather.

Slowly, she turned around and he could see a look of excited passion on her face. He found it hard not to near her, but he wanted to see more.

She arched her back and let out a tiny giggle as she again soaped her breasts and continued to massage the silky bubbles between her legs.

Suddenly, she turned and with the soap in her hand she again went to her favorite spot in the lake and dove in.

He could see her silhouette in the, soapy, milky water. After finding a clear spot in the water, he watched her find a secure section, on the sandy bottom, where she stood up and washed her hair with the soap. She then tossed the soap to the shore line and dove in again to rinse her hair.

Finished bathing, she left the water and grabbed her towel. She went to the soft quilt, and only for a second looked around, and then lay down to let the sun dry her.

He thought this was his chance to satisfy his aroused male emotions. She had stimulated his erotic cravings and in his mind he believed she would be the one to end his desires.

Quietly, he looked around and slowly removed his clothing and without hesitation, neared her.

He could not take his eyes from her completely naked body, as she lay flat on her back. She had one hand behind her to support her head and one leg slightly bent at the knee. Slowly, she caressed her breasts and was moving her hand closer to her navel when he gently caught her hand with his.

"I'll take over from here," he whispered. He was heavily breathing.

She nonchalantly opened her eyes. "You sure took your time," She teased him. She giggled and turned onto her side with her one leg still bent.

"Are you sure you want me? It looked like..." he was saying. After witnessing her seemingly satisfied play.

She gently stroked his hand. "Always," she purred. She placed her lips on his and they deeply kissed. He then kissed her neck and she started to squirm. "I never knew love could be this wonderful," she whispered. She snuggled in his arms close to his naked body.

"I love you with all my heart," he hoarsely said. His body ached for her. "You're an incredible woman. You give me more pleasure than I ever could've dreamed of," he whispered in her ear and then nibbled it.

"Honey, you know this is all new to me and I know I'm really naïve about love making, but if something else is supposed to happen..." Curiously she looked at him. "Well, you'll have to teach me?" She ran the tips of her fingers on his muscular, bare chest.

"Yes there's more and I was hoping when we got together things would work themselves out...maybe we should've waited to get married...you shouldn't have..." he was saying, but then hesitated.

"Mitch, I'm your wife you can tell me anything," Colleen said. She looked at him with only admiration and love in her eyes. "No matter what, I know I was meant to spend the rest of my life with you," She put her hand under her chin and continued to look at him with great love.

"I talked this over with Geoff before we got married, and he said my problem probably stems from the bee stings and me being unconscious for so long. He said it will most likely fix itself in time..." A look of embarrassment reddened his face. "I was hoping we wouldn't have to have this conversation, but..." He gave her a pitiful look.

"What we have is enough for me. Honey, you're a great lover and the rest will come in time," She pressed her body close to his. "Enough of this talk...you know what I'm going to do..." She got up and went to her saddle bags. "You stay right there," Teasingly, she shook her finger at him. She picked up her saddle bags and started to fumble around in them until she found the article she wanted. She then took a cloth from her bag and went to the lake.

"What are you up to..." he laughed. He noticed she soaked the cloth in the lake and seemed to be looking for something when he saw her stoop down and then walk back to him.

"I'm going to give you a shave," she said. Still stark naked, she stood in front of him with her hands on her hips.

He thought she almost looked like a little girl getting ready to play with her favorite toy. "Oh Honey, I don't know, you look a little too eager," He scooted back on the quilt.

"Come on baby, I can do it," shc said. She had the soap she had tossed to the shore from the lake already lathered in one hand, while she un-wrapped the cloth where she had placed a straight razor. "You know your whiskers have been kind of scratching me," She knelt next to him and tried to coax him into submission. "I'll let you do around your cute little dimples. They're so cute I could fill them up with cement and keep them all to myself," She neared him with her face right in his. Softly, she pinched both of his cheeks.

"Now don't make fun of my dimples. I'll have you know, in times past of course, some women thought of them as a rather come on," He was purposely trying to make her have a jealous feeling.

"Is that right...well they're all mine now..." She again gently pinched his cheeks. "Come on Honey, I know I can do this," She slithered and purred around him like an innocent pussy cat, until she saw a submissive look in his eyes.

"You'll need a lot of soap. I'll go get a pan from the wagon and some water," He got up and went for his supplies.

"Take your time, I'm not going anywhere," she said. While watching him, she playfully tossed the bar of soap in the air several times catching it each time; then casually lay back on the quilt.

When he returned he looked at her lounging on the quilt. "Are you sure?" He sat next to her. "I guess I should've taken care of this myself. You do look a little red in certain areas," He slightly blushed.

She started to giggle. "Well, I'll just get rid of these whiskers so you can glide into those certain areas a little easier," she cooed. She knelt on the quilt and dipped the cloth in the water and placed it on his beard to soften it. "Just relax," She worked the soap to a rich lather and massaged it into his beard. "Here, put your head back a bit and I'll try not to slice your neck," She noticed his eyes widen. "Golly, I'm just kidding…I mean I'll gently start here," She giggled.

He felt her soft breasts on his arm. "Feels pretty nice so far," he said. He gave her a wink of his eye and enjoyed the soft press of her flesh on him.

"No talking," she teased. She continued her task. "You're a handsome man," She admired him as she knelt in between his legs while he sat in front of her. "Here, now you shave the dimples," She handed him the razor.

"You know, I think I should shave your legs too. I've got some stubble marks myself," he said. He finished shaving around his dimples.

She handed him the damp cloth. "Fine with me, I'd enjoy the pampering," She deeply sighed when he soaped her legs and caringly shaved them. "You know, not being able to take care of the hair under my arms doesn't bother me as much as it does on my legs. Is that silly or what?" She lay back and peacefully enjoyed watching him.

"I love everything about you, even the hair on your legs. So if you're silly then so am I," He looked at her and saw that familiar look of passion he had fallen in love with about her.

"Honey, you give me so much love and pleasure I'm sure I can try to give you just a little more in return," she purred. She knelt next to him and then straddled him. Slowly, she caressed his chest and gently pushed him back down on the quilt. She then reached for his out stretched arms, as her breasts brushed across his chest and she reached his lips with hers and deeply kissed him.

"Colleen, I don't think I can…" he was saying.

She silenced him with another kiss and then knelt next to him again and kissed his belly. "Come, my husband," She gently took his hand and pulled him to his feet.

"What are you up to?" he curiously asked.

She quickly removed their gear from the quilt. Silently she took his hand. She then stooped and grabbed the quilt and dragged it behind her as she led him towards the side of the lake.

"This is our honeymoon and we're going to enjoy ourselves as husband and wife," she said. She squeezed his hand and then neared his naked body with hers as they walked to the lake.

"You're quite a woman," He looked down at her. His heart swelled as he admired her as his wife and a woman he could completely trust. "I'm all yours wife," His voice slightly cracked when she looked up at him.

She gave him a quick wink of her eye. "Yes you are," she said. She unfolded the quilt as she was dropping it to the ground and the bar of soap fell from it. She then slowly, bent to pick up the soap. "You're all mine," she purred. She dipped the soap into the water and worked it to a foamy lather, as she had before, but this time with another purpose in mind.

He could hear the water and soap mix together as she worked it between her hands. She then stepped in front of him and started to massage his chest and then with the soap still in her hands she lowered her reach to his back side and gently massaged him.

She turned her back to him and purposely bent down again in front of him to wet the foamy soap to another thick, creamy lather. But when she returned to him her hands bathed the man as her husband.

***

Later, feeling playful they both jumped into the lake and caringly washed each other. "I'm a lucky man," He held her close in his arms as they stood waist deep in the water. He softly stroked her cheek.

"Me to," she whispered.

They gently kissed and hugged. They then, without a word, took each other's hand and waded out of the water to the quilt.

"I've never felt so complete," she said. She cuddled in his arms with her head on his chest. "Honey, we can work things out together," she whispered. She softly kissed his chest and lay back in his arms.

"I know I'm not all man yet, but…" he was saying.

She hushed his lips with a gently touch of her fingers. "You're all the man I've ever wanted and a man I'm proud to call my husband. If we don't have babies, then that's the way it's meant to be. I love you completely and forever and nothing can ever take that away," she lovingly said. She had a bit of a stern voice. "You know this might be our only time, for a long time, to have privacy…" she was saying.

He shook his head in agreement. "It was a gift from the heart, when everyone agreed to give us this time before we start on our trip again," he commented.

She softly wiggled in his arms. "I know. And wasn't Ricky so cute, as your best man. I don't think you could've given him a greater gift than to ask him to stand up for you as a man. He already thinks he's a man and now he believes everyone else knows it too," she said. She lightly chuckled.

"At first I thought I might have put too much responsibility on him, but he did a fine job," Mitch said.

"Yes he did. And even when you first brought it up; I believed he could handle it. It seems that after Pavel, he's grown up pretty fast. His heart has had its first taste of grief, and that's something no one can protect him from. And I think with all the male guidance he'll have around here, he'll grow to be a kind, capable man," She looked up at him and stroked his clean shaven cheek. "And I hope you know, that besides your brother and BD, you're one of the most important male role models for him," She again snuggled in against him.

"How did I get so lucky?" He gently caressed the back of her head and hugged her in his arms.

"And wasn't that whistling he did after the ceremony something else. Did you see Abby's eyes light up while he whistled his tune. She has a tremendous crush on him," Colleen said. She was remembering how Ricky didn't show a hint of his shy side at all as he stepped up in front of everyone and announced his gift to them.

Right after the ceremony he stepped to the side of the bride and groom. "Ladies and gentlemen," She remembered Ricky saying. He surprised everyone with his out of the blue bluntness. "For some time now my grandfather, BD has been teaching me not only how to whistle, but also this little tune that I want to share with you all as my wedding gift to Aunt Colleen and Uncle Mitch," he announced and started to whistle 'Twinkle Twinkle

Little Star'. He showed a self-confidence Colleen had never seen in him before.

And then he surprised them all even more when he asked everyone to join him and sing along as he whistled and then BD also chimed in with his harmonica.

"That was so much fun," Colleen said to Mitch. They continued to lay in each other's arms reminiscing about their wedding ceremony.

"And then when Omar started up with BD's guitar, I just couldn't believe it," she said. She smiled to herself and stroked her husband's bare chest. "They must've been secretly practicing for some time. Ricky was so cute. And when Abby came up and held his hand I thought he would faint," she said.

They both started to laugh. "I don't think I've ever seen that deep of a red on anybody's face before," Mitch commented.

They both turned and faced each other on the blanket and laughed until they cried. "I just love that boy," Colleen said. She composed herself and sat next to him with her arms folded in front of her. "But, do you know what was my favorite thing about our wedding ceremony?" she looked at him.

He wanted to tease her. "When I said I do" he said.

"That was wonderful, but what stays in my mind is when you said, I will keep myself only for you..." She had a shy look in her eyes.

"That is a pretty big statement...and Honey I will..." Tenderly, he caressed her cheek.

Tears welled in her eyes. "Our 'I do' is very important... something for the rest of our lives," she whispered.

"I don't think there's another love in this world the same as ours. And I'll always remember our 'I do'..." He whispered. And at that very moment they made certain they did.

***

It was a lazy day and they enjoyed every second of their privacy. "Honey, what's your take on Omar? I know I feel he's a great asset to the train," She knew they would soon have to go back to real life and continue their journey.

"He's a good man, Colleen. He not only fought for Theresa but for us. He lost more than any person should. And after seeing how those bandits acted I know he's seen things no man should have to witness..." Mitch was saying. He got a faraway look in his eyes.

"No more talk about this. Let's enjoy our honeymoon husband," She tickled his side. "I'm really famished. Let's fix some lunch," She noticed the sun was nearly right above them. "We've played the morning away," She got on her knees and quickly kissed him.

"Come here wife," He tried to reach for her but she evaded his grip.

"Kiss later, eat now," She teased him and went for her clothes and started to put them on.

"Come here baby," He was trying to tempt her back in his arms.

"You're bad. Come on with me..." She reached her hand out to him to help him up.

"Yeah, that's what I'm talking about..." His eyes passionately pleaded with her. "I'm completely in love with you..." He gently tugged her to him.

"You're too much," she smiled at him. "You know I can't resist your love..." She let him pull her into his arms and they again enjoyed the passions of their love.

***

Well into the evening they made love and satisfied their hunger with each other. With the chill of the night filtering in around them they covered their naked bodies with another thick quilt and watched the stars fill the heavens above them.

"Look there's the star Ricky gave us after his song," Colleen said. She pointed to the star in the dark sky. "Every night we'll always have his love to look at with that star," She felt a warm tear on her cheek. "I can't help but love that boy. He makes my heart sing," She felt her throat constrict.

Mitch held her close to him. "I know what you mean. He's really touched my heart strings too. He just has a way about him, and I think a lot of that has to do with how you raised him…" he was saying.

She wiggled in his arms. "Thanks Honey, you couldn't have said anything nicer. I really don't know anybody who doesn't like him," Joy filled her heart.

They both stared at the night sky. "Look a falling star," Mitch said. He pointed to the streaking light.

"There goes another one," Colleen shouted and pointed in its direction. They both opened their eyes wide to take in this night show. "And look at that slower one. I've seen something like it before. They don't have the same kind of bright tail," She again pointed towards the starlit sky.

"I know I've seen them too…" he was saying. They cuddled close and continued to watch natures wedding gift to them. "I'll never look at a meteor shower in the same way," Mitch said, holding his wife as close as he could.

"Me either," Colleen whispered. She was completely mesmerized as the flashes continued all around them. "It's breathtaking," She did not want to close her eyes. "I want this to go on forever," She looked at him and kissed his cheek.

"I love you wife," he whispered in her ear.

"I love you too, my husband," she purred back to him.

For a while they lay in silence. "You sleeping?" she asked.

"No...just relaxing..." he said.

"I was wondering what you remember...you know growing up and some of the tales about how life used to be..." She turned on her side.

"My dad told me some things. I mean about how it used to be. One thing he told me about the most was how pure and easy it was to have water," he was relating.

"My mom has talked about that too..." she commented. "She also said a lot was said about a lot of earthquakes because one of the planets moon's exploded back then when the planets lined up..." She covered her head. "But she said that was about thirty three years before she was born. She said it took that long for the debris from that moon to get close to earth and start some more havoc..." She continued to talk to him with her head still covered. "I was always told not to talk or ask questions about that, but I think I can talk about it with you..." She peeked from under the covers, but then again covered her head.

"I've heard so many different stories that I don't know exactly what happened. And like you a lot of people just don't want to talk about it," He put his head under the quilt. "Boo..." he said. He took her in his arms.

"You're so funny," She took the quilt off of their heads. "Why do you think a lot of people who went through it are so hush hush about it...?" She spoke of things she had always wondered. She knew even her mother never wanted to talk about it.

"I think some people thought it might have been caused by man...you know some kind of war of the world. I don't really know. I just live with what we have today," He held her tightly in his arms.

"When you met me on Driftwood that was all I knew. Except for that short time when I lived with my sister, Jeanette and Geoff and we were going to go west. That was a hard time, but we were ready to be pioneers," She had an adventurous look in her eyes.

"Colleen, I don't think I've ever met a woman who I believed could take on any kind of challenge like you do," he smiled.

"And look at you…the biggest challenge of my life," She tickled him. "I think we'll both be able to handle anything that comes our way…" She took his hand.

"Yep," he said.

"Honey, I just remembered about what my mom told me just after she and BD married," She looked at him. "Well, on that day my mom for the first time told me things she never told me before. She said she doesn't even know if her parents are alive or dead. She was too young to remember a lot of things, but she was old enough to understand life had changed…" She sat up next to him. "But she didn't make a big deal about it. Here…wait a bit…" She got up and went to their wagon.

He watched as she came back. "What are you up to?" he asked.

"She gave me this," She showed him the chest that her mom asked her not to open.

"Looks old," he said.

"It is old. Mom's aunt gave it to her and said it was from my mom's mother," she related.

"Wow," he said.

"And then my mom told me not to open it until I get to a place called compost, or at least understand what compost is…" She had a look of anticipation in her eyes. "Do you want to open it?" She held her hand on the chest.

"Colleen, your mom said…" he was saying.

"I know, but she's not here right now, and I'm curious. What could possibly be in here?" She looked at him. She saw a hurt look in his eyes. "I guess you're right. I should abide by her wishes. But if I don't find out who, what or where this compost is; well then, this little treasure is all yours..." She set the chest in his hands. She had a feeling of relief in her heart. "You know, that feels good. Now you can worry about keeping this thing safe too," She started to laugh. "She gave me this key on a chain. I keep it in the box under the bed in my...I mean our wagon," She winked at him. "I'll put it back don't go away," She left him.

When she went to the wagon, she hesitated for a moment. 'We've been telling each other so many things. Maybe I could tell him about the blue light,' she thought. "I don't know, maybe some other time..." She spoke out-loud. "It would take a lot of explaining, and I'd rather spend our time doing other things," She grinned, when thoughts of their love making entered her head. "We have the rest of our lives to talk about that," She replaced the lid on the box and slid it under the bed.

He looked up and saw that she was coming from the wagon. He was covered up with the quilt. "Here wife," He lifted the cover for her to snuggle in with him.

Silently, they lay in each other's arms. After a short while the hypnotic trance from the falling stars and dark night found them drifting to sleep with only feelings of love and hope filling their dreams. They were joined as man and wife and only allowed thoughts of happy tomorrows for their united future.

Chapter Eight

Wagons Roll On

Following the southern edge to the end of Lake Polymer took them almost three months of travel from the Bee Apiary. They were about to embark on another one hundred mile trek to the next western body of fresh water in the district.

"You know it's funny, but this always seems to happen around this time of year, at this spot," Omar was saying to Mitch.

They stood next to each other in the pouring rain. "It's been some time since my last crossing, so I can't say I remember the weather being this bad, but I do remember this stockade," Mitch said. He bowed his head and the rain water poured off his hat to the ground.

"The building will help protect us until the storm passes. It usually last around a week or so..." Omar was saying. They both had checked the stock and were on their way to the main building, where everyone was gathered. "Mr. Timms, with his wife and family are caretakers here. They keep the fort stocked and in repair. That's their home over there," Omar pointed in their direction. "And other families or hired hands live on the other side," He pointed to the opposite side of the yard.

"The Moss family was here last time I came through. They had all the supplies we needed back then, and I'm sure we can do some trading with the honey and wax we brought from the Apiary" Mitch replied.

They opened the door to the building. The large, rectangle open room with its low ceiling had stone fireplaces in the center of each of the four walls. There were long wooden tables and benches appropriately placed in the center of the room to allow everyone some access to the fireplaces with candle chandeliers hanging over the tables.

"Yeah, I'm sure the Timms will be up to trading our supplies, especially those bushels of apples we brought…" Omar was saying.

Ricky ran up next to Mitch. "Uncle Mitch, you'll never guess what?" Ricky was so excited that he didn't care that Mitch had picked him up as a child and held him in his arms.

"What's that Partner?" Mitch asked. He noticed his wife with her mother at the far end of the room so they walked in that direction.

"Look around," Ricky said. He openly raised his arm in front of Mitch as he looked up and around the room. "All this lumber is from Driftwood, can you believe it?" His eyes lit up and he wiggled out of his uncles arms.

"I've dealt with Driftwood. Of course it wasn't directly, but from a southern store," Omar said, to the two of them. "Quality stock and products, I never heard anyone ever complain. Are you associated with Driftwood?" Omar was asking.

Ricky eagerly interrupted him. "We are Driftwood," Ricky looked at him as he walked backwards in front of Mitch to Omar's side. "I made my first sale of lumber to my uncle Mitch here when he came to Driftwood to get this wagon train set up," He was so excited. "When we left, my uncles took over Driftwood for my grandma," His eyes showed how proud he was of his heritage.

"Looks like quality lumber all around here," Omar commented.

Ricky could not have felt prouder. "Sure is, even the tables and benches," Ricky said.

They reached the tables and benches where Colleen and her family were set up. "I see Ricky told you about Driftwood..." Colleen was saying.

They noticed Ricky turn one of the benches over to show Omar the Driftwood mark.

"He's sure excited about it," Mitch said. He took his bride in his arms and gave her a welcomed kiss on the lips.

"It sure brings back memories of home," Beatrice said. She was caring for Joseph with BD right at her side.

"Omar says he's bought some Driftwood products, Grammy," Ricky told them. He came next to her and held onto Joseph's finger. "Strong, grip! Yep, I remember, I'll teach you how to make fire," Ricky was saying to Joseph as if the baby had asked him the question.

"Ricky, you're so funny," Beatrice said. She ruffled her grandson's hair and watched while he rubbed noses with the baby. "So you had some dealings with Driftwood?" She turned her conversation to Omar.

"Yes ma'am, in the southern region. Horses and cattle for the trail, and some of the finest drift I've ever seen," he told her.

Beatrice sat up with pride in her stance. "Thank you for the compliment. We always take pride in the quality. My two older boys are working the business now..." she was saying, as Joseph started to cry for attention. "Come here my boy," She lifted him from the make shift crib BD had made for him.

"Here, let me take him," BD said. He always tried to tend his son and take care of other chores for his wife. "You continue your conversation with Omar. I'm going to walk this little guy around for a bit," He took Joseph from his wife's arms.

Ricky came to BD's side and they walked away. "Grammy looked a little sad, when Omar talked about Driftwood," Ricky said. He looked back at his grandmother and spoke when they were out of ear shot of Beatrice.

"Driftwood's always been a part of her life and I guess talking about it brings back old memories," BD said.

They passed through in front of the O'Donnell family's set up. "Hi Ricky," Abby said. She came next to him and wanted to join in their walk around the room.

"Hi," was all Ricky said, in a nonchalant manner. "We're kind of having a private conversation," he then said to the infatuated, young girl. He did not want her to walk with them.

"Oh, I see," Abby sadly said. She bowed her head, turned and went to sit next to her parents on the bench next to the table.

"That really wasn't necessary Ricky. Abby could've joined us," BD said. He noticed the boy's face turned bright red.

Ricky looked at BD. "She always wants to be with me. Gosh, she's a girl. Me and Pavel, we were buddy's. She can't be my buddy. I just don't see why she can't understand that," He turned and looked at Abby sitting with a look of rejection written all over her face.

"Maybe you could start out slowly. You know you could teach her how to make fire. It's very important and everyone really should know," BD said. He looked at Ricky with only kindness in his eyes.

"I guess," Ricky replied. He again turned and gave Abby a quick glance. He thought he could almost feel her dejection.

They continued their walk. "Look at your Dad over there," BD motioned for Ricky to look in his father's direction. "He's always ready to lend a helping hand," BD said, as they both looked to where Geoff was sitting with a group around him. "I bet he's talking with Mr. Timms and figuring something out about trading our supplies from the Apiary…" he was saying. "Oh look, Olivier LaFarge is with them. Don't see much of him around…" BD commented.

"I know he's a loner and a weird kind of guy. He's always messing around with some kind of an experiment or other kinds of things…he's an odd sort," Ricky said. "He stays with Omar and the Bolovich boys. He said his wagon's too crowded. I heard Mrs. LaFarge say with all of his gadgets he should've had his own wagon…" Ricky was saying.

"Have you ever seen any of his experiments?" BD asked.

"One time, he was working on some kind of a contraption that he said could catch waves from space…" He gave BD a curious look.

"You mean radio waves?" BD asked.

"Yeah, that's it. He said there are all kinds of them out in space, and all he would have to do is catch one…" Ricky laughed. "Like I said he's kind of weird. I don't understand his talk and he's got a lot of books and stuff," He shrugged his shoulders.

"Books don't hurt. We all could keep up with some reading and learn new ideas," He gave Ricky a serious look.

"I know; Aunt Collie says the same thing. But I've just about read all of her books…I know…I could start reading some of my Dad's medical books," He had a big grin on his lips that lit up his face. He loved anything that had to do with his dad.

"Couldn't hurt. We could use another doctor around here," BD said. He noticed Joseph needed some diaper attention. "Better head back,"They finally returned to their own set up and BD gave his son to his mother's opened arms.

He noticed that Omar had left their spot. "Omar's such a nice man," Beatrice said. She watched as Ricky flopped in the seat next to her. "What's with you?" she asked, looking at her grandson.

"Not much to do around here," Ricky said. He let out a deep sigh of boredom.

"I don't know, maybe this is a good time for that fire starting teaching project we were just talking about," BD said. He noticed

Ricky fidgeted in his seat. "We're going to be here a while," he added.

Ricky looked at his grandfather and begrudgingly went for his saddle bags. "I guess so," was all he said. He turned towards the O'Donnell set up without another word said to them.

"Teaching project?" Beatrice asked her husband. She finished changing her son's diaper and started to breast feed him.

"Abby, how to make fire," BD said. They both looked at each other and started to chuckle. "He'll be fine," BD said. He sat next to his wife and child.

"While you were gone, I was telling Omar about little Pavel. It made him understand why Yerik stayed with his younger boy's at the Apiary," she said.

Colleen came next to her. "Mama, Mitch and I are going to our wagon for a bit. Could you keep an eye on supper?" Colleen asked.

Her mother just nodded a yes to her daughter. "They're so cute together," Beatrice said. She watched her daughter walk arm-in-arm with her husband and BD only nodded in agreement. "But, you know, I still can't get used to Colleen's hair being so short or Mitch's for that matter. They must've had some kind of a honeymoon taking care and grooming each other..." she was saying. She saw her daughter put her head on her husband's shoulder as they continued to walk out of the building.

"Yeah, they're a cute couple. I'm glad they finally got together. We had a lot of fun at their wedding reception. Ricky was so excited. He's a quick learner. Picked up on the fire starting and the whistling..." He smiled and so did his wife.

"Has a good teacher," She smiled at her husband.

"You know, earlier, I was thinking about Yerik. I sure do miss his contagious laughter. And I wasn't at all surprised that he wanted to stay at the Apiary," BD said. He continued their conversation. "Did you know he was also getting to know the beekeeper's sister, Agnes?" he added.

This surprised Beatrice. "No I didn't know that. But she's a good woman. They're all good people. You know in the short time we were with them it seemed like we all lived a lifetime together," she said. She knew he agreed with her without saying a word about it. "Isn't it funny how we always refer to the Warren's as the beekeepers? You know the beekeeper, the beekeeper's wife and…" she was saying.

BD laughed. "Yeah, I always thought that was funny too. Yerik and his young'uns will fit in just fine. Yerik's easy to be around, and I know it really took a load off his mind when Omar agreed to travel with his older boys. I'm sure they'll all get back together again one day," BD said. He went to check on the supper.

"And the LaFarge family just loves Theresa living with them. Even though Omar's in another wagon it's really kind of like he's just in another room. I'm sure he knows a woman's influence and care are important to his daughter," she said. She noticed her husband again nodded in agreement. "And it was a blessing that those bandits didn't completely succeed with their abuse to Antoinette," she softly whispered for her husband's ears only to hear. She remembered the look of relief on Camille LaFarge's face when Geoff told her that her daughter had not been completely sexually violated, and did not lose her virginity. "I know it will take time for her to put it out of her mind, but with all of our support and the love of her family, I'm sure she'll be okay," She looked at her son. "You're such a good baby," Beatrice said. She finished breast feeding Joseph and laid him in his cradle. She noticed he smiled at her when she tucked him in.

"Good afternoon," Camille LaFarge said. She came next to Beatrice with Antoinette right behind her holding Theresa.

"Good afternoon. Nice weather we're having," Beatrice said.

They all laughed knowing it surely was not nice outside. "You can always make me laugh Bea. How's the boy today?" Camille asked. She looked in the crib.

"Just fine," Beatrice said, looking at little Theresa in Antoinette's arms. She thought the baby looked somewhat jaundice. "How's Theresa doing?" she asked.

Antoinette came to her side and let Beatrice take her from her. "She doesn't seem to like the cow's milk. She eats, but I don't think she's getting enough," Antoinette said.

The baby squirmed in Beatrice's arms. "Oh dear, I think she can smell my milk. I just fed Joseph, but I think there could be enough for Theresa. What'd you think?" she asked. She looked at her husband and then at the two woman in front of her.

"I truly was hoping you'd think that. She really needs some nourishment," Camille said. She watched Beatrice start to breast feed the baby.

"God's gift," Beatrice said, as Theresa greedily ate, while BD watched with a smile on his lips and then continued to tend their supper.

"She's really a good baby," Antoinette said. She sat next to Beatrice while she fed Theresa. "I love caring for her. It makes me feel good to care for her; especially after all Omar did for me," She caressed the baby's head.

"Children are a gift and should be protected and loved by all," Beatrice said, as Camille shook her head in agreement.

Geoff joined them. "Afternoon, everyone," he said. He went next to BD.

"Afternoon Geoff," they all chimed to him.

"How's the supper going BD?" he asked. He noticed the women continued their conversation so he came closer to BD. "Just to let you know, Mr. Timms was telling us there's been some big cat problems around here lately," he whispered to BD.

"Is that so? Is it serious enough to consider a hunt?" BD whispered back to Geoff not wanting to fear the women.

"That would be to our advantage. We wouldn't want to deal with it out in the open," Geoff said. He noticed BD shook his head in agreement. "No disrespect BD, but with your condition, I…" Geoff was saying.

BD interrupted him. "You don't have to spell it out to me Geoff. I've learned how to work this ole body of mine," he replied. He slightly grinned.

"I'm glad BD. But we'll have to let everyone know to be on guard," Geoff said. He noticed BD nodded in agreement.

Geoff went to stoke the fire; while BD took his harmonica from his pocket and started a soothing tune. He went next to his wife, who had finished feeding baby Theresa and returned her to Antoinette.

As the evening went on; they continued to enjoy BD's serene tunes. The room filled with mixed aromas of evening meals and soft mumbles of personal conversations.

***

Later that night the rain had not let up. Keeping alert with thoughts of the cats; some kept watch, while others tried to keep warm and cozy in their own wagons for a good night's sleep. The soft rhythm of the steady rain created a relaxing atmosphere and the camp seemed peaceful.

After midnight, with the grace of a performing acrobat he jumped and scaled the wooden walls of the stockade. Slowly, without a sound he leaped from the wall. His cunning senses led him to his prey.

The bawling was ear piercing. In a matter of seconds all of the men, armed and ready, were out of their wagons. Most of them went directly to the corralled animals. It all happened so fast.

"Omar...look out..." BD yelled.

Omar swayed to avoid the full blunt of the beast, but not before the large animal pounced on him and clawed his arm. BD came next to him, but like a bolt of lightning the phantom like creature evaded them and retrieved his prey.

"They're too far away..." Omar whispered to BD. They could hear the other men at the far end near the coral calling to each other. "Don't move; I can hear him..." Omar whispered to BD.

Huddled together in the dark; both men stood perfectly still. The cat's frightening presence made their hair stand on end. As it fearlessly passed behind them, they could hear the low threatening gurgles coming from the creature. They heard its heavy breathing and could smell the over powering, putrid odor of the animal's wet fur mixed with the sweet metallic smell of its victim's blood.

The rain drenched them. They felt frozen to the spot, while with the silent grace of a tiny church mouse they barely heard the fierce beast scale the wall of the stockade, as he carried off his heavy prey.

"BD, Omar, thank God you're all right..." Mitch was shouting. He approached them with Geoff and the others right behind him.

"If you say so..." BD mumbled. He could feel his bowels weaken, as he almost wet on himself. "It attached Omar, he needs help..." BD slowly spoke. He weakly turned towards Mitch.

They both watched as Omar promptly fell to the ground. "Geoff, hurry..." Mitch yelled to his brother.

They all came on the scene. "Get him to his wagon. And Mitch get my bag," Geoff barked to his brother, as the men picked up the large man and carried his unconscious body to his wagon.

At the same time that the giant cat was terrorizing the occupants of the stockade with his nightly hunt for survival; Hania, the Spirit Warrior, was hunting his own prey for the survival of his family.

***

The following morning, the rain had washed the blood from the scene, but the terror from the night invader left its mark on all. Paranoia became tangible and could be seen on everyone's face. No one felt safe.

"How's Omar?" BD asked Geoff.

Geoff and Ricky joined the family for breakfast and Ricky went directly to Joseph where he lay in his crib.

"Mitch and Collie are with him now. The cuts are deep and the stitches are holding. He'll be fine if I can keep the infection down," Geoff said. He sat down and Beatrice brought him a cup of hot coffee. "Thanks Bea," he said. She gently patted his shoulder.

"You can almost cut the tension in here this morning. Everyone's scared to death," BD whispered to Geoff.

"It's understandable. Omar could've been killed. Not to mention you," Geoff said. He noticed Beatrice glanced at them and nodded towards Ricky.

"Bring your coffee. Let's take a walk around," BD said.

He neared his wife and whispered something to her and then gently kissed her cheek. "That's fine Honey," Beatrice said. She continued making their meal.

Both men left and walked to the O'Donnell set up. "Morning Brady, Briana," BD said. They entered their space, and they all greeted each other with a handshake.

BD came next to Abby. "Abby, Ricky said you're really catching on with your fire making," He caringly spoke to the young girl.

The shy girl was sitting on the bench. "I sure try," Abby replied. She had a slight smile on her lips. "He's a good teacher," she added. Both BD and Geoff noticed a slight pink color brighten her cheeks.

"My wife made some honey cakes and I'm sure there's one with your name on it. That is if it's okay with your parents," BD said.

Abby's eyes lit up and she looked at her parents. "Well, if you're sure, it's fine with me," Briana said. She looked at her husband and he nodded in agreement and Abby ran off towards Beatrice, and mostly Ricky.

"We didn't want to frighten the child with our talk," BD said. He noticed Brady and Briana straightened up on their seats. "Can you join us in a walk and talk along?" he asked, as the O'Donnell's rose from their seats and they all started slowly walking.

"Good morning Camille, Claude," Geoff said, when they reached the LaFarge site. Everyone tipped their heads in greeting. "Are your children around? They should be included..." he was saying. He noticed their son, Olivier walking with Antoinette with baby Theresa in her arms. They were walking closer towards Beatrice in the room. "Oh, I see them," He commented. "We can talk with them later," he added.

Camille and Briana started to chatter. "This is scary..." Camille said, as Briana nodded in agreement. "My children are very edgy..." Camille was saying.

Geoff interrupted them. "Let's include the Bolovich family in our conversation. I see the Timms are already over there..." Geoff was saying.

They all walked to join them. "Morning everyone," BD said, in his usual happy way.

"Morning," they all chimed back.

"I'd say we all can't get last night's events off our minds, and as well as it should be. I know I sure can't..." BD continued to say.

"Thinking of what you went through scares me to death. And Omar could've been killed," Camille said, with fright sounding in her voice. "He's a large man. If it had been one of the children..." she cried.

Briana came next to her and held her in her arms. "We know, the outcome could've been worse," Briana said. She had a look of fright in her eyes. "I'm sure my Abby weighs less than that calf," she blurted out. Her tears flowed from her eyes as the two women tried to console each other.

"That's why we have to get him before he can attack again. We have to have the upper hand and keep control of the situation..." BD was saying.

Mr. Timms interrupted. "These cats have hunted in our area before, but this is the first time one has entered our fort," he said.

This did not make them feel any better. "We're not any safer in here than we would be out in the open. We can't stay in this building all the time..." Briana was saying.

Suddenly, the front door opened and Hania, the Spirit Warrior, walked in taking them all by surprise. He looked like a bear in his oversized, dark colored animal fur that covered him from head to toe, but was used to protect him from the elements.

At first sight of him the room was full of chaos until Mr. Timms spoke up. "Everyone, please this is our friend Hania," Mr. Timms shouted in a calming voice.

Hania neared him and the group around him. Quickly, Mr. Timms helped Hania take off his rain drenched outer wear. He was dressed in a soft tanned, light colored, animal hide shirt and pants, with a pair of hard leather soled moccasins. His long, dark hair was pulled back with a leather strip and hung as a long pony tail to his waist. He held a rifle in one hand, and a deadly looking, handmade, sharpened stone axe in his other. He wore a belt with two knives sheathed at his side, and a pouch for his ammunition and supplies.

"My family and a few from our Peaceful Valley, who have joined in our hunt, are outside," Hania hurriedly said. His shiny, black eyes were pleading for help.

Mr. Timms immediately went to the door and let them in. Geoff quickly went to them with the women in the group right behind him.

"Oh dear God, she's pregnant," Camille shouted. She helped Hania's wife disrobe her outerwear. "Hurry, she needs help," Camille shouted.

Geoff came to her side. "Get some bedding. We'll set up a makeshift bed over here," Geoff barked out orders as everyone in ear shot started to clear a spot.

BD went to his wagon for some supplies. He then poked his head in the Bolovich wagon. "Just to let you know, we have some Indian guests in the lodge and one young woman's pregnant and looks like she's about ready to delivery," BD advised Mitch and Colleen on the situation. They were keeping watch over the sleeping Omar.

"I'll come with you," Colleen whispered. She glanced at her husband.

He nodded his agreement. "We'll be fine," Mitch said.

Colleen quickly bent and kissed her husband. She momentarily shut her eyes as they showed this short expression of love. Her husband looked at her with deep admiration and then she hastily departed with BD.

Rushing into the room Colleen followed BD right in front of Hania and his family. "The Portal…" Kuruk, Hania's father exclaimed when he saw Colleen.

Colleen looked directly in Kuruk's dark, understanding eyes and then, after a slight hesitation, she went directly to help Geoff with the delivery of the baby.

Part 2

❀

Chapter Nine

13 Years Later Memories of Cats at Timms Stockade

The bright green fields of alfalfa glowed from the distance. This was Peaceful Valley. The land was fertile for crops of wheat, soybeans, peas and potatoes; and everyone took part in their harvest. Life was good and full of plenty for all who had settled here.

'My God, I can't keep my eyes off of her…' He thought. He was riding his horse; as he watched her skillfully ride her horse through the tall grass. She rode with the ease and grace of a great horsewoman.

He looked at his friend, who was riding his horse next to him. 'He can't keep his eyes off of her either,' He felt a jealous flash hit his heart.

She stopped far ahead of them. As she bent to hug the neck of her mare he noticed he could not tell where her naturally wavy hair stopped when it mixed with the beautiful golden color of her Palomino.

At the same time they reached her they watched her laugh and easily dismount her horse. "I told you I'd win," she breathlessly said. She was laughing and talking at the same time. Her bright blue eyes sparkled with her happiness. She went next to her horse and patted her side. "Good girl," she happily said.

He watched, as she continued to rub her horse's side and gently kiss the tip of the horse's nose. "Good girl Topper, I knew we could do it," she lovingly purred.

He looked from her to his friend still mounted on his horse next to him. "Good win Abby, at least ten lengths I'd say, wouldn't you Ricky?" Andrey Bolovich was asking Ricky.

Ricky saw a look in his friend's eyes that almost frightened him. It was the same look he felt in his heart for Abby. 'What a fool I've been. I should've let her know a long time ago how I feel about her,' he was thinking. He and Andrey dismounted their horses. He watched Andrey lead his horse next to hers. "Yeah, good win Abby ten lengths or more, I'd say…" Ricky was saying.

Andrey neared Abby and hugged her. "You guys didn't let me win, now did you?" she asked. She had a sly look in her eyes, but she knew in her heart they did not.

"You know we didn't," Ricky said. He gave her his usual, nonchalant, I don't give-a-care look like he always had over the years.

Next week Abby would turn eighteen and Ricky would soon be twenty one. 'When will I stop acting like a kid with her? She's been a thorn in my side for as long as I can remember,' Ricky was thinking.

Andrey and Abby started to chatter and walk away from him with their horses' right behind. "Abby you ride like a whisper in the wind…" Andrey was saying. He looked at her with a look of deep fondness in his dark, black eyes.

"Andy, you always say such profound things," Abby said, using his nickname they all used. "How do you come up with these things?" She glanced over her shoulder and tried to get a handle on how Ricky was feeling, but as always he had that unconcerned look on his face.

"You inspire me. Your grace, your loveliness makes me want to write a sonnet in your honor…" Andrey was saying in the way they all had become accustomed to with him.

"You're so funny," Abby said. She noticed his face redden. "I'm sorry Andy, I know your poems and sonnets are important to you, and they're so nice to read. I know I could never even think of a word to put down on a piece of paper..." She wished Ricky would come to her rescue and join in their conversation. But he looked like he was in his own world, so she knew she was on her own. "Hey look Kuruk's coming in from his hunt," She pointed towards him. "And it looks like he has a good catch for supper," She was thankful to change the subject.

"That doesn't look like supper to me," Ricky said. He quickly mounted his horse and rode in Kuruk's direction with Abby and Andy also astride, close behind him.

"The cats are back," Kuruk said. He was pointing to a large, black female mountain lion draped over his pack mule.

***

Later, some in the stockade gathered at Colleen and Mitch's home. That familiar paranoia was apparent on their faces.

"Remember at the Timms stockade, Omar was almost killed," Antoinette said to all present. She went next to Omar and placed her hand on his arm.

Kuruk tried to curb their fears, but still keep them on guard. "I tracked them. There are not as many as back then, but they will hunt us the same," Kuruk softly said. They all just looked at each other. "We know their cunning all too well," the elderly man then said. He noticed they started to speak among themselves.

He came next to Colleen. "It was many years ago," Colleen, with a fear showing in her eyes, said to Kuruk.

"Yes it was. But for me it feels like yesterday..." Kuruk was saying. He slowly sat next to her on the tall hearth in front of the cold fireplace and stretched out his right leg for comfort. "Ah, that's better,"The older man said, in a lethargic way.

Colleen only smiled at him. "I remember. Back then at the Timms Stockade, it was a time for new life and a time for death," She gave him a sad understanding look.

They both watched the others mingle around her and Mitch's large living room of their log home.

"It was at that first meeting, when I first saw you; that I knew you were The Portal..." Kuruk said. He smiled at her. His leg started to stiffen, so he started to rub it.

"Would you like to sit someplace else?" she caringly asked.

"No, I love the hearth. My favorite spot, even if it is hard on the bottom,"They both chuckled.

"You know back then, when we first met and you called me The Portal; something in me understood what you meant," Colleen gently patted his hand in memory of that time. "I'm still not completely clear about everything about the orbs or me as The Portal, but I can understand a little about what you tried to explain to me over the years," she looked at him. "You remember I told you I first experienced the blue orbs during the death of my sister," She knew after all these years of conversation, he would understand her thoughts.

"Colleen, it's hard for others to understand the ways of The Portal. But it is a gift and should be thought of that way. Just take it in faith and know you are showing the way to those-in-need," Kuruk always spoke to her in a whisper and he always seemed to have a faraway look in his eyes.

"You know more about me than I know myself..." Colleen was saying. "Over the years, I've tried to talk to my mom or Mitch, and even BD about the things that happen to me or what I've seen, but the time was never right, and then what happened was over and I would forget about it until it happened again..."

she explained. "And now, just like back when the cats attacked us at the Timms Stockade and I experienced the passing of the spirits of those who died and the blue lights; it seems I might experience them again..." She had hesitation in her voice.

"If it does happen, let's hope your gift of The Portal doesn't come to be with the force of the cats, but in the natural, more peaceful way," Kuruk had a calming way about him. "My dear, energy is all around us, and our body's possess a very special active energy until the day this physical body dies..." He looked at her. "It is this special, active energy, that some call the divine gift of the soul or the spirit; and that is where your gift as The Portal comes into the picture of life," He noticed she looked directly into his eyes as he spoke to her. "This powerful source that life possesses must pass out of the deceased body," He knew they had spoken of these things in the past. But he also knew she was a gentle novice regarding the blue orbs and her role as The Portal. "It is nothing to fear. It is a gift you were given to provide directions to life's spirits to His spirit," He knew her fear. "It is a challenge to accept that what you are seeing is real. But don't fear it; embrace it as a part of you," He noticed she had an understanding look in her eyes.

Mitch approached them. "Care for some apple cider or tea?" Mitch had a tray of refreshments.

"Thanks Honey," Colleen said. She took a prepared cup of the cider, and handed one to Kuruk. "We're talking about..." She slightly hesitated. "About the Timms and..." She was going to bring up the blue orbs again.

Mitch interrupted her. "Everyone is. I think we're going to be more prepared this time," He left them and went to pass out more refreshments.

"Like I was saying; you are about the only one I really talk to about the orbs or what you say is my gift as The Portal," She took a sip of the cider. "Mitch and I were talking the other day and he pointed towards something and I noticed it looked like silver and gold coins flew out of his hand…" She had a concerned look in her eyes. "And sometimes I see different size; deep blue balls come from the sides of people's heads…" She knew she had never told Kuruk about these balls. "I never said anything because…" She could feel tears welling in her eyes.

"They are essence, not Portal...they pop out like perking bubbles…" His calming eyes relaxed her. "Like we were talking about before; we all possess energy; and you have the ability to see it…" He winked at her. "Colleen, don't fret about it. Just…" He had a fun look in his eyes.

"I know, like you always say; just go with the flow," They both laughed.

"On a more serious note, we know the cats are fierce animals, but we have human intelligence on our side," Kuruk said. He had a kind look in his eyes. She noticed he was also listening to the others.

"My dear, that night when we first met at the Timms Stockade was a night for Alo, the spiritual guide, and also for you my dear," Kuruk softly whispered. But then, he turned his gaze from her. She could tell he was remembering, as was she, about that night of terror, so many years ago, when blood was spilled and life was lost.

***

It was the morning at the Timms Stockade after the wild cat killed the calf and marred Omar's arm.

Kuruk's son, Hania had arrived with his wife, Muraco, to the Timms Stockade. And with the help of Geoff and Colleen, Muraco gave birth to a daughter, they called Manipi, which they explained meant, she was an amazing child, born to the Spirit Warrior and the woman of the White Moon. This was also the first meeting of Kuruk, meaning the Bear and his wife, Langundo, which they explained later meant Peaceful to man. They were pursuing the cats that had attacked their village, they called Peaceful Valley, and all of the cat's signs led them to the Timms Stockade.

Hania with his band of braves were intentionally dressed to hunt. They had prepared to stay in the wilds until the cats were killed or driven away. But first, Hania had to make sure his family was safe. After the birth of his daughter he prayed with his father and mother for the safety and a peaceful end for all in the stockade and for those who would hunt the terrorizing beasts.

Later, they all met in the courtyard of the Timms Stockade, with the wagons surrounding them and some men on the walls keeping watch. "We are lucky at this time that the rains have stopped," Kuruk loudly spoke for all to hear. He noticed that some of the women came to listen with the men who had gathered for the hunt. "My son, Hania, knows the way of the beast and will explain what he knows," Kuruk explained.

The group quieted and listened intently to Hania. "This is an integrated cat family. They fight for their lives like we do. Do not underestimate their cunning," Hania told them. His words sent a shock wave down BD's back, and brought back the intense fear he felt when the creature passed behind him and Omar.

"What do you mean integrated?" Claude LaFarge asked. He knew the word meant united or mixed, but he did not understand what it meant in the cat family.

"I will let my father give his thoughts on how and when this took place," Hania said. He was trying to curb his impatience to hunt. He knew the challenges they were going to face should be prepared for to ensure success, so, for the time being, he would watch and listen.

"It started many years ago, after what we have called the great crack," Kuruk spoke to them. He noticed his words did not shock some who listened to him. "As many of you have heard or have witnessed, our earth split and the waters changed the land as we then knew it. Our people call it the new Cenozoic epoch, a new creation of continents," He saw recognition in some eyes. "Our lands and waters were repositioned. This was a disaster that took many lives. Many who witnessed and lived through this time thought it might have been a strategy created by those in power, who used their scientific abilities to arrange this devastation, that went further than expected," He noticed many nodded their heads in agreement. "But, I'm sure you also know that others believed the powers of the heaven's aligned planets created such a powerful magnetic force making our known environment almost turn upside down and go haywire with many continental drifts," Kuruk was relating.

"I've heard tell of these things…But, what of the cats?" A frustrated bystander yelled out. "I don't see what that has to do with the cats…" he yelled and some started to get agitated around him.

"It has a lot to do with the cats. No matter what; during the circumstances of that time, someone or something went wrong and it got out of control and went awry…" Kuruk went on to say. He then purposely extended his hand to their surroundings to make his point. "We know that now where we stand was once part of a great sea, but now is as we live with it," He was repeating words that they all had known or been told by their ancestors. "This way of life is a drastic change for some, who like our family, had to return to former ways of life; but to the young, who know no better, this is their way of life," He knew to fight these creatures, new ideas had to be observed by the seasoned hunter and taught to the young.

"I have hunted cats all my life; but after my experience last night, I realize we have to understand the new ways of the cats..." BD said. He knew even though the cat acted fearlessly; it also acted like it possessed some kind of a sense about his and Omar's actions. This thought scared him and made him want to know more about the cats. "Please, tell us more," He looked at Kuruk.

"When we travel this vast desert we can find rich earth and plenty of fresh water holding wells like the artificial, prismatic lakes in the Gyre District," Kuruk continued. Some of these words were new to these pioneers, who were traveling away from the lands they were familiar with. They listened as attentive school children hoping to learn his words of wisdom, which might help some of them, understand the old tales they had heard in the past, and hopefully understand the threat of the cats that faced them.

"It was said that discarded hardened materials of past times were trapped in the oceans under currents. These materials formed gigantic deep basins. These basins swirled around and around in the deep ocean, until after the great crack when the ocean water subsided, these basins fell to the once sea floor," Kuruk spoke of the past. "It was when the water was gone that the rich soil settled and these great unnatural basins filled with fresh rain water, and became the lakes as we know them today," He noticed some irritation in the eyes of the young not caring about things of the past, but confirmation in the eyes of the older adults.

"We know some of these things, but what of the cats? Why does our past influence how we deal with these killers?" Gavrie Bolovich asked. It was a question that others were also thinking.

Kuruk tried to ignore any outbreaks. He wanted them to completely understand what they were up against. "Our families settled not far from here, in a place we call Peaceful Valley. Our valley is full of rich soil and fresh water. It is usually undisturbed and there is plenty for many to join us there," he spoke softly. "But with this plenty also comes the occasional predator seeking our abundance," Kuruk explained, while his son, Hania stood completely still with the look of a British Guard standing at attention in front of a great palace.

"Our families must be protected...we must act now. I don't see why we have to do all this talking about our past to go hunt this cat down and kill the bastard," Gavrie raised his voice and started to stir up some of the others.

"Like I'm sure all of you know when you cross, and in some cases settle in what used to be our great Ocean, you will come across renegades, who terrorize and steal," he was saying. Saying this reminded them of the wrath of the Queen and her bandits, as they unanimously shook their heads and spoke in agreement.

"It is like that with the cats. Like us humans they have joined families and forces for their survival..." Kuruk was saying. He hoped they could learn what he and his family had been living all these years. "The lions and tigers from the East have integrated with the cougars and mountain lions of the West. They are a different breed now. Normally, they live peacefully in a valley not unlike where we live with the fast growing Mimosa and Poplar forests; where over these many years the ground squirrels have carried the acorns and the mighty oak forests are rapidly growing. This fertile ground has also attracted much wild life, like deer and other small game for the survival of all..." he was saying. He noticed they all started to murmur their concerns to each other. "And like us who enjoy this plenty, sometimes hungry renegade cats leave their overpopulated, peaceful pride and threaten other lives, like ours," Kuruk softly said.

All listening went silent. They wanted to understand more about the creatures they would be facing. "They kill to survive with a skill that is frightening..." Kuruk continued. He noticed they all started to get agitated and the women had looks of fear on their faces. "Please, please, everyone understand, I only say this so we all are aware of what we're up against..." Kuruk tried to explain.

Mitch took over for the moment. "Everyone, please...stay calm. I'm sure Kuruk is only trying to let us know about these beasts so we can hunt them intelligently and save our lives," Mitch said. He was trying to settle their nerves. "After last night, we all know these cats are cunning and we have to be prepared to keep our wits about us and keep focused when we're out there hunting them..." He noticed they seemed to calm down.

Kuruk continued. "Our village knows only too well how ferocious these conniving beasts can be. Many have died during the fight, and luckily in times past, we've always won our battles," Kuruk said. He knew he was not really settling their fears. "It is good to have fear, because it keeps you alert and on guard. It is when you think you completely know the beast that you will fail..." He intently looked at the eyes that stared at him knowing some would die.

"I can't emphasize enough that this is a new breed. If you have ever hunted the North American mountain lion or the African lions and tigers you know how clever they can be. But this new breed has watched man as we've watched them, and they know how we react. So we have to be pro-active," Kuruk said. He saw many questions in their eyes, as they started to stir and mumble between each other. "Please let my son explain," He shouted in a controlled voice.

"Everyone, please listen carefully," Hania shouted. He was not the teacher like his father, but knew he had to try to make them listen. They all quieted down to hear his words. "All adult cats, males and females hunt for the renegade pride. The young stay at a distance to watch and learn,"He explained his experience to them. He was well aware, by their silence and intent looks, that he had their complete attention. "Every man, woman and child has to be on guard. Remember, we are not the only ones hunting," Hania said. They all remembered how the cat must have scaled the walls of the stockade to kill and take the calf. "They are fully aware of their keen night vision and have taken full advantage of it and hunt when they know we are at that disadvantage..." he was saying. They all nodded in agreement remembering the crafty way the cat entered and left the stockade while only encountering Omar and BD during its brief hunt.

"Not only do they communicate with each other when they use their loud roars and ear piercing cat calls, but they also intimidate. They want to scare you to death and make you sweat and lose your focus of the hunt. But stay the course. Try to remain calm. And never, under any circumstances run, because if you run you are running into a trap," Hania said.

His words sent another shock wave down BD's back. He could almost smell the cat again. "Omar and I stood perfectly still while the cat passed right behind us. I could hear him gurgle as he slowly left," BD said, as they all listened.

"Had you moved or ran he would have dropped his prey and killed you both on the spot. And believe me he could have done that and went back to his prey or worse," he was saying, as they all understood what he meant. "From what Mr. Timms has told me most of you were at the corral when the cat was leaving and passed behind you and Omar. Am I right?" Hania asked BD.

BD nodded that he was right. "The cats did that on purpose. After looking over the area, even after the rain messed up some of their tracks; I'm certain there were at least four cats in the stockade last night...you just saw one," Hania explained. He noticed they all looked at each other with fear evident in their eyes. "That's the shifty way they operate. They divide your groups, while one of the cats hunts and takes the prey. At first they're not greedy, but will kill again if the chosen cat, who hunts, alerts them that his take was unsuccessful," He could tell they were fully engrossed in every word that came out of his mouth.

"So, if I understand what you're saying, they'll most likely be back here tonight?" Mitch said, as the women huddled next to their men. "What can we do to prepare for them?" He knew they had to learn and act.

Quietly, they all gathered to hear and set the ground work for their hunt. Looking around, each person knew in their heart that when the sun set that night some one that faced them now might be the next pursued victim, maybe even themselves.

It was arranged that the women and children armed and ready would all stay in the stockade building for the night. Large bonfires were started in the courtyard and would have to be tended throughout the night.

Even though no place was thought to be safe only older teenage and men were in the outside hunting party. It was a different world beyond the walls of the stockade and those that would hunt in the wilds had to take extra precautions to protect themselves from becoming prey.

Hania had brought with him from their village the rendered fat from his last cat kill. To disguise their scent, men who would hunt outside the stockade covered their entire bodies under their clothes, with the fat; and for camouflage they rubbed black tar on any exposed skin. Like Hania, they all were fully armed.

Just before sunset they would travel in groups of four. Trying to cover the entire perimeter, and using their compasses, one group would go northeast, one group northwest another southwest with the last southeast. Hania explained that for safety, it was important to remember where each group would be located. No one wanted to experience friendly, deadly gun fire.

When they all understood the tactics of the hunt; the outside hunters said their farewells to their families. They watched the gray clouds cover the setting sun. Finally, with the shutting of the stockade door; the outside hunting parties felt a deep, skin penetrating chill in the air.

"Remember no one's safe...keep alert," Hania loudly, whispered to the huddled, joined forces.

"How many do you think are out there?" Gavrie asked. He looked at Hania and then at his younger brother Andrey, who was crouched next to him.

"I'm thinking might be around fifty," Hania said.

His words sent looks of astonishment to all in the group. "Oh my God, that many," Mitch whispered. He then thought he should not have said that aloud. He prayed for their safety. He looked back at the stockade wishing he could take his wife in his arms one more time.

"Does everyone have all the supplies we talked about?" Hania asked. Purposely he disregarded Mitch's fearful response. He wanted to keep the men in control and ready for the task before them.

"Yes, and we all know how to use them," Mitch then said in a steadier voice. He knew a lot of the men looked up to him for guidance.

"Then let's check our compasses and note the time. We will make our attack as we planned. Is everyone ready?" Hania asked. He noticed the groups nodded in agreement. Quietly, they all went their separate ways.

Kuruk and BD, with six men from the village and Mr. Timms lined the walls and kept the bonfires glowing. "Even if the weather changes, we have to keep the fires going. The bright red light will show like a beacon in the sky. And because our hunters know the exact location of the stockade, their compasses will lead them back to us," Kuruk said to BD, as they both stoked the fires.

"Not to mention lets us see what's going on with the beasts," BD said. He saw Kuruk nod in agreement.

Inside the building, a bed had been made up for Omar. He was wide awake, but still too injured from the cat's deep claw wounds to join the hunt outside.

"I should be outside to protect…" Omar was saying to Antoinette.

Antoinette interrupted him. "Your wounds would open and you would be no good to anyone. At least in here you have a better chance. We all have to protect each other," she said in a caring way. She went next to him, with Theresa in her arms and sat next to him.

"You're a good woman. I can never thank you enough for the love and caring you've shown my daughter," Omar said. A tiny tear sparkled in his dark, kind eyes.

"You're a brave man," She gently caressed his cheek. She noticed the tiny tear drip from his eye. She took a cloth and wiped it from his face.

"You're the brave one," Omar whispered. He slightly moved for Antoinette to place his sleeping daughter next to him.

Colleen approached them both. "Everything okay here? Do you want me to change the dressing on your arm Omar?" she asked, as Antoinette moved to allow Colleen to come closer to Omar.

"I'm fine. Antoinette has taken care of me," Omar replied.

Colleen looked at Antoinette and could see a look of love in her eyes for the man. "Yes, I can see that you're just fine," Colleen said. She got up from the cot. "Just call if you need anything," she said.

She left them and went by her mother and Ricky. "Hi Camille, I can see your daughter is taking good care of Omar. We might have another nurse on hand," Colleen said to Camille, who had joined Beatrice at their site.

"Yes, she tends his every need," Camille said. She watched her daughter from the distance.

"Ricky, you keeping an eye on things over here?" Colleen asked her nephew. She knew he always craved others to acknowledge his taking charge of things without being told to take on the responsibility.

"Everything's fine Collie," Ricky said. He stood up showing her his holstered pistols and sheathed knife. "I'm ready," He went next to the crib to watch over Joseph.

Beatrice came next to her daughter. "The way he keeps an eye on Joseph you'd think he was twenty instead of only nine," They both smiled when they looked at Ricky. "I think I'll heat up some milk and honey for him and Abby. Might soothe their nerves…" Beatrice whispered to her daughter.

Colleen came closer next to her mother. "Mama this is so scary, make a little for me too. I'll send Abby over. I want to see if Geoff needs any help with Muraco's newborn," Colleen said. She patted her mother's shoulder and went to get Abby.

"Hi ladies," Colleen cheerfully said to Abby and her mother, Briana. "Briana, Mom's making some honey milk and asked if you and Abby might want to come have some," Colleen said. She knew Briana was not really included in the initial invitation, but when she saw the terrifying look on the woman's face she decided to ask her too.

"Oh, thank you Colleen that sounds wonderful. Maybe take our minds off what's going on for a minute," Briana said. She noticed Colleen gave her a bit of a stern look. "Don't worry, we know to be alert, don't we Abby," Briana looked at her daughter.

Abby stood up straight and held her head up high. "Yes we do Mama," The little girl said. She showed the same intense bravery that Joan of Arc showed when she liberated the city of Orleans from the English many many years ago.

"Good girl Abby," Colleen said. She went to the young girl and gave her a brief hug. "Go get that drink," she said.

Abby looked up to her and smiled. "Thank you," she replied. She gave Colleen a tiny curtsey and then turned and ran towards Ricky.

"Thanks Colleen. And you know we're always alert and ready," Briana said. She patted the rifle in her arm and then her pouch of ammunition. "Your family's always been so kind to us, and we really appreciate that," Briana said.

They hugged each other, and with their eyes explained what words could never say, and then went their separate ways.

"How's it going here brother," Colleen said to Geoff.

He was sitting with Muraco, while she breast fed her newborn and her mother-in-law Langundo sat near her. "Your brother is a wonderful doctor. From what's been told to me we surely would have died had he not performed the operation to save us," Muraco softly said. She caressed the small head of her daughter. "She's so tiny and look at all that black hair, just like her father's, so soft and silky," she continued to happily breast feed her daughter.

"She's a beauty. But I have to tell you Geoff's really my..." Colleen was about to say brother-in-law.

Muraco interrupted her. "Yes, I know the facts, but in the heart he is your brother," Muraco spoke in a whisper, as if her words were sacred.

"Yes, I believe you're right. We're kindred spirits and have a lot of history, don't we brother," Colleen said. Tears brightened her eyes when she looked at Geoff.

"We have named her Manipi, which means, she is an amazing child," Muraco said.

Her mother-in-law, Langundo came next to her with a soft cloth to tend her granddaughter when she finished her feeding. "We have been blessed and God will watch over us through this time," Langundo said. She held her arms out to take the baby. "She is beautiful like you my daughter, and I can see the brave spirit of her father, my son, in her eyes. She will live a long, giving life," Langundo said. She showed a brave face to them.

Even though they knew the risks that now faced them, it seemed this time held a silent spirit, on guard, to protect them.

Meanwhile, in the wilds, outside the stockade, the groups of hunters stayed alert. The clouds were partially dissipating and the waning, Gibbous moon lit up like an intermittent strobe light.

"Thank God for this small amount of light. I can see my compass better," Andrey said to his brother Gavrie as they waited with the group in the northwest section.

"I wish you would've stayed behind. I worry about you," Gavrie said to his younger brother, Andrey without looking at him.

"Don't worry about me. I can take care of myself," Andrey said. He was trying to take the responsibility his older brother always felt for him off his shoulders.

"I'll always worry about you. Family's in my blood so you're stuck with it," Gavrie looked at his brother. He always spoke like this to his younger brother. "I'd say it's almost 2:30 and about time for our first round, so keep your head about you," he softly whispered.

"Keep it quiet over there," Mitch whispered to the pair.

Gavrie looked at his little brother with that reprimanded look in his eyes, and they both softly giggled a bit knowing they were thinking of their father, Yerik just then, and how strict he was with them.

Just then a thunderous roar echoed throughout the night as shock waves shot down the spines of all the hunters.

"That was towards the northeast section," Mitch said, as all present stood still, wide eyed and alert. "Get ready, remember we hunt as they do," he then said.

They all prepared for their defense, as a deafening, body shaking shrill broke the silence and resounded from the southwest section. "They're checking locals. Stay close," Mitch whispered to his group.

They knew all of the hunting groups, in their different sections, were taking their orders from the cats, as Hania had explained to them. "They're cater-cornered," Mitch hurriedly whispered.

All of a sudden an explosion of ear splitting bawling erupted from the west. "Now," Mitch yelled.

They struck their flints and started the sage brush they had gathered with the char cloth and kindling wood they brought with them. The fires from all the sections could be seen from the stockade and from each group's section. With the moon and fire lights everything almost looked like daylight.

The cat's screeching wails and bellows seemed to be coming from everywhere and it was then that Hania felt his blood go cold. In the limited light he saw at least fifty long slithering shadows heading towards the stockade, which prompted him to send out his own shrilling howl that signaled the pre-designated section to kill the cubs. Earlier he had explained to them that, from his experience, he was certain the cubs would be watching from the northern ridge.

Immediately, after Hania's signal, Mitch's group hurried to the northern ridge. Within minutes they reached the cubs.

Mentally challenged they performed their deadly duty knowing with certainty that the savage beast warriors would soon be there to defend their young. In seconds the distress whines from the cubs were heard by the adults and half of the cat raiding party circled back towards the ridge.

Seeing this, Hania knew the cats would seek out their cubs, so he let out his second call that prompted the southwest group to join the northwest group to fight this crucial war with the cats, at the battle on the ridge.

Earlier, during the night, Hania's southeast section and the northeast section had built larger stacks of brush and kindling ready to be lit on command.

Hania felt like a steam engine going full throttle, his blood was pumping throughout his body. His temples were pounding as he, with all that he had in him, shrieked out his final call to action. With this order they lit the stacks to encircle the remaining beasts between them and the stockade.

Again, he watched the cats split and he knew now the bloody battle of the wedge would begin. His section would try to keep in close knit groups, but he knew, as they all did, that it was truly every man for himself.

The cats feared the fire, and the smoke was thick, and made it hard for both man and beast to see.

Finally, unable to see him, and only hearing the sound of the huge paws hitting the earth and the terrified shrills coming closer to him, the fearful tiger emerged from the smoky fog and leaped over the wall of flames. And then another and another until there were ten.

Hania, raised his rifle, aimed and in seconds killed five. He knew he was alone. The smoke swirled around him but also gave him the advantage of surprise. He was calm and felt like he was on familiar ground. He believed he knew them as well as himself.

And then he heard the gurgle, the low growl that alerted him to pull his pistol turn and shoot as another beast fell to his death near him.

He fought for his family. "I will help bring peace my mother, I will free our people to live without fear," he shouted.

With the force of the warrior he was he took on many cats. He used every ounce of skill he was taught by his father to save his family until all, but one of his resources was used up. "My baby will live. My family will be saved," he shouted.

A black mountain lion toyed with him as if he knew him. With a keen eye the cat slowly circled him. Hania knew the beast had the advantage, but he was not going to let him see his fear. Looking deep in the beast's yellow eyes he could see the reflected flickering fire light, but then he saw something that terrified him even more, he saw intelligence.

Then, with a loud shrill the cat made a catapulting leap into the air knocking Hania to the ground, but not before Hania was able to use his axe with a blow so hard he nearly took the lions head off.

At this same time, Gavrie was fighting for his life, as three cougars were circling him, after he had just killed a giant tigress. Quickly, he looked around for his brother, Andrey. He watched as one of the cougars that had been circling Andrey had just tossed Andrey like a sack of potatoes, and Andrey lay limp on the ground. Garvie pulled out his pistol; he took aim at the cougar and killed him dead with a shot between the eyes. Gavrie, thinking only of his brother, ran to him with another cougar close behind him.

As he reached his brother, Andrey opened his eyes and saw Gavrie coming to him. "Behind you!" Andrey yelled.

Gavrie turned and shot the cat as it leaped through the air over him and fell dead on his brother. With the weight of the beast on him Andrey could not move.

Helpless, Andrey lay, unable to speak as he heard his brother take on and kill many cats. Thinking his brother Andrey was dead, Gavrie screamed at the savage beasts. "Come get me you bastards. You want me come get me!" he screamed. He found a strength in him that helped him fight with courage until the end when he plunged his knife deep inside the last cat, but not before the king of the beasts clawed him to death.

At the stockade the cats were not wasting any time as they approached with lightning speed and the men lining the walls were able to only kill ten of the twenty five. Just like the humans the cats knew this was a war and they all would battle it to the end.

The remaining cats scaled the walls with fierce fury. The roars and screams were deafening to all.

Those in the building stayed alert but felt shaken, as they could only wait. "Oh God, they're going to break in," Muraco cried to her mother-in-law, Langundo, as Muraco held her newborn baby close to her.

"Have faith daughter," Langundo peacefully said to Muraco. She slowly caressed her grandbaby's cheek. "You and your beautiful little daughter, my grandbaby will be safe," she caringly said. She had a quieting look in her eyes that calmed Muraco. "Here you go baby get under here and hold her tight," Langundo softly said to Muraco. She lovingly helped Muraco, in her immobile state, to move as fast as she could, with her baby in her arms, to bed down.

Only when she knew Muraco and her grandbaby were completely comfortable and settled in did Langundo leave their side. She quickly began to pull tables and benches in front of Muraco and her granddaughter. "Stay here," Langundo slowly whispered in Muraco's ear. She had completely covered them with blankets and reluctantly left them. "I'm going to help the others block the door," With all the chaos in the room she had to shout to Muraco.

Everyone in the building was dragging the benches and tables towards the door. Colleen saw Langundo going to the door. Just then a bright blue ball flashed right in front of her and she could feel the spirit of Gavrie pass straight up through her. "Langundo, wait," Colleen yelled. She noticed another large, bright blue orb streak around the room and then towards her.

Langundo screamed, as she also watched the giant ball enter at Colleen's feet. "My son," Langundo let out such a lamenting cry that Muraco uncovered her head to see what was going on. "Get down," Langundo shouted. She looked straight into Muraco's eyes, and Muraco immediately did what she was told.

Langundo went to the door and slightly opened it to see what was going on in the courtyard. "Langundo, don't go," Colleen shouted. She watched the woman look at her with a peaceful stare of purpose in her eyes. Colleen knew the woman was going to leave the building and help outside. But then Colleen realized that Langundo was also witnessing her son, Hania's spirit draw up and out of Colleen's body.

"God's speed, Colleen, peace be with you!" the older woman cried out. She looked towards the heavens as she hurriedly slipped outside and quickly closed the door behind her knowing they would barricade her retreat.

Langundo saw her husband, Kuruk was fighting like the brave man she knew him to be. With her pistols drawn she knew she was fully armed and capable to fight the brutes. Just then, a yellow and black spotted female cat jumped in front of her. "You look about my size," Unafraid, she spat at the furious, feline.

The enraged cat lifted her head and let out an ear piercing roar, as she pawed away the earth behind her. "Roar all you want," Langundo yelled. Both woman and cat looked each other square in the eyes. "Trying to size me up are ya?" Langundo spat at the pursuing cat. She squatted down in front of the savage beast and stared directly into the blue eyes of the creature.

It was at that moment that her husband Kuruk saw his wife facing the cat. In a split second, he watched how she aimed her pistol and killed the animal. As he rushed to her aid, another, larger male jumped his wife from behind. Quickly, she took her other pistol and killed that giant cat and with a tremendous strength was able to toss it off of her and to her side.

Kuruk immediately went to his wife and they fought back to back with their knives and hatchets until one large tigress leaped towards them both. Kuruk, seeing her approach them instantly thrust out his leg and tripped the tiger to the ground, but not before she deeply clawed his leg.

Injured, Kuruk fell to the ground. He tried to get up but could not. He could only watch as the screaming cat rolled in the mud and fiercely jumped up on all fours and vaulted over him and then pounced on Langundo knocking her to the ground.

From the far side of the stockade, BD saw the cat land on Langundo. Quickly, he ran to help her, but as he plunged his knife into the neck of the beast, immediately killing the tiger, he could see that Langundo was already dead.

***

These were the images Kuruk and Colleen were remembering now. With the cats on the hunt again those terrifying flashbacks of that time of death at the Timms Stockade, was all they could talk about, as they gathered at Mitch and Colleen's, where they now lived in Peaceful Valley.

It was that terrible time that was again highlighted in their minds and forced them to recollect the war with the beasts. "Yes, I remember it was the night for Alo, the spiritual guide," Colleen said, bringing them back from that time so many years ago. "And you're right, it does seem like it was just yesterday for me too, when the renegade cats attacked us at the Timms Stockade," Colleen caringly said to Kuruk.

They continued to sit on the hearth and lowly speak to each other as the others in the room also softly spoke of that night. Then she noticed Ricky, sitting by himself. She had noticed over the years that he had grown and learned a lot about life and death after the cats attack at the Timms Stockade, but lately she thought maybe he missed his dad more. Maybe life had changed too much and it was hard for him to adjust. She thought even though he was almost twenty one there were times that he seemed to need some of her TLC. She made a mental note to try and spend more time with him and talk like they used to do in the old days.

"I know I have told you many times over the years, that when your son Hania passed how I believed Langundo also saw his blue orb, but you never told me why she could see it but…" Colleen was saying.

Kuruk interrupted her. "My dear, only The Portal can ascend the spirit. It seems those who care can only see, but do not appear to have the gift to transfer the spirit that you do as The Portal," He explained his theory to her, for the first time since she had met him, what he believed her gift of The Portal meant to him, and those who believed in it.

"And your wife, Langundo, when she passed, she was a white orb. I had never seen a white orb before," She gave him a curious look.

This was a question she had also asked him many times over the years, but for some reason he always avoided answering her. But now he seemed willing to explain this phenomenon in more detail than he ever had before. "She is a spirit guide. She possesses the bright light and is a strong spirit. She will continue to lead until all that she loves have returned," Kuruk said, not pausing before he added. "Her guiding light led white moon to our son and from that union our amazing granddaughter came," He looked at her.

She could see he was speaking words from his heart. "Back then, after Hania's death, Muraco was in a bad way; even though, after time, life was good for us here in Peaceful Valley," he looked at her. "As you know after the great crack many of the forests were uprooted and with the oceans back lash drifted the wood to the eastern shores. We were blessed when we were joined with your group and re-built this settlement with the quality lumber from your Driftwood..." he was saying. "My family lived in the West. Life changed as the waters spilled but then covered the low lands. We were lucky to live in the mountainous range. But after such a drastic change our land was not fertile; and we had to find a different way to live. We did not know if the sailing ships we built would bring us to a new land or just a water world. But we had to move on," Kuruk always spoke of his past life with his family. It was a part of him. "Thinking about the cats is bringing up a lot of memories," He shrugged his shoulders.

"I know what you mean. I look at Ricky and I can see him as a baby and this young man before me. My life has not been as changing as yours. My mom only remembers small parts, but you lived through it," She looked at him and then at Ricky. "These cats are bringing up all sorts of mixed up thoughts..." She looked at Kuruk.

"Yes, when one's way of life is threatened all kinds of thoughts go through your head. Maybe, one day life will return as it was; and maybe even better..." Kuruk commented.

He continued to look around the room and listen to other conversations. "When I think about my wife; I cannot help but think about Muraco; and how Langundo has loved her with her guiding light not only once but twice and who knows how many other times…" His eyes glistened.

"With her bravery, your wife saved many lives when the cats attacked us at the Timms," She envisioned Langundo leaving the Timms Stockade, knowing the danger of the cat's outside.

"But what comes to my mind now is how safe and secure Muraco's home was when we settled again in Peaceful Valley. I truly believed she had dealt with her sorrow after the deaths of her husband Hania and my wife Langundo. I know she thought of Langundo as her mother," He looked at Colleen.

"I thought she was living each day, not just coping. After so much time had passed she seemed happy," Colleen had a sad look in her eyes. "I know Muraco never should've gone out in that blizzard back then…" Colleen was saying. She looked at Kuruk and could tell he also was reminiscing about that time.

***

Back then, unknown to most of them, Muraco found life almost unbearable after losing, not only her loving husband, Hania the father of her newborn baby girl, Manipi, but also Langundo, the woman in her life she always called mother. She went into a deep depression and had to fight with herself to take care of her baby and tend to her own personal needs. But she believed she hid that fact from those around her. It was six years after the deaths, when she felt her daughter was old enough to live without her, that she mentally planned her escape from, what she believed to be her dreadful life of anguish.

She found it easy to disguise her pain and pretend that everything was perfectly normal. She attentively cared for her daughter, as she thought they would want her to. She dressed herself very neatly and made certain she looked almost manicured, because that was how she felt, chiseled from stone.

She almost fooled them all. But Geoff could see her pain. It was a trip back to his past, after the loss of his wife. The look in her eyes gave him an intense slap of grief. He could almost feel her frozen heart. But he knew what he saw was something only Muraco could cure. His heart hung low as he watched her try to live a lie.

Chapter Ten

Memories of Muraco's Decision

It was the winter many had decided to live in the tranquil surroundings of Peaceful Valley. The same tranquil, home-place Kuruk had spoken about to them when they were at the Timms Stockade. Muraco and her baby daughter, Manipi stayed with Kuruk, Muraco's father-in-law at the home she used to share with her husband, Hania. Muraco's heart could not forget the times she was with her husband; and now she felt she was another woman and those loving times were only thoughts of another lifetime. In her despaired mind she planned her escape from her misery with thoughts of joining her husband.

A wagon train of logs and milled drift lumber had been transported to the area from Driftwood; and before this particular winter set in many cabins had been erected for those who followed Kuruk and his family to set up residence at Peaceful Valley.

For their protection in Peaceful Valley they had also built a small stockade where they could gather and feel safe. They also had a general store, which actually looked like a barn. They took turns manning the store and traded with the Timms and traveling wagon trains for personal and luxury goods. After the cat invasions at the Timms Stockade, they knew they would need more protection than just the walls and the small building, so they also dug out and built refuge cellars. It was a peaceful community.

It was the winter of the worst blizzard that many had experienced in years. They all were thankful for their new homes in Peaceful Valley. "I sure do miss Mama," Colleen somberly said to Mitch and Geoff.

They were sitting in Colleen's kitchen drinking mugs of hot tea. "It had to be Honey, you know how she was about getting older and wondering about her ancestors…" Mitch commented.

Colleen interrupted him. "I know, like Mama always kept saying, 'I'm not getting any younger'…" she sighed. "But it's so nice here at Peaceful Valley. I just wish they could've…" she was saying.

Geoff interrupted her. "She had to go see if her parents or any of their families are still alive. Things are changing and from the way it sounds from travelers passing through, small cities and townships are uniting and technology is finding its way back into societies," Geoff commented. He took a sip of his tea and then reached for the honey Colleen always kept on the table.

"You never can get enough of that stuff can you?" Colleen teased.

"Speaking of technology; have you noticed Olivier's radio receiver. That boy's got talent and tenacity…" Mitch said.

They all laughed. "I know, even with all the racket his contraption makes, he still keeps trying to make it work. There has to be something out there that could make it work," Colleen added.

"Well, if there is, he'll find it. Whenever a peddler comes along he's the first to check out his wares; and he scrounges around just like BD," Mitch said. They all laughed.

"I know BD helped him out some before he left with Mom," Colleen added.

Ricky came in the room. “Dad, I’m going to visit Andy for a while,” Ricky said. He had a completely bored look on his face.

“Okay. And Son, with the storm coming you might want to get home before dark. And if it starts snowing you might want to go right home. I’ll be leaving here in a little while…” Geoff was saying.

Ricky was putting on his coat and scarf. “Don’t forget your gloves,” Colleen said in her always motherly way.

He reached in his pocket and pulled them out. “I’m always prepared Collie,” Ricky said. “You guys still treat me like a kid,” He chuckled and they laughed with him. He came next to Colleen and hugged her. “See you later Dad,” he said. He picked up his saddle bags and headed out the front door.

“Jeanette would’ve loved that boy to death,” Colleen said. She noticed Geoff only turned and smiled at her.

“I’m sure she would’ve been a great mom,” Mitch said. He went to the stove and poured himself another mug of steeped tea. “Anybody else ready?” he asked. He held up the pot but they both nodded in disagreement. “I’m glad he still takes his saddle bags with him,” Mitch added. He came back and joined them at the table. “I think I’m going to add a little spirits this time,” he said. He poured a jigger of whiskey in his tea.

“I’ll take a shot,” Geoff said. Mitch poured it in his brother’s cup. “You know I think carrying our saddle bags around is something we’ll most likely do for the rest of our lives,” Geoff said, as they all softly laughed and agreed with him. Geoff took a sip of his whiskey. “Great stuff, takes the chill off,” He finished the spiked tea.

He eyed the whiskey bottle. “Help yourself…” Colleen said. She poured a bit in her cup and passed it to her brother-in-law.

“What’s your take on Muraco?” Geoff asked. He knew they would understand he meant her state of mind like they had often talked about over the years, after the loss of her husband and mother-in-law.

"She really seems to have moved on. She's very attentive to Manipi and she looks great…" Colleen was saying. Mitch nodded in agreement with her.

"I don't know. There's just something not right. I can't quite put my finger on it, but to me she acts like she's hiding something," Geoff said.

Colleen gave him a puzzling look. "I don't think so. She's always so happy to see me when I visit, and she's always making over Manipi," Colleen said. She reached for a honey bun she had in a covered dish on the table.

"Well, enough of this talk…I think it's about time for me to head home. Ricky will be home in a while and I want to get some supper going," Geoff said. He got up from his seat and reached for his coat and bags.

"Want a couple buns for dessert?" Colleen asked. She reached for the dish.

"Sounds good," Geoff said. Colleen wrapped them in a napkin and gave them to him. He put the buns in his coat pocket.

They all walked to the front door. "Looks like you have enough wood stocked up for the storm," Geoff said with a chuckle.

They all started laughing when he pointed out all they had stacked against the walls and in the box. "Yep, sure do…you too?" Mitch asked, with a laugh in his voice. They all knew they both had made certain everyone in the community had ample supplies in their homes and at their stockade.

"If it gets too deep, don't look for us for a while," Geoff said. He started out the door. "It's starting," he said. He walked into the twilight as the snow was falling. "I see Ricky made it home and started the fires already," He turned and told them. He then pulled his scarf over his nose and started for his nearby home.

"He needs a woman," Mitch said. He held his wife close to him.

They both watched the lonely man walk to his home. "He'll be fine," Colleen said. She watched Geoff turn and wave to them and then continue his walk. They then closed the heavy wooden door which shut the cold outside.

"Whew," Geoff said. He entered their cabin and briskly shook his head as he removed his knitted black sock cap. "It's really starting up out there. Looks like we're in for a big one," He started to take off his coat.

"Dad on my way home I saw Muraco," Ricky said, with concern in his voice.

"Oh, how was she?" Geoff asked. He came next to his son.

"I don't know I called out to her but she didn't answer. I know she could hear me I wasn't that far away from her, but she kept on walking," Ricky said. He started to stir the left over stew that was bubbling in the pot on their wood stove.

"Which way was she walking?" Geoff quietly asked. He started to feel a fear grip him deep in the pit of his stomach.

"She didn't look like she was going to see anyone, she was going out towards the fields," Ricky said. He noticed his father's caring look turn to panic. "What's going on Dad, do you think something's wrong with her?" Ricky asked. He took the pot off the stove.

His father went to their cedar chest. "Son, I'm going after her. I think she's in a bad way. You know, even after all these years she still misses her husband and Langundo…" Geoff was saying. He reached for his leather pouches, knives and pistols. "Can you get me some jerky and hardtack? I don't know how long this will take. I'm taking the lantern too," he said.

His son took one of the pouches from his father and did as he asked. "But Dad the blizzard," Ricky said. He was scared of the thought of his father out in the storm.

"Ricky this woman needs help. You give me an hour, and if I'm not back with her by then, you go tell Uncle Mitch what's going on," Geoff said. He zipped up his pants after putting on his long underwear. "She might have just walked to the field. You know, to get some fresh air before the storm gets too bad, and keeps us all homebound. If so nothing to worry about," He looked at Ricky. "We'll stop by here before I take her back home. Okay son," he said, convincing his son that everything would be just fine.

"Okay Dad, but just one hour, and then I'm going to Uncle Mitch's," Ricky said, with conviction in his voice.

"That's fine son," Geoff said. He headed for the door and then turned and went back to his son. "You're a good boy. I don't think I say that enough. I couldn't have asked for a better son than you are. I love you son…" he was saying. He hugged him and kissed his forehead.

"Dad…" Ricky was saying. Geoff immediately turned and went out the door with Ricky right on his heels. "Don't forget one hour," Ricky shouted as his father disappeared in the falling snow.

Ricky shut the door. "Oh God he didn't pick up his compass," Ricky ran to the door, opened it, and shouted for his father to return, but did not get a reply. 'I don't know if I should wait the hour. He'll need his compass,' he thought to himself. "No I'll give him the hour but no more," he said out loud.

Out in the night the snow hit Geoff's face making him bow down and force himself onward. The snow blew and drifted faster than he had expected it would, but he kept trudging on. Looking up he saw a dim light in the distance and believed she must have taken a lantern with her so he followed it.

'I don't know how she's got this planned, but from the way she's going it seems she's decided to go to the cave down by the stream,' he thought. He again saw the light off in the distance. 'I'm lucky I can see that light with all this snow. I guess it's bouncing off the snow kind of like a prism,' he was thinking,

He noticed the light change directions. "Now where's she going," he said out loud. He reached in his pocket for his compass and realized he didn't have it. 'I hope she's got on plenty of outer wear,' he thought. But then thought with what was on her mind she really did not care what she was wearing.

"Okay, now she's back on track. Or with only my mental compass to go by, I'm guessing she is…hell, I'm no better off than she is...God we need some help down here," he prayed.

He noticed the light seemed to stop and get brighter so he continued to follow it. 'I guess I've been out here for over the hour I told Ricky about and Mitch is on my trail, but how will he know where to go,' he was thinking. A bit of panic hit him. 'Can't worry about that right now, just have to get to her,' he thought, with a prayer in his heart that he would reach her in time.

Even as the snow came down so thick that he could hardly see where he was going; in the distance he noticed the light was getting brighter and brighter until he finally reached the cave.

Entering the cave his sole lantern cast a dim light in the small opening. The room had a low ceiling but was high enough to walk upright in. It was a great protection from the snow and the cold.

"Muraco," he called out, in a low soft voice. But she did not answer him. He looked around. "Where's her lantern…' he thought. He took off one glove and rubbed his eyes and tried to focus on her lantern. "Muraco," he again whispered. He thought she had to hear him. "I know you're in here I saw your light," he said. He heard something move to his left.

Slowly he turned and moved in that direction. "Leave me…" she cried out. She noticed he was coming closer to her. "Just leave me. I can't go on any more. Can't you just let me be…" she was saying.

He could tell she was crying but then he stopped in horror. She was huddled next to the wall. She did not have a stitch of clothes on nor did he see her lantern. "The cave's dark," he said. He continued to look around for her lantern but did not see it.

"Yes it's dark. Why can't you just leave me alone? You're always hovering around me. You make me sick…" She spat at him. She tried to cover her face when he neared her with his lantern. "Get that damn thing out of my face," she screamed. She reached for his lantern.

He backed away and she ran to the rear of the cave. "Muraco, you can't do this. Come back with me…" he was saying, but then thought that was most likely out of the question right now with the blizzard and with her naked condition.

"You go back," she shouted. "Just get the hell out of here…" she was saying.

They both heard a low whine come from the other side of the cave. Taking his lantern Geoff neared the area where he heard the sound. "Good God, where did you come from?" he quietly asked. He neared a pregnant dog. "I haven't seen a dog in a long time," he was saying. He looked back at Muraco and could see that she was watching him near the dog. Suddenly the dog's whining got louder and she started howling. Geoff noticed she was giving birth to a puppy. "What the hell. Boy nothing's ever easy around here," he commented. He put his hand to his cap and pulled it off and wiped his brow, but then put the cap back on his head.

Just then the mother dog yelped in agony. "Help her. You're the doctor…" Muraco shouted. She had a vehement tone in her voice.

"Why the hell do you care about this damn dog, you don't even care about what you're doing to your own flesh and blood," he yelled back at her. "You want me to help a pitiful dog, while you kick your own daughter to fend for herself," he yelled. He neared the animal but could only watch as she gave birth. He knew in the dog's present state, her first instinct might be to look at his attempt to help her as a ploy to fight or kill her while she was down, so for the moment, he just watched.

"You with your perfect little family, always knowing what to say and how to act, you make me sick," Muraco said, with hate in her voice. "I lost everything. Everybody just expected me to love my baby and act like nothing happened. Well something did happen and it changed my whole world," she shouted. The dog howled again and the first puppy was born. "Can't you just take that bitch out of here and leave me the hell alone?" she screamed. She squirmed back to the side of the cave and tried to huddle away from him.

"Oh boy, here we go again," Geoff said. He neared the dog and she went into labor again, but this time she seemed more at ease with him and allowed him to near her and tend to the already born puppy. But then he heard another low growl and saw another dog coming close to him. "Oh boy, now what… guess I better let you two take care of this yourselves…" he was saying.

A male dog came close to the first born and picked it up with his mouth and carried it away. "Well it looks like you know what you're doing…" he was saying. Just then the mother dog let out a painful wail and gave birth to a second pup. "Good girl," Geoff said, in a low caring voice. He watched her lick her newborn.

Looking around Geoff thought it seemed warmer in the cave than he thought it should be. "This place feels warm to me," he said out loud. He did not really expect Muraco to respond. "What's this back here," he then said. He took his lantern and walked a short distance towards the back of the cave. "Wow, a hot spring. All this time we never knew there was a hot spring in this cave," He neared the steaming pool of water. "I guess we just never explored it," he said out loud, knowing Muraco would not respond.

"This will help girl," Geoff said. He went to his saddlebags and took out a cloth. He then went back to the spring and dipped the cloth in the water, and went next to the female dog and helped attend her male pup. "Looks like you're doing a good job mama, but here let me give you a hand," He gently caressed the tiny creature and cleaned the mucus from his eyes and mouth. "I think I'll just let Papa take care of his daughter," He noticed while the male dog was tending the female he was also keeping a keen eye on Geoff while he cared for the newborn male pup's needs.

"I wonder where you two came from," Geoff commented. He purposely ignored Muraco while he spoke to the animals. "Not a very good night to be out is it girl…" He sat down next to the female and placed her pup near her.

The female immediately started to clean him up with her tongue. "It always amazes me how nature seems to take care of itself. If you could talk I bet you would have a lot to say," Geoff took a chance and started to pet her. "Good girl," he gently said. He glanced at the male and thankfully noticed he seemed unconcerned. "I can tell you two are not wild," He thought they must belong to someone. "I guess we have some guests on the way to the settlement," He got up and took two pieces of jerky from his bags. "There you go Papa…" Keeping a safe distance he tossed the dried meat to him. "And this is for you Mama," he softly said. He again sat next to the female and she gently took it from his hand. "That's it…" he was saying.

Muraco started to softly cry. She was crouched down near a corner in the cave. She started to feel the cold, and she held her arms around herself. "Why couldn't you just leave me alone? I could be with my husband now if you had just left me alone," she sobbed. She continued to watch him caress the animal.

"Did you hear that girl?" Geoff caringly started to pet the mama dog. "I think you accomplished something I don't think I ever could…" he was saying.

The male dog got up and picked up the female pup with his mouth and brought her near the mother dog and she began to nurse both pups. "Are you telling me you trust me now?" Geoff looked in the male dog's eyes, and watched as the dog quietly lay down near Geoff and his canine family. "Trust…that's a quality a lot of men have a hard time with," He sat back and folded his arms.

He then noticed Muraco's clothes thrown in a pile near the entrance of the cave. He went and picked them up. "Here put these on," He walked near her with his lantern in his other hand and put the clothes next to her. "I'm going to conserve my fuel…" He walked back to the dogs and sat down next to them and turned off his lantern. In the dark he could hear her wrestling with her clothes. "Where's your lantern?" he softly whispered.

He noticed she finally settled down and he could tell she was resting against the wall of the cave. "I didn't bring one. I didn't need one. I just happened on the cave," she coldly replied. She did not care what he said or thought about her. "You know this isn't over…" She had an unfeeling tone in her voice.

"That's up to you," he said. He understood, only to well, the mental torture she was putting on herself. "You know what puzzles me…" In the dark he could almost feel her glare at him. "Colleen and I have spoken about Kuruk's explanation of the orbs. She never talks much about it, but I do know that if you believe as Kuruk does and your family did, you should know that you will one day join them…" he was saying.

He could feel a greater tension in the room. "You self-righteous…" she shouted. She started to sob uncontrollably. "I'm already dead. I died when they died…but this body…this body just keeps on going," she almost inaudibly screamed. "What do you know of my pain? You have your perfect little world…" She could not see his tears flowing from his eyes and down his cheeks. "Every time I look at Manipi I see her father and her grandmother. It's unbearable…there was a time I wanted to take her and just…" She felt her throat constrict.

Suddenly, she noticed a tiny light near the entrance of the cave. "I thought you turned that damn lantern off. And can't you stay put," she yelled.

He whispered from where he was sitting with the dogs. "I'm still over here, and it is off" he said.

She realized he was still with the dogs near the back of the cave and not by the entrance. "I thought I saw a light at the front," she said. Unexpectedly, she got the hic-cups. Trying to get rid of them she got up and started to stamp her feet.

Looking towards the cave entrance Geoff also saw the tiny light. "I see it. Might be Mitch coming to find us," He groped for his lantern and lit it. "I'll set this by the entrance so he can see it," He placed the lantern.

He returned to the dogs. "Take a couple deep breaths and then hold it," he explained. He sat down by the head of the mama dog.

"What the hell are you talking about," She shouted with a hic-cup in between each word.

"It'll help get rid of the hic-cups. Just do it!" He shouted back at her.

He could tell she was doing as he said. "Muraco, my life isn't that perfect world you think it is. I went through what you're going through. That's why I could see it in you," In the limited light he could see that she had a confused look on her face. And then she held her hand over her mouth. "I lost my wife when Ricky was born..." He felt a sharp sting hit his heart as he remembered Jeanette living her last hours in his arms. "If I told you that the pain goes away I'd be lying because it doesn't, but with God's help you find a way to live with it..." He knew she would have to deal with those feelings herself.

"You say this isn't over and all I can say about that is I hope it is, because you have so much to live for..." He noticed she put her hands over her face and softly wept. "You have free will and only you can say it's over. I learned that a long time ago," He tried to wipe the tears from his eyes.

She looked at him and saw his tear stained face. "I didn't know..." She had compassion in her voice.

"It doesn't matter. I manage one day at a time and I give all my love to my son because I don't know what tomorrow might bring. A friend once told me God doesn't make junk..." he was saying.

She came closer to him. "And I'm not junk," she said. She sat down near the head of the female dog.

He looked at her. "No, you're not and neither am I. How can you look at how our earth has come back to care for us, and not think there is a greater power out there helping us. I know I sound like a preacher, but God helped me learn how to live again..." He noticed she had started to pet the mama dog. "Hey, your hic-cups are gone," he said, with a bit of a chuckle in his voice.

"So they are. I guess you're a good doctor," she quietly said. She had a slight grin on her lips. "I think I can try," she softly whispered. Her warm tears flowed from her eyes as she lay next to the female dog and the little pups nuzzled next to her and their mother.

"Maybe you could also try to get a little sleep. I guess that wasn't Mitch but I'll keep watch for a while..." he was saying. He reached in his pocket. "Oh man I forgot about these," He took out the honey buns Colleen had given him earlier. "They're a little mashed, but I'm sure they're still good," He offered her one.

"All of a sudden I'm famished," she said. She took one of the buns and looked at him with a slight smile on her lips.

"Famished becomes you," he teased. He noticed a soft look in her eyes that gave him hope that she would be all right.

***

After the hour Ricky promised his Dad he would wait; he went directly to Mitch and Colleen's cabin. "We have to try Uncle Mitch. They could die out there," Ricky said. He was pacing the floor. His words sent a surge of fear through them. Colleen could hardly bear watching him. She gently persuaded him to sit next to her.

"We can't go now. We'd all die out there now," Mitch said. He understood every fear his nephew was feeling.

"Mitch is right the storm would not let us find them. Right now we can only wait and pray," Kuruk, said. When he realized Muraco had been gone too long he had come to their cabin, in search of his daughter-in-law. He sat near his granddaughter, Manipi, where she peacefully slept on the soft sofa in the living room.

"He doesn't have his compass. He could never find his way back," A nervous Ricky said. He left Colleen's side and flopped on a chair near the fireplace.

"My brother's like me; we have a natural sense of direction. He'll find his way back, if not tonight, soon. But I'm guessing, when he finds her if he can't make it back here, they'll make their way to the cave," Mitch hopefully explained his theory.

Colleen went to the kitchen and brought them all some of the left over honey buns. Together, they all sat in silence and could only wait out the storm or Geoff and Muraco's return.

***

Back at the cave, the morning light slowly seeped its way into the cave waking Geoff and the male dog first. "How you doing fella?" he quietly asked the dog. He glanced towards Muraco, who was fast asleep next to the mama dog and her pups. She still had the blanket from his saddle bags on top of her. "Thank God we're always prepared," He went next to her and tucked the blanket around her, but did not rouse her.

"I'm right behind you," Geoff whispered to the male dog. The dog got up and went to the entrance of the cave with Geoff right on his heels. "Looks like we have the same thing on our minds…" Geoff was saying. He looked over at the dog relieving himself just outside the entrance to the cave.

'Thank God it's over,' Geoff thought. He watched the morning sun rise with a pink glow filtering through the gray clouds. 'But I don't think we're going anywhere for a while,' he then thought. He looked out over the white landscape of deep, glistening snow.

***

On the second day after the blizzard, they all met at their stockade. "We all know what we're up against," Mitch said, as they all sat around in the building. To conserve wood only one fire in the pot belly stove warmed them. "The frigid temperature will keep this snow on the ground for some time…" he was saying. He noticed they all nodded and murmured in agreement.

"It was only with luck that we made it here just as the storm hit," A familiar voice spoke out to them.

"And we're all happy to see you and your family Yerik..." Colleen was saying. She watched as Yerik hugged his new wife Agnes, who held their young daughter Polly. "I just wish it were under better circumstances," Colleen added.

Andrey came next to his father. "My boy," Yerik said. He pulled Andrey close to his side with tears welling in both their eyes. His brothers Bohdan and Alek stood close to Andrey. "We all have experienced loss," Yerik said.

They all knew he was speaking of his sons Pavel and Gavrie and the others lost during the cat raid at the Timms stockade. "Yes, I'm sure we all remember that time," Colleen was saying

"We were lucky to see the lights from here. I'm sorry Mitch, it was really bad out there," Yerik said, as his wife huddled closer to him. "This storm came up on us. Otherwise we wouldn't have made the trip," he added.

They all could only look at each other. "And we're glad you made it," Colleen added. She came next to Agnes, who continued to hold daughter Polly. Colleen caressed the child's red cheek. "I have some lotion for her chapped skin here in my bags," Colleen said. She and Agnes went near the stove and sat next to it.

"My dogs are out in this mess too," Yerik then said. "The female was about to have her pups. I guess she went off looking for some place to have her pups and the male followed," Yerik said. They all were shedding some of their wet outer garments and trying to warm up.

"Hope they make it..." Mitch was saying. He motioned for Yerik to follow him outside.

"Care for a chaw?" Yerik asked when they were outside. He offered Mitch a bite of his jerky.

"Sure, thanks," Mitch said. Taking it he put part of it in his mouth and saved the other for later. "My brother would look for shelter, and there's a cave out there," He situated the bite of jerky in his mouth. "But knowing Geoff, he would not even take shelter until he knew she was safe. I'm really not feeling good about this…" he was saying.

They started to hear wails from the dog out in the snow. "That's my Pepper. I'd know his howl anywhere," Yerik commented.

They looked at each other knowing they could not leave the compound to search for the dog. "This is crazy. The sun's out; the sky's as blue as the ocean; and the snow's as deep as a mountain glazed like some kind of icy lake…" Mitch was saying. He had a sad heart. "The howl sounds so close, but might as well be a million miles away…" he continued to say.

They could only hopelessly look at each other. "Mitch, my boy, you gave me a great idea," Yerik said. His eyes lit up like sparklers. "Come, let's see if we can make this work," He put his arm around Mitch's shoulders. They both went back inside the stockade.

***

In the cave Geoff and Muraco were surviving the best they could. "He keeps on howling. He's driving me crazy…" Muraco was saying. She gently held the female puppy and tenderly petted the soft fur.

"He might lead the others to us. Think of his howling as a signal," Geoff was saying. He had to speak up with the loud howl also hurting his eardrums.

"Won't they just think it's the howl of some wild animal?" she asked. She had a distant look in her eyes. She turned her head from his. She had an unconcerned look about her. "I don't know if I want to be found," She turned red with a look of embarrassment on her face.

"I thought you…" Geoff was saying. He had a bit of panic in his voice, thinking she still might have suicidal feelings.

"Geoff, you've been a God save, but this has been a part of me for so long that I don't know how to act…they'll know what I was going to…" she was saying. She felt warm tears flow down her cheeks.

"No one will judge you. You are loved by your family and everyone has only had good things to say about you. Just be yourself…" he was saying.

The dog stopped his howling for the moment. "Thank God," Muraco said, thankful that the dog stopped and for what Geoff had said to her. "You're a good man," she then said. She looked at him.

He noticed she had a touch of joy in her eyes. "I like that look," Geoff said. "You're a good woman too," He smiled at her.

She nervously giggled and snuggled her head in the fur of the puppy as the dog outside started to howl again. "I'm sorry I got you involved in this," Muraco said, changing the subject.

"Nowhere else I'd rather be," he said. He shrugged his shoulders.

She felt her spirits lift. "You lie," she teased him. The puppy squirmed in her arms and she laid her next to her mama and watched as she started to nurse the pup.

"Well the circumstances could be better, but not the company," he said. He wondered how he got the courage to say that. He always thought of her as a beautiful woman with a tender heart just like his own, but now he was seeing her as someone who could possibly bring out the love that had been hidden in his heart.

"Do you think we can survive?" she asked. Her heart took a giant leap in her chest; she felt a deep belief in her come alive; that was the first time in a long time she truly meant what she said. "I really do want to live for my daughter," The dog stopped its howling. She looked at him and smiled. "You made me see that I would disrespect the lives of my husband and his mother had I done what I…" She started to say but could not finish.

"You know I don't think God would have led us this far only to take us. I did see that light that brought me to this cave and you didn't have a lantern…" he was saying. He saw a look of bewilderment on her face. "You don't remember about the light. I thought it was your lantern, but you didn't have one," he was saying.

She started to laugh, like he had never seen her do before. "Langundo…She brought you to me," Muraco said. She could feel goose bumps rise on her arms. "She knew, and she would not let me…" She put her arms around her and could feel warm tears again on her cheeks. "My mother-in-law brought my husband and me together so long ago, and now I know she still watches over me," She tried to wipe the tears from her face.

Geoff came next to her. "She was a wonderful, loving woman," he said. He was not really surprised at the way she spoke about Langundo. "Why should we only believe in what we can see? I have felt my wife next to me, and sometimes I get a little nudge that feels like her touch. So why can't we believe Langundo has the power to show us a light to safety?" he said. The dog started to howl again. "And maybe we can also believe that this barking dog is another miracle and right now Mitch is on his way to us…" he was saying. He looked outside and knew his words might not be true; as the day was turning into night.

He knew they had to prepare for another frigid night in the cave. "Here take this," Geoff said.

He handed her a piece of jerky. "I can't eat it. It's your food," she said. She turned her head knowing he was offering her his short supply.

"It isn't much, but if we conserve we can make it last for a while," he said. He looked at her with trust in his eyes. "Take it," He saw hesitation in her eyes. "For your daughter," He held the jerky out to her.

She took the piece of dried meat. "You're a good, generous man. Thank you," Was all she said. She took the hard meat. "The only thing I've ever liked about this stuff is that it takes your mind away from food because you can chew on it forever," She smiled.

He started to laugh. "You know you're right. The longer you chew the bigger it gets," They both chuckled and chewed at the same time.

The dog continued to howl outside and the mama dog tended her pups. They were trying to make the most of this bad circumstance. And if seen by a stranger they would have looked more like a couple enjoying a picnic instead of a life threatening situation.

Chapter Eleven

Memories of Yerik's Return

Colleen and Kuruk continued to sit on the hearth and talk about the past and the present. It seemed Kuruk always brought up situations from the past when trouble was brewing, as it was now with the return of the cats to Peaceful Valley. He believed they could learn from their mistakes, and Colleen agreed with him.

"After that terrible blizzard Ricky may have lost the constant companionship of his dad, but he got his puppy, Rex..." Colleen was saying to Kuruk. They both spotted Ricky leading Rex around the room.

Ricky seemed to be looking for someone in particular. "I think I know his intent," Kuruk said. He winked at Colleen. They both knew he was looking for Abby.

Just then Rex took a playful leap in front of his sister, Queenie. "They still play like puppies," Colleen commented. They both watched the large dogs play in the middle of the floor, while all watched and gave them plenty of room.

"It was the constant howling of their father that led us to them..." Kuruk was saying. He and Colleen again thought about that harsh winter when Yerik returned and Geoff and Muraco were lost in the blizzard.

But then, Antoinette interrupted their thoughts when she came next to Colleen and Kuruk. "My husband would give his life for all of us, but with his arm still…" Antoinette was saying. She knew the cats were a threat to all of them at Peaceful Valley, but with Omar's maimed arm his contribution would be minimal.

Colleen interjected. "We know Omar will protect you and your girls as well as all of us. He has proven that to us many times…" Colleen was saying. She looked at the big man where he sat with his daughters huddled around him. She noticed he hung his head low. Then she remembered it was a happy day when he and Antoinette married, a day that Antoinette's mother, Camille openly celebrated. Not like when she first met Omar, when she did not like his black color; but with complete rejection of any racial prejudice. And on their wedding day Camille totally welcomed Omar and his precious daughter, Theresa into their family. "The protection of those inside the compound is just as important as those on the outside. And we all know with him inside at least four more men can hunt outside," Colleen said, as Kuruk nodded in agreement.

"Yes, he's a strong man; but his marred arm makes the hunt outside…" Antoinette was trying to explain why her husband was unable to hunt the cats outside.

"He will join me on the inside…" Kuruk lifted his injured leg.

Antoinette placed her hand on Kuruk's shoulder. "Thank you. I know you understand," She then looked at Colleen. "You know, I believe I loved Omar the moment I saw him. And when he saved me from the bandits I knew my love would last a life time," Antoinette had love in her eyes. She looked at Omar as he sat with Theresa and their daughter. "We have our beautiful daughter and his Theresa is as close to my heart as ever…" She smiled as she looked at her family. But she could feel her husband's despair knowing he was incapable to join in the fight outside. He was still suffering after the cat's claw so many years before had left his arm impaired.

"You've grown a true woman's heart," Colleen said. She smiled, when she remembered the time Antoinette's desires were set on Mitch.

"I can speak with him," Kuruk commented. He grabbed his leg and grunted as he rose from his seat on the hearth.

"I think he would like that," Antoinette said. She then took Kuruk's seat next to Colleen. "You know, I was a young, spoiled brat back then. It may have taken a while, but a good man can make a girl change her way of thinking," Antoinette bowed her head. She had a flush of pink turning to red on her cheeks. "I was a little vixen in my day," She then added with a nervous laugh.

"Yes, you certainly were," Colleen added. Both women looked at each other and started to laugh. "But now you have a beautiful family," Colleen patted Antoinette's hand. They both looked over where Kuruk was speaking with Omar and they saw Omar extend his black hand to Kuruk and with a big grin on his face shake the Indian's hand.

"Kuruk sure has a way about him," Antoinette said. She let out a deep sigh. She rose from her seat to join her family with Kuruk. "Talk with you later Colleen," Antoinette left Colleen on the hearth alone.

Mitch walked up to Colleen and joined her on the hearth. "Everyone's concerned about the return of the cats, but they all seem to be in control,"They both noticed everyone seemed more quiet. "You seemed in deep conversation with Kuruk. Did he say any more about the cats?" he curiously asked Colleen.

"Believe it or not we were talking about the first time we met and how he knew about The Portal in me," Colleen glanced at her husband. She knew his understanding of her as a Portal was unclear to him but that because it was a part of her he accepted it.

"Oh," was all he said. He then looked at Kuruk, who waved an acknowledgement to him and continued to speak with Omar.

"Omar is concerned that he will only protect from inside the walls," Colleen explained to him. 'He's still as handsome as when I first met him,' she thought of Mitch when he looked at her.

"You have a look on your face," Mitch smiled at her. "We'll beat them again," He believed her look to be her concern about the cats.

"I know. But I was thinking how lucky I am to have such a loving, not to mention good looking husband," She had a tender look in her eyes.

"Back then, when I left the stockade to fight the cats at the Timms, my last thoughts, before we went out, were about you," To get comfortable, as a person only could on the hard surface, he shifted his weight on the hearth. "I wished I had held you in my arms one more time..." He smiled and had a sincere look in his eyes.

She gently touched his lips with her fingers. "We're always here," She took his hand and pressed it to his chest and then cuddled it in her hand next to her heart. "Forever," She winked at him. They looked deep in each other's eyes and could feel the love between them.

Ricky came up to them by the hearth. "Aunt Collie..." he was saying. He had a calm tone in his voice.

"Hi there..." Colleen greeted Ricky with a hug. 'I still can't get used to his deep voice. Oh well, part of growing up...' she thought. "This must be serious you called me Aunt..." she slightly smiled.

Ricky seemed somewhat eager as he stood in front of Colleen and Mitch. "You know I'm not a kid anymore; I'm almost twenty one, and old enough to fight outside this time," he said.

Colleen felt a cloud cover her. "Ricky," was all Colleen could say. She looked at her husband with pleading eyes.

"I think we can talk about that later. I don't know what your Dad would think about it..." Mitch was saying.

Ricky interjected. "Dad always said us Banks always look out for others," he looked at Colleen with concern in his eyes. "Dad showed me many times how to care for myself and other people..." He had a mature manner about him. "I especially remember how much he cared when he searched for Muraco during that blizzard..." Ricky was saying.

Colleen spoke up. "I can't believe you said that. Kuruk and I were just talking about that time. I guess when our peaceful way of life is threatened we remember past times of danger," Colleen said.

Mitch joined in the conversation. "Yeah, I remember back then when Yerik and Agnes had made it here just before the snowstorm really hit us hard, but his dogs were out in it..." Mitch was saying.

"Yeah, I was young back then, but I remember I thought Yerik's idea to save Dad and Muraco was farfetched," Ricky said. "And I also thought if you went out there to try and find them, and his idea didn't work; well, I was scared I might lose you too..." He looked at Mitch. "I guess us Banks' always have others on our minds..." Ricky said. He turned his head. He wanted to emphasize that the Banks family always put others first.

Colleen noticed Ricky looked towards Abby. He had a look she had never before seen in his eyes. "I think you're right. You guys are brave and always look after others. And that might be why I can't help but love the Banks' men so much..." Colleen was saying. She noticed, like he always had in the past, Ricky perked up when she included him as a Banks man. "But, I think, even though a person's brave; it's the unknown that's the most scary," she added.

"And I think that's where faith comes in..." Ricky looked at her.

"Maybe you are old enough for the hunt," Colleen had tears in her eyes.

"We all have each other's backs..." Mitch said. He hugged his wife. "And back then, Yerik sure had our backs during that blizzard. The cave wasn't that far away, but with the mountains of ice and snow it seemed like it was a hundred miles away. I can still see the look in Yerik's eyes when he thought about how we could save Geoff and Muraco..." he looked at Ricky and Colleen. He could tell they were also remembering about that life threatening blizzard all those years ago when lives were threatened by Mother Nature.

***

Mitch and Yerik had just re-entered Peaceful Valley's stockade after their one-on-one discussion outside.

"Everyone may we have your attention please..." Yerik was saying. He raised his arms. "My wife and family know that the treacherous storm has most likely stranded Geoff and Muraco. But I come from a land of deep snow and ice. So I believe with your help we can possibly make a way to search for them now before it's too late," Yerik said, getting everyone's undivided attention.

"Yerik said his dogs are out in this also, and we just heard his dog, Pepper howling near the cave," Mitch said, as the place went silent.

"I know my dogs. The female's pregnant. They would find shelter, and most likely Geoff and Muraco are with them..." Yerik was saying. "If we can gather the supplies we need, I know I can make implements to help us save them..." Yerik was saying. They all gathered close and listened to him and started on the project to bring Geoff and Muraco home.

***

Meanwhile Geoff and Muraco were doing their best to stay alive. "It's been almost four days," Muraco said to Geoff. "At least Papa dog's kept his family in meat…" she was saying. The dogs were finishing a rabbit that the male dog had caught for his family.

"They would have starved otherwise," Geoff said. "We only have enough jerky for us and that's getting pretty scarce," he only said to let her know, but not to make her feel she was not worthy of the food.

"I can't say it enough. I am so sorry for getting you involved in this. Now that I want to live I probably won't. And I won't see my baby girl grow to be a beautiful woman…" she was saying. Her tears started to flow down her cheeks like rain.

"Muraco you will live. Don't tell me how I know it but I do. We both are fighters, and we will get through this…" He came next to her and held her gently in his arms.

"You give me faith…" She looked deep in his eyes and saw something she knew she could trust. "Geoff, I see love in your eyes," She could not stop looking in his eyes.

"I think you're right. And I hope that's the same thing I see in your eyes too?" he whispered.

She gently caressed his cheek. "If God saves us from this I can only hope this lives in us forever," She lay her head on his chest and they hugged each other, as the Papa dog went to the entrance of the cave and again started his insatiable howling.

***

That blizzard, all those years ago was a tough time, and the waiting and wondering was the worst part of it. Knowing their loved ones were in a life or death situation took a toll on all of them. But in the end, when their fate was known, all that was left were the tales to be told of the adventure. And that was what they were continuing to do now.

"Yeah, Ricky what your Dad said was right; we all fight to protect our loved ones," Mitch cleared his throat and tried to conceal a slight chuckle. "I can still see the look on my brother's face when we all entered the cave..." he was saying to Ricky and Colleen. He looked across the room in search of his brother. "He kind of had that same silly grin on his face like he does right; you know, kind of shocked and happy at the same time. All I can say is I'm sure glad things turned out the way they did. And one of the best things is that the two of them found someone to love again..." He saw that Geoff noticed he was looking at him. Geoff winked at his brother. Mitch watched Geoff squeeze his wife, Muraco and whisper in her ear. She smiled and looked right at Mitch. She was holding their young baby girl.

Mitch started to openly laugh. He could not get the image of his brother out of his mind when they first entered the cave and found him with Muraco. He remembered Geoff was huddled with Muraco and the dogs at the back of the cave. "When we first entered the cave we all could smell the wet fur; so our first thought was grizzly bear..." Mitch continued to look at Geoff. "Of course we didn't think about the dogs making that smell. I guess fear just comes naturally sometimes..." Colleen and Ricky started to laugh with him. "And when Geoff first stood up, unshaven, with his blanket draped over him..." He held his stomach he was laughing so hard. "I'm telling you he sure did look like a bear..." He noticed Geoff and Muraco started to walk towards them. "...And all of us coming to save the day wearing Yerik's snow-shoes..." He looked at Ricky and Colleen.

They were getting involved in his story. "The shape of those lanky shoes with the leather straps made sense. But they were so big they almost looked more like sleds than shoes..." Colleen laughed.

Ricky was also getting involved. "I know it took us a while to make them but it was sure worth it..." Ricky said. He looked over at his dad.

They all laughed, as Mitch went on with the story. "But when Geoff saw them on our feet; he just busted out laughing..." he said.

Geoff and Muraco came next to them by the hearth. "I can tell you're talking about me looking like a bear again," Geoff smiled at them.

"I wish I had a picture of you...then you'd understand..." Mitch tried to subdue his laughter. He rose for Muraco to take his seat.

"I was so cold I'm surprised I could even get up so fast," Geoff said. He winked at Muraco.

Muraco buried her head next to her baby daughter and cuddled her close to her chest. "You were my protector..." Muraco said. She had an evident blush on her face. She knew Geoff never mentioned her true intent, to anyone, about why she walked out into the snow storm that night.

"Everyone's getting ready for the hunt..." Geoff said changing the subject.

"You two sure don't look like the cats put the fear in you..." Mitch was saying to his brother, Geoff and Muraco.

Geoff put his hand on his wife, Muraco's shoulder. "I don't want to say we're not afraid, because we both know we have to be on our guard and always alert with the cats. But, it seems that since we beat the odds against a sure death out in the wilds we both have a greater trust in God. And we believe that when the time comes that we meet our maker...well...what can I say, we're ready for it..." Geoff was saying. He noticed Muraco looked up at him and shook her head in agreement. "That was one of the reasons we married so soon after that incident..." he winked at his wife.

Muraco joined in his conversation. "Life's too short, and we knew we never wanted to wake up alone again," she winked back to her husband.

Just then, Ricky's dog, Rex started to bark and come towards them with his sister, Abby's female shepherd Queenie. Abby was right behind the dogs. Yerik had given Ricky the male and Abby the female offspring of his dogs that were born in the blizzard. "Queenie keeps on whining...I think she wants to play again..." Abby commented.

The two dogs started to the middle of the floor again. "Rex, be careful," Ricky shouted. He and Abby followed the dogs and they both started to laugh as they watched the dogs playing.

"Geoff, I can tell Ricky's been acting kind of left out lately," Colleen said. She noticed Muraco shook her head in agreement.

"I think it's more like puppy love," Geoff then said.

They all looked at Ricky and Abby and could see love was in the air. "I have a feeling it's more than that..." Colleen said. She noticed Muraco shook her head in agreement.

"When this is all over I'm going to have a long father son talk with him..." Geoff was saying.

Soon, the tone in the room turned tense when they all directed their attention to the importance of their meeting and started to make plans to congregate and again battle the force of the threatening cats.

Chapter Twelve

BD Returns

The citizens of Peaceful Valley, fully armed were making their final preparations against the deadly cats that threatened them. They gathered at the stockade's community center making ready to leave for the hunt. Suddenly, there was a loud knock on the door and the door abruptly opened. "Oh my God it's BD," Colleen shouted. She ran to her stepfather. "Dad…" she shouted.

Quickly, she looked behind him. "Not on this trip Collie," BD told her. He knew she was looking for his wife, Beatrice, Colleen's mother, and Colleen's half-brother, Joseph. "But our group did bring in something I think you're all going to really be happy about…" he started out the door.

All in the room went silent and followed him outside. "Thank God…looks like the leader…" Colleen came next to a big cat draped over one of the pack mules. "I think you can smell trouble," She came next to BD and gave him a generous hug.

"You know, I think you're right…when something's not right, I can almost feel it in the air. So I packed up and…" BD neared the giant cat as everyone cheered.

"Wow Grandpa this is great, any more out there?" Ricky asked. He hugged his grandfather.

"Besides this monster, I guess you can say we left a lot of food out there for the buzzards," BD put his arm around his grandson. "Lucky thing for us is; I think by coming from the opposite direction, we took them off guard and surprised them." He watched everyone gather around the large beast.

"You saved a lot of lives..." Mitch said. "Look at the size of those paws. Just thinking about his claws makes my skin crawl..." He looked at his wife, and she came next to him and hugged him.

Omar came next to them holding his arm. "Me too...some things just won't let you forget," Omar said. He came next to BD and shook his hand.

BD had an understanding look in his eyes. "I'm not going to say it was easy..." BD was saying.

Omar looked him in the eyes. "You don't have to explain. I've a pretty good idea we all know where you're coming from," Omar said. He went up to examine the large cat.

BD started to look around the crowd that had gathered. "Colleen is Olivier around?" he asked. He walked towards one of the covered wagons.

Camille LaFarge heard him. "I believe he's in his workshop," She came next to BD.

"Always working on something..." BD continued to look for something in the wagon when he heard a faint whimper. "I didn't forget about you all..." He uncovered and pulled out two large caged kennels. "Here you go..." He opened the cages and five dogs jumped to the ground from each of the cages.

"Mercy..." Camille shouted.

BD reached for two of the dogs in front of him. "Collie..." he shouted.

Colleen and Mitch came next to him. "Golly, puppies," Colleen shouted. She had excitement in her voice.

"These two German shepherds are for you and Mitch. In Ricky's last letter he told us about Rex and Abby's Queenie.

These two are not related, so now you can start some families," He picked up the dogs and placed one in Colleen's arms and the other in Mitch's.

"How cute...Thank you so much...I've always wanted a dog of my own..." Colleen cuddled the puppy. "See now you're free from that ole pen," She looked at BD and then to Mitch. "That's her name Free," She nuzzled her new friend. "Oh look she wants her buddy..." Colleen almost lost her grip on Free when she leaped for the male dog in Mitch's arms.

Both dogs started to lick each other. "Well, I guess you named him too," Mitch said. He noticed Colleen did not understand what he meant. "You said Free wants her buddy..." he was saying.

They both laughed. "Buddy..." They simultaneously said.

BD laughed with them. "The other pups are up for grabs," he said. He noticed Camille looking them over. "If you want one; I'd take that female collie mix over there. She's gentle and would make a great pet," He watched Camille pick up the pup.

"Thank you. She's a sweetie," She looked around for her husband, but Claude was nowhere to be found. "BD is this why you asked me to come over by the wagon?" Camille asked. She noticed BD was still searching for something in the wagon.

"Well, I was wondering where Olivier is. I have some supplies for him," He continued his search.

"He said he was working on some kind of a weapon against the cats," Camille told him. "He's always trying to figure out some kind of..." she continued.

BD interrupted her. "I know, and I have something that might help him," BD found the crate he was looking for. He went near Colleen and Mitch. "Can you find Geoff and Ricky and bring them to Olivier's workshop?" he asked them.

"What's up?" Colleen asked. She noticed the crate he was holding. She had many questions in her eyes.

"I'll let you know when you get there; and could you also bring Kuruk?" He was following Camille to Olivier's workshop.

"We'll be right there," Colleen looked at Mitch and they left to find Geoff, Ricky and Kuruk.

BD and Camille reached the workshop. "Wow, what the heck does he have on the roof?" BD asked Camille. The roof of the work shop was sectioned with glass panels.

Camille looked at BD. "He gets his heat from the sun…and other uses…" She tried to hurry BD inside the workshop.

But BD continued to examine the panels. "I'll have to ask him where he got the glass. It's a commodity we don't see around much out here. What a mind he has…" A wide grin lit up his face. "Solar panels…something very unusual out here…" He looked at Camille.

Camille was happy about the way BD spoke of her son. She was used to people thinking and speaking of him as a weird recluse. "They work. But like you said not enough materials around to make them," She smiled at him, and they entered the workshop Olivier never locked.

Olivier always poured his heart in his work. He completely focused on his idea at hand and found it hard to even communicate with others when he was deeply involved in a project. Even when his mother, Camille and BD entered his workshop he continued with his task until they overtly made themselves known to him.

"Olivier," Camille shouted. "Olivier…" she again shouted. When she saw what he was working on she did not near her son.

BD loudly banged on the door. Olivier stopped his work. "BD…" he shouted. He put down a jagged arrow he was sharpening. "How good to see you my friend…" He acknowledged his mother only with a nod; and then vigorously shook BD's hand. "It's been too long…" He wanted to return to his project, but nervously stood in front of them.

"I see you could kill many cats with that catapult..." BD went next to the weapon Olivier was working on. "Do you think you could put it aside for the moment?" He knew the intense motivation behind the man; and how focused he could be.

"Son...BD killed the beasts..." Camille calmly said. She looked at Olivier. She thought he looked in shock.

Olivier could feel a hot sweat cover his body. He had worked so diligently that he had not even taken breaks to eat, drink or relieve himself. "This will work...I'm certain..." He urged BD to come and look at his catapult. "You see I have many sharp spears. And look we won't have to go near the cats...this will save many lives..." he was saying. "All we have to do is position it where we want out there...I fixed up this crystal radio receiver that will detonate this gun powder and hurl the spears..." he was saying. He did not hear what his mother said about BD's annihilation of the beasts that had threatened them.

"Olivier..." Camille again tried to get her son's attention. She also knew how devoted he was to his work. "BD killed the beasts. We do not have to fight this time..." she was softly saying. She wanted to hold her son in her arms.

"Dead...all of them..." Olivier looked from his mother to BD.

"Yes Olivier, all of them..." BD positively nodded his head and confirmed it to him.

Olivier started to scratch his head and look for his chair near his desk. His workshop was always cluttered with his experiments, but he knew each one of them by heart. This was not clutter to him. In his mind each area was a special organized undertaking. "Wow, that's great," He sat down on his chair. "Forgive me; I know I look a fright..." Olivier started to shiver. Suddenly, he understood what they were saying and a great relief came over him.

BD came next to him. "Your catapult will work, just not today," He quietly said. He put his hand on Olivier's shoulder.

"Yes it will," Olivier whispered. "But thank God, not today..." He put his head in his hands and wept.

BD calmly spoke to him. "Let's go get you cleaned up," BD whispered. Just then Colleen and Mitch, Geoff and Muraco and Ricky and Kuruk entered the workshop. "We'll be right back... can you wait here?" BD asked them. He then took Olivier by the arm and they left.

Camille had a passive look on her face. "Ricky, could you find Claude and bring him here?" Camille asked.

Ricky quickly left. They all looked around the workshop. Some of them had never visited Olivier in his shop. But Kuruk was not one of them. He had visited Olivier many times. "This is incredible..." Kuruk was admiring the catapult.

"He works so hard..." Camille said. She still held the puppy in her arms. 'He never even noticed me holding my puppy,' she thought.

"We know..." Colleen said. She came next to Camille. "He's a genius," she added. "What a cutie..." She petted Camille's new puppy.

Camille smiled. "She is a cutie..." She let the puppy lick her face. "Does that sound like a good name...Cutie?" She looked at Colleen.

"Well she sure is one. Hey Cutie meet Free," They both put the puppies down and they joined Ricky's Rex and Mitch's Buddy.

Camille came next to Colleen. "I don't understand all of this stuff, but Olivier believes in all of it," She looked around the large room.

Ricky returned with Claude. "What's going on?" Claude asked.

He came next to his wife. "BD wanted to bring this to Olivier," She showed him the chest. "And our son was working on this..." Camille led Claude to the catapult.

Kuruk was examining the spear hurling apparatus. "I don't quite understand his firing mechanism, but the rest will work..." Kuruk was saying. "Ingenious...how he did this in such a short time; and the unique parts he used..." he continued to inspect the catapult.

Camille and Claude came next to him. "You know how he scrounges. Look at the arrow heads on his spears. He said you taught him..." Camille was saying.

Kuruk picked up one of the spears. "Yes he learns well..." he commented. "The flint and agate of the different arrow heads are cut perfectly," He turned the spear around in his fingertips. "Balance seems right too..." he was saying.

In the meantime BD was waiting while Olivier freshened up. "These are unusual..." BD was examining some project parts Olivier was working on in his room at the LaFarge home.

Olivier was in a dressing closet changing his clothes. "They are for the crystal radio..." He spoke to BD from behind the closed door. "You wouldn't believe my idea..." He came out of the closet. He was buttoning up his shirt.

"I think I would believe anything you said," BD commented. "This material for the antenna; does it work?" he asked.

"You know copper was my downfall, not much to find or use; so I had an idea," he looked at BD. "It worked; I think it's the fiber. I never thought of it as fiber, but it works...it's not copper, but it works..." Olivier felt a sense of relief. BD and Kuruk were his mentors and his sounding boards. They understood where his ideas came from and always gave him support for his projects.

BD gave him an inquisitive look. "What works...what is it?" BD asked.

"Don't laugh..." Olivier sat on the edge of his bed and put on his socks and shoes. He looked at BD and knew he could trust him. "Hair..." he smiled broadly at BD.

"Hair," BD twirled the antenna in his hand.

"Yes, I found that the hearty tensile strength of the fibrous material works. I really never worked with copper, so I don't have anything to compare it with, but I do know that it works," Olivier took a bite of a sandwich BD took the liberty to make for him while he was freshening up. "Thanks, by the way," He held up the sandwich.

"No problem..." BD continued to look at the long, light weight antenna. "So you're saying the inside of this is made up of hair?" He had an amazed look on his face. "It must have taken a long time to collect this much..." he continued to look at Olivier.

"You'd be surprised at how much is lost in just one day. And no one ever questioned me they just gathered it and I collected it," A big grin lit up Olivier's face. "It's a mix...you know human and animal..." he was saying.

"What's this on the outside?" BD asked.

"I had a hard time trying to figure that one out; then I started thinking about papyrus, but I used mashed leaves with a mixture of flour and water. It's something like papier-mâché," He noticed BD nodded that he understood him. "It takes some time to shape it over the fibers, but what else do I have..." He slightly laughed. "I braided the longer strains as connectors. That one might not work the way I want it to...but who knows..." he grinned. "I found that the longer the antenna the better the reception...you know on my crystal radio," He had a questioning look in his eyes. He knew not everyone was aware of his working with the radio or even why he spent so much time with it or any of his projects.

"I know some of the aspects behind the works of the crystal radio..." BD was saying. "I know the power comes from the crystals and it's only a receiver," He explained what he knew.

Olivier felt relieved to speak with BD about his projects. "Yes, that's right, and a lot of the information you sent me really helped me to reverse it; and now I believe I can also use it as transmitter," Olivier said. He was overly excited. "Well, I know if I can reach a quality high quantum radio wave frequency, I might be able to send a voice message...I've been working with the parts on those speakers and microphones you sent me with the head phones," His eyes were opened wide. "I've stayed up late many a night trying to hook into somebody else out there possibly using the amplitude modulation radio waves." He noticed BD did not understand where he was coming from. "Way back, before my time...you know, before the crack...Well, from what I've read, what were called, ham operators used the lower amplitude modulation, you know AM frequency radio waves. It's a lower amplification and is usually used mostly at night when wave traffic isn't as congested. So I've been trying to get a handle on it..." Olivier found it hard to explain all of his thoughts.

He was certain his ideas would work, but he did not know how to perfectly explain everything he had been working on for so many years. "Well, one thing I did was instead of using the crystal diodes, I fixed up some crystal triodes with the impure property of the hair to amplify an electrical signal that oscillates; you know, goes back and forth; so now, if its working properly; not only can I receive, but also send out voice messages...I think it's worked already, but I haven't gotten any responses," He was thrilled to talk with BD. "I'll tell you; it isn't easy. This special technique of adding my pure crystal semiconductor materials to the right amount of impurities didn't happen overnight," He scratched his head and looked at BD. "But I believe I've found a magnetic radio wave that has the quantum frequency I need, but I just have to be able to tune in to it. In other words…my sending grid needs to find a receiving grid…" He was excited. "I know I talk a lot…but…" He looked at BD.

"It's okay, and guess what…I think I met your match out there…and found that receiving grid you're talking about," BD gave Olivier a curious look.

"You what…" Olivier shouted. "You can't know how happy that makes me…somebody with knowledge of technology. We can collaborate…" Olivier jumped into BD's arms. "You really don't know how happy you've made me…" He almost squealed.

"I think I have some idea…" BD hugged him.

"How…who…" Olivier asked. He started to settle down.

"There are other set ups along the way here. And this one I'm talking about is operated exactly like yours…and with the same kind of enthusiasm as you have," BD was telling Olivier. "Hey, maybe we'd better get over to your workshop; everyone's waiting on us," He added.

"Yeah, okay, but can you elaborate on that other operation. You can't know how exciting it is to know someone is out there like me doing the same thing," Olivier said.

They started for his workshop. "Well, on our way here many of the settlements along the way are showing great signs of technological advancement," He looked at Olivier. "And I was introduced to a young inventor, around your age, just like yourself," He noticed Olivier's face flushed a full red color.

"Oh God, thank you," Olivier shouted. He was not a kid anymore, but at that moment he sure felt like one. "Tell me, what's his name?" Olivier stopped walking for the moment.

"Well, for one thing, he's a she and her name's…" BD was saying.

Olivier jumped up so high BD thought he might fall flat on his face. "Oh God, thank you God..." He tried to compose himself as he stood in front of BD; and his eyes asked BD to tell him her name.

"Her name's Wilhelmina Gates," BD told him.

Olivier had a completely serene look on his face. "Wilhelmina...surrender my heart," He had tears in his eyes.

"I know this might sound somewhat weird, but after I told her about you she insisted I give you this note...But now that I see how you act I think maybe it's not so weird," BD reached inside his coat pocket and withdrew the note and handed it to Olivier.

Olivier held the note in his hand. "I've been waiting for this all my life; I savor the moment..." He looked at BD. "I'll read it later; we have pending issues right now," Olivier quietly said. He completely subdued his feelings and had a reserved tone in his voice.

BD could not believe how Olivier changed his thoughts and actions so quickly. 'He's quite a remarkable man,' he thought.

They again started for the workshop. "Golly, I still can't believe it about the cats..." Olivier glanced at BD. "I know my catapult would've worked..." He surmised.

"Olivier, I know it will work. We can save it for another time. But for now let me tell you you're going to be really happy when you see what I've brought you. Wilhelmina put them together for you. She left a lot of instructions, so I know they will help you," They were reaching Olivier's workshop where everyone was waiting for them. BD noticed on one hand, Olivier seemed completely in charge of his thoughts, but on the other hand; he seemed to be thinking of his future research. "They're just parts, but I'm sure with your technology and her instructions you'll get them to work..." BD looked at Olivier, who quietly smiled at him as he opened the door to his work shop.

***

After BD gave Olivier the chest of parts from Wilhelmina Gates; everyone could tell the inventor in Olivier needed his time alone.

"BD, I can never thank you enough for all that you've done for me. All of these supplies and mostly for this..." Olivier patted his chest where he had placed his note from Wilhelmina.

BD understood what he meant and he reached to shake Olivier's hand. "No problem my friend; we all have to take care of each other..." BD was saying.

Colleen came next to them. "I can tell Olivier wants to continue his experiments, so would everyone like to come on over to our house?" she asked them.

"That works for me; I have a lot to tell you..." BD started for the door.

Ricky came next to Colleen. "Collie, I have something to do. Is it okay if I come by later?" He seemed a bit anxious.

"That's fine Ricky. Have supper with us..." She hugged her nephew. "Come on everyone. Camille, want to help me with a must go supper?" Colleen asked, with a chuckle in her voice.

Camille had an inquisitive look on her face. "Must go?" Camille asked.

"Sure, everything left over must go..." She hooked her arm in Camille's arm.

"Colleen, you're so funny..." Camille laughed. "Let's get on with it..." They all left Olivier to his inventions.

Olivier wanted to savor this moment. He was over thirty years old and life seemed to be passing him by. He patted his chest where Wilhelmina's note was tucked in close to his heart. "I can almost feel you," he said.

He reached for the note. "Dearest Olivier," he read. "BD told me about your crystal radio set up and I would like to commend you on your inventive curiosity..." He felt his heart skip a beat. Someone understood him.

He read on. "With the parts and instructions BD is giving you it will be possible for you and me to communicate..." Wilhelmina wrote.

Olivier jumped to his feet. "I knew there was a way. And now I know I can do it..." he shouted. He kissed the note.

He continued to read. "After you follow the instructions I have enclosed in the chest of parts; please direct your signals as follows: My call signal is Q98. For our radio communications, you are Q99. Every night from midnight till six in the morning I will be tuning in on the AM frequency waves. The secret to our communication are satellites. The solar batteries in the orbiting satellites have kept them active over all these years. If you follow my codes, your signal will transmit to the satellite and then back to the frequency modulation, where I will be waiting for your call signal. Good luck, Q98 signing off," she concluded her note.

Olivier quickly put her note down. He went to the chest and opened it. "Instructions, just like she said," He carefully took out the top covered parts and read her instructions. "Holy cow, I can do this...keep focused boy...just keep focused. Maybe by tomorrow night I'll hear her sweet voice..." He could almost feel her next to him urging him in the right directions. He started his new project. It was a new trek that would take him to his next step in life; a step that might be a winding road, but if it turned out like he planned it, his future would be blessed and he would finally find a way to settle down.

Chapter Fourteen

Ricky's Proposal/Plans Are Made

Later, on the same evening of BD's return to Peaceful Valley, everyone felt the quiet peace return to their valley after the annihilation of the cats. A cool fog was forming over the lake and the bright; full moon was made for young lovers.

Ricky and Abby were strolling near the stream by the lake. "You were going to fight the cats weren't you?" Abby stopped and looked at Ricky.

He looked in her eyes. "Yes. I had to. I've been thinking about a lot of things lately, and one of them is how much I want to take care of people…and things…and…" He was stumbling on his own words. He really wanted to take her in his arms, kiss her and tell her she was the most important one he wanted to keep safe; and that she was the one he would do anything for. 'God, she's so beautiful,' he thought.

She took hold of his hand. "Ricky, I've loved you from the first day I saw you," She did not shy away from him. For many years she had seen a love in his eyes for her and knew he had a hard time trying to explain it to her.

When she took his hand he felt a spark go directly to his heart; but he did not remove his hand from hers. "Things seem to come easy for you," He hoped he did not sound like an idiot. "I had a hard time after Pavel. We were so close; and I know you wanted to be my..." He could not even say the word buddy. In his mind she was something way more than a buddy; but he was thinking about how he never wanted to get close to her. "I don't know if it really was because you're a girl or maybe because I didn't want my heart to break again by getting close to someone I might have to lose one day," He was pouring his heart out to her, and it made him feel good that she did not flinch or act like what he was saying was silly.

"I know exactly what you mean. We have learned a lot over the years. And we have learned these things together..." She squeezed his hand. "But Ricky, I'm not that little girl anymore...I'm a woman...I have a woman's heart that loves you deeply..." She came closer to him. "I could tell by the look in your eyes that you were going to go hunt. I didn't know what to do. I knew I couldn't beg you not to go; you're not a boy anymore, and I know we both have to take on greater responsibilities. But I'll tell you something; I was going to tell you before you left how I felt about you. I didn't want anything to happen..." She buried her head in his chest and started to sob.

He held her close. She looked up at him and quieted her sobs. While looking in her eyes he took his hand and wiped away her tears. "I guess those cats did a good thing after all, because I was going to tell you the same thing..." He felt his eyes moisten with tears. "I love you too. And I have for some time now, but being the stubborn..." he was saying.

She put her fingers to his lips. "Yes, I know your stubborn side. I've seen it many times over the years," They both laughed. "But I've also seen your kind, loving side; and you know what's really funny..." She looked at him with her deep love showing in her eyes. She thought he looked a little scared at what she was going to say. "Honey I love it all; the stubborn and the loving.

They're you and I love you…" She reached behind his head and gently pulled him close to her.

Their lips touched with a tender kiss. They separated and looked in each other's eyes. They hugged. "Would I be taking a big risk if I took this time to ask you to marry me?" Ricky had only a slight bit of hesitation in his voice.

"I'd be completely hurt if you didn't. So…"While waiting she coyly looked at him.

"Will you…" he was saying.

"Yes…yes…yes…" She did not let him finish. And then she jumped to hug him.

"Wow…" he said. He picked her up into his arms. "I love you…I love you…" he kept on saying. It was his heart shouting something he had wanted to say for a long time. "Let's go tell our folks," He put her down but could not take his arm from her.

"Let's…" she said. She put her head on his chest. "I'm the happiest woman in the world…" She squeezed his hand and they went to tell their families their good news.

***

Meanwhile back at Colleen and Mitch's, after their supper, Camille and Claude along with their new puppy Cutie had left for home. "Look how peaceful they look…" Colleen pointed to the puppies, Free and Buddy, on a rug near the fireplace.

Kuruk, Geoff and Muraco with their daughter, Alegro, had stayed for after dinner drinks and conversation with BD's news.

Colleen picked up Free and went to sit on her cushioned rocker. "She's just precious," She petted her puppy.

Buddy came next to them. "Are you jealous Buddy," Colleen said, but Buddy lay down next to the rocker.

Mitch came and sat on the hearth. "I think he just likes being close..." He smiled at his wife. "Takes after me," He winked at Colleen and took a drink of his whiskey.

Colleen looked at BD. "So Mama's okay..." She knew if anything was wrong he would have told her by now.

"Colleen," He slightly hesitated. "Your mother wanted me to tell you that she knows what the compost is," He thought she would fall off the rocker.

"What...why didn't you say so sooner..." She shouted. When the puppy started to yelp; she tried to compose herself.

"She told me to tell you when the time was right...well, now I think the time's right," BD commented. "This is something that I know only a few people are aware of," He looked at Kuruk.

Kuruk stretched his stiff leg. "I know a little about it. Not really much to know..." he said.

"I've told him about the chest Mama left with me; it's really not much of a secret. Especially when I don't know any more about it than anyone else does; that is until now...So what is it?" Colleen asked. She tried not to act to hastily.

"Well, I'm not to privy too it myself. And I don't know if you and Mitch are going to be ready for my next question...but it's a question from your mother," BD noticed Colleen's face was turning red and he knew she was getting agitated. "Well, your Mom would like you to come West and bring the chest and key with you," He thought he had better hurry and tell them all that his wife Beatrice had asked him to relate to them. "She said the only way to find out about the contents is to bring it to the compost..." BD finished what his wife asked him to say to them.

Colleen gave him a curious look. "That doesn't help much. She didn't tell you what the compost is...or anything..." She looked confused. "That's an awful long way to go for something we don't even know about," she looked at Mitch.

He also had a confused look on his face. "I'm with Colleen. That's pretty far away…" He took a gulp of his drink. He knew he did not want to leave the comforts of the home he had finally settled into with his wife.

BD looked at Colleen and Mitch. "Your mom doesn't know what's in the chest either. She wants to open it up with you…" he was saying.

Mitch noticed Geoff was looking at him. "I don't think Bea would ask you to come if it wasn't important to her. And none of us are getting any younger," Geoff said.

"It's not that I don't want to see Mom. But we're so settled, and we have our home and gardens; not to mention all the fields for the settlement…" Colleen felt responsible to help everyone. They were an undivided community; and everyone took care of each other.

Kuruk had been listening to their personal conversation. He normally never interrupted or commented unless he was asked to do so. But now he felt compelled to speak his thoughts. "Colleen, things are changing out there. Technology and ways of living are growing. You can learn new ways and share them with our community," Kuruk said.

"I don't know. We would be gone a long time…" She felt pulled in two directions. She would love to visit her mother and learn about the mystery of the chest, but she also felt obliged to her community and her home.

Just then Ricky and Abby came into the house. "You all look deep in thought," Ricky said. They startled them.

Colleen noticed Ricky was holding Abby's hand. "Oh my God…" She went to them. "You two…finally?" She looked in Ricky's eyes.

Ricky put an arm around Abby and squeezed her. "Yes… finally…" Ricky said.

"Let me see if you still have any teeth in there..." Colleen took his cheeks in her hand and gently squeezed them in a playful way.

Abby started to laugh. "It didn't hurt him too much to finally tell me how he feels about me," Abby shyly said. She knew she had spoken with Colleen over the years about her unreciprocated feelings for Ricky.

Colleen hugged them both. "He's just stubborn..." She hugged them again.

Ricky and Abby looked at each other and laughed. "That's me stubborn..." Ricky was saying.

Geoff came next to them. Ricky went to hug him. "My boy..." Geoff had tears rolling down his cheeks. He held his arms open. Colleen and Abby joined in his hug with Ricky.

BD rose from his seat. "Bea sent some bottles of wine with me...I'll be right back..." He left to get the wine.

They all settled down. "Have you set a date?" Colleen asked. She saw Abby and Ricky turn bright shades of red. "You did mean that you're getting married...right?" She thought maybe she had misread what they meant about getting together.

Ricky seemed to stiffen up. "Well, yes I asked. And yes she accepted. But her parents want a long engagement and a big wedding..." Ricky looked almost beside himself, and Abby looked the same way.

"I explained that we wanted to marry right away, but..." Abby blushed again.

"Briana knows how much you love Ricky, and I'm sure Brady really doesn't have any doubts about that..." Colleen looked confused.

"It has to do with me being their only child and wanting the best for me, or that's what they're telling us. I don't know... maybe it just shocked them when we told them..." Abby said.

BD returned with two bottles of wine. "Great for celebrating," he held up the bottles. "Bea even sent this cork screw. She thinks of everything…" He could tell they all seemed more sedate than when he left. "What's going on? Aren't we going to toast the happy couple?" He looked at them.

"Well, it seems Abby's parent's want her to wait a while; they want a big, elaborate wedding for their daughter," Colleen said.

There was a loud knock at the front door. Mitch went to see who was at the door. "Olivier…come on in…" he was saying.

Olivier hesitated for a moment when he saw that his parents were not still visiting with them. "My parents have left?" he asked.

"Yes, but come on in and visit for a while," Mitch said.

Olivier came in and Mitch led him to the hearth where they both sat down. "Well, I actually wanted to speak to BD about when he would be making his return trip," Olivier said.

"That's funny, because before Ricky and Abby came and told us they might be getting married soon that's exactly what we were talking about…" Mitch was saying.

Olivier perked up. "Married…wow, that's great," he rose from his seat. "Congratulations you two," he shook Ricky's hand and slightly bowed in front of Abby.

"Thanks Olivier," Ricky said. "But what's this about BD. Are you going back so soon?" Ricky asked his grandfather. He sat with Abby on a short sofa.

"Well, hopefully not alone. Some who came with me are going to settle here, and some came just for the trading, but your grandmother would like for Colleen and Mitch to come back with me for a visit," BD said. He did not want to get into it again about the contents of the mysterious chest or the compost.

"Wow, I would like to see Grammy too…" Ricky was saying. He looked at Abby. He thought she had that same look of dejection he had seen in her eyes many times over the years. "Of course I mean after we marry and we can go together," he added. He was not used to including someone else in his plans.

The talk of traveling urged Kuruk to speak out. "BD, if you have room, I'd also like to make the trip. Like Geoff said we're not getting any younger," he said.

"There's plenty of room if you want to make the trip. I'd like the company," BD said.

Abby started to fidget in her seat. "When are you planning to leave?" she asked.

"Actually, as soon as I can get an answer from these two," BD looked at Colleen and Mitch.

Geoff spoke up. "If you're worrying about your house and garden; we can take care of them for you," he said to Colleen and Mitch. Muraco nodded in agreement.

Colleen was feeling pressured. "It's not just that. Now we have Ricky and Abby to consider. I would love for Mom to see how happy they are..." She could feel her tears building as her throat constricted.

Abby looked at Ricky. "I'm a woman now. I'm eighteen and I want to marry you now," She stood in front of him with her hands on her hips.

Ricky had a sideways look in his eyes. "Wow, what can I say. I'm ready when you are..." He took her outstretched hand. "I think we're going somewhere..." he laughed.

Abby was leading him from the house. "We're going to tell my parents we're getting married now..." Abby shouted. She and Ricky held on to each other, and while laughing they left them.

"Well, if that goes like they want it to; we will be leaving here pretty soon," BD said. "Wouldn't you two agree?" He looked at Colleen and then Mitch.

"I'd say that's an affirmative," Colleen said. She looked at Mitch.

He lifted his glass of whiskey. "I'd say yes," He tilted the glass towards his wife and then to BD.

"This is great. I'll have to let my parents know and get my wagon ready," Olivier said. He then looked at BD. "I should've asked; we will be stopping by Wilhelmina's settlement?" he asked.

"Of course Olivier; they're on the way..." BD said.

Olivier got up from his seat on the hearth. "Well, I'll be going. I have a lot to do tonight. I've just about got all the parts together and I may be in touch with her tonight..." he said. "I'll catch up with you all later," he said. He left.

Colleen looked at BD. "Wilhelmina...who's Wilhelmina," She had a confused look on her face as did everyone in the room.

"She's a carbon copy of Olivier. She sent the parts I gave to him before. And I'm telling you, she thinks, acts and most likely breathes the same as he does. Those two have to meet because they were made for each other," BD said. "I guess we can't open these until the kids get back right?" He lifted the two wine bottles.

Colleen went next to him. "Neither of them drinks alcohol; so I guess we could open one and save the other for later. I think it might settle my nerves..." She sat next to Mitch on the hearth. He hugged her and she put her head on his shoulder.

All that was left were plans to make for the trip. Colleen felt her heart skip a beat when she thought of seeing her mother again. It had been too long, and she was sure her half-brother, Joseph must have grown as fast as a string bean. Time would be on their side and the numbers would not be too many for them not to be together again.

Chapter Fifteen

Olivier's First Contact

Ricky and Abby had a beautiful wedding. BD again played 'Twinkle Twinkle Little Star' on his harmonica with Omar accompanying him on the guitar. But this time Colleen pointed out a star as a gift to them.

A few days later, knowing they would return; Briana and Brady happily said their good-bye's to their daughter, Abaigeal and their son-in-law, Ricky, when they left on their covered wagon.

Colleen and Mitch felt almost at home as they sat side-by-side on the seat of their wagon; with BD and Kuruk sharing the wagon in front of them. "I don't think Ricky and Abby have a problem following so far behind. Not only can they keep away from the dust, but they can have a little honeymoon privacy," Colleen said. She snuggled up to Mitch.

He smiled at her. "Too bad they couldn't have had as much time for their honeymoon as we did, but time and weather wait for no man..." Mitch was saying.

"I know. And as it is we'll be hard pressed to make it before winter," She held on to his arm. She then turned and looked behind their wagon. "Looks like Olivier's doing okay," She waved at him and he waved back to her. "Did you notice all the equipment he packed? You know we'll have to feed him. Camille gave me trading goods and food. She knows her son…" They both laughed.

Later that evening; they were sitting around the campfire enjoying the last of Colleen's honey buns. "I sure have missed your honey buns. You're mom has a different recipe," BD said. "Now, don't quote me, but yours do seem lighter…Oh boy now I'm in trouble," He took off his hat and slapped it on his leg.

"It's mom's recipe so they should taste the same, but your words will never leave my lips…" Colleen laughed. She then looked at Olivier. "Things okay with you Olivier," she asked. "Maybe you should get some sleep. I'll wake you," she said.

"I thought I would've been in contact with her long ago. We'll be at their settlement before I can even hear a word from her," Olivier said.

"We still have a few weeks to go," BD said.

"Well maybe I will get some sleep. You will wake me just after midnight?" Olivier asked Colleen.

"Yes I will," Colleen said. Olivier went to his wagon. "Do you think maybe it really doesn't work like he thinks it should… Gosh I feel sorry for him," she looked at them.

Kuruk stretched his leg. "I believe he'll be in touch. Other than some devoted ancestors, I have never seen a man with such committed devotion," he said.

"You're right. It's almost like a marriage," Colleen commented.

"Speaking of marriage; I'm surprised Ricky and Abby even had time for supper…" Mitch chuckled. He looked at his wife.

"Quit teasing. They're on their honeymoon. And as I recall you wouldn't have taken the time for supper, so…" She gave him a sly glance.

"You're right…" He cleared his throat.

"Oh to be young again…" BD smiled and scratched the whiskers on his chin. They all laughed.

He then took out his harmonica. He rubbed it on his vest to shine it. "We'll be coming to Cavern City sometime tomorrow afternoon," BD said.

Colleen snuggled up with Mitch. "That sounds intriguing…" She looked at BD.

"It is. Their outside housing is similar to yours at Peaceful Valley. The cavern is used as a storm shelter, and their stores and other retail businesses are set up in it. It's huge. It's the first place I've seen where they use gold for trading. Gold and other metals are used pretty heavily the farther west you go. It takes time to get used to it. We started out trading and then people paid for our services with gold and diamonds. Some only want to trade goods for services or vice versa. It kind of depends on the availability of the commodity…" He continued to polish and slightly blow on his harmonica.

Colleen looked at him. "I love Peaceful Valley. We get along just fine…" She squeezed her husband's arm.

"I think we have a good system. Everyone works the fields and we all share the meats that are hunted or raised on the farms. We trade goods with peddlers…" Mitch was saying. "It seems the only things we're missing are the modern conveniences' and new techniques," He noticed Kuruk agreed with him.

"Peaceful Valley is a good place to live. I too believe we have a good system," he said. "But I think my son, Hania, had he lived, may have traveled west looking for other ways of life. He had a searching spirit…" Kuruk said. He smiled and slightly laughed. They all went silent for a time.

"Cavern City even has a dining restaurant," BD told them.

"Wow, no cooking for a change; I would like to try that out," Colleen said. "Look at Free and Buddy. I'm glad they're not related; when it's time they'll give us some pretty puppies," She watched the pair cuddle close while they slept.

"In my next life I'm coming back in one of your pups," Kuruk said. He started to laugh. "I'd love to be spoiled by you two..." He looked at them and winked.

"So you believe in reincarnation?" Colleen asked.

"Sure I do. My spirit will never quit; it has a lot more to do..." he smiled.

"Don't we all. Just seems like there's never enough time in the day..." Colleen said. She sat up straight and looked at BD. "Are you going to play that thing or not..." She laughed and then snuggled back into her husband's arms.

BD smiled and put his harmonica to his lips. He started with a soothing tune. They sat around the fire and enjoyed each other's company and the peaceful melodies that echoed throughout the night air.

But for Olivier this was not a quiet evening. He tried to sleep, but his eyes were wide open. It was just after midnight. He went to his radio. He had two set ups; one for sending and one for receiving. He placed his antenna on a long pole he had bolted to the side of his wagon. He put on his headset and worked the tuner to the codes Wilhelmina had given him. He could hear loud static and whining, so he knew he was connected to the wave. "Q98 this is Q99, come in please..." He listened. "No response..." This was the tenth time he had tried to get through to her that evening. He was getting frustrated. He knew he was using the right codes that Wilhelmina had given him; so he tried her signal over and over again to no avail.

So he decided to just talk to Wilhelmina. "Q98 Wilhelmina this is Q99 Ollie here, he gave himself a nickname. If you can hear me I want to tell you I have waited all of my life for someone who could understand the inventor in me," He felt a warm sensation just saying those words. "Mina," He used a pet name he picked out for her. "I put my heart in everything I do. And when I first held your note in my hand I don't know how to explain this, but I felt strange," He felt his heart open up. "I have never thought of another that I might love," He stopped talking. He felt his palms get wet. "God Mina, I have never said that word to another human being…forgive me, but I don't think I even spoke that word to either of my parents or my sister," He stood up and took off the headset.

"Get hold of yourself man…" He went outside to the water barrel attached to the side of his wagon and dipped out some water. "That feels good," He splashed some on his face and took a generous drink. "I haven't even met her and I'm talking love…I must be a bit nuts…" He laughed at himself. "Mom would give me one of her looks with that comment…" He laughed again and went back inside his wagon.

"I can't sleep," He put the headset back on. "Q98 this is Q99 come in please," He kept repeating for over an hour. He took other times to just talk to Q98, his Mina, as if she were sitting right next to him.

Finally, Colleen came and shouted from the outside the back of his wagon. "Olivier, its Colleen, are you up?" she asked.

He opened the back flap. "Thanks Colleen; I'm awake. No word yet," he told her.

"Did you get any sleep?" she asked him.

"I can't. I don't understand this. I know everything's working but she's not responding…" he was saying.

"Well, we'll get Mitch to drive for you tomorrow; and then you'll have to get some sleep…okay…" She almost sounded like his mother.

"Yes ma'am…" He smiled at her.

She left and he went on with his transmitting. "Q98 this is Q99 come in please," he said over and over again.

It was around three o'clock in the morning. He felt somewhat hoarse. "Q98 this is Q99 come in please…" he said again.

The static went away and he thought he heard a slight hum in the receiver. "Q99 this is Q98…is that you Olivier?" she said.

His eyes widened and he thought he would fall off the side of his cot. "Q98 this is Q99…yes it's me Wilhelmina…" he was saying. "I've been trying to get you forever…" he said.

"Q99 we've had a terrible storm here; my equipment almost had to be reinvented, I could only receive not send. But Ollie you have to get to cover; the storm is headed directly to you, and you could never survive in wagons out in the open…over…" she said.

He felt his perspiration go cold. "Q98 this is Q99, can you tell me what kind of storms?" he asked.

"Q99 this is Q98; Ollie we had hurricane force wind; hail and flooding rain; you must take shelter as soon as possible," she explained.

"Q98 this is Q99; I will sign off now and we will take shelter. I will try to contact you again tomorrow around this same time," he said.

"Q99 this is Q98; God go with you all Ollie," She signed off. Olivier took off his headset and took down his antenna. "I have to get them going…" he said aloud.

He started for Colleen and Mitch's wagon. "She called me Ollie…" he then said. "She said she could only receive…she heard everything I said," He had a large grin lighting up his face. "God get us through this…" he prayed. "I have got to meet this woman," He ran to their wagon.

"Colleen, Mitch…" he shouted.

Mitch opened the back flap of their wagon. "What's the matter?" Mitch shouted. He saw a terrified look in Olivier's eyes.

"I got through to Wilhelmina, and she said we must seek shelter as soon as possible; a terrible storm is headed towards us.

Colleen came next to Mitch. Mitch looked at her and then to Olivier. "Go wake the others we'll get ready," Mitch said. He looked at Colleen and they both dressed and made ready to depart the camp.

After waking the others Olivier went and prepared his wagon. They were lined up and ready to go just as the sun came over the horizon.

There were only two other wagons from the group that had come with BD to Peaceful Valley; and they were in the lead. Colleen insisted that Ricky and Abby start their party of the wagon train right after the main group; then Olivier, BD and Kuruk, with her and Mitch at the end.

BD assured them if they sped their horses at a slow trot, and rested and slightly watered them every hour they could most likely make Cavern City in less than six hours. They did not know exactly how much time they had before the storm hit; but they would survive the best way they could on the open land.

Colleen stayed in the bed of the wagon with their pups. She noticed the wind was picking up. "Wow, getting bumpy back here…" She shouted to Mitch.

He turned and looked at her. "Looks like they're taking another break…" Mitch shouted back to her.

The train formed a circle. Mitch went to water their horses; while Colleen went to check on Ricky and Abby. "How're you two doing?" Colleen asked.

Ricky jumped down and started to water their horses. "Okay Collie," Ricky shouted.

Abby jumped down from her seat on the wagon. "Wow, what a ride…" Abby said. She thought Colleen looked somewhat pale. "Are you alright, you look almost green…" She came next to Colleen.

Colleen put her hand to her mouth. "I think it's all this bouncing around…" She suddenly felt sick to her stomach.

She ran away from Abby and immediately threw up. She then went back to Abby's side. "Oh golly, I'm so sorry…" she was saying.

Abby put her arm around her. "Not your fault; I don't feel so good myself. Like you said must be all this jerking around…" Abby was saying.

Ricky joined them. "The wind's sure picking up," he said. "I think I'll go see what Olivier found out about this storm that's coming," Ricky left them.

Colleen and Abby started to message their backs. "Riding a wagon is one thing, but this fast rock and roll is sure hard on the back side," Abby said. She was trying to take Colleen's mind off of getting sick in front of her.

"I've never done that in front of anybody before…" Colleen apologized.

"We're in this together…no matter what…right?" Abby said.

"Right," Colleen said. "You're a sweetheart," She hugged Abby.

Ricky came back. "Olivier said the storm has hurricane winds; with lots of rain and hail," He glanced at Abby. He thought she had fear in her eyes. "BD says we can make it to Cavern City before another rest; but we're going to have to pick up the pace," He noticed Abby looked at Colleen.

Mitch came next to Colleen. "Ready," He put his arm around his wife.

Colleen winked at Abby. "Ready…" Colleen said. "We'll be fine," She went to Abby and gave her a quick hug.

"You know it…" Abby said. She hugged her back.

Ricky helped Abby get seated on the wagon. "Maybe it would be better if you ride in the back this time," He helped her climb in the back of their wagon. "Everything okay with you and Colleen?" Ricky asked.

Abby poked her head from behind the canvas. "Yes, don't worry about it. And here put on your poncho in case it starts raining," She handed him his rain gear.

"Thanks Honey," He took the poncho and kissed his wife. "Hang on…here we go," Ricky shouted. He flipped the reigns as they followed the leader out of the circle.

The wind was picking up and the rain was starting. They were about a mile away from Cavern City. They were running the horses faster this time.

Mitch noticed BD's wagon hit a rock and slightly tip sideways. "Oh no…" he shouted.

Colleen heard him and poked her head out. "What happened?" she screamed. The wind was howling around them making it hard to hear.

"BD's wagon tipped and now it tipped the other way… shit…" he yelled. "Whoa," He pulled back hard on the reigns and stopped his horses.

"What…" Colleen screamed.

"Someone fell off the wagon…" Mitch yelled. He noticed BD's wagon stopped.

Mitch jumped from the wagon right next to Kuruk. He was humped face down in the mud. Colleen came next to them.

BD ran from his wagon. "Let's get him in the back of your wagon. We don't have that much further to go…" BD yelled. "The storm's coming fast…" He looked around and then helped Mitch lift Kuruk into the wagon, with Colleen right behind them. They placed him on the small bed, but did not have time to check out his injuries. They actually did not know if he was dead or alive.

BD went back to his wagon. "Watch out for that bolder up here…" he yelled.

Mitch waved to him, and then jumped back on the seat of his wagon and snapped the reigns. The horses took off. The intermittent force of the wind caused the teeming rain to blow sideways and hit him with the feel of face slapping pellets.

Colleen noticed the puppies were lying around Kuruk's head. She was about to place them in the boxed bed they had for them. "Leave them…" Kuruk said. "They give me peace…" He placed his hand behind his head and brought the puppies around to his stomach. "Colleen, its bad…" he whispered. Even with his pain he softly petted the puppies.

"What can I do for you?" Colleen asked. "BD said it's not much farther. They might have a doctor…" She had to shout over the noise of the rain pelting the canvas.

"I don't know…" He had a smile on his lips. "I saw her light…" he whispered. He knew Colleen would understand him.

"Oh Kuruk…" Colleen could feel warm tears on her face. It seemed as if she were in a trance. She could no longer feel the jolts from the racing wagon or hear the thunderous rain. She felt a genuine peace all around her.

Kuruk motioned her to him. "You will have a girl…" He patted her hand.

"Oh my…so that's it…that's why I'm sick…" She had an amazing feeling in the pit of her stomach. "Oh Kuruk…" she cried.

The dogs started to squirm in his arms. Colleen noticed he had a serene look in his eyes. He then pointed up with his finger. Colleen looked up. She saw a bright, white light fill the wagon. It was as if someone had lit a lantern. And then she thought she could smell the strong scent of gardenias. "Jeanette's favorite…" she thought.

"They come for me…" he whispered. "You are The Portal…I am ready…" he then whispered.

Colleen looked up. She saw a shooting blue orb, larger than she had ever seen before; it circled in front of her and then through her. Immediately she felt the spirit of Kuruk. The white light still lit up the wagon. But then something happened that shocked her. As the blue orb left her it circled around her and entered her puppy Buddy. "Oh my..." Colleen shouted. Buddy looked at her.

But then the white light turned into an orb; it circled her and entered Free. "What's this all about..." she looked at Kuruk. He still had the serene look on his face; but his eyes showed no signs of life. She gently closed his eyes and covered his head with the blanket.

She could feel the wagon slowing down. "We're here Colleen," Mitch yelled to her. The wagon stopped. He poked his head in from the front of the wagon. He noticed Kuruk's covered body. "Oh no..." he shouted. He jumped from the wagon and came in from the back. "Oh Colleen..." He put his arm around her.

Colleen did not cry for the loss of her friend. "He's fine...he's at peace..." Mitch held her close. She still felt in a trance. She looked at her puppies. After she had covered Kuruk's body they had hopped from his side and were huddled together in their boxed bed.

Mitch continued to hold on to her. "Are you okay; I know he's your dear friend?" Mitch looked in her eyes. He thought she might be in shock.

"Mitch, before he died...he..." She did not know how to explain what had happened.

"He what Honey..." Mitch was saying.

BD came to the back of their wagon. "Hold on. I'll drive your wagon into the cavern. They have a place for us to wait out the storm..." he shouted to them. He saw Kuruk's covered body. "Damn..." he whispered. "He was a good man..." he whispered. He motioned for them to get ready.

BD drove the wagon to the spot he was instructed to by the curator. He came to the back of the wagon and opened the flap. "What a tragedy..." he was saying.

Colleen looked at BD. "He's at peace with Langundo," She did not have the energy to say anymore. She stood up and fainted in Mitch's arms.

***

The room was completely still and silent. She felt like she was walking out of a dense fog. "Am I dreaming," she said.

Mitch came next to her. "Honey it's me…" He took her hand in his.

She tried to get up, but fell back on the bed. "Mitch…" she whispered.

"Yes Honey, don't try to get up," he said.

She put her hand to her head. "What happened? Is the storm over…" She tried to open her eyes, but her eyelids felt like they had lead on them.

"You fainted. You've been out for about a day. And the storm's over," he told her.

"Kuruk…" she whispered. "He's…" she was saying.

"Yes, he's passed on…" he said. "Honey, you have to get some rest. They have a doctor here and he examined you, and…" he was telling her.

She interrupted him. "I'm going to have your baby girl," She opened her eyes and saw an amazed look in his eyes.

"Yes, that's what he said…well part of it, not the girl part," He looked at her with questions in his eyes.

She sat up against the pillow. "Just before he passed," She started to remember about the white light and Kuruk's orb. "Well, he told me I was going to have a baby girl. I know I haven't been feeling quite myself lately, and I did get sick the other day, but I never in a million years thought I might be pregnant…" she smiled at him.

"Well, you are…we are. Isn't it great?" he kissed her cheek.

She smiled at him. "It sure is great. After all these years I thought it was just going to be the two of us…" she was saying.

He squeezed her hand. "I know what you mean…" He winked at her. "Do you think you could eat something? Abby has a nice stew with some corn bread. Unless you think you might want to try the restaurant?" he asked her.

"I'll try Abby's stew. She went to all the trouble…" she said.

He got up. "I'll be right back. Everyone's going to be so happy you're feeling better…" He left the room.

Chapter Sixteen

Gates Settlement

Two days later, they were on the way again. For this trek Ricky and Abby followed the first group; with Olivier next, and then Mitch and Colleen, and BD trailing. The storm damage was very evident. "We were lucky to make it to Cavern City in time…" Mitch said. He and Colleen were riding on the wagon. She did not answer him.

He looked at her. He thought she looked in deep thought. "You're thinking about Kuruk," he said. "I'm sorry for your loss. I know he was your good friend," he commented.

She patted his hand. "He was everybody's friend," she smiled. "But, he just helped me in so many ways. He was like a father to me…" she said. "I was happy to see we left his remains in such a beautiful spot," She slightly glanced his way. "And since we believe I know his spirit is in a special place too…" She felt in a trance.

He noticed she turned her head. "He was a great man, who will be sorely missed…" he was saying.

She turned her head and could not look at him. She did not know how to explain about what had happened when Kuruk's spirit left his body. How could she explain something she had trouble trying to figure out herself?

After some time she looked inside the wagon. The dogs were peacefully cuddled together, asleep in their box bed. She could not help but stare at them. 'Did I see what I think I saw…' she thought. She remembered how the two orbs appeared to enter the dog's bodies.

Mitch looked at her. "You look strange," he said.

She closed the flap on the wagon. "Just checking out the pups…" she said to him. 'Now why didn't I tell him what's on my mind. Do I think it's so farfetched that even my husband wouldn't believe it…' she thought. 'Reincarnation…I believe in it, just never saw it; or did I?' she thought. 'I think I'll just let this alone and see what goes on…' she smiled.

From the corner of his eye, he saw her smile. "Now that's my girl…" He patted her hand. "BD said we'll be at Wilhelmina's settlement in a couple days," he told her.

"Great…I'm okay, but I'm sure ready for a break," She hooked her arm in his, as they slowly trudged on.

Finally, they pulled into the Gate's Settlement. The lead group led them to the holding corral. This was the settlement's parking lot, where travelers kept their wagons while visiting the settlement.

Mitch looked at Colleen. "Nice and clean," he said.

Colleen looked around. "Sure is. After the storm they must've had a lot to do to get it to look this ship shape," She continued to look around the compound.

Mitch asked her to wait while he came to help her down from the wagon. "You're going to treat me like a queen, aren't you…" she giggled.

"You know it…" He reached for her.

She slid into his arms. "I could really get used to this…" she giggled again.

He kissed her neck. "And I could get used to doing it…" They hugged each other.

BD, Ricky and Abby with Olivier following came next to them. "Quite a large settlement…" Olivier said. "I didn't know it was the Gates' Settlement," He looked around.

"It's one of the biggest; Cavern City is huge but this place is colossal," BD told them. "Wilhelmina is their daughter," he explained.

Olivier slightly blushed. "I see," He felt rather common.

BD saw him blush. "They're down to earth, ordinary people. Don't worry..." BD said to Olivier.

Olivier looked at him. "Where'd you buy your crystal ball? That's exactly what I was thinking...you know kind of out of my league," He slightly grinned. He happened to look towards the gate of the compound, and saw a young woman running towards them. "Oh my God," Olivier shouted. His heart skipped a beat. He watched her long, dish water blonde, braided ponytail sway with each step she took. She was wearing brown breaches tucked into leather boots; with a smart looking white blouse tucked into her trousers. "Be still my aching heart..." he almost inaudibly said. He blinked and rubbed his eyes. "Wilhelmina..." he then whispered. He stood perfectly still. Not because that was what he wanted to do, but because he could not move his body.

They all turned to look at who he was talking about. Breathless, she paused at the gate and rested for a second. She spotted Olivier and ran to him. "Ollie," She jumped into his arms that finally found movement. "Q99...Q98...over..." She laughed and took liberty to kiss him right on the lips.

Olivier's eyes opened wide, but then he picked her up and kissed her back. "Q98...Q99...here..."They laughed and danced around in circles. They acted like reunited lovers.

She ruffled his hair. "I knew it would be mousy brown; and that your eyes would be deep brown..." she smiled.

Olivier blushed. "And I knew you would have almost blonde hair; and that your eyes would have different shades of green and blue...God you're beautiful..." he said.

They were so in to each other that they forgot about where they were or who was around them. "Excuse us..." BD coughed and cleared his throat to get their attention.

They both stopped their joyous meeting. "BD, I'm so sorry... but..." Wilhelmina was saying.

BD took off his hat. "I think we all understand," he said. "Wilhelmina Gates may I introduce..." He was about to introduce them to her.

Wilhelmina saw Colleen and came directly in front of her. "The Portal..." she said. "You will have a girl..." she then added.

Colleen could not believe her ears. She could almost feel Kuruk next to her. She looked down and saw Buddy at her feet; she thought it looked like he winked at her. "Did you see that?" Colleen felt completely happy. She looked right at Wilhelmina.

Wilhelmina stooped and picked up Buddy. "I saw it..." She petted him behind the ears. "You're special, aren't you?" She smiled at Colleen. She then went next to Olivier. "Ollie, pick up his lady would you?" She sweetly smiled at Olivier, and he picked up Free.

BD then took over the rest of the introductions as they started for the community center.

Olivier and Wilhelmina straggled behind with the puppies in one arm and the other arm around each other's waists.

Chapter Seventeen

Wagons Roll On

After two days of rest they continued their journey west. They were not surprised that Olivier wanted to stay with Wilhelmina, at the Gates' Settlement.

They were having their evening meal. The night air was starting to get a familiar chill in it. "Autumn's on the way..." BD said. "We're right on time..." he added. "Just about two more weeks..." he scratched the whiskers on his chin.

Ricky and Abby were snuggled together with a blanket around them. "This has really been a wild trip," Ricky said.

Abby tickled him under the blanket. "I'm really tired...do you think..." She had a loving look in her eyes when she looked at her husband.

Ricky felt his face go warm. "I'll help with the dishes and then..." he was saying. He started to get up and out of the blanket.

BD and Mitch got up from their seats. "You two run along. We'll get the dishes tonight..." BD said, while Mitch nodded in agreement.

Abby jumped up and put the blanket around Ricky. "Well if you're sure..." Ricky slightly coughed. He had a false reluctance in his voice.

Mitch started to laugh. "Get out of here..." he said. He went to start the water to boil.

Ricky and Abby left for their wagon. "They're so cute together..." Colleen said. She felt satisfied after the evening meal.

BD was over by his wagon getting the dish pan ready and Mitch came next to Colleen. "We never really talked about our first meeting with Wilhelmina..." he looked at Colleen.

She slightly fidgeted on the hard bench. "She saw The Portal in me..." she was saying. "I felt so lost after Kuruk died. He understood The Portal..." She had a caring look in her eyes. "I know it's hard to understand what it's about...it's hard for me to completely understand; and that's why I find it hard to talk to you about it. But when someone can understand it and see it, and..." She wanted to also tell him about the reincarnation part, but found it hard to relate to him.

He sat next to her. "I understand..." he said. "I don't know about it, but I can accept the fact that others can see The Portal you talk about in you. I wish I had the gift of sight, but I guess it's just not meant to be..." He hugged her. "You're getting cold. Why don't you go to our wagon; I'll be along when we finish up out here..." he said. He smiled at her.

She caressed his cheek. "You're the best," she said. She got up and went to their wagon.

Inside the wagon, she lit their lantern. "You two settle down. It was a good thing Geoff and Muraco took care of Rex and Queenie," She put a small quilt in the box bed with the pups. "Just go to sleep..." she commanded. Both dogs lifted their heads and stared at her. "Please..." she added. She noticed they looked relaxed and closed their eyes. "Interesting," she said.

She tried to put them out of her mind. She knelt next to the bed. She felt under the bed and finally reached the chest. "Soon, the mystery will be solved," she said. She touched the lid. "Your secrets will finally be known..." she whispered. She placed the chest back under the bed. "And the compost…soon, after all these years, all the pieces of this gig-saw puzzle will come together; and we'll finally find out what this mysterious compost is…" she laughed. She started to get ready for bed. "I can't wait to fit in the final piece," She went to her saddlebags and found the key on the necklace. She tossed it in the air and caught it in her hand. "The final piece of the puzzle," she giggled. "We're almost there Mama…we're almost there…" she whispered. She finished getting ready for bed; and climbed in between the cold sheets.

Chapter Eighteen

Journey's End (For Now)

The full moon was a bright orange as it came over the horizon. They were close, but did not want to chance a night ride. "Just over that ridge and it all will be over," Colleen had a sad note in her voice.

Ricky looked at her. "I know what you mean. It kind of reminds me of the carrot on the rope in front of the donkey..." he slightly laughed. "You know he keeps going towards it but it's always out of his reach..." He looked at Abby. He shrugged his shoulders. "I guess that was kind of a silly comparison..." he added.

Colleen looked at him. "Not really. That's about how I feel. Mama's right over that ridge and..." She felt like she could cry.

BD came next to her. "Colleen, we couldn't get anywhere tonight anyway..." he calmly said.

She looked at him. "Why not, it's not like its midnight it's only around seven or so..." she had a baffled look on her face.

"Well, things are different here. This is a metropolitan city. Places open and close for business..." he was saying.

She gave him a curious look. "You know more about this compost than you let on...don't you?" She tried to get him to admit to something she believed he knew when he first arrived at Peaceful Valley and eliminated the threat of the cats.

BD shuffled his feet. He took off his hat and hit it against his leg. "Colleen…your mother…she's a pretty forceful woman…" He almost stuttered.

Colleen laughed. "You almost act like you're scared of her…" She continued to laugh.

Ricky looked at him. "I can understand where he's coming from…" Ricky came next to BD. "Grandpa, us men have to stick together…" He put his arm around BD's shoulder. He whispered something in BD's ear. They both laughed.

In a teasing way Colleen reprimanded their laughter. "You two…" She tried to copy her mother's "look".

Ricky continued to keep his arm around BD's shoulder. "Oh boy Grandpa, look familiar?" They laughed some more, while Colleen continued to give them the "look". "Just some male bonding Collie…I know how you like that…" He winked at his aunt and then went next to Abby.

"Bonding's good, but not at my mother's expense…" She pretended to scold them, but then she laughed and they laughed with her.

Mitch came next to Colleen. "Last night in the wilderness; want to carouse…" he whispered for only her to hear.

Colleen looked at him. "Sounds nice," she said. "We're going to take a moonlit stroll. See you all in the morning," She took a hold of Mitch's hand. They left them by the fire. "Let's get some quilts. We can look at the stars like we did on our honeymoon," she said. "I'm kind of glad the rest of the group went on ahead of us this morning. They're used to the ground…" she was saying.

"Yeah, and that gives us more privacy," he said.

They retrieved the quilts and were leaving their wagon. "You two stay in the wagon…" Mitch commanded the pups. But they were already nestled in their warm box bed. "Those two are funny…" he said to Colleen. "Every time I try to train them or command them they stop and..." He sounded unsure of how to say what he wanted.

She interrupted him. "They look at you like they know what you're going to say?" She paused and then laughed when she saw the look on his face.

"Yeah..." he was saying.

She hesitated, but thought right now she did not want to talk with him about something that would take that long to explain. She had more amorous ideas on her mind. "They're smart pups..." she only said. 'Maybe one day I'll talk about that but not tonight,' she thought. 'I still have my own skepticism to deal with...' She looked at him with love in her eyes.

The stars twinkled down on them, and they shared a night of love making under their downy quilts. Tomorrow would explain itself.

***

This was a metropolis. Businesses were on either sides of the gravel road that seemed to go on forever. Colleen did not see anything that looked like a house that someone could live in. This was a city of commerce. They followed BD to a holding corral.

Mitch helped her down from the wagon and they all gathered around BD. "I thought you lived here?" she asked. "Mama wouldn't live in a place like this..." she was saying.

BD knew they all were confused. He had to tell him what was going on. "Colleen, our home is out of the city, but the compost is here..." he said. "We're in St. Louis. This is the new East of what had been the United States of America. Earth's lands are lived on by all men and animals, and where we're standing, used to be a part of Central America; but is now called the new East of America. America now begins here in what is still called St. Louis," he said. "From Driftwood to here is now as we just left it," BD said.

"You could tell me we're in Tim Buck Two and I wouldn't know the difference," Colleen said.

BD had a sad heart. "I don't think folks know exactly what happened back then. Maybe like Kuruk explained when we first met him at The Timms Stockade, after the planets lined up a moon in the great beyond exploded and crashed years later into the earth," He raised his eyebrows. "Or maybe it was some kind of war between countries that led to such a travesty. Who knows? But in my mind it doesn't matter…it happened," He wiped his brow. "The great crack almost consumed the entire Appalachian mountain range that we should have traveled over…" He looked beaten.

Colleen was getting impatient. "I think my hormones are making me impatient. I'm sorry for what you're saying, but you sure picked a fine time to start talking about the past. All my life I've asked questions about the past and nobody ever wanted to talk about it; and now when I have all this compost stuff on my mind you want to give us a history lesson…" She loved BD, but he was truly annoying her. "And where's Mama; you said she would be here…" She was trying to hold her emotions in place.

"I just think a little knowledge at this point might help," He had a determined look on his face. He did not want to speak about Beatrice at this time.

Colleen knew he was going to finish what he wanted to say to them. "Well, do we have to set up camp for this?" She did not understand why BD insisted on talking about the past. She looked at Mitch.

Mitch seemed to have an agreeable look on his face. "I know what he means…the old eastern part of the states are gone…

where we stand is Missouri, the new east, where the states now begin," He looked at Colleen. "When we left Driftwood we crossed the great wilderness that once was the Atlantic Ocean. Your home, Driftwood was located on the western boarder of old Europe and relied on debris that was left from the drained ocean," A loving, kindness showed in his eyes. "And farther to the east of Driftwood, is what is now called the Russian Ocean. When it was land, Yerik told me that's where he and his family's ancestors were once from," Mitch explained his ideas. "But now, as I understand it, we're in the eastern part of what used to be Central America," He felt humbled. "We survived a great travesty…" he almost whispered.

"A lot of that is true. The ocean parted and the rushing waters flowed through the many sea floor caverns, like the one at Cavern City," BD explained his theory.

They all were becoming intrigued. "Wow…" Ricky said. "When we were there, I was talking with a young fellow, and he told me the cavern of Cavern City goes on for hundreds of miles to an ocean of water…" He looked at Colleen.

Colleen was settling down. She knew this conversation was going to go on so she tried to get it straight in her mind. She had heard bits and pieces about their past and what happened; and some of what she heard was now starting to make sense to her. "So then you're saying a huge mountain range fell into the great crack and the force of that earthquake parted the ocean," She looked at BD.

BD just raised an eyebrow. "That's pretty close…" he said.

Colleen continued with how she interpreted what he told them. "So then, from how you explain it; when the ocean was separated, some of the ocean's water rushed into the great crack, and then some of it was forced through these sea caverns where it then settled?" Colleen looked amazed.

BD's face turned red and he bowed his head. "That's pretty close to how I believe it happened…" he said. "It was heartbreaking…all the loss," He had tears forming in his eyes. "I was a wet nosed kid back then, but I was one of those folks who remember it and lived through it; I just don't like to talk about it…" He took out his handkerchief and wiped his eyes and nose. "I just want you to be prepared because this is a town that remembers and tells all," he looked at Colleen. "You don't know this, but we should have crossed a great river before we entered this metropolis, but it too has been re-directed; so to speak. Folks here have seen and lived through a lot of devastation; but now they're rebuilding a great society…" he said.

He came next to Colleen and put his arm around her. "Colleen, the chest has a lot to do with the past and the present. And that's why your mother wanted me to wait until now, to give you that, what you called a history lesson…" he said.

Colleen bowed her head. "Thanks Dad…" She hugged him. Colleen wanted to be with her mother. "But Mama…" She felt a tinge of fear in her heart.

BD intervened. "She'll be here. Come on, we have about six blocks to walk to the compost…" he said.

They followed him from the corral. The streets were busy with consumers selling and buying or trading in some of the open aired markets. Colleen carried the light chest; while Ricky carried Free, and Mitch carried Buddy. "I feel like some kind of a hillbilly…" Colleen said. She looked at the patrons dressed in fashionable clothes.

BD came next to her as they continued to walk. "They take their shoes off one at a time just like we do…" he chuckled. "Check out the buildings…" he was saying. "Every building is built over its own deep entry to an underground city," he could tell they were confused. "Predominate, granite caves are in this area. They housed many; and still protect to this day," he commented. "This entire city is built over a cave," They reached their destination. "Here we go...the compost..." He pointed out the building.

Colleen looked up. "The Communication Post," she read aloud. "So that's it...com for communication...who would've thought..." She laughed and looked at Mitch. "I wish Mama was here," she whispered to him.

BD opened the door for them. "Yep, this is it," he said. "What was left of the downtown St. Louis Jefferson Memorial and then refurbished," They followed him inside. He went directly to the main information desk. "Good morning; we're here to see..." he was saying.

The clerk interrupted him. "Oh yes, Mr. Dollar, I remember you. Please take a seat. Miss Nichols will be right with you," She left them to seat themselves.

They looked around the large, lavish furnished office building. All of the clerks were seated at neat desks, with instruments in front of them. They had tiny microphones attached to their heads. "Olivier would love this place," Ricky said. They all quietly giggled. "Looks like they're talking into space..." he then said. "And look..." He pointed to the lighted ceiling lights.

BD smiled. "They use the sun and wind for their power. You all are in for some innovative developments; a whole lot different than what you have in Peaceful Valley..." BD said. They continued to look around the large, open office area.

The clerk returned. "Please, will you all follow me," She escorted them to a large steel door. She opened it and led them down what seemed to be a cave under the building. "This is the bunker..." the clerk was saying.

"Wow," Ricky commented. "And lights too," he added. The winding stone stairwell was lit with dim, yellow lights.

"What you see is a new indoor, solar lighting system. We are one of the first to use it in this fashion," The clerk turned and smiled at them as they continued down the stairwell.

She then unlocked and opened another steel door. Inside, the walls of the bunker looked like they were built out of a hard steel material. It was a huge room with tiny office cubicles. They finally came to Miss Nichols' enclosed, private office. The clerk was about to knock when all of a sudden the room started to shake and the lights blinked and then the room went black.

The office staff remained completely quiet, while BD gathered his family and they huddled together and tried to stay calm. "We have small quakes and aftershocks all the time. Don't worry we always lose the lights. They'll come back on in a second or so…" the clerk said in a soothing way which gave them more settling feelings.

"You all hear what the clerk said?" BD asked.

"Yes…" they all said in unison.

Finally, the lights flickered, starting with a low yellow and then a spark of blue light beamed throughout the room and then the lights were on.

"Wow…" Ricky said. "Those lights have a funny way of coming back on…" He held Abby close to his chest.

"They sure do…" Abby added.

The clerk came next to them. "Well, like I said before we're used to this. Shall we continue?" She raised her arm and again led them to the steel door. She knocked once opened the door and they entered the office.

Miss Nichols rose from the seat behind her desk. "BD, good to see you again," She shook his hand. She was a young, high spirited woman not much older than Abby. Her brown hair was tied into a bow with a black ribbon at the nape of her neck. She was dressed in a gray, tailor made pant suit and wore flat, black leather shoes. A great smile lit up her clear blue eyes as she approached Colleen. "And this must be Colleen," She came next to Colleen knowing Colleen was the older of the two women in front of her. "Sylvia Nichols," she introduced herself. "Welcome to my grotto..." She extended her arm to her underground surroundings. "Most of what you see survived the great quake..." She nonchalantly spoke of the great travesty. Not experiencing it first hand and never knowing another way of living; she was comfortable in these top secure surroundings. This was the normal way to live.

Colleen extended her hand. "Yes, I'm Colleen. Nice to meet you Miss Nichols," she said.

"Please, call me Sylvia," Miss Nichols replied. She could not help but look at the chest Colleen was holding. "And that's the chest?" she asked. She almost looked like she could devour it.

Colleen felt like she had to defend it. "Yes, this is the chest my mother entrusted to me," she said.

Sylvia did not approach her. "And you have the key..." She curiously looked Colleen over.

Colleen looked at BD. "You said Mama would be here when we open it..." she said. She still felt like she had to defend her release of the chest.

BD could understand Colleen's defense. "Colleen this is part of the mystery of the chest. You're mothers in the chest..." he said.

Colleen backed away from him. "Are you nuts..." she almost screamed. Everyone else remained silent.

BD stood where he was. He knew this was all new and baffling to all of them, but especially to Colleen. "You have to trust me..." BD softly said.

Colleen looked at Mitch. She noticed he had an understanding look in his eyes. "You think it's okay to let her have the key; even if Mama's not here," she asked.

Mitch handed Buddy to BD and came next to her. "I guess like BD said, we'll have to trust him…" he whispered.

Colleen looked at BD and then to Sylvia. She noticed Sylvia cleared a space on her desk and pointed for her to place the chest on the desk.

Colleen placed the chest on the desk. She then took the necklace off that held the key to the chest, and placed it in Sylvia's hand. "Oh Mama…Mama should be here…" Colleen almost cried. She turned away from the chest.

Sylvia placed the key in the keyhole and turned it. They all heard it click. She then opened the chest. She removed several layers of packing and then what appeared to be a wooden lid. "Similar to the others," she commented. She did not take it out of the chest. She looked at Colleen. "It is for you," she softly said. She backed away from the chest and her desk.

Colleen looked at BD and then to Mitch. She felt frozen to the spot. "I can't look…" She put her hands to her eyes and started to sob.

Mitch came next to her and held her in his arms. Ricky and Abby could feel tears on their cheeks as they watched Colleen go through this personal turmoil.

"Don't be afraid of this…" Sylvia said. She could see a fear of the unknown in Colleen's eyes. "This is a part of your inheritance. It has been passed down from generation to generation," she explained. She did not force Colleen to approach the chest.

"I really don't think I'm afraid; it's just that I truly feel my mother should be here for this," she looked at BD. "And for you to say Mama's in the chest just doesn't make sense," She continued to stare at BD while Mitch held her close in his arms.

"Collie, please trust me. Do yourself a big favor and…" BD nodded towards the chest.

Colleen looked up at Mitch. His love was in his eyes and gave her courage. Slowly, she turned towards the chest and left his hold on her. She looked at him and nodded that she could do this alone. He stooped and kissed her cheek.

She looked at Sylvia, who stepped further away from her desk and the chest. Sylvia only smiled at her.

Nearing the chest, she thought she felt some kind of a magnetic pull draw her to it. She looked back at Mitch, who still had the look of love in his eyes. He nodded to her.

She was in front of the chest; she put her hands on it but did not look at what was inside. She looked up. She saw Ricky holding Abby with one arm with Free cuddled between them; it looked like they all had tears in their eyes. Wanting them to believe she was okay; she winked at them. She saw Buddy in BD's arms. BD was petting Buddy. Buddy, quietly stared at her.

She closed her eyes, tilted her head and then opened her eyes. She looked amazed and only a bit puzzled. She looked back at Sylvia.

"Yes, it is for you..." Sylvia said. Knowing that Colleen truly wanted her mother to be present; she could understand her hesitation and need for permission to continue.

"It's beautiful," Colleen had a peaceful look on her face. She noticed a delicate chain. She reached for it and gently tugged it. Caringly, she removed what was attached to the chain from its velvety home of many, many years. In front of them she held up what appeared to be a huge, perfectly cut diamond set in what looked like gold. "It looks like a diamond necklace," she said. In the limited light the stone seemed to come to life. The prisms from the stone twinkled all around the room. "Incredible," She looked at the many colors that filled the room.

Sylvia came next to her. "As I said, this is your inheritance. It is a precious stone from your birthplace..." she said. She smiled at Colleen.

"And Mama, BD said Mama..." Colleen questioned Sylvia about her mother not being present. She again wondered how this could have anything to do with her mother.

"Before we speak of your mother; I must explain a little of what will transpire..." Sylvia spoke in a cryptic way as she put her hand on Colleen's elbow. She then gestured for Colleen and them all to be seated on the small sofas that crowded the room.

Colleen continued to hold the gem up and they all could not help but take in the magical display of colors that filled the room. "Breathtaking..." Abby whispered.

Sylvia went to her desk and picked up the chest and brought it to Colleen. "For now Colleen; before we speak of your mother, could you please return the stone to the chest," She pleasantly asked Colleen. She placed the chest on Colleen's lap.

Colleen carefully returned the sparkling stone to its velvety cradle in the chest and closed the lid. Immediately, the prismatic colors were gone.

Sylvia returned to her desk and sat on its edge in front of them. "Now for life's lesson of love," She looked at them all. "What Colleen holds is not only her heritage, but is also for all of you," She noticed, other than BD, they looked at each other with evident confusion written all over their faces.

"So, are you saying this diamond or stone is also from our birthplace?" Ricky asked.

"Let me explain. As humans we all have the mark of His spirit of love that leads us..." She went behind her desk and sat on the comfortable cushioned chair. 'This is going to take a while,' she thought.

"Wow," Ricky said. He set Free down on the floor next to where BD had sat Buddy.

Sylvia noticed Colleen and the others seemed somewhat more relaxed. "To completely explain this I must go back to the 1940's when the knowledge of this spiritual existence of love was first documented. This is not like other interpretations mainly written as parables, or stories that depict certain ideas. What I'm talking about started in a place some of you may know or read about as Roswell or area 51," She said. She noticed they looked somewhat confused.

BD stood up. "Would you mind if I took it from there?" he asked.

"I think you might be able to explain it to them better than I could," Sylvia said. She knew he knew them better than she.

BD cleared his throat. "Actually, it is really simple, and I believe the only reason it is hard to explain is because, it is not common knowledge," He started. "First off, don't fear what you don't know. What I'm about to explain, I've known all of my life. It was a knowledge that in our family was passed down from generation to generation. It wasn't until I was older that I found out not everyone was aware of it," He noticed they started to get agitated and squirmed in their seats.

"This is another history lesson isn't it? Colleen asked. She sat back on the sofa.

"More like a life lesson," BD looked at Sylvia and cleared his throat again. "I know all of us in this room are Christians, and we all believe in a higher power..." he was saying.

"So this is a religious thing...what's in the chest is some kind of a relic?" Colleen asked. They all started to chatter.

BD held up his hands. "Let's just regroup for a minute. Remember where we are. Colleen, you were asked not to open the chest until you reached or knew what the compost is. Well, now you know it means communications post…" He slightly shouted over their chatter.

"So what does religion, Roswell, and area 51 have to do with communications?" Mitch asked.

"Without losing your complete faith in me; I will try to explain what it all has to do with communications…" he told them.

BD sat on the edge of Sylvia's desk. "Earth is not our first home," he said. He noticed they all looked at each other. "Roswell made certain we would remember where we all came from. When this physical body dies…" He put his hand on his chest. "…the spirit is free to choose another life. Sometimes that form is taken quickly and sometimes we wait for another choice. But the important word here is free choice. The greatest gift to us, as humans, is the freedom to choose," He folded his arms in front of him.

Ricky looked at BD and saw him in a different light. He looked younger yet seemed like an old sage teaching his family the secrets of life. "I've always felt like a free man…" Ricky said.

"We all are free. We are not forced to choose a kind, giving way of life, or a fair way. We could choose the evil way, and some do. But, no matter which way is chosen; we all start from the same Spirit of love…" BD continued to say.

Mitch spoke up. "What did you mean when you said Earth is not our first home?" he asked. Colleen squeezed his hand she was holding.

BD let out a deep sigh. "Roswell was the first time when the history of spirits were completely documented. This documented knowledge was hidden from ordinary people, such as ourselves. Bits and pieces were leaked out to us making us believe that area 51 was some kind of a landing spot for UFO's, you know, unidentified flying objects. The area was completely controlled by political powers that did not want us ordinary people to know exactly what was going on in our lives, on Earth, or the universe. They did not want us to know the powers we also possess," he readjusted himself on the desk.

"I can only tell you about it in the way I understand it." He scratched his brow. "Although we all start from this same Spirit of love, which I believe is God; we have the freedom of choice. Then, individually, with His help, our own spirit is created. You know, the way you act, feel and relate with others. This spirit is then joined to a physical body of our spirit's choice. And when our physical body ceases to exist, our spirit leaves the body and crosses over into its new, selected form," BD slightly hesitated. "I know, at first, after the cross over, my knowledge of my true spirit was unknown to me." He could tell he had their full attention. "Like with myself, you have the choice to learn of it or not. Some never learn of the true spirit ways and some don't want to learn. Some question it, but never find the truth," he was saying.

"So if I'm getting this right, you're saying, as spirits, we came to Earth from another Earth or planet?" Colleen asked. She felt goosebumps on her arms.

"Wow, spaceships..." Ricky looked at Abby. "Don't look so scared. I think it's neat..." He put his arm around her.

"Well not really spaceships..." Sylvia spoke up. "May I?" she looked at BD. Her eyes asked him if she could continue. "Actually, it is a gift from a higher existence, that allows our physical beings or our human forms to be transferred through our own ability of the mind to move matter, a form called Telekinesis," she said. They quieted down. "Through this higher power, in a millisecond, travel is possible," she explained.

"I'm really trying to take this all in. And I've always had thoughts about how man began, but you're saying our human forms and our spirits are a gift from a higher power?" Mitch asked.

"I've always wondered about those things too..." Colleen added. She noticed Ricky and Abby also shook their heads.

"When you look around; how can you not believe that our existence has to come from a higher power of love? Our bodies are almost completely self-sufficient. If you look at the night sky or a beautiful sunset the gift of life makes sense. All of the beauties of life are experienced through our bodies," Sylvia explained.

"I can agree with that..." Mitch sat back next to Colleen.

"And like BD said we always have the freedom to choose good or evil. And sometimes those who choose evil ways always want more power. And to get that they believe they have to have the resources to keep them on top," Sylvia told them.

"So, to stay in power those who are evil steal what is needed for us to survive," Mitch commented.

"And then we have to pay them for what we need to survive," Colleen added.

"Yes, and we all know the prices we pay to survive..." Mitch said.

"If what you say about this higher power is true, why doesn't this power just give us what we need to survive?" Abby whispered.

"I think that's where freedom comes in again..." Ricky said. He looked at his wife. He squeezed her and she put her head on his shoulder.

"Abby, that is a question that man has debated over for centuries. And, from what I've been told not only on this Earth but other homes..." Sylvia said.

"Okay, so if we can digest this and take it as true," Colleen looked at BD and then Sylvia. "I again ask; where is my mother? And, if communications is the meaning of the compost, what kind of communications?" Colleen asked. They all sat on the edges of the small sofas.

Sylvia rose from her seat. "If we had just blurted out the information we have just given you or shown it to you all without an explanation; well…" She looked at BD.

"What she's trying to say is what you've seen so far is just a fraction of what is about to be revealed…" BD was saying. "Before we go on does anyone have any questions?" he asked. He had a caring look of love in his eyes.

Mitch stood up. "Well, all of my life I have wondered about all of the different races and languages in the world. Where did we all come from? I've read the bible that was saved by my family, about the Tower of Babel, and I've tried to take it with faith, but…" he looked around hoping he was making some sort of sense to them.

"I think I know where you're going with this Mitch." BD chimed in. "When you think about it it's a mystery. Where did all of these different ethnic individuals that live in our world come from?" He started to pace in front of them. "All the different languages, colors and looks; how did they first start?" He stopped his pacing. "When you think about it where did Adam and Eve come from? And after Cain killed his brother Abel, where did Cain's wife come from? These are questions that have been studied by scholars for centuries; but I believe only could have come about through a higher power; the supreme power only He has. And we should thank our lucky stars that he allows us our freedom." BD let out a sigh.

"I might be speaking out of turn but what comes to my mind is it sounds like you're saying these different ethnic groups come from different worlds? But how? How can their bodies get here?" Ricky asked.

"That again has to come from the spirit of a higher power." Sylvia explained. "I believe that can only be the true answer.

Although the different groups look and talk in their own ways our bodies all are human. We have the same body make-up. And that in itself is what I call a miracle that only God can create." She looked at them with tears forming in her eyes. "And with His almighty power our body, in the form that it is, with its spirit is mysteriously transported for whatever unknown reason. And those here chose Earth to be their home." She felt completely drained.

"Wow Collie!" Ricky shouted. "Without even knowing it, I may have picked out the star I came from and gave it to you as a wedding gift." They all laughed.

"Could be true." BD chuckled. "And, here's another can of worms I'm gonna open," he said. "We know the bible is not the first record of history. And I'm thinking over 2 million years ago the first humans emerged before modern humans or Homo sapiens appeared. So is our Earth God's first garden, or just another island in the sky?" He asked them.

"Please, let's not go back to the first, one cell amoeba!" Mitch replied.

"NO!" They all shouted.

"But I do kind of remember, when I had a chance, reading about the Sumerians and Greeks recording history, and the tombs of the Egyptians with the hieroglyphics on the walls." BD said. "Gosh, I've even met some archaeologists who talked about old buildings or structures, and how they could figure out how people at certain times used to live." BD was on a roll. "And there was this one young lady Geologist I met, who learned from her father how to study the earth and figure out the different periods in time." He added with a slap to his knee.

"I think you've never met a stranger." Colleen said with a chuckle.

"Oh, I think you're right." BD scratched his head. "Here's another one that might fit in with all of this, the Botanist." BD added.

"Of course." Colleen said. "Fossil Vegetation is very important too."

"Can't forget the Zoologist." Ricky threw in his thoughts.

"Yep, the animals are important." BD agreed.

Sylvia chimed in. "I think the knowledge of all these things are pieces of His puzzle, and a gift to humans and creatures alike."

"And, if you ask me, we have to include the entire universe." BD related, as they all nodded in agreement. "And the list goes on and on." He added. "But all of this historic knowledge always leads back to His first gift of?" BD gave them a musical conductor's wave of his arms.

And they all shouted: "Telekinesis!" They all started to laugh and talk between themselves.

"This is deeper conversation than I was truly expecting. My brain's trying to take it all in." Colleen looked at her family. "But what about Mama? I think we just want to know all about her right now?" She felt she spoke for them all when they all nodded and spoke in agreement.

"Well then, Colleen will you bring the chest back up and place it on my desk?" Sylvia asked. She motioned to the spot for her to place the chest. "Will everyone please rise and come around the desk?" She watched them all encircle her desk. She did not have to ask another question.

Immediately, Colleen again felt the magnetic pull towards the chest, but this time the lid opened without her help. The gem floated from the chest and into her hand. She looked at them with an amazed look on her face. "Wow…" she said. The prismatic colors again filled the room.

"That goes for me too…" Ricky commented. Looking around he could see everyone could not take their eyes from the stone or the beautiful colors.

"The stone is your communication tool," Sylvia explained.

Colleen gave her a perplexed look. "How…" She thought the stone seemed warm and vibrated with a soft tingly sound.

BD felt he had to prepare her. "Colleen, before you continue please understand that all that will happen was learned by your mother when we arrived here. She asked me to explain this all the best way I knew how," He softly spoke to her. "It was never her intention not to tell you these things; but had she known about them or what the future held she would have done this all in a different way…" He had tears in his eyes and his voice quivered when he spoke.

"I think you're starting to scare me…" She looked into BD's eyes and saw a love in them that calmed her.

"BD, I think it is time…" Sylvia said.

Colleen did not take her eyes from BD. "Cover the stone with your other hand…" BD said. He did not take his eyes from Colleen's eyes. "The stone will feel warmer, but do not worry it would never burn you…" His eyes showed a greater love and he winked at her.

"Mama…" Colleen whispered. She could feel, smell and hear her mother as if she were standing right next to her.

"Yes daughter it's Mama," She heard in her mother's voice.

"Oh Mama, where are you?" Colleen whispered. She looked at Mitch and then to BD.

"We all can hear her," Sylvia said. "But not in the conventional way, but through mental telepathy," She explained, but did not move her mouth.

"Wow," Colleen thought. Everyone laughed.

"Double wow," Ricky thought. They laughed.

"Oh Mama, what's going on?" Colleen said aloud.

"With the prism's light enveloped around you; everyone in this room at this very moment is at the place we call home," Beatrice said. "This is a place that has been verified many times and now it is our turn," she explained to their minds.

"Everyone in this room?" Sylvia asked. Now she had a look of confusion on her face.

"That's news to me too..." BD said. He looked for a place to sit on the sofa.

"This special place is His gift of love and has kept the spirits in the human body always alive," Beatrice said.

"So are you saying your spirit is in this stone?" Colleen asked. She started to hear a barrage of noise. She thought everyone in the room was shouting at her. She saw that everyone had their hands over their ears.

"For now, until your telepathic abilities are mastered, could everyone try to keep their thoughts under control and only speak orally?" Beatrice softly asked. She had a sound of empathy in the tone of her voice.

They happily looked at each other. The noise stopped.

"And to answer your question...yes daughter my spirit is in this stone. This is my home for now and one day will also be all of yours..." Beatrice explained. The noise filled their heads again. "Please, for your own sakes try to control your thoughts," she again softly whispered.

Sylvia spoke up. "Why are you speaking to me? I'm just a communications director. Other stones have come to my attention and I've led them...but..." She had to sit down in her chair.

"This time the stone is for all in the room and also for you," the spirit of Beatrice explained. "And before you say or think it... yes you too my husband..." she said.

"Sure hope my thoughts don't offend anyone; I'm trying to control them and my use of foul language," BD said. He sat back on the sofa and scratched his head.

"So Mama you're…" Colleen could not say dead.

"I've crossed daughter…as my last human request; my husband buried my human remains at our new home not far from here," the spirit of Beatrice explained.

Colleen held on to Mitch's hand and led him to sit on the sofa next to BD. "You had a hard secret to keep," she said to BD. She put her head on his shoulder.

"Your mother has a strong will in all ways," BD said.

"My spirit will move on as we spoke of before. But for now I have been given this gift to explain what is going to happen to all of you…" the spirit of Beatrice said.

"All of us?" Abby asked. She looked at Ricky with a bit of fear and doubt in her eyes.

Ricky held her in his arms. "Grammy would never hurt us…" Ricky softly said to his wife.

"None of you should fear any of what I am going to explain to you," the spirit of Beatrice said.

"I guess from now on you have the floor…" Sylvia said to Beatrice. She looked at them and then to Colleen.

Colleen still held the stone in her hand as the prismatic colors continued to fill the room.

"You can release the stone," the spirit of Beatrice said to Colleen.

Colleen opened her hands. The stone floated above them. The soft colors seemed to embrace them with great joy. Any fears or doubts were released from them.

"At this time, twelve are named as The Portal for this stone. And those named, in one way or another, are in this room…" the spirit of Beatrice said.

"Kuruk told me I was The Portal a long time ago..." Colleen said. "It's a hard thing to talk about. But since he understood all the crazy things that I saw and..." Colleen looked at Mitch and tried to explain why she could never tell him all of the experiences of the blue orbs in her life.

"You do not have to explain Colleen. Everyone in this room has had similar encounters in their human lifetime," the spirit of Beatrice said.

"So if I tell everyone that Kuruk and Langundo's spirits have been reincarnated in Free and Buddy here nobody will laugh..." Colleen shyly asked. She pointed to the dogs lying on the floor by the sofa.

"Awesome," Ricky shouted. "I always thought they had a human way about them," He picked up Free and handed her to Abby and then he picked up Buddy. "Truly real," he said. "Now what I feel makes sense," He stroked Buddy and scratched behind his ears.

"You're right, this is awesome," Abby petted Free. "I feel something too," She looked at Ricky. "I think a lot of things are starting to make sense," She looked at Colleen. "Remember when Pavel died and I came to you and wanted to be Ricky's buddy; but he was so against a girl as his buddy?" She knew Colleen remembered that day. "Well, when Ricky threw the handful of dirt into the grave I saw white balls all around him. I was drawn to him and knew I would love him all of my life. I knew, like you said he needed time; and I also knew I would wait forever to win his love. I didn't understand the white balls, and after a while; just like the blue ones, they became a part of my life," Abby said. She felt relieved to speak of these things.

"So you've seen the blue balls too..." Colleen looked at Abby.

"Yes..." Abby said.

"In some way or another, everyone in this room has experienced a trait of the Spirit," the spirit of Beatrice said.

"But you said twelve for this stone. Counting you, Kuruk and Langundo in the pups, there are only nine of us here..." Mitch said.

"My daughter is going to have..." the spirit of Beatrice was saying.

"Not triplets..." Colleen shouted.

"No Daughter. Like Kuruk explained you are going to have a baby girl," the spirit of Beatrice stopped.

Sylvia stood up. "I think she means Abby's going to have twins," She looked at Ricky and Abby.

"Really," Abby said. She looked stunned.

"Awesome," Ricky excited could not help but use his now favorite word.

"A great grandson will be born to Ricky and Abby," the spirit of Beatrice said. "And..." she stopped.

"Me..." Sylvia held her hand on her head. She also looked stunned. "That explains all this morning sickness and mood swings...my husband...boy do I have a lot to tell him..." she was saying.

"In time, you will tell your husband about the baby boy,"The spirit of Beatrice detected shock in Sylvia. "But when I leave, none of you will remember all of this; only bits and pieces will be left in your subconscious and brought to mind in a subliminal way," the spirit of Beatrice said.

"I also remember Wilhelmina knew me as The Portal," Colleen said.

"Yes she did because she is also in another family of Portals. It is her responsibility to explain it to Olivier and the others who will join her in their stone..." the spirit of Beatrice said.

"Golly..." Ricky said.

Colleen had a worried look on her face. "But what about the stone, what will happen to you and the stone…" Colleen started to sweat and get a feeling of loss.

"As for the stone; Colleen, it will remain in the chest and be passed on to your daughter, Chelsea…" the spirit of Beatrice said.

"Chelsea. What a beautiful name," Colleen looked at Mitch.

"Yes it is…" Mitch had tears in his eyes.

"And you Mama…" Colleen could feel her throat constrict.

"A part of the essence of my spirit will always be with you all…" she stopped. A sigh of relief was heard from them all. "But we all must move on. And, as was mentioned before, our spirits have the free will to choose where we go. But I must relate that a higher power is always present when we call for help; all we have to do is ask…this knowledge will always be present…teach it to your children…" the spirit of Beatrice said.

"You said Wilhelmina was also a Portal. Are there other stones out there, and how did this stone…" Mitch was going to ask how the stone came to be.

"As Miss Nichols has explained; other stones have surfaced and The Portals have found their ways to them; while other intended Portals continue to search for them. It is a never ending quest," the spirit of Beatrice explained.

"And it's through a form of Telekinesis that our spirits and physical bodies along with the stones are transported from planet to planet and universe to universe. And with mental telepathy, this quest goes on and eventually is explained to The Portals," BD whispered. He seemed to lethargically lie back on the sofa.

"Mama, what exactly is The Portal?" Colleen asked.

"Well, daughter it has been explained that what we know of as time has been established by humans. Humans need stability, but the Spirit is forever. Time to the Spirit of the higher power is nonexistent; in other words time to the Spirit of the higher power has no beginning and no end…" she was saying.

"So then, if our spirits are from the Spirit of the higher power…" Colleen was trying to figure out what her mother was explaining.

"Our spirits are the essence of the Spirit of a higher power, which transport or cross over from our human existence to another chosen existence through The Portal," the spirit of Beatrice explained.

"So then some humans are not Portals," Colleen asked.

"That is right. But even if they are not Portals they are still the essence of the Spirit of a higher power; and when the human body they abide in dies the spirit finds direction from The Portal and then can use free will to reincarnate the essence of its spirit into another existence," the spirit of Beatrice explained.

"Wow. I think that makes us pretty special," Ricky said.

"All life is special," They heard BD say.

"But Grammy, I still don't quite understand about you in the stone. Are you crammed in there?" Ricky asked.

Abby looked at him. "I believe she means that since we're Portals we are somehow different, and when our human bodies die, as Portals we use the stone as our portal…" she whispered.

"That is one of the best explanations I have ever heard," Sylvia said.

"Like I said before; it is really very simple," BD said.

"Sure, it's simple; if you let it be as it should be and don't analyze it. But I keep thinking about what you said about us not remembering most of this. So how will we know when to search for the stone or when we…" Mitch held his wife close. He did not want to think about dying when his life was so full.

"First, let me answer Ricky's question if I am crammed in the stone…the answer is no. I am a free spirit," she explained.

"And Mitch, to answer your question and explain to all of you; our Higher Source of Spirit understands our human need for a physical presence, and the stone represents this need, and its existence is only used as a guiding tool. So, only when it is your turn; all of you, as my spirit was led to the stone; the Spirit of the higher power will also lead you," the spirit of Beatrice said.

"I also remember when you spoke about Roswell you said powers we possess were being hidden from us. What kind of powers and by whom," Mitch asked.

"When I crossed to the stone I became aware of many things. And one of these things was the power of mind over matter and telepathy; these are powers that evil spirits don't want kind spirits to become aware of. Kind spirits are more complacent and usually only find out about their unique powers when they or those they love are threatened; and even then, when the powers occur, the kind spirit will always say, 'Thank God…' the kind spirit never believes in his own power, His gift…" thc spirit of Beatrice said.

"So we also have these powers?" Mitch asked.

"Yes, but like I explained before, your memories of all you are learning right now will remain in your subconscious and will only be remembered when you are led to the stone…" the spirit of Beatrice said. "In other words; what I am speaking about to you now is a prelude of what will come; life as you know it will continue until it is time for us to meet again…" the spirit of Beatrice explained in a soft voice. Her spirit felt almost tangible.

"I can feel you, but I wish I could physically hug you Mama," Colleen whispered.

"Stand up and close your eyes daughter," Colleen heard in her mind from her mother.

Colleen did as her mother asked and could feel a loving embrace hold her close and she could smell her mother's scent.

"Thank you..." Colleen whispered. Tears fell from her eyes. But then the embrace was gone.

"Now I must tell you, that for the time being, the spirits of Kuruk and Langundo wish to remain reincarnate in the canines..." the spirit of Beatrice told them.

"Wonderful..." Ricky said. He bent and petted both dogs.

"It is time my husband..." the spirit of Beatrice then said.

They all looked at BD. He was slumped over on the sofa. "BD..." Colleen seeing him, came next to him, but immediately knew his body was dead.

"It is okay Colleen..." the spirit of Beatrice said. Suddenly, a great blue orb soared through the room and into each of them and then directly into the stone. The colors of the prism from the stone grew stronger and brighter.

"Benjamin and I are together until we decide to move on," the spirit of Beatrice informed them.

"Until we meet..." They all, mentally, heard in BD's voice.

They looked at each other and then watched as the stone returned to the chest; the prisms faded and the lid on the chest closed.

All at once the lights in the room started to blink and the room started to shake. "Just another quake..." Sylvia said. "Just remain calm until it is over..." she told them.

They all rose and came together and embraced each other. The lights went off and the room became pitch black. "I can still feel BD as if he was right next to me..." Colleen said. The lights flickered with many strobes. "Those lights make me almost feel like I'm in some kind of a hypnotic trance," Colleen closed her eyes. "I'm telling you, I can still feel BD next to me..." she said again.

The lights came back on. "Where else would I be," BD said to her.

They were right outside the last steel door to Miss Nichols office. "Huh," Colleen looked around. "How did we get..." she was saying.

The clerk approached them. "I'm sorry, sometimes when the lights go out during one of the tremors, certain people get somewhat disoriented..." she explained. "Shall we continue to Miss Nichols' office?" She motioned for them all to follow her.

Colleen looked around the room. They were in the office area with the clerk they had first met when they arrived at the compost, who was leading them to Miss Nichols' office. "If I told you something that I think just happened; I don't think you'd believe me..." She looked at BD and whispered.

Hearing her, Mitch hugged her waist. "Something tells me I might..." he whispered in her ear. "Something like déjà vu?" He looked at her.

"Yeah, like we've been here before..." She gave him a sideways glance. "But..." She did not finish her words.

BD winked at them, and then herded them from behind to follow the clerk into Miss Nichols' office.

"I feel like we were..." Colleen wanted to say she felt like they had already been in Miss Nichols office, but then she looked at everyone and thought she must have just imagined it.

Miss Nichols rose from the seat behind her desk. "BD, good to see you again," She shook his hand. She was a young, high spirited woman not much older than Abby. "And this must be Colleen," She came next to Colleen knowing Colleen was the older of the two women in front of her. In greeting she offered her hand to Colleen. On touching hands they both felt a static electric spark. "Ouch...sorry that's never happened before," Miss Nichols said. Both women immediately pulled back their hands.

Miss Nichols looked directly into Colleen's eyes. "I really am sorry about that…have we met before?" she asked Colleen. She also experienced a déjà vu moment.

Colleen again had the same feeling of déjà vu when she looked directly into Miss Nichols' eyes. "I don't believe so… unless you've been farther east than St. Louis…" Colleen said. She had a questioning look in her eyes and could not shake the feeling that maybe she had met her at some time in her life.

"No, born and raised here. Well, no matter…welcome to my grotto…" Miss Nichols nonchalantly extended her arm to her surroundings and continued her practiced greeting. In the few years of working at The Communication Post, she had met many people who she thought of as, 'baby techs', new to technology. "Most of what you see here survived the great quake…" She casually spoke of the great travesty. Not experiencing it first hand and never knowing another way of living; she was comfortable in these top secure surroundings knowing this to be a normal way to live.

Miss Nichols looked at the chest Colleen was holding. "And that's the chest?" she asked. She almost looked like she could devour it.

Colleen felt like she had to defend it. "Yes, this is the chest my mother entrusted to me," she said.

Miss Nichols did not approach her. "And you have the key…" She curiously looked Colleen over.

Colleen looked at BD. "You said Mama would be here when we open it…" she said. She still felt like she had to defend her release of the chest.

BD could understand Colleen's defense. "Colleen this is part of the mystery of the chest. Your mother's in the chest…" he said.

Colleen backed away from him. "Are you nuts…" she almost screamed.

BD stood where he was. He knew this was all new and baffling to all of them, but especially to Colleen. "You have to trust me…" BD softly said.

Colleen looked at Mitch. She noticed he had an understanding look in his eyes. "You think it's okay to let her have the key; even if Mama's not here," she asked. Subconsciously, those words sounded very familiar to her. She tried to put those thoughts out of her mind. She knew she had never met or been in Miss Nichols' office. 'Maybe my hormones are playing tricks on me,' she thought.

Mitch came next to her. "I guess like BD said, we'll have to trust him…" he whispered.

Colleen looked at BD and then at Miss Nichols. She noticed Miss Nichols cleared a space on her desk and pointed for her to place the chest on the desk.

Colleen placed the chest on the desk. She then took the necklace off that held thc kcy to the chest, and placed it in Miss Nichols' hand. "Oh Mama…Mama should be here…" Colleen almost cried.

Miss Nichols placed the key in the keyhole and turned it. They all heard it click. She then opened the chest. She took out an old looking, wrapped package, she un-wrapped it. "Perfect, it's in the original package. Great, the instruction manual…" she said. She had a big smile on her lips. "I know it will work. I just have to program it and get the code…" she was saying. "I'll be right back," She left them for a moment.

Colleen looked at BD. "Oh God, I can't look at it…" She rolled her eyes. She was too afraid to even look at what was in the chest.

BD tried to calm her. "If this works; we'll be…" He did not finish what he wanted to tell them.

Miss Nichols returned to the room. "Let's see," she said.

They could not see what she was doing or what she was working on. The wrapping paper from the package covered it from their view and no one wanted to go near the chest. In Miss Nichols' hands, it seemed like a foreign object.

Miss Nichols almost looked like a surgeon. "The SIM card's in perfect condition and I programmed it with its circuit card; so it looks like we're good to go…" She looked completely happy. "I don't see many in this good of condition. You know you're really lucky…" She acted like they should understand what she was talking about. "Here we go," she said. "Everything you see here would not work if it were not for the solar batteries used on the orbiting satellites," She again acted like they should understand what she was talking about. "And with this little baby…" She pointed to the object on the desk.

Colleen looked at BD. "What's she mean about solar batteries. What is it?" She had many questions.

Miss Nichols spoke up. "Okay, now for the numbers; let's take a look at the note…" she said. She picked up a piece of paper from inside the chest.

Colleen looked at Mitch. "Note…" Colleen mouthed. She had a feeling that Miss Nichols had another kind of trick up her sleeve. She noticed Mitch just shrugged his shoulders. She then gave Buddy a sideways glance, thinking he might look supportive; but his dog eyes were tired and he seemed to be sleeping in Mitch's arms.

Miss Nichols looked at Colleen. "According to the note, I am instructed to ask you the following questions," she said. "What's your mother's birth date?" she asked.

Colleen had to think for a moment. "March 18th…" she was saying.

"And the rest; you know the year?" Miss Nichols asked.

"Two thousand forty five, I think…" She looked at BD.

"Yes, two thousand forty five," BD agreed.

"And her maiden name," Miss Nichols then asked.

"Wayne," Colleen said.

"And your full name; including your maiden name and your birth date?" she asked. She wrote down what Colleen told her. "I'm just asking some of these questions for verification," Miss Nichols continued to work on what they could not see. "Here we go. Hmm…that's unusual…only a set of seven digits, but, looks like we have a hit…" she almost shouted. "Elaine Wayne at code 3182045, yep that's the code right here," she told them.

"That's my mother's aunt's name," Colleen said. She looked at Mitch with raised eyebrows. "How do you know all this?" she asked.

Miss Nichols held up a tiny object. "With the information you gave me everything will work with what's programmed in here…" she was saying.

Colleen felt deflated. "That little thing's what all the mystery's about…" She could not believe her eyes. "What is it?" she asked. She was completely amazed. She looked at BD.

"Your Mom made me promise not to say a word. And I'm a man of my word…" he was saying. "Now just wait…" he added. He nodded his head towards Miss Nichols.

"Mama should be here with us…" Colleen kept shaking her head. Colleen thought it looked like Miss Nichols was playing with the tiny object. "What is it anyway?" she again asked. She had a completely confused look on her face.

Miss Nichols again held it up. "This, my dear is a PPVTR, in other words a Portable Polarized Voice Transporter Receiver. It oscillates images and voice," She could see they looked confused. "That means images and voices come through it one way and go back to a similar PPVTR at the other end," She knew she did not satisfy their curiosity. "It was commonly called a cell phone, and; I'd say it's from around 2040 or so. This type was popular in those days," she explained.

"I'm to the point where I don't care what you call that thing. I just want to know where my mother is right at this very moment...you said Mama would be here for this...Mama's not here..." Colleen said. She looked directly at BD. "BD..." She almost shouted. She looked like she might explode.

He again nodded towards Miss Nichols. "She will be..." BD said.

Miss Nichols continued to read the instruction manual. "Oh, now I understand input of the code is orally," She spoke the birth date and year of Colleen's mother, Beatrice. "This is Miss Nichols..." she was saying. The phone almost came to life. "Yes ma'am, they're all here. Okay, here we go..." She put the device on her desk.

A projected liquid looking wall appeared in front of them. "Collie, daughter, its Mama..." Beatrice almost yelled.

"I'm here Mama...I'm here..." Colleen shouted. She came near the projection. "I can see you Mama, but where are you?" She waved her hand through the projection.

"BD will bring you to me Honey. It will take some time we live several days west of St. Louis..." Beatrice was saying.

"Mama, I'm going to have a baby girl..." Colleen said. Her entire face lit up like a Christmas tree. They all came around her while she continued to speak with Beatrice.

"How wonderful, a baby girl...This is fantastic, I can see all of you..." They watched Beatrice wipe her eyes. "Ricky, Abby is your lovely bride..." She blew them a kiss.

"Yes she is Grammy," Ricky squeezed Abby in his arms.

"How is this possible?" Colleen asked her mother.

"Well, daughter I believe when my parents left me to spend the summer at my aunt and uncle's home they must've had a premonition that they might never see me again; and that was why my mother left the chest with this communications device in it. I was really too young to remember everything back then. But like I explained to you my aunt said it could only be opened when the compost was understood. I don't think they thought it would take me this long to find it all out," Beatrice belted out one of her contagious laughs.

They all laughed with her. "Well, when Benjamin and I found out what the compost was we made plans to come for you," Beatrice said.

"It took us a while to settle down and get a place of our own," BD added.

"This is truly amazing," Colleen said. She again passed her hand through the projection.

"After we spoke with Miss Nichols and she informed us that all of the codes were made up by my mother and had something to do with me; all that was left to do was for you to bring in the chest with the device so we could get it to work," she explained.

"Now I know what BD meant when he said you were in the chest," Colleen smiled at BD.

BD winked at her. "Since we didn't exactly know what kind of device was in the chest Miss Nichols picked out one for us to use from around the time Bea was born, and as we see the similar device works..." BD smiled and looked at his wife in the projection.

They were a family from a place where life was a battle to survive and now they were witnessing a technology from their past. This would change their future lives forever.

Miss Nichols watched them with much gratification. Then she looked at Colleen. The technical side of her brain wondered; if Colleen truly was pregnant, how could she possibly know for sure, that she was going to have a baby girl. She had read about ultra-Sonogram machines that could determine the sex of a child, but the equipment for that technology had been destroyed long ago; and at this time parts for the mechanism were out of the question. In her business, of information technology, Miss Nichols had met many different types of people. She enjoyed showing them old and new techniques. She thought one day she would write a book about how people responded when she explained past and present procedures and communication devices to them.

She remembered the déjà vu moment. But then she thought; this woman in front of her was a first. She continued to watch the elated daughter speak with her mother over the communications device that, when knowing where she had just come from, she, undoubtedly, had never seen or used before. With questionable eyes, Miss Nichols continued to study Colleen and those around her. She did not think about what made up the woman, or the adventures that were a part of her life; she only saw Colleen, as a simple woman.

Silently, Miss Nichols compared Colleen with herself. 'How could this plain looking woman have such a knockout of a man standing next to her?' she thought. 'My husband's a wonderful man, but I'm also married to my career' she thought. It appeared to her that Colleen seemed completely comfortable dressed in denim coveralls and a checkered shirt; with her pants tucked into her leather boots. 'I look great…' She smoothed her fashionably tailored pantsuit and looked at her flat shoes. 'I'm certain she's never seen the luxuries of running water or solar powered lights…' She continued to size Colleen up. 'Coming from the prairie she most likely doesn't always have a solid roof above her head…she doesn't act like it, but knowing where she's from, I'm sure there's been times she's feared for her life,' She looked around her office. 'I'm an educated woman,' She believed she was a successful scientist of technology. 'What kind of career can she have out there?' She noticed Colleen looked at her. Miss Nichols blushed when she saw the look of love in Colleen's eyes as with her family, she continued to speak with her mother.

But then Miss Nichols' inquisitive mind again wondered how this country girl, from the prairie could possibly say with complete certainty that she was having a baby girl. But then a flash of recognition invaded her thoughts. As she watched them she felt drawn to them with a feeling she had for her own family. She felt, in some way, a type of kindred spirit joined her with them. 'How could this be? I just met them' she thought. 'I need to get some rest. Maybe I should go to the doctor like my husband said. I have been feeling sick in the morning,' Miss Nichols smiled at them while they continued to speak with Beatrice and watch her through a device Miss Nichols had shown to many others over the years.

But this family was different. She wrote a little note to keep in touch with the family of Colleen Armstrong Banks.

Colleen smiled at Miss Nichols. She turned from her and continued to speak with Beatrice.

Colleen was not a simple woman; she was simply a woman who loved the man she married. She loved his baby girl she now carried. She loved her family and her way of life. She would continue to search out the mysterious ways she had witnessed in her life. And although, at this time it was unknown to her; at another point in her human life, she would join all of those now present around her; and again recognize and remember the complete truth of her role as The Portal.

Bibliography

www.wikipedia.com
Ann and Jane Taylor "Twinkle Twinkle Little Star"
Geography

The World Book Encyclopedia copyright 1977, USA
Radio Information
Geography
Cats

Editors:
Carol O'Brien (nee Villani)
Dennis O'Brien
James E. Eimer, Sr.
Constance M. Voss (nee Eimer)

Review Requested:

We'd like to know if you enjoyed the book.
Please consider leaving a review on the platform
from which you purchased the book.

Printed in the USA
CPSIA information can be obtained
at www.ICGtesting.com
LVHW040535080724
784629LV00001B/4